# Never Go Back

It started with a kiss . . .

Well, not exactly. More a look of passionate hunger, when I dreamed up an imaginary hot-headed 1960's East End of London girl (Annie Bailey) who had a massive crush on local up-and-coming gangster Max Carter. Straight away, I understood Annie's feelings when Max ended up engaged to her goody-two-shoes sister Ruthie, I understood how badly Annie behaved and how cataclysmic that 'crush' became when she was perched between one rival gang (Max's) and another (the Delaneys).

Reader, I couldn't get the thing down on paper fast enough! I rattled it off in no time, forgot to number the pages, shivered in my shoes at my own audacity while I stood in the Post Office queue and sent it off to six agents.

I waited.

I shivered a bit more, because I was living in a council flat and couldn't afford to run the heating. I'd typed the whole of *Dirty Game* while wearing an overcoat and using a monitor lent to me by a kind neighbour because I couldn't afford to buy a new one when my own packed up. I was told by well-meaning people that I should Get A Proper Job. Seriously! When I knew I was holding this story, this *fabulous* story of conflict and hate and desire, in my hands and that someone *had* to put it into print.

Well, someone did. Also, someone paid me a six-figure sum for *Dirty Game* plus two more Annie books – *Black Widow* and *Scarlet Women*.

So, my writing career began.

The truth was, I'd always wanted to be a writer. As a child I'd scribbled down stories, or told stories in needlework class, or put on puppet shows I'd scripted. All through my teenage years I'd written westerns and adventures and sci-fi pieces. All through my twenties I'd written romantic comedies. I'd even tried to get a few of those published, only to fall at the last hurdle. One exasperated agent said to me when I'd pestered him once too often: 'Why don't you write straight crime? Why fiddle around trying to be funny?'

So, straight crime it was. And finally, miraculously, I found my writing voice and Annie Bailey sauntered into my head and stopped there. Seven books about her followed, and three about another very gutsy heroine Ruby Darke, and seven stand-alone novels too. Then my editor pointed out to me that it's 15 years since that very first Annie book *Dirty Game* was published. She's right! I wish I knew where all that time's gone, but I have to say, it's been a lot of fun. I've bought a house, slogged over the keyboard, sold a house, slogged a bit more, bought another house, moved, slogged on . . . you get the picture. Mostly, it's been the perfect life for a homebody introvert who likes to just plod along at her own pace. I've been blessed with great helpers and fantastic fans. So thank you, one and all. Now I've got to get back to the keyboard, I sense another book coming . . .

Love

Jessie x

*By Jessie Keane*

### THE ANNIE CARTER NOVELS
Dirty Game
Black Widow
Scarlet Women
Playing Dead
Ruthless
Stay Dead

### THE RUBY DARKE NOVELS
Nameless
Lawless
The Edge

### OTHER NOVELS
Jail Bird
The Make
Dangerous
Fearless
The Knock
The Manor
Diamond

JESSIE KEANE

# Never Go Back

HODDER &
STOUGHTON

First published in Great Britain in 2023 by Hodder & Stoughton
An Hachette UK company

1

Copyright © Jessie Keane 2023

A CIP catalogue record for this title is available from the British Library

Hardback ISBN 978 1 529 36309 8
Trade Paperback ISBN 978 1 529 36310 4
eBook ISBN 978 1 529 36311 1

Typeset in Plantin by Manipal Technologies Limited

Printed and bound in Great Britain by Clays Ltd, Elcograf S.p.A.

Hodder & Stoughton policy is to use papers that are natural, renewable and
recyclable products and made from wood grown in sustainable forests.
The logging and manufacturing processes are expected to conform to
the environmental regulations of the country of origin.

Hodder & Stoughton Ltd
Carmelite House
50 Victoria Embankment
London EC4Y 0DZ

www.hodder.co.uk

*To Cliff*

# AUTHOR'S NOTE

Annie Carter is one of those strong, compulsive female characters that I love to write, and judging from all the five-star reviews that my series of books about her have received, it's extremely gratifying to see that my readers love her too. This novel – *Never Go Back* – dives deep into Annie's background and Max's backstory too, spanning both their lives and the lives of their families from East End 1950s poverty right through to the 1990s.

# PART ONE

# Caesar's Code

268
16242223
2341514
641515
168
23118
242324415
1915468
16413182164
16427

# I

Queenie Carter and her sister had always despised one another.

'She's such a moaner,' Queenie said about Nora.

'She's a bit of a *tart*,' Nora sniffed, disapproving of Queenie's liking for Bill Haley when he got up on stage with that ridiculous kiss-curl of his and belted out 'Shake Rattle and Roll'.

Nora had married early, and her husband, a dock worker called Ted Dawkins, had very tidily dropped dead one night after exiting the docks, falling gracefully into the gutter not six months after their wedding. He left Nora a young widow, with a small sum that she took down to Brighton, to set up a bed and breakfast establishment and make a bit of money off the tourists.

Queenie was warm-hearted, bold, loud and loving – the polar opposite of her plain, prudish older sister. Queenie fell recklessly in love and married an East End boy, a Carter who, much to her eventual disappointment, did *not* drop dead but lived on – and on – lazy, feckless, *useless* son of a bitch that he was.

She named them all herself, her three boys, her beloved sons, because her ale-soaked liability of a husband was neither use nor ornament – and by the time he made his mind up about anything, she'd already made the decision and acted upon it. He lounged day after day in his chair, complaining about the government, drinking beer and doing a fabulous impression of fuck-all. Marriage was a huge disappointment to Queenie. She grew bitter and resentful and she quickly lost interest in the once-handsome man she'd wed back in her optimistic girlhood, when she'd still had hopes and dreams to cling to. Bit by bit, all her passion for the man drained away in the face of his apathy. But she had to have *some* focus, so as the years went by, all her attention was lavished upon her sons.

Queenie's boys were her pride and joy. They were great boys, lovely boys, and she'd chew the head off anyone who said different. Her husband had at least managed three good things in his life – he'd given her delicate baby Edward, and Jonjo the rough-and-tumble middle son. And – best of all – there was the eldest, Max, the handsome one, the brightest too. Max was her favourite really, but you mustn't show favouritism. She knew that, so she did her best to hide it. Two years between each of them, and although Queenie was skint for a great part of the time – the war was not long over and there was still rationing – she made sure her boys wanted for little. She often went hungry herself to achieve that.

Boys were always into mischief. They weren't like girls. She'd wanted a girl of course – what mother did not? – but that hadn't happened. So she had to content herself with her three boys, and yes, they were often getting into trouble – Max especially. First with him it was a flat refusal to be told what to do at school. Then he'd be skiving off, leading his little brothers on wild chases, and the school inspector would be round and they'd have to turn the radio off and all be quiet and hide until the fucker went away.

'You little . . .' Dad would say, hoisting himself out of his chair long enough to raise a threatening hand to his eldest.

'You leave him alone!' Queenie would snap as Max darted out of reach behind her, too quick to be caught by his slothful father.

So, Max was the leader, the young prince, the heir apparent. Lumpish, slow-thinking Jonjo trailed after him, and Edward – Eddie – tried to keep up, but couldn't. Max was slight as a boy, not tall, not thick-set, but he had a commanding way about him. Jonjo was bigger, bulkier, but lacked Max's brain. You could imagine Jonjo running to fat in his middle years; his sheer size meant that he found it easy to intimidate smaller, weaker boys – like Eddie, who was almost girlish in his fragility. Jonjo often mocked him for it.

'We can't all be the same,' Queenie often said, pulling Eddie in for a cuddle. 'Jonjo, go out and play with Max and stop pushing our Eddie in the nettles while you're out there, all right? Or you'll see the back of my hand and no bloody supper.'

For a long while, the three boys thought their mum might even be one of those peculiar vegetarian types, because they had meat to eat, but she never touched it. It was only later on, as they grew older, that they realised she was simply giving the best of the food to them and doing without herself.

So, they grew. Max left school early on and joined one of the East End gyms for the boxing.

'He's so bloody scrawny, he'll get knocked to fuck,' said his dad, laughing, relishing the idea of the pushy little sod getting a pasting.

But Max didn't. He became stronger and he fought dirty. Queensbury rules? He laughed at the very idea. Slowly, the weedy boy with the thousand-yard stare grew muscular. And his dad gave up trying to take a swipe at him. Maybe Max wouldn't strike back at his own father, but his dad wasn't prepared to chance it. Sensing his wife's preference for her eldest son, Max's dad was often tempted to give the bolshie nipper a smack. But he suspected he might one of these fine days get knocked flat on his arse if he did, not only by Max himself but by Queenie too, who could be a right dragon when the mood was on her.

Jonjo joined the gym too, encouraged by Max's example. Not little Eddie, though – it was all a bit too physical, too rough, for him.

Then one day Max came home and found Queenie weeping in the front room.

'What is it, Mum?' he asked.

Dad was gone. He'd packed a bag that morning and fucked off. Queenie wouldn't miss him – Max knew that – but Dad had earned a bit on the Corona lorries sometimes and now they didn't have even that small wage coming in. Queenie quickly got another job cleaning. That made three jobs she had on the go, so she could at least still put food on the table for her lads. But she was never there when they needed her. Jonjo and Eddie were dragging themselves up, more or less. And as the man of the house now, the head of the household, Max was making up his own rules as he went along.

The Carters were barely scratching a living, hiding from the rent man, buying stuff on tick and then struggling to pay for it. Max hated that. He hated his father for running out on them and making a bad situation even worse than it already was. He was determined that this wasn't going to last. One way or another, he was going to break out of this downbeat endless struggle that made up their lives. He was going to be *rich*.

# 2

All through his growing up and into adulthood, Max felt the weight of the world upon his shoulders. He worried constantly about Mum. She wasn't strong. He looked at her pale, tired face and drooping shoulders and felt under intense pressure, felt that he should, he *must*, do something to change their situation. He was forever thinking up new and inventive ways of bringing in cash, because he could see quite clearly that Queenie was just about working herself to death. She was in and out of the house at all hours with her cleaning jobs. He knew she was struggling and he was determined to help out.

Max knew that he didn't have the application to turn pro as a boxer. He was altogether too bright and too wary of managers and promoters, too concerned about ending up punch-drunk and addled like so many did in that business. Jonjo might have given it a shot, if only he'd had the merest bit of self-discipline, which he did not. Boxing or crime – those were the only ways out of penury on the dirt-poor streets of the post-war East End, so Max decided that crime it was going to have to be.

Max and his old gang from schooldays still hung around together, loitering around the dance halls, getting into trouble. Steve Taylor had been working as a self-employed window cleaner. He even had his own round, he was sorted, but Max's siren call was loud and it was lucrative, so Steve chucked that in and joined Max's firm as a breaker. Tone Barton's father earned good money around Bermondsey on the docks, and for a while it looked like Tone might follow his dad into that, because it paid well enough. Dock worker's houses had fitted carpets, TVs and the latest radiograms – and every so often a crate of goods got damaged by being dropped onto the concrete unloading bay – usually deliberately – and so there was always a surfeit of marketable stuff to sell.

But Tone didn't fancy that work and he could see the way things were going around London, dock work thinning out by the day. He liked – because of his dad's comfy lifestyle – the luxury of having money on the hip. But more than that, he liked cars. He dreamed of being Stirling Moss one day. Fat chance, but he could dream. So when Max asked Tone if he wanted to join up as driver for the firm, and offered him a cut of any profits for the privilege, Tone jumped at it.

Sometimes the firm stole wages from shops and factories, using skeleton keys an old lag down The Grapes had sold to Max. The keys worked a treat, usually – hardly any of the businesses had alarms fitted.

'Piece of piss,' said Tone, parking a van he'd appropriated outside a hardware store.

Steve hopped out and went and tried a skeleton key in the shop lock. It didn't work. Glancing left and right, he got out his matches and let the black smoke run over the key. Then he put it back in the lock, waggled it, drew it back out. Now he could see from the smoke's outline where the thing was jamming. He went back to the van where Max and Jonjo were waiting, with Tone at the wheel.

'No good?' asked Max.

'Don't fit. Can't get it in,' said Steve.

'Ought to stick some hair round it, you'd find the opening quick enough then,' said Jonjo with a grin.

Max took the key and applied the file. 'That should do it,' he said, and handed it back to Steve.

Steve jumped down out of the van and went back to the shop door. This time, it worked. He nodded back at the van. Max and Jonjo piled out but Tone stayed put, with the motor running.

The three of them went inside the hardware shop. They moved around among the piles of screws, hammers, paint pots and saws, noting what was worth taking and intending to set off any hidden alarms. Then they went back outside, locked up and sat in the van again. Tone moved it down the road a safe distance, just on the remote possibility that the place was connected to the local nick. When the police failed to show up within half an hour, Max knew the coast was clear, and the place was theirs for the taking. That place – and many, many others.

An even easier game was the protection rackets, and Max got into that very early, setting up fights in clubs all around the city and then coming in with his tasty mates after the event with offers of coverage, for a price. Mostly the owners jumped at the chance, not realising they'd been set up, so Max started earning better. Apart from getting established in the protection business, he was also getting to be an expert thief.

He looted Dorothy Perkins one day, nabbing a fistful of fivers from inside the cashier's box and legging it out to the door to where his mate Tone was waiting behind the wheel of an old Armstrong Siddeley car. That worked out fine, but Max didn't like the risk and he didn't attempt it again. You could only do so many sudden little jobs like that, then sooner or later the Bill were going to be aware and then they'd grab you and there'd be a three-person cell in Wandsworth with your name on it. And there was no way Max was *ever* going to prison.

# 3

'Gawd! She looks like *him*, don't she?'

While the teenage Max Carter was busy out on the rob, Auntie Maureen, Connie Bailey's sister, was leaning over Annie Bailey's cradle and looking disapproving.

Annie was a dark-haired, red-faced little scrap, newly born, who bawled the place down night and day. Annie heard the same thing said about her when she was five years old, and ten, and fifteen. Somehow, she had committed the crime of the century by the simple act of arriving on earth looking like her own father.

Connie, Annie's mother, had another daughter too. Ruthie was two years older than Annie, and a sweeter, more obedient child altogether. Ruthie played quietly with her toys, Ruthie studied at school, Ruthie toed the line. Ruthie was pale, mousy-haired, wouldn't say boo to a goose. Annie was Technicolor while Ruthie was black and white. The more cuffs around the ear Annie got for being disobedient, the more she misbehaved. She didn't care. Dad called her his little princess and she was happy. So what if Mum hated her?

But then Dad left.

'You are *just* like your father!' Connie would rage at her youngest daughter.

After Dad's departure, Annie learned to keep well out of Connie's way.

'She don't mean it,' Ruthie would whisper to her in the night. 'Not really.'

But Annie thought that Connie *did* mean it. When she wasn't drinking and cursing her husband for having it away on his toes, she was taking a swipe at Annie over just about anything, because – Annie could never be allowed to forget – she looked like her father, and that, in the Bailey household, was unforgivable.

'She's the dead spit of him, that girl,' Auntie Maureen would hiss. 'Ain't she? Got that look in her eye like she don't give a damn for nothing.'

Annie grew up and became used to the fact that even the sight of her seemed to aggravate her mother.

'Maybe ease up on the drink,' Maureen said to Connie.

Drunk or sober, Connie would always take one look at Annie, see her missing husband staring back at her, and hit the roof.

So Annie grew a hard shell around her heart.

She'd loved her dad and he'd abandoned her. Maybe all the men in her future life would be nothing but a search for that missing father figure, the beloved Daddy who'd run out on her. She hated her mother and was despised in return. So what? She would cope. She grew into a beauty, eclipsing poor little goody-two-shoes Ruthie. And she grew up hard. She had to.

# 4

For Max, there was always anxiety over Queenie. He didn't like his mum working so hard, and he was earning good now, coining it. He told her that she needn't bother anymore.

'I'm a working woman, darlin',' she told him. 'I like to keep busy.'

Then one of her friends who worked down The Grapes was off sick, and the landlord said she'd suggested Queenie for a stand-in. So now – as well as the cleaning stuff during the day – she'd got this new evening job too, as a barmaid. For that, she had to dress up – 'make herself look shipshape', she said, laughing about it, trying to make light of it, while Max gritted his teeth and got into ever more dodgy stuff, more *lucrative* stuff, so that he could say to her, 'You can stop all this, Mum. We've got enough to keep us going now. Fuck the cleaning and fuck the bar work too.'

But Queenie wouldn't have it. She was a strong-willed woman and she relished a measure of independence. God knew, married to their father, she'd had little enough of that. Now, she was enjoying life. *Loving* it.

Despite Max's best efforts, there still never seemed to be quite enough cash coming in. Maybe someday soon, there would be. But not yet. So he carried on trying everything he could to alter the family situation, and Queenie carried on cleaning and going out to her job down The Grapes, first just evenings and then lunchtimes too. She'd be all dolled up, her hair in a fancy chignon, her tea dress tight around her waist, hugging her curves. She looked damned good for a woman with grown-up kids, and she knew it. She had a swagger about her and a mouth like the Mersey tunnel. Sometimes the Bill came round with questions about things 'her' boys had been up to, but she always saw them off with shrieks and yells of outrage.

'My boys are good boys!' she'd roar. 'They work hard and all they get off you lot is ruddy persecution!'

Queenie frightened the younger lawmen to bits. They always slunk away, defeated by the sheer scale of her verbal assaults. The older ones knew better. They chased Jonjo all the way back home one day, and out the backyard and through the gate. Queenie faced them down with a yard brush and a scowl of temper and saw them off.

'No wonder her husband ran for the hills,' the Bill muttered among themselves. 'Poor bastard, I'd run too from that loud-mouthed bitch.'

Not able to afford stockings, instead she painted lines up the backs of her legs with gravy browning, as she had done in the war, before slipping on her one good pair of high-heeled shoes, snatching up her handbag and going out the door to the barmaid job she seemed – much to Max's annoyance – to love.

She'd never dressed like that when Dad was here.

'You're overdoing it, I reckon,' said Max, uneasy. He didn't like her working in The Grapes. He didn't like the punters down the pub eyeing up his mother, flirting with her, the lairy bastards. It cheapened her. She flirted right back at them, and Max started to wonder what the hell she was up to, acting the tart like that.

'Don't be silly, son. Got to get earning, ain't we?' She'd smile, dabbing on red lippy and blusher before leaving Eddie and Jonjo in his care, who invariably started fighting. Half the time there was a battle on Max's hands, just keeping Jonjo off Eddie's back. Then one day Jonjo found Eddie mucking about with Queenie's make-up, dabbing on lippy like he'd seen their mum do.

'You bent little fucker!' roared Jonjo and started laying into Eddie.

Max heard the commotion from downstairs and ran up, two at a time. He pulled Jonjo off, pushed him away.

'Leave him be,' Max ordered. 'He's not hurting you, is he?'

Jonjo was panting, his face contorted with rage. He pointed at Eddie and Eddie flinched back. One of Jonjo's punches had smeared Queenie's lipstick all over Eddie's face. He looked both comical and pathetic, like a clown. 'It's fucking disgusting. He ain't a girl.'

'Leave it. I mean it.'

Max had more important things on his mind. He went in The Grapes and saw the men chatting his mother up and it made him want to puke. This was his *mother*. But she was doing it for the money, and she was obstinate. She'd never give the job up, and so he had to shift himself, bring in more and more loot – and then perhaps she'd stop and maybe just be content even with a couple of little cleaning jobs. Or stop altogether, just let him support her? That was what he wanted, ideally. It irritated him that her mate who'd been off sick didn't come back to the job at The Grapes, which meant that Queenie, to her obvious delight, stayed on.

Max started shifting dodgy motors around the manor and sold as much stolen gear as he could lay his hands on, like the big load of nicked police shoes that he offloaded in Smith-field meat market. He had a lorry load of fashion goods that had been bound for West End shops that his gang sold off all around the manor, and a load of furniture that had come up from Southampton docks. He grafted longer hours than anybody, thieving and selling, sometimes buying cheap and selling dear, covering the clubs, making whatever he could *however* he could, to build up a pot of money so that Mum could see sense, that she should stop the pub work and the cleaning stuff too, and relax a bit more.

Soon – much to his relief – he was able to tell Queenie he had enough to keep the Carters; she didn't have to graft like she did. They argued about it and Queenie relented. She gave up her cleaning jobs, but said she enjoyed the bar work – and there was no way she was stopping doing that, not to please him, not to please *anybody*.

'Now let's not fall out over this,' Queenie said to her eldest son.

'We won't,' said Max.

'Yes we bloody will. Unless you fucking well drop it, my lad.'

'All right, all right! I won't mention it again,' said Max, who could smell trouble long before it ever materialised. How did it reflect on him and on the business he was steadily building up, his mother being a barmaid? It irked him, *tormented* him.

'You swear?' said Queenie.

'I swear it. All right?'

'Good!'

Then one day what Max had feared would happen actually did. Queenie brought home one of the punters, Clive Jensen. He was a flashy salesman from up north who – to Max's intense annoyance – made her giggle and flirt like he had never seen her do with Dad.

Max and his brothers had been used to seeing Queenie with her mouth turned down, wearing drab unflattering gear, cursing Dad as the useless waster sat there in his armchair, reading the *Racing Post* and smoking roll-ups. But this was a new Queenie – pouting, laughing, enticing her new beau.

'It's fucking sickening to see,' said Jonjo.

Max agreed. He was seriously pissed off. He had been working his arse off to allow Mum to stop with all this, to concentrate instead on being a steady, reliable housewife, a mother to her adult sons, one of whom had a strong and fast-growing reputation in the area to think about. Clive took to lounging around the Carter house, staying for his tea, getting in Max's face, smirking at him. But if Max poked Clive on the jaw – as he longed to do – he could see that Queenie was only going to come roaring to the bastard's defence. So he left it, hoping – praying – that it would fizzle out.

And eventually it did, and Max was thankful. Not that Queenie was. Suddenly, Clive was gone – and Queenie was moping about the place, drinking too much gin, crying in the night when she thought they couldn't hear her; but they could. Without Max's prompting and much to his astonishment, she then gave up the job at The Grapes and sat about looking dismal. Gone were the flattering clothes, the giggly demeanour. Now she wore big shape-covering items that did nothing to flatter her. She tied her hair back in a rough bun and forgot about make-up. This was worse than the Queenie of old, the bored and put-upon wife she'd been when Dad was here.

Max jollied her along, took her out to dinner at the swanky places he could now afford. But nothing seemed to snap Queenie out of her mood. She was depressed. She drank far too much. She fell asleep on the sofa. The mum they'd always known had disappeared, and it was a worry for them all – but mostly for Max.

# 5

Queenie knew she'd been a fool. Having been used to a married life full of nothing but dull misery, she could admit – only to herself, mind – that she had gone a little wild when all that was over. Suddenly, free of matrimonial tedium, she felt like a woman again and it was wonderful; men paid her attention. Most particularly one man: Clive. The only man – ever – who could make a purring pussycat out of the snarling tigress she knew herself to be. He'd shown up in The Grapes, suited and booted, handsome, merry-eyed, a commercial traveller with a seductive line in patter. Clive really could charm the birds from the trees; to her own surprise, he charmed Queenie.

Like one of those old snake oil sellers in the western movies, he laid out his wares – encyclopaedias, silk stockings, ornaments, brushes – and the housewives flocked around, interested, blushing at his words as he teased them, lured them into spending their husbands' hard-earned money, which many of them could ill afford, on his goods. Queenie knew that Max didn't like Clive hanging around, but for God's sake! Didn't she deserve a little bit of pleasure, after all the dross she'd been through in her life?

Clive might have had a way with all the ladies, but to Queenie's surprise he seemed to single her out for his special attention. He treated her nicely, and she wasn't used to that. She found herself smiling more. Whistling on her way in to do her shift. She wasn't in love – she was getting a bit too long in the tooth for that stuff – but there was a powerful physical pull from Clive, like magnetism. When Queenie listened to Al Martino crooning out 'Here in My Heart' on the pub radio, she always thought of Clive.

They kissed a few times, out in the tiny beer garden at the back of the pub, the kisses becoming increasingly desperate. If people came out there, they had to spring apart, they had to be discreet. She was still a married woman even if her husband had cleared off. She was still the mother of Max Carter who was a rising star in the East End and she had to consider that, be careful never to cause Max embarrassment.

'You know I want you, don't you,' Clive whispered in her ear. 'I want you so much.'

'Yes, but we have to be careful,' Queenie told him. She didn't feel she wanted to be careful, but she *had* to be.

'Please,' he moaned against her throat, causing ripples of sensation to shimmer up her spine. 'Please, honey, we must.'

And then one night she weakened and – to her shame – he coaxed her out into the alley behind the pub. Suddenly he was kissing her, over and over, rendering her weak, blissful, uncaring. His hands were all over her and she wanted that; she wanted it so much that when he pulled down her underwear and freed his manhood from his trousers she could only raise the thinnest of objections.

'Clive, no . . .' she groaned, but it was too late, he was frantic and so was she; she felt him searching, groping, finding her and then heard his gasp of triumph as he pushed himself eagerly into her waiting flesh. She was ready for him, *more* than ready. He did it to her right there in the dark, holding her up against the wall, arousing something in her that she could only vaguely remember, an animal passion that had long ago been a part of her life. Now, it was back with a vengeance. Sex had been off limits for years with the boys' father and she had felt herself sinking into a miserable middle age, sitting in an armchair and waiting to grow older, waiting for the grim reaper to show up with his scythe and put an end to it all.

She had accepted that situation. But now – incredibly – she was free of it! After the time in the alley behind The Grapes, she went willingly, carelessly, to the rooms Clive rented and spent hot, lusty afternoons in his bed.

She felt like a girl again. It was nothing short of a miracle when he brought her to orgasm after orgasm, stifling her ecstatic cries under his hand, kissing her breasts, whispering how much he loved her. She was astonished at her own responses. She was enjoying this, loving it. Already her periods had stuttered almost to a halt; she'd thought that sex was behind her, a thing of the past, but now she thanked God every day that it was not.

Sex with Clive was a revelation. Her husband had never been all that in the sack – but Clive was a maestro. He touched her and she caught fire. Time after time they lay there in each other's arms, exhausted from lovemaking, the scent of brandy and sex and cigars coiling around them like incense. This was how it should always have been, she realised. Her life with her useless husband had been a criminal waste, when she could have had a live wire like Clive instead. And Clive actually *talked* to her. Clive had big dreams that he told her about. He made her feel that somehow she could be a part of his future.

'I'm going to take over the company,' he said. 'The owner's retiring, and I've got just enough to buy the business off him. Then I could employ salesmen of my own and sit in a fine big office somewhere letting *them* do all the rep work.'

She loved to hear him talk, and his plans did sound exciting. Almost as exciting as he was in bed.

Her husband – that miserable bastard – had never really
been too bothered about the sexual side of things. Three kids
and then he'd thrown the towel in, given up. For a while,
Queenie had felt hurt by that, rejected. She'd even tried making overtures to him but was always brushed away, which
was humiliating. Soon she hadn't even bothered to try. It had
all got lost in the everyday business of living. After all, she
wasn't a hopeful girl anymore, she was a mature woman. Yes,
middle-aged. Washed up. Over the hill.

But with Clive, everything was different. Suddenly there
was a spring in her step, a new light in her eyes.

'I love you,' he whispered to her as they lay dazed in the
afterglow of lovemaking.

She never said it back; she was afraid to. The times they
shared were precious, and she didn't want to think about
the future, about where this might be heading. She was only
interested in the *now*, being here with him, holding him, feeling loved, safe, secure, a woman again after so many years
of nothingness.

Then – as suddenly as he had appeared – Clive Jensen was
gone.

For days she waited in puzzlement for him to show up at
The Grapes with his flashy suits and his smile and his laughing blue eyes. Had he been in an accident maybe? She was
anxious, worried for him. Then she started asking the regulars, had they seen him?

No one had.

'He's moved on I reckon,' said one, stabbing her straight
through the heart with his casual words. 'That's what they
do, ain't it, commercial travellers. They bomb out an area

until there's no more pickings to be had, then they move on to the next.'

No. That couldn't be right. She knew it couldn't. Clive loved her.

She asked around at some of the other boozers in the area, but no one had seen or heard a thing about him. She went to the flat he'd rented, where an old harridan with knowing eyes informed her that Mr Jensen had paid up last week and gone.

Aware that one or two of the regulars in The Grapes were starting to look at her askance, perhaps suspecting what had been happening between the travelling salesman and the bar-maid, Queenie stopped asking. She couldn't bear any of this getting out. She had her sons to think of, and most particu-larly Max's standing in the neighbourhood. She was mother to the Carter boys and people respected that. These days she always got served first in the corner shop, people stepped aside for her. She *was* a queen, a queen of the East End, because of her eldest, Max, who was doing so very well for himself these days. There was no way, no way at all, that she could embarrass him.

So – Clive was gone. Queenie still stood behind the bar, taking orders, chatting to the punters, but feeling numb, like someone had cut out her heart, but somehow she still had to function.

She hadn't loved him. Of course not. She told herself that, over and over. Love? That was for youngsters, for impres-sionable girls. But not seeing him, not knowing that there would be that magic happening between them – it killed her.

So she stopped wearing pretty dresses; stopped painting lines up the backs of her legs. She felt sick and tired and worst of all she felt a fool. He had used her. She could see that now. He'd been here doing business and he'd wanted sex – and he'd quickly realised that she was desperate for it. He'd sensed it on her, smelled it on her like musk off a female beast in heat. She'd been *such a bloody fool.*

So, chalk it up to experience, she thought. It was over. Life went on. There wouldn't be any more ruddy men. She'd been a bored wife and – so briefly, so heartbreakingly briefly – she'd been alive and thrilled, a sensual creature all over again just like she'd been in her youth. She had believed herself to be adored. But there would be no more of that. She put her glad rags away and cursed herself for her stupidity. No more.

She was Queenie Carter, the middle-aged mother of grown men. Max, Jonjo and Eddie. Time for her to grow up too, put all that sex nonsense in the past where it belonged.

She was determined to do that. In the chilly light of this new reality, she realised that it was disgusting, *common*, the way she'd been carrying on. What had she been thinking? What if her relatives or her neighbours ever knew? What if – God forbid – her sons should ever find out the carryings-on their mother had been up to, rolling around in bed getting her end away, screaming with pleasure, being kissed all over her squirming and treacherously responsive body by a chancer like Clive?

Still, she cried in the night, thinking of him and his laughing blue eyes. She dreamed of his arms around her and woke up bereft, wanting him back, *willing* him back with her.

But he never came.

He was gone, on to the next area, the next woman.

So be it. Her heart was broken into a thousand pieces but she would live with it.

She would grow a tough shell over the hurt and the disappointment. Somehow, she would go on as normal.

But then she realised she was pregnant.

# 6

Having found out that she was up the duff, Queenie Carter knew there was nothing for it but to take herself off down to her sister Nora's in Brighton. Nora was a pain in the arse, but she was her sister and Queenie had no one else she could turn to in her hour of need. Certainly, she couldn't stop at home and be humiliated when her pregnancy became obvious to all. Everyone around the East End knew that her hubby had abandoned ship a long, long time ago. They would add up the facts and easily come to the conclusion that she, a woman past her prime who ought to know better and to conduct herself in a decent fashion, had been out hooking her pearly with some arsehole she should have left well alone.

Then of course all the regulars down The Grapes would quickly realise that the baby's father was Clive. And word would spread; her name would be mud, she would be embarrassed, Max and Jonjo and Eddie would get into fights over people bad-mouthing her. And Max might track Clive down and do him damage. Despise Clive though she might, she found that she didn't want that to happen. She didn't want any harm coming to him. How soft did that make her? But this was the worst thing – her boys would know. And she couldn't take that. She really couldn't.

Not that they were boys anymore. They were men full grown, and they would be disgusted with her over this. Of course they would. And this was awful, too awful to contemplate – that Max, who was her pride and joy, would realise his own mother was nothing but a slag. It wouldn't matter to him or Jonjo or even Eddie that she'd fallen in love – yes, she could admit now that it had been love – at such an inappropriate time of life. They would hear the coarse laughs and the rumours and they would get into all sorts of scrapes trying to defend her, but really they would be ashamed of her, which was no more than she deserved.

She couldn't let that happen.

She *couldn't*.

So somehow she had to get herself out of this situation – and the only thing she could come up with was Nora.

She wrote to Nora, asking if she could come and stay with her for a bit. As the weeks passed her anxiety grew. She checked the post every day, hurrying to intercept it before her boys could get it. Queenie wasn't in the habit of staying in regular contact with her sister – after all, they'd never seen eye to eye – so she knew a letter with a Brighton postmark on it would instantly arouse curiosity.

She couldn't let that happen, either.

Then – one miraculous day – there was an answer. Yes, Nora said, she could come and stay. Was there something wrong?

Queenie didn't bother to reply to that. Her condition was becoming ever more obvious, and soon she wouldn't be able to persuade anyone that she wasn't in the family way. She was always careful now to wear loose, concealing clothes, but she was blowing up like a ruddy Zeppelin and soon it was going to be too obvious to conceal.

So she had to pack up and tell Max she was off to Brighton for a while, change of scene, she was tired and she needed a rest. He called in at teatime – as he often did – to find her taxi waiting outside. He went into the house and there was Queenie, standing in the hall with a bag packed.

'What's this?' he asked.

'I'm going down to your Aunt Nora's place for a few weeks. You three can manage, can't you?'

Max was surprised, to say the least. Queenie and Nora weren't close; but he reasoned that it would do Mum good to get away, take in the sea air. He felt he couldn't stand much more of her hanging around the place looking fed up over the loss of that waster Clive.

''Course we can manage,' he told her, kissing her cheek. Then he frowned. 'There's nothing wrong, is there?'

Just lately, her health hadn't seemed at all good. He knew she'd been sickly as a child with scarlet fever. She caught colds easily, and where once she had simply shrugged them off, now she seemed to take ages to recover.

'Nothing that a bit of rest won't cure,' she said, with a faint suggestion of her old sassy grin.

'You have a good time then,' he said, and watched her out the door and down the path.

He watched her get into the taxi, talk to the driver. Watched the car speed away. He'd been right all along – she *had* been overdoing it. She needed a break.

Max turned back to the house. He, however, couldn't afford the luxury of time off. He had deals going down all over the city these days. He'd grown up on his wits from helpless child to feisty boy and now he was a tough, competent, *fearsome* man who could take on anything and anybody. And Davey Delaney, one of the big gang bosses over Battersea way, had been in touch, saying he might have some work to put Max's way. So – at last – things were looking up.

# 7

Once she was in the taxi Queenie dared to relax for the first time in far too long. Then it was the train, then another taxi and finally she was on Brighton's blustery seafront, tapping on the door of Nora's tall narrow bow-fronted and cream-painted terrace house that she ran as a B & B. There was a 'vacancies' sign up in the window beside the highly polished turquoise door.

'Hello, sis,' said Nora, dour as always, thin and pinch-faced. She cast a sharp eye over her sister. 'What's up then, kid? You got trouble?'

It was Nora's long-forgotten pet name for her that did it. *Kid.* Nora, being the older sister by two years, had always called Queenie 'kid', or 'our Queen'. Queenie stood there on the doorstep and, having intended to conduct herself with absolute dignity, started to cry.

'Blimey!' said Nora in alarm. Then she lowered her voice. 'Don't stand there bloody howling. I got guests staying. Come in for the love of God. What's up with you?'

'I'm in the family way,' said Queenie past her sobs. She could barely get the words out.

Nora stood there, open-mouthed. Her eyes swept up and then down over Queenie's form. Then she gathered herself and said: 'But that useless old man of yours left ages ago. Didn't he?'

'He did,' said Queenie.

'Oh.' Nora's thin mouth tightened to a line of disapproval. 'Then . . . it's not his?'

Queenie sniffed, hard. The tears stopped and suddenly her eyes were like flint. 'Of course it bloody isn't. Don't be stupid.'

'Then whose is it?'

'Nobody you know.'

Queenie stood there, bereft, exhausted, wrung out with emotion and now she was getting the third bloody degree. This was so typical of Nora. Always the precise one, the one who always had to have the fine detail spelled out for her. Never caring about feelings, the way people actually were under the skin, the magic that could happen, the passion that could ignite when a man and a woman came together. She'd say that was filthy lust, that it was disgusting. But Queenie knew, in her heart, that what she'd had with Clive had been anything but. It had been beautiful. It had been heaven. It had been – yes – *love*. But now she was paying a price for that, and the price was far too bloody dear.

'God's sake!' muttered Nora. 'Well come in. Don't just stand there on the fucking doorstep.'

★

'The obvious thing is to give it up to the adoption people,' said Nora when she and her sister sat down for a cup of tea late that evening.

They were in the kitchen where Nora prepared all the breakfasts for her guests. Above them, Queenie could hear people moving around the bedrooms, settling in for the night after a day or the pier or shopping in the Lanes or picnicking on the shingly Brighton beach.

Queenie nodded. Of course. That was the only thing they could do. Wasn't it?

Of course it was.

Nora had gone straight to the solution, easy as that. It seemed to Queenie that Nora had been born to be a widow. Even as a girl, she'd had that prune-faced look about her, repelling most advances from boys until she was snapped up by the late and not-much-lamented Ted Dawkins. Queenie suspected that Ted hadn't had a single good fuck in him, the poor skinny bastard. She knew her sister and she knew that Nora's marriage to poor Ted had been mostly financially driven, being that dock workers earned so well.

There was no doubt that Nora had worked hard after Ted had collapsed into the gutter and left this world. She'd wisely used the nest egg he'd left her to get this house so that she could run it and make some money – whereas Queenie had fallen in love with a no-hoper and had her own small cache of savings snatched away and pissed up against the wall by her worthless husband. Then she had laboured long and hard at menial jobs, struggling to bring up her three sons with little assistance. She'd got cleaning jobs, then *more* cleaning jobs after her husband had run out on her, then the bar work on top of it all. And then finally – worst of all – she'd gone and got herself banged up.

'That's all women's work,' her husband had always grumbled when Queenie had suggested he might, in some small way, lend her a hand around the house.

And then – just like that – he'd up and gone, taken off for God knew where and just left her to it. Her life had been one long uphill battle, until the bliss she'd found with Clive. Ah, she knew she'd been a fool. But for a while, she'd been happy.

'Tried the gin, have you?' asked Nora, coughing delicately as they sat there into the night, drinking tea and trying to work out the best solution to the problem. 'Lots of gin and a good hot soak – that's what I heard.'

'That's bollocks,' said Queenie. 'Yes I've tried it. And no, it don't work.'

Nora drained her cup and lowered her eyes to the tabletop. 'I heard there are women who do things – you know, to get rid of a problem like this. If we could find one . . .'

'No, I'm not bloody doing that,' said Queenie with a shudder, thinking of metal hooks tearing at her insides. 'Forget that. I'm not doing it.'

Nora cast a critical eye over her sister's form – what she could see of it, anyway. Queenie was wearing a huge assortment of loose draperies – it was impossible to see whether she was pregnant or not.

'You're sure about it?' she asked. 'You couldn't be mistaken?'

'Yeah. Dead sure,' sighed Queenie, thinking that this was crippling her with embarrassment. She'd been caught out, like a teenager. Her! A sensible, hard-working woman. 'I've had three kids already, Nor. They're adults for Christ's sake. Look, I know what I know.'

Nora put both hands on the table and slapped the surface briskly. 'So how far gone are you then?' she asked, her lips pursed in distaste.

'Over five months I reckon,' said Queenie, who had done the dates.

'That much! But you don't show too bad, do you?'

'I never showed much with the first three,' said Queenie. She clutched her head. 'Jesus! That was so long ago. Boys carry at the front, don't they. Just a small bump. This one's shaping up to be just the same. Damn it, Nora, I didn't think it was possible to get pregnant at this age or I would have taken precautions.'

'I don't want the fine details,' said Nora primly.

'Oh shut up, Nora,' said Queenie.

'You don't half get yourself into some scrapes, our Queen. I was always sort of glad I never fell for a baby before poor Ted fell off the twig like he did. Seeing the mess you're in now, I'm gladder still.'

'Oh thanks,' said Queenie, thinking that 'poor Ted' had probably had a merciful release from a long and stone-cold existence with his cheerless, nit-picking little wife. 'That's a great help.'

'There's nothing to be done. You just have the kid, and then we get the authorities to take it.'

Queenie nodded. It would be easy. It would also be appalling, painful, embarrassing – but then, she'd lived through worse. And once it was done and the kid out of the way, she could go back to her life sadder and wiser – and carry on.

# 8

Once her schooldays were over, Annie Bailey suffered through the inevitable 'final report' scene with Connie.

'Look what it says here. She's intelligent and she could be something special if she'd only make the effort!' Connie raged.

'I'm sure Annie tried her best, Mum,' Ruthie said, trying to be helpful to her younger sister.

'Her best? Her *best*? She don't know the meaning of the word. She's just an idle little cow!' Connie threw the report in Annie's face. 'You know your trouble?' she roared.

*Let me guess,* thought Annie.

'You are just like your bloody father!' yelled Connie.

Annie sat there, obstinate, unmoving, and took it. School was over, thank God. She'd plodded through that, acquired a minimal amount of education, scarcely even paying attention to any of it, and now she was out on the loose. A job would be good. Down the biscuit factory. In the local hairdresser's maybe. Maybe in one of those swish boutiques up Carnaby Street. Or the corner shop – they were advertising for a shop assistant. Annie had little interest in jobs, just like she'd had little interest in school, but what *did* interest her was earning, and keeping out of her mother's way. Anywhere that was pulling in a bit of cash and was out from under Connie's drunken stumbling feet was just fine with Annie.

*Have another drink, you old wreck,* she thought. *That'll shut you up.*

Connie had another drink and passed out on the sofa. Ruthie left her job at the tyre factory and found another in one of the clubs up west. Annie burned her school report out in the back yard.

Right. She'd settle for the corner shop. Why not?

And there were other diversions too. One day as she came out of the house she saw a small boy across the street, being beaten about the head by two older lads. Cars cruised by, their occupants uncaring. Then one stopped and out stepped this sharply dressed black-haired bloke. He caught hold of each of the bigger lads by the scruffs of their necks and yanked them away from the smaller boy.

'Oi!' he yelled out. 'Enough, all right, the pair of you! Piss off, yeah?'

And the two boys scarpered. Another man stepped out of the car as the black-haired man hauled the little boy back to his feet.

'He all right is he, Max?' asked the one who'd just got out of the car.

'Yeah, he's fine. Aintcha Timmy?' He slapped the boy on the shoulder and the boy ran off.

A door opened along the street and an aproned woman with her hair in curlers peered out. The boy ran into her arms.

'Wha . . . ?' she started, then looked along to where the two men were standing. 'Oh! Morning, Mr Carter,' she said.

'All right, Vi?' said the stunner with the black hair.

'Fine.' She smiled.

'Tell Bert I've got that thing I promised him,' said the black-haired one.

'I will. Thank you.'

The two men got back in the car.

Annie stood there staring after it as it moved away, up the street, turned the corner and was gone.

She felt like she'd been hit.

*Max Carter.*

# 9

Davey Delaney was cock of the walk, king of Battersea, a very big noise on the London streets. He'd come over with his wife Molly from Ireland years back and set himself up doing deals and getting his family firmly entrenched in the area. In between making himself a fortune, he trawled the East End gyms looking for likely lads who had talent and were soft enough to be made use of, or had brains and needed seeing off.

Anything that earned, Max was up for. He'd never liked his old lady working her fingers to the bone. Truthfully, poverty had completely blighted his early years. Queenie's kids had often gone hungry, little Eddie sucking a halfpenny Oxo on his way to school instead of getting a good breakfast down him, Max and Jonjo filching their food from wherever they could. They'd grown up coping, surviving, and it was in them now, running in their blood. None of them could forget their poor upbringing, or ever be truly free of its grip.

'I got work for a lad like you,' Delaney told Max, and Max was tempted.

Davey Delaney was a greasy old Irish mobster with a plume of shocking red hair turning grey around his big sticking-out ears. His nose looked overlong and bent to one side, broken in a fight no doubt, and his green eyes were warm as a lizard's. He'd come and stand by the ring down the boxing club and watch the lads taking punches off the trainer, giving a few back. His own grown-up kids were rarely seen around Bow but Max knew he had five – Tory, Pat, Kieron, and a set of twins – Redmond and Orla. Max always thought of his own dad's face whenever he landed a punch in the ring. He would never, ever forgive the bastard, clearing off like that, leaving their mum to fend for herself, leaving his kids to go hungry.

'What sort of work?' he asked Davey.

'The sort that pays well,' came the reply. 'Time to move up a gear, my lad. You're playing with the big boys now.'

Max could believe that. Delaney was always dolled up to the nines, flashing a lot of gold jewellery about, krugerrands set in thick gold rings, medallions, thick Belcher chain brace-lets. He wore loud, big-checked and immaculately tailored outfits. Max and Jonjo and Steve and Tone were only a bit removed from the ragtag band of up-and-coming kids they'd once been, but Delaney and his thuggish boys were already a step up from that. Max's crew still smelled of desperation. Delaney smelled of cologne and he had the impermeable gloss of riches – and Max wanted that for himself.

'Any of you lot know how to drive?' Delaney asked the lit-tle group of young men when their training session was over and they were gathered around, chatting.

'Why?' asked Max, ever the suspicious one.

'Because my driver's gone off sick. Got a job down Newhaven, collecting some items. Pay's good.'

'Tone can drive.' Jonjo smirked. Tone shoved him and Jonjo laughed. Tone had done a short spell last year in the young offender's gaff for twocking – taking a car without the owner's consent. Tone was a demon behind the wheel; he had a knack for it.

'Any good?' asked Delaney.

'Fair,' said Tone modestly. All his mates knew that Tone could make a car – any car – turn on a sixpence.

'I'll drop a motor off round Whitney Street this aft at four,' said Delaney. 'Keys'll be inside. Deal?'

He spat in his hand, held it out to Max. Max stared into Delaney's eyes for a second, then spat and shook. 'Deal,' he said.

'Then you got a job, you lot. You three—' he looked at Max, Jonjo and Steve '—you all go along, in case there's trouble.' He turned his attention to Max again, who was obviously the leader of this motley crew. 'You pick up the holdalls off Carl Bentley the skipper of the *Rebecca*. He'll meet you at eight out behind the Lamb and Flag in Newhaven high street. You leave the car with the keys in the ignition back in Whitney Street. And you bring the goods back to me here on Thursday at ten in the morning. Then I'll pay you.'

'How much?' asked Max, thinking that this was odd; at the very least, Delaney should have wanted one of his crew along for the ride, if only to make sure they didn't make off with the loot themselves and make a far prettier penny than whatever he was going to promise them.

'More than you're worth.' Delaney laughed. 'You'll be well rewarded, don't you worry.'

'And if we get caught?' asked Jonjo.

'You don't mention my name. You're like the secret service – you got that? You get caught, you're on your own.'

'It's a fit-up,' Steve said, when Delaney had left.

'Or a test,' said Max.

'I don't like it,' said Jonjo.

'Tough, we're doing it,' said Max. If this jaunt to Newhaven proved their worth to Delaney – who was one of the big bosses, noted among the Richardsons, the Krays, the Foremans – people with a lot of clout – then they were seriously on the up.

They met in Whitney Street. One of the big muscle-bound yobs who always hung around Davey Delaney was there, looking enough like him for Max to identify him as Pat, the second-eldest Delaney son. Pat was lounging against the door of a tired-looking old Jaguar motor. He said: 'Tank's full,' then he opened the car door, showed them the keys with a grin, and left them to it.

They piled in, Tone at the wheel, Max riding shotgun in the front passenger seat, Steve and Jonjo in the back.

'I don't much like this,' said Jonjo.

Max didn't entirely like it either. He was thinking that maybe someone had tipped old man Delaney off to a rising young gang assembling itself in the boxing hall, and he was now intent on killing off any possible competition. Maybe by drafting them into his own firm – yes, that was possible. Or maybe by stitching them up on a dummy job so they got their arses caned by Old Bill.

Maybe Davey Delaney had got wind of some sort of trouble involving these shipments and he wasn't about to risk his own crew being involved if things went tits up. Either way, Delaney won and Max and his boys could lose big style. Weighing it all up, Max decided he'd take the chance, hope for the best outcome but prepare for the worst. They had to get in the Lamb and Flag and out again with the holdalls double quick, no messing about.

Tone drove them down to Newhaven, not speeding. 'This accelerator's as rough as arseholes,' he told them in disgust when they were halfway there. 'And the brakes are just about shot.'

'Just get us there and let's get this over,' said Max.

They reached the Lamb and Flag and Tone parked up. They went through the public bar and straight out into the courtyard at the back where the empty barrels were stacked, ready to go back to the brewery. There was a tall stick-thin man standing there, wearing a seaman's cap and a grubby navy reefer jacket. He was clutching a big brown holdall in each hand.

Max approached him. 'You here for us?' he asked. 'What's your name?'

'Carl Bentley. Skipper off the *Rebecca*. Who sent you?'

'Delaney,' said Max.

'You're not the usual fellas.'

'No, we're doing this one job for him.'

'Fair enough.' Bentley shrugged, uncaring. He handed over the holdalls to Jonjo and Steve, then shot out through the back gate. Max and his crew went back through the public bar, but as they got to the front door Max froze. Uniformed customs men were coming in, blocking their escape route.

'If you can stop right there please, sir,' said one. 'We have reason to believe . . .'

But Max shoved past him, knocked his companion to the floor, and was gone.

# 10

Amid shouts and punches and yells, Max's crew – being younger, fitter and desperate – all surged out, following Max past the customs men and away to the motor where Tone was waiting behind the wheel with the engine ticking over.

'What the fuck?' he asked as they piled in at a run.

'*Drive*,' said Max, looking out the back window and seeing the customs officials getting into another car right behind theirs.

Rubber burned as Tone floored the accelerator and the Jag flew off along the street. The customs were instantly in hot pursuit. 'Get this moving faster, Tone,' said Max urgently. So it *was* a set-up. Delaney must have got wind of possible trouble and thrown them to the wolves rather than risk his own arse.

That *bastard*.

'I'm trying,' said Tone, sweat beading his brow despite the chill of the night air. 'Thing's a bloody wreck.'

The Jag screamed along, out through the town and into the countryside. At odd corners they lost the customs men, but they were persistent, appearing again, always there, always coming.

'They're not going to give this up,' said Steve when they once more thought they were clear, only to see the headlights of the customs car rounding another bend, creeping ever closer.

Then there was a loud clunk and Tone swore as the Jag started to slow.

'What is it?' demanded Max.

'Fucking thing,' said Tone, and swerved the car into the side of the road, killing the engine.

Jonjo was staring nervously out the back window. For the moment, they were clear. But now the car was kaput, their only hope was to leave the thing and leg it for all they were worth.

Steve grabbed a torch and stepped out into the road. 'Get the bonnet up Tone,' he said, and went around the front of the car.

Max wound his window down and sat there listening for the customs car. So far, nothing. This was turning into a bloody disaster. Tone popped the bonnet and they watched with bated breath while Steve peered around under there by torchlight.

'Fuck!' said Steve.

'What is it?' asked Max. He could hear something coming. The bloody customs car. They were done for. They'd have to abandon this heap of scrap and run.

'Accelerator arm's bust,' said Steve. 'Start the damned engine, Tone. I'll hold it.'

'He can't hold it,' said Jonjo, panting with nerves. 'How the fuck can he?'

'They're coming,' said Max grimly.

Tone started the engine. Steve piled in under the bonnet, clutching the broken parts of the accelerator arm together, and pulled the bonnet down on top of him. Tone floored the accelerator and the car – thank God! – started to move. Soon they were motoring along the country lane again, until Tone steered the car into a farmer's field, killed the lights and the engine. They stayed there, hidden by a hedge, as the customs men shot past, away.

Everyone breathed a sigh of relief. Steve came around to the back of the car and flopped down inside. He was covered in smuts and oil stains. His coat was in ribbons.

'Jesus,' he said. 'That was close.'

'Yeah, it was,' said Max. Steve had been nothing less than a bloody hero tonight.

'Delaney saw that coming,' said Jonjo angrily.

Max knew that for once in his pea-brained life, Jonjo was right. They'd been set up for a fall.

# I I

The day dawned, as Queenie knew it must – the day when she was lumbering her swollen form up the stairs with bedsheets in hand to change over the linen for the next set of tourists when she stopped, doubled over and clutched at her belly.

'Jesus!' she shrieked.

Nora came haring out of the kitchen in alarm, just in time to see Queenie's waters cascading down, all over her stair runner.

'I cleaned that this morning,' she howled in outrage.

Queenie slumped on the stairs, her stomach cramping fiercely. All the clean sheets were scattered, sodden with wetness. The contractions had started. She gritted her teeth, unable to speak a word, and when the first of them was past Nora was there on the stairs with her, hitching an arm around her sister's waist.

'Can you stand? The folks'll be back soon and I don't want them finding you here like this.'

Queenie grimaced and a sob escaped her. The pain was coming again. Jesus, this baby was going to come in a hurry. But then – all her boys had. Thinking of that made her think of Max, of how sickened he would be if he knew what sort of a loose cow his mother truly was. She heaved herself upright, sagging against Nora's skinny form and nearly toppling them both down the stairs into the hallway.

'Come on, let's get you to bed,' said Nora, and together they puffed and panted up the stairs and got Queenie into the bedroom she'd been occupying these past months.

'It's early,' said Queenie. 'It's too early.'

'Just a couple of weeks,' Nora told her firmly. 'Better get it done, yes? Get it over with.'

\*

The baby arrived two hours later. Queenie had been right – it was another boy. She was destined never to have girls; that much was obvious. Had it been a girl – a little girl in her own image, a companion for life – would she have somehow found a way to hold on to the baby? But no – she couldn't. And it being a boy took the agony of that decision away from her. The kid had to go. And there would be no more kids, not now, not ever. No more romances. No more bloody men.

'It's a pretty little thing,' said Nora, when the baby was delivered.

Nora never having had kids, Queenie had talked her through what she had to do, cutting the cord in the right way, cleaning away the afterbirth. Now Nora was peering at the baby as it lay on the bed wrapped in a blanket, beside its exhausted mother. 'Shame about that bloody birthmark, but still. Look, Queen. That kid'll break a few hearts, don't you think?'

Queenie wouldn't look at it. She *glanced* at the baby, saw a scruff of dark hair, dark just like Max's had been when he was born, and very dark blue eyes – also like Max's. She saw the strawberry birthmark on the child's left cheek, round as a penny.

*The mark of Cain,* she thought. The baby was cursed, unwanted, a disaster.

Quickly she looked away. She focused on her sister, clutched her arm, squeezed it hard.

'Ow! What, Queen?' Nora demanded.

'We agreed,' said Queenie through gritted teeth. 'The minute it arrived, we said, you would take it straight down the police station and you would say that someone dumped it on the doorstep. That's what we said.' She turned her head away from the baby, who was making mewling noises. Her breasts ached at the sound. Best not to look. She didn't want to start getting attached to it. She couldn't do that. 'Now go on. I've done my bit. Time for you to do yours.'

★

Nora went out nearly an hour later, in the teeth of a gale-force wind that spat rain on her, with the kid wrapped up and clutched against her chest. She walked quickly, head down, hoping she wouldn't see any of her church associates about, because how could she possibly explain *this*?

On the pavement in front of the police station where the blue lamp glowed, she paused. The baby in her arms whimpered and stirred.

She was going to have to do this.

She walked up the steps to the station.

★

Queenie was back in London within a week of the birth, wearing a strip of old towelling around her breasts to soak up the milk. It had been a hard time in Brighton, waiting for the kid to put in its appearance.

Once the child was disposed of as agreed, there was no reason for Queenie to delay her return to the Smoke. She packed her bags, thanked her sister, and left. She felt battered, humiliated, like the guilt of what she'd been up to was imprinted all over her. But Max, Jonjo and Eddie greeted her as if she'd never been away.

'How is Nora the Witch?' Jonjo asked after Aunt Nora. Queenie's sons had always called her that. She'd never been a warm or affectionate aunt to any of them. None of them had developed a fondness for her.

'Nora's fine,' said Queenie as they sat in the parlour and Max chucked logs on the fire. More logs than they could afford to burn, she thought. 'And don't call her that! Ah, she's the same as ever. What you lot been up to then?'

'This and that,' said Max.

He didn't tell her about Davey Delaney and the Newhaven job.

He had yet to deal with that.

But he would.

# 12

'You're playing with the big boys now.'

That was what Davey Delaney, the double-crossing old scrote, had told them when he'd dangled the juicy carrot of a big payout for their little jaunt down to Newhaven.

Now, they stood in the gym – Max, Jonjo, Steve and Tone – and waited for him to show up. He was prompt – you had to give him that. Smack on ten on Thursday morning, Delaney came in the front doors with two massive men at his back. He did look slightly surprised to see them all there, but Max thought that on the whole he covered it pretty well.

'How'd it go then?' he asked Max.

'Fine,' said Max. He was holding a rag-covered item, about two foot by six inches, in his right hand.

Delaney gave a look around the place, weaving his head left and right. He shrugged, holding out his hands, palms up. 'So! Where's the watches then. Where are the bags?'

Max had been up to a jeweller's he knew in Hatton Garden and had the watches valued. Fifty thousand quid, his mate had told him, but they were so red-hot they were smoking.

'I could shift these, mind you. Easy,' he'd told Max.

'Do it then,' Max told him, almost dizzy at the idea of so much money when he'd been raised with so little. The times were changing. He was going places.

'The car wasn't where you were supposed to leave it,' pointed out Delaney. 'Whitney Street we said, when it was all done and dusted.'

'We did say that, yeah. But we had to change our plans around. We burned out the Jag in a farmer's field. Here's the number plates. Didn't want them tracing it back to you, now did we? But then I suppose the car's hot anyway, yes? Nicked from some poor mug? We noticed the ID on the engine'd been rubbed out.'

Max threw the rag-covered bundle he held onto the floor at Delaney's feet. The soot-blackened number plates clattered out onto the concrete, dislodging the rag.

'So what happened?' asked Delaney, coolly looking down at the plates and then back up at Max's face.

'What happened?' Max was gazing at him, very direct. 'I'll tell you. The customs nabbed us in the Lamb and Flag. It was almost as if – and if I were a suspicious person I would definitely think this – almost as if you'd got wind of some bother and were putting in a gang of patsies to cover your arse, just in case the thing blew up. And then, the Jag. The bloody thing's a pile of junk – best thing that could happen to it, getting burned out. Scrapped would have been even better. Preferably before me and my associates got in it and tried to drive the fucking thing around the lanes of Sussex.'

Davey Delaney gave a crooked smile. His eyes never left Max's face. 'You accusing me of something here?'

'Your goods are gone,' said Max.

Delaney stiffened. 'Gone where?'

Max shrugged. 'Had to abandon them. Burned up in the car. Shame, yeah?'

Delaney's smile dropped from his face like a fright mask put aside. 'You don't want to fuck with me. I'd be careful of that, if I were you.'

'I'll bear it in mind. But this one? Maybe we'll just chalk it up to experience. For both of us.'

Davey Delaney was silent. He shifted on his feet and Max thought, *Uh-oh, here we go.*

'You want to make an enemy out of me, boyo?' said Delaney softly.

'I didn't,' said Max. 'But now? I think we've already picked which side we're on. Don't you?'

'You uppy little bastard,' said Davey, gesturing to his two heavies.

They started forward.

'I wouldn't,' said Max calmly.

Slowly, men were emerging from the shadows all around the gym, coming out into the light. All of them had been born in the East End. All of them had been forged in the fires of poverty. Max had nurtured them, been good to them and all their families. They carried hammers and baseball bats. The Delaney boys were outnumbered, outgunned and outside their own turf – in Max Carter's domain.

'This isn't over,' said Davey Delaney.

'Didn't think it was,' said Max. 'Now fuck off.'

# 13

Annie Bailey, not knowing what on earth she was going to do with her life, got a very boring job in the corner shop where she chatted to equally bored housewives. She hated her job, pushing a mop around the dirty lino, wearing a horrible scratchy, sweaty overall, weighing out this and that, bored to tears. Sometimes her cousin Kath called in, and they had a bit of a laugh. Sometimes – and this was interesting – Max Carter's mother came in, the gimlet-eyed and pretty damned scary Queenie, buying up the store as she could no doubt afford to do.

When Queenie Carter came in, all the other housewives backed away.

'You first,' they'd say, making room at the front of the queue for her.

'Thank you,' she'd say graciously, her head in the air, and the shop's owner would serve her, oiling his way around her, being *nice* to her like he rarely bothered to be to anyone else.

Certainly he was never nice to his sole employee, Annie Bailey. He worked her like a dog and tried to feel her up whenever she was careless enough to loiter in the stockroom. So whenever trade was slow, Annie stood at the open doorway of the shop and looked out for *him*.

*He* was Max Carter, Queenie Carter's son, and Annie had a massive crush on him.

Not that he would ever look twice at her.

He was older than her, for starters. And he was rich, of course. And dodgy. The dodgy bit didn't put her off. It added to his allure. He looked *dangerous* and she liked that. So she stood there in the shop doorway with her little red transistor radio tucked in the pocket of her overall, listening to it whenever the shopkeeper was out of earshot, listening to 'I'll Never Find Another You' by Billy Fury and 'Cryin' in the Rain' by the Everlys. She waited and waited for Max Carter's Jag to go past, and if it did, that made her day.

'Gawd, you ain't half got it bad,' Kath always teased her.

Annie knew she had.

She also knew that she was dreaming.

Her and Max Carter?

Now how the hell could *that* ever happen?

# 14

For Max it had always been a simple choice, really – go robbing and make good money; get his brains pulverised in the boxing ring; or schlepp off to a day job and spend the rest of his life grafting hard for bugger-all. Max had no education to speak of and neither did his crew, but he was bright, street-smart, super-tough and there was an unbreakable brothers-in-arms trust between Max and his men. They knew each other, covered for each other, were tight as a drum.

They weren't scared of the Delaney crew. And the jeweller came good on the haul from Newhaven. Not fifty grand's worth but forty-five, and things started to get a lot more comfortable for Max Carter and his lads. Word spread quickly that he was on the up. He'd stood against Davey Delaney and he'd stepped away with a tidy profit.

When they were still out on increasingly rare jobs in the Transit, Tone always had a high-speed car nearby in case of trouble – a Ford Zodiac or a Zephyr, and Tone was fiddling under the bonnet of his motors all the time, fine-tuning their performance so they always ran sweet as a nut, not like that useless pile of junk Delaney had tried to stiff them with.

Max knew that he was right – Davey Delaney had sussed them out as up-and-coming competition and decided to chuck them to the wolves. Only his plan had backfired and he had underestimated Max, making a powerful enemy – and, now, a wealthy one.

Max grew. His firm grew with him. Delaney had people trying to infiltrate the ranks, pull them down, but Max had a sixth sense and he usually sussed them out. Pretty soon Max was swanning around in his very own brand-new chauffeur-driven Mark X Jag, Tone at the wheel – and he was looking over clubs to buy.

On the day when he stood in the Palermo Lounge and knew it was his, he felt so proud that his heart could have burst. He'd bought out the previous owner at a bargain price, the owner having been unable to cope with all the fights that had been occurring in the club – fights that had been mostly engineered by Max himself.

The club was a wreck. Undeterred, he hired in builders, painters and decorators, interior designers. Work began on getting the old club up to the new standards of the day. And then, triumphantly, there came the opening night. Max was there, Queenie his dear old mum on his arm with a new mink stole around her shoulders and a little clip-on fascinator hat atop her brand-new perm. Her dress was designer, bought and paid for by Max.

'What do you think then, Mum?' Max asked her.

'It's wonderful,' said Queenie, and it was.

'I've got another surprise for you too,' said Max, pleased.

'Oh? What's that then?' Max loved giving Queenie surprises. She knew that. Thankfully, she had never given him any – particularly not the most humiliating one of all, that dark secret; the baby she and Nora had given away.

'I'll show you,' said Max as the four-piece band struck up 'That's Amore'. 'Tomorrow.'

The place was buzzing. The Krays were in, patting him on the shoulder, shaking his hand. Babs Windsor came over and kissed his cheek and said, 'Well done, darlin'.' The band moved on to 'Mambo Italiano' and he thought, *I've arrived. This is it. This is the big time.* He had money to burn and people were looking up to him.

Next day, he had Tone drive him and Queenie down to Surrey.

'This is the surprise then, I take it?' Queenie said as the Jag sped along the open road.

'Wait and see,' said Max, and the car purred along the highways and down into country lanes frothing with cow parsley, passing huge houses set back behind vast billowing green hedges. At one of these, Tone turned the car in and went up a long winding drive. The house that awaited them was high, gabled, and its entire frontage was draped in a rampantly flowering and highly scented purple wisteria. Queenie caught her breath.

'What's this?' she gasped out.

She'd never seen anything so lovely. Back up in the Smoke, she had her little terrace house, the crowded streets, the gossiping neighbours, the corner shop, and that was her little world, the one she understood. This was something surely only millionaires could own, this place. Had he brought her here to visit some of his new well-to-do friends? She knew he was mixing with lords and politicians and all sorts now. He'd told her to dress up for this outing, just as he had for last night's club opening. That must be it.

'This is my new gaff,' said Max as Tone stopped the engine.

Max got out and came around to the passenger door and helped Queenie out. She stood there, staring up at the house, marvelling at it.

'And there's more,' he said, and tucked her hand in the crook of his arm and led her around the side of the house. There was another smaller place there – built in the same elaborate country-cottage style as the main house and draped in deliciously fragrant pink roses. Max stopped at the front door under its dainty little porch and handed Queenie a key tied to a red silk tassel.

'What . . . ?' Queenie was smiling at him, her brows knitted together in confusion.

'It's yours, Mum. This annexe. All yours.'

'Oh!' Queenie stared at her son's beloved face. He meant it! Suddenly she was in tears.

'Hey, hey!' Max was laughing, pulling her in for a quick hug. 'No need for that. Come on, let's take a look.'

It was beautiful. He'd furnished it just as she would have wished. But it was so far from home, so far from where she truly belonged. Well, she couldn't tell him that. He'd be devastated. She could see what this meant to him, gifting her with something so extravagant.

'What do you think?' he asked, after he had shown her all around the place. They paused in the sitting room to gaze out at a small, exquisitely planted lawned garden that was hers and hers alone.

'Any time you want to come down here, Tone'll drive you,' Max told her. He was watching her face. 'You don't have to go to Nora's. I know the two of you don't get on.'

'I think it's beautiful,' said Queenie at last, squirming at the reference to Max's aunt. The place *was* beautiful, it really was: but it wasn't her. 'I can't thank you enough, son. I really can't,' she said, to please him.

Max relaxed. His mum loved it.

Max bought two more struggling clubs and renamed them the Blue Parrot and the Shalimar. The Palermo Lounge was up and running and when the two new clubs were finished to his satisfaction, he was coining it. He counted himself lucky and started to distance himself from the old games he'd played, out on the rob. Now he stuck to the protection rackets and the clubs.

Once, everything had been a struggle, but now the cash was rolling in and all was well; life was easy. It was straightforward. There was still the Delaneys, but fuck them; they could go to hell.

Max had extended his influence out around Bow and into Limehouse. Beside the club business, people still paid him to keep their businesses intact, keep the rubbish out. People were treating him with respect.

'Now you got this big posh house in the country, ain't it time you settled down, my lad?' Queenie said, kissing his cheek. 'Don't you think?'

It would break her heart, of course, and he knew it; he was 'her boy'. Her favourite. And he had the gilded, impermeable self-confidence which seemed to go with that. He wore a gold ring on his little finger now, Egyptian cartouches engraved upon it, inset with a slab of lapis lazuli. He wore tailored suits, expensive shoes. When he was in a room, he filled it. He'd *arrived*.

But Max didn't want to settle down. Marriage, so far as he could see, was a miserable experience. He'd seen his parents' union and it made him shudder. One partner rubbing up against another, that dreaded word 'compromise'? Most of the time both of them unhappy because they couldn't live life their own way. No. He relished his freedom. Marriage? Forget it.

So for a while he enjoyed himself to the hilt, living the rich-bachelor life, holidaying abroad with his mates or with one or two very expensive female companions. At home he was fending off eager young women and even some very keen older ones. He dated some of Babs's showgirl friends. He didn't settle down in any way, shape or form.

Then, inch by inch, he tired of the life and started to think that maybe Queenie might even be right. He could have kids, a woman of his own, someone to be *there* for him.

But it would have to be someone quite different to his mum, who could be – he knew this was true – overbearing and a constant worry, with a tendency to treat him and Jonjo and Eddie like they were still little kids. Queenie seemed to think that if she shouted loudly enough, her will would always prevail. Well, it might with young Eddie, who was soft as butter, and maybe even with Jonjo, but never with Max.

So when he finally started looking for wifely candidates, he was unconsciously searching for a woman who was the farthest thing imaginable from his own mother – a quiet girl, a plain girl, homely – someone who would never answer back or embarrass him in public.

One day – just like magic! – this girl turned up at the Blue Parrot looking for work. There was a vacancy for a cloak-room girl. She was perfect for the job so he offered it to her and she accepted. Her name was Ruthie Bailey. She was a bit on the dull side, but she was – even Queenie admitted this – perfect wife material.

# 15

Truth mattered to Nora. Telling the absolute truth was one of the rules she lived by. She'd become a devout member of the Christian church, a keen supporter of the Salvation Army, always whipping up funds for the local church steeple or the nave or the Sally Army's welfare arm, always glad to do her bit. She was a generous woman; that's how she saw herself.

She'd gone above and beyond, lots of times. Like the time she'd stood outside the cop shop with Queenie's kid, ready to hand it in, and decided that no, that would not be the right thing, the *Christian* thing, to do. And so she'd brought up her sister's kid, unasked. Didn't that prove what a good Christian soul she was? You should never be 'loose' (as her sister Queenie had been, the cow, and just look where that had got her) and you should always, *always*, tell the truth.

Nora had told the truth about the kid to the Reverend Payne. She told him about Queenie's unfortunate 'mistake' and her own part in it; she told him that she had agreed with Queenie to take the kid to the police station, and she'd almost *got* there, really she had, but she hadn't gone through with it: the *truth* was, Nora had kept Queenie's illegitimate child and raised him and named him Bruno.

'You've done a bad thing,' said the vicar when Nora poured out the story to him. 'You've deceived your sister and you have deprived the child of a *proper* upbringing . . .'

'He wouldn't have got that. Not with her. She wouldn't have kept him anyway. How could she? It would have been a disgrace.'

'With foster parents then. A proper family with a father and a mother. Stability for him. Nora – you don't know that she wouldn't have kept the child, not for sure.'

'I do.'

'Nora, you've done a terrible thing.'

Nora felt chastened. 'So . . . what should I do now? Tell me. I'll do it.'

'It's obvious, isn't it?' Reverend Payne's pale blue eyes bored into hers. 'You must tell your sister what you've done. But first . . .'

'First? First what?'

'Tell the boy. He has a right to know.'

So one day Nora sat the child down – he was nine years old – and told him *his* truth.

He sat at the table, his dark waving hair neatly brushed (she insisted on neatness, and cleanliness) and his face shining from a recent scrub with the dishcloth. The penny-sized strawberry birthmark on his cheek was a shame, Nora thought. It stood out, spoiling what could otherwise have been a very attractive face, but no matter. Bruno's dark blue eyes were fastened to her face. To his *mother's* face, because that was what he had always believed her to be, hadn't he. And why not? She had been a mother to him, after all. She had sent him to school, sent him to *Sunday* school too. She had done right by him, hadn't she? It wasn't her fault if he was difficult.

'Child,' she said, seating herself opposite him, 'I am not your mother.'

Bruno looked at her. Was she joking?

But no. He dismissed that idea. Nora never joked. If you knew Nora at all, you knew that she had no sense of humour whatsoever.

'Well, what have you to say about it?' she asked, plainly irritated by his bewildered silence.

'Who is then?' he asked.

Nora hadn't been prepared for this. She had been pre-pared for shocked tears, disappointment. Instead, a demand for information.

And there was the truth, staring her in the face. He was Queenie's child and he had a right to know that. Of course he did.

'My sister, Queenie,' Nora told him.

'Then where is she?' He looked around, almost as if Queenie was going to jump out at him from behind the furniture.

'She's in London, Bruno. She ain't here.'

Bruno's face screwed up. Was he going to cry? But no. He was puzzled, not distressed.

'Why ain't she here?' he asked.

'She lives in London.'

'But . . . well, why am I not there, then? With her?'

'She didn't want you, son,' said Nora.

The truth was a dish best served cold, just like revenge. And maybe this *was* a type of revenge on ebullient, larger-than-life Queenie. She'd had kids and then she'd got herself in trouble and abandoned this one. Her dirty secret. Nora'd had none of that and she felt superior to her sister because of it. *Cleaner*, sort of. Untouched, that was her. She'd lived all her life a virgin, her brief marriage to Ted had never actually been consummated. She had never really known any man.

But somehow, when she'd held Bruno for the first time, something had been triggered inside her. Maybe a tiny seed of maternal longing – or maybe just a stab of jealousy for all that Queenie had known in life, when she had known so little.

She'd done good by this unwanted boy; she knew she had. Later, she would get him sorted out with a bank account, pay in a little to get him started. She would do *right* by him. Not like Queenie. Nora had the superior high ground here, and she hugged it to her, self-satisfied.

'Why didn't she want me?' asked Bruno.

Nora told him about Queenie. That she was doing well for herself in London, that her three sons Max, Jonjo and Eddie were all grown-up men, gangster types, and doing good business, running their own firm, looking after their mother. A woman who worked in The Grapes, Max's local, had passed on the information to Nora – for a price – that Max had bought a big house in the country, with an annexe for Queenie to stay in whenever she wanted.

Nora thought that if Max knew his mother's *true* nature, he wouldn't be so bloody keen to accommodate her. That was for sure.

Bruno was silent again. Taking it all in. Nora could almost see the thoughts fizzing through his brain.

'But why haven't I got all that then? Like they have?'

Nora felt surprised and then affronted. 'Haven't you been happy here then, son?' she asked.

Bruno didn't answer that and she thought no, he hasn't been happy. Or maybe he has – until now. Until I've told him how the other half live. His *real* family. A flicker of unease coursed through her at that. Maybe she'd done the wrong thing, telling him. But the truth will out. Didn't they say that?

They did.

No, she hadn't done anything wrong. No matter what Reverend Payne said, she *hadn't*.

'They're no big deal,' she sniffed. 'Nothing to be impressed with. Criminals, that's what they are, done up in suits. Thugs in fancy clothes. Running nightclubs and breaking heads. And they don't have their troubles to seek. I'm told they've been stepping on the toes of a big Irish family and there's trouble brewing.'

'Who are these Irish?' asked Bruno.

'Delaneys, they're called. They're the Battersea mob.' Nora sat back. 'Well, that's it then, son. I just thought you had a right to know the truth. It didn't seem fair, keeping it from you any longer.'

'Right,' said Bruno. He pushed his chair back, stood up. Said nothing else.

'So . . . this need make no difference,' said Nora. His silence was making her uneasy now.

'No,' said Bruno with a thin smile. ''Course not.'

'You don't . . . *mind*, living here with me do you, Bruno? I mean, you've been happy enough?'

'Yeah,' said Bruno. ''Course.'

He was very hard to read sometimes, Nora thought. Bruno had been a quiet child, reading books – Bible books, of course; Nora wouldn't allow anything else in the house – in his room. He'd never mixed much with other kids.

Maybe he had been lonely, living here with her, seeing the tourists passing through the B & B, strangers drifting through his life and no real company except for Nora herself. An only child, to all intents and purposes.

Only, not really. Really? He had three older brothers.

But now the truth was out, and life would go on. There was no reason for anything to change, Nora thought, lying sleepless that night after she'd told him about his real mother. All would be well, all would be just as it *had* been, for so long.

Next – the Reverend Payne was right – she ought to tell Queenie.

# 16

It was late in the afternoon and Max was on his way out of Queenie's little terrace house when the doorbell rang. He called in often, but he lived across town now; he had a flat over the Palermo. Jonjo had a place over in Frith Street, and Eddie – well, it was best never to enquire about where Eddie went of a night-time.

Max opened the front door, surprised to see Aunt Nora standing there. Nora hadn't visited London in a long, long, time. He could remember her pushing in once or twice at Christmas when he'd been very young, eating them out of house and home and drilling them over the Sally Army, making all their lives a misery – the implication being that Queenie and her husband and offspring were a bunch of devil-worshippers or the next best thing. Nora was very 'church on Sunday' – and Queenie most definitely was not.

On those past Christmases, when Mum finally got sick of Nora's miserable mush – which she always did – and gave her her marching orders, everyone had breathed a sigh of relief.

Now here Nora was – again. Older and greyer but still essentially the same, with that pursed cat's-bum mouth of hers, disapproval writ large on her face. She was standing on the stoop with an overnight bag in her hand, and Max had the feeling that the instant before he'd opened the door, she'd been running a finger over its paintwork to see how dirty it was.

'Aunt Nora,' he said, without a great deal of warmth. 'Hello.'

'Well that ain't much of a welcome,' said Nora, bustling past him and inside. 'Give your aunt a kiss, then.'

She held up her wrinkled monkey-face to Max's. Dutifully, unwillingly, he kissed her cheek.

'Who is it . . . ?' asked Mum, coming into the hall from the kitchen.

Queenie stopped short when she saw Nora standing there.

'Gawd, you look like you've seen a ghost,' said Nora with a thin smile. She strode over to Queenie. 'Give us a kiss then, girl.'

Queenie obliged.

'I'm off then,' said Max, stepped out the front door and glancing behind him. He was going to check out the clubs, do a few deals, then he was going to take Ruthie Bailey out to dinner. 'Bye, Mum.'

Queenie nodded to Max and then, with him gone, she stood there staring at her sister. 'What the fuck?' she asked finally.

'Stick the kettle on then our Queen, I'm parched,' said Nora.

'What you doing here?' asked Queenie.

'Let me get in the door first will you? I got something important to tell you.'

Queenie eyed her sister in puzzlement. 'All right.' She nodded to the half-open front door. 'Stick the wood in the hole, will you? And come on through.'

★

'So what you got to tell me that couldn't be put in a letter?' asked Queenie when they sat at the kitchen table, tea and biscuits in front of them.

Queenie wasn't surprised to see wafer-thin Nora ploughing her way through the biscuits. Nora ate like a horse but stayed thin as a coat hanger. It didn't seem fair, when Queenie had to watch what she ate or look like she'd swallowed a sofa. Not that she cared too much these days. She was into her fifties and all that business about turning men's heads was well in the past. Her health didn't seem that good anymore. That dose of scarlet fever she'd contracted as a child? The doctors said it had damaged the muscles of her heart. She still sometimes thought of Clive, of his blue eyes and his teasing smile, but that brought her nothing but pain and regret, so what was the point?

Nora was crunching her way through another biscuit, swilling it down with tea. She was staring at the tabletop, not looking at Queenie's face.

'Well?' Queenie prompted.

Nora shoved her teacup over to the pot. 'Pour us another then, girl,' she said.

Queenie poured, pushed the cup back to Nora. She waited. Nora drank, took another biscuit. Queenie remembered that Nora always, when she was a girl, ate more whenever she was worried. Maybe she still did that, because the biscuits were going down fast. Maybe Nora was ill too. Maybe that was it. Maybe she was about to cark it, and she'd come here in person to tell her sister so.

When Nora reached for yet another biscuit, Queenie slapped the lid back on.

'Nora!' she burst out.

'What? You nearly had my bloody hand off.'

'Spit it out. Whatever you've come all this way for, it must be important or you wouldn't have bothered, would you. So come on. Tell me. What's up? You ill? Or is it the business? Has it gone west or something like that?'

Nora shook her head. Hesitated.

'*Nora*,' said Queenie, infuriated.

'It's the kid,' she snapped out.

'It's . . . *what*?' Of all the things Queenie had expected to come out of Nora's mouth, *that* had certainly not been among them. 'The kid?' She lowered her voice. '*What* kid for God's sake?'

Nora was staring at her sister, saying nothing.

'What you talking about?' said Queenie.

'I mean *your* kid.'

'I don't understand.' Queenie glanced nervously out to the hallway. She got up, went over, closed the kitchen door. She came back and sat at the table and looked at Nora. 'What are you saying? What about the kid?'

'Your son,' said Nora, her mouth pursed in prudish disapproval, like she was judge and jury. 'The one you *left behind*.'

Queenie was staring at her sister in bewilderment. 'That's not something I ever thought you'd want to be discussing. *I* certainly don't. It was a mistake, and – as you rightly say – I've left it behind. And *you* left the kid behind too, the day you took it to the police station and handed it in to the rozzers. Didn't you.'

Nora's eyes flicked up, held Queenie's.

'But that's it, our Queen,' she said stiffly.

'What? What the hell . . . ?'

'I didn't hand the kid in.' Now Nora was – and this shocked Queenie more than anything – staring at her with tear-filled eyes.

'You *what?*' Queenie couldn't believe what she was hearing. 'But . . . but you did. You went to the police station, you said you were going to hand it in. You went out, you took the kid out with you . . .'

Nora slapped the table and rolled her eyes. 'No, Queen. I'm . . . oh fuck.' Nora hated to swear. She crossed herself instantly. 'I kept the kid,' she said.

'What . . . ?' Queenie felt like she'd been gut-punched.

'You heard me, Queen,' said Nora, and now her voice was steady and her gaze was straight. 'I kept him. I kept your son, God forgive me. I called him Bruno and I kept him for my own.'

# 17

Queenie was so poleaxed by what Nora had told her that she didn't know what to say. She sat there gulping like a landed fish, trying to get her panicky thoughts together, to get some words out. For a long while, she couldn't. Then finally she said: 'God's sake, Nora, what'd you want to go and do that for?'

'I said, didn't I? I told you at the time, it weren't right, what you were doing. It wasn't a Christian thing to do, was it. Abandoning your own flesh and blood.'

Queenie was shaking her head. 'For the love of God!' she burst out. 'You and your bloody church mates, you'll be the death of me. You mean, all this time, you've had the kid with you?'

'Your *son*, yes. Not "the kid". He's your son, and his name's Bruno.'

'I don't give a shit if his name's King Farouk!' Queenie scraped her chair back and came to her feet. She pounded the table with her fists. Nora jumped. 'Jesus!'

'Don't take the Lord's name in vain,' said Nora primly.

'*Bruno?* Hold on! Didn't your old man Ted have a dog once called Bruno?'

'What if he did? I liked that dog. I like the name.'

'You named the kid after a *dog*?'

Nora shrugged, looked away.

This was a bloody *nightmare*. Queenie had thought all this gone, way in the past, dead and buried. She had closed her mind to it, closed her heart. Now, it was coming back to bite her. She stared at Nora. She'd never liked her sister. *Never*. But this was such a betrayal, such a truly terrible thing, that Queenie looked at Nora with utter, uncomprehending hatred.

'Did you . . . so what happened? You took it to the station, and what? What happened then?'

Nora shook her head. 'I got to the station but I couldn't go in. It just wasn't *right*. So I took it to a friend of mine. A *church* friend, and she looked after the baby until you went back to London, and then I . . . well, I kept him.'

'Did you register the birth then?' Queenie asked, drymouthed, horrified.

Nora shook her head once: no.

'I've looked after your kid for you all these years, Queen,' Nora ploughed on. 'I've fed him. Raised him.'

'What – *you*?' Queenie snorted. 'I wouldn't trust you to look after a fucking budgie! You don't have it in you to actually *care* for anything.'

Nora snapped back in her seat like she'd been struck.

'What – and you do? You cruel cow. All you wanted was to offload the kid, and you did.'

'I couldn't . . .' started Queenie.

'I know, I know! I've heard it all before. Mustn't upset the boys, must we? Mustn't let them know their mum's the next best thing to a whore.'

Queenie blanched. She felt her heart stall in her chest and she swallowed hard, pulled in a breath, *tried* to compose herself.

'You know what happened. You know how difficult it was. All I wanted was some support from you, my sister,' she snapped out. 'And what do I bloody get? You're a treacherous evil cow, Nora Dawkins.'

'Yeah? Well I raised *your* child. I even opened a bank account for him, put fifty pounds – *fifty pounds of my own money* – in his name. What do you think of *that*?'

'What do I think? I think you're a tight bitch and you only did it to feel good about yourself. You and your church buddies, you all love it, don't you? Get a pat on the back from the vicar, store up points for heaven! Well you done wrong this time, Nora. You've fucked up, you silly cow!'

'Queen . . .'

'No! Shut up! Don't you know nothing? Don't you understand? I had the kid when I shouldn't. At the wrong time of life and out of wedlock. By a . . . by a travelling salesman. I had adult kids and *this* was just a bloody abomination, something that never should have happened to anyone in their middle years, not when they had their reputation to think of. What do you think Max or Jonjo or Eddie would make of it if they found out? Their mother who is supposed to be a respectable woman, that she had a leg-over out of wedlock and got herself up the duff? I told you what I wanted to be done, and you *didn't bloody do it!* I can't believe you, Nora, I really can't. You've bloody *done* for me, haven't you. And now what the hell have you come here for, to tell me this?'

'I've heard that Max is doing well these days,' said Nora.

Queenie fell silent, staring at her sister. Slowly, she sank back down into her chair. Placed her shaking hands on the table. 'What?'

Nora shrugged. 'Business has dried up at the boarding house. It's *winter*. People don't come. Times are getting hard, Queen, and friends are few. I have the nipper to keep fed and watered and clothed. And – to be honest – he's not an easy kid. Not at all.'

'That's *your* bloody look-out, Nora. That was your decision. It certainly wasn't mine.'

'But *you're* doing all right, aintcha, Queen? Max has got half the town paying him money, I heard. I been in The Grapes listening to the talk, and it's all about Mr High and Mighty Max Carter, who runs these streets, who everybody looks up to.' Nora's eyed rested, shrewd and sharp, on her sister's shocked face. 'Wonder what Max would say, eh? If he knew he had a bastard brother hiding away down on the coast.'

Now Queenie understood. She looked at her sister, her *blood*. Nora had betrayed her trust and now she wanted hush money. She had to swallow hard before she could get more words out.

'How much?' she asked. 'Come on, Nora. How much is this going to cost me, to keep you quiet?'

Nora named her price.

Queenie sat across from her sister and knew she was going to have to pay it.

'And then there'll be no more demands, all right? It was your decision to keep the kid . . .'

'*Bruno*,' said Nora sharply.

'*The kid*,' retorted Queenie. 'You wanted him, you got him. I pay this, then we hear no more about it. All right?'

'Deal,' said Nora, and held out her hand to shake.

Queenie stood up again. She ignored her sister's hand.

'And now, if you don't mind, I have things to do.'

'When will I get my money?' asked Nora.

'By the end of the week. All right?' Queenie's face was hard as she glanced at Nora's overnight bag there on the floor. 'And you can forget staying here. The Grapes has a couple of rooms. And once this is settled, I never want to see or hear from you again.'

# 18

Bruno Dawkins was a loner. An only, lonely child. His very earliest memory was of sitting in a cold wet nappy on the freezing-cold kitchen lino of Nora's Brighton boarding house, crying his eyes out and being ignored – until she dashed in and slapped a bottle of cold tea in one of his hands, a sliver of pink ham in the other.

'Now will you just *shut up*?' she'd hissed at him, shocking him into frightened silence.

After that, he didn't cry anymore. There was no point.

As Bruno grew, he took to wandering around Brighton, down on the seafront and around the Royal Pavilion grounds, around the Lanes, peering in the shops there. He never had much pocket money. Nora was tight as a duck's arse. Tight with money just like she was with physical contact. People passed through the B & B but mostly he lived a solitary life with charmless, God-bothering Nora. He rarely turned up for school, never made friends. He lived with Nora and once, after she'd told him about his real mother in London, he asked for more details. She beat him with a stick and told him not to be bloody nosy, to be grateful he had her and a roof over his head, and food to eat.

After that, he stopped asking. He wandered about the town, always alone. And then something interesting happened. Maytime came and with the bright sunny spring weather there arrived two big gangs – the mods on their Vespa scooters with their parka jackets and their knives and their trendy short haircuts, and the rockers with their duck's-arse greased-down quiffs, leather bomber jackets, bike chains and high-powered motorbikes.

It was a hell of a clash. The police were caught unawares and soon they were entangled in the midst of a bloody war. Black Mariahs were summoned and tons of interlopers were shovelled inside and carted off to the station. Ambulances came and scooped up the wounded, of which there were a fair few. The locals recoiled in shock, astonished at what had happened to their previously peaceful town.

Bruno went down that night onto the beach when he was sure the last of the Bill had gone, and poked around with a hand torch among the debris. He found motorbike parts, bloodstained clothes and – most fascinating of all – a set of three needle-sharp stiletto knives with smooth sharkskin hilts. Bruno picked them up, weighed them in his hands. Then he tucked them away in his pocket, and left the beach.

Next day the newspapers ran garish pictures of the clash between the mods and rockers, and Nora exclaimed over it all in shock and horror.

'God-forgotten vandals,' she hissed, reading the *Brighton Echo*.

Bruno went out, taking his new-found treasures with him. He found a quiet spot, well away from the beach, which was still heaving with interested onlookers and a copper or two, and he practised throwing the knives. Accuracy was a lot harder than he had supposed it would be. He tried to hit the same patch of dirt ten feet away, over and over. There was a rhythm to it, an intensity. Mostly he missed. But he came back the next day, and the next, and tried again, and slowly, slowly, he started to hit the target.

'Can I have a dartboard?' he asked Nora one day. 'In my room?'

Nora was surprised. The boy never asked for anything.

Actually, she often wished that she'd never given in to the temptation to 'do the right thing' and kept the kid. She didn't know much about children, and having Bruno underfoot made her realise that she had no aptitude and no true warmth in her when it came to childcare. Truth was, she *didn't* care much. She'd acted out of a sense of Christian duty in keeping Bruno and the truth – oh, the truth! – was that in a very short while she had found him irritating, an encumbrance. The feeding. The nappy changes. The fretful months of teething, the endless demands on her time when she had so little time to spare.

She hadn't expected it to be such bloody hard work and she often felt sorry she'd bothered, which she realised was a sin. She'd told some of her church pals that her sister had died and left Bruno in her care. They sympathised while the Reverend Payne eyed her sadly, accusingly, knowing it was all a lie. The churchgoers called in with children's clothes, toys, puzzles. No dartboards though.

'I don't see why we can't get you a dartboard,' said Nora.

Nora was quite used to making trips up to London to cash in on her sister's 'little mistake'. She'd ignored Queenie's declaration that the payment should be a one-off. She'd been back there several times, each time demanding more money – and of course, to keep her sister silent, Queenie had been obliged to pay up.

Nora was feeling flush. She could afford a dartboard for the kid; why not? 'So long as you don't disturb the guests at night,' she warned him.

'I won't,' he said.

So a dartboard was procured. Bruno banged in a nail and hung it from the door in his room. He tossed the matching Union Jack darts aside in a drawer, uninterested in them. Instead, he lay on his bed and took out the trio of needle-thin scalpel-sharp stiletto knives he'd found on the beach after the battle between the mods and the rockers. He aimed for the Bull, the centre of the dartboard.

It wasn't easy.

He practised again and again and again. Accuracy was what he strived for. He had to become adapted to the weight of the blades; they had to become like an extension of his own hand.

He practised, day and evening – never at night. Mustn't disturb the guests. Slowly, inch by inch, he improved. It became his obsession, *thunking* the knives into the board, challenging himself. Try for the two. Hit the Bull. Hit that, then that, then that.

He grew better and better.

# 19

A blackmailer will always make mistakes, in the end. Mistake number one – being too greedy. And Nora was surprised to find that she was just that. It was a sin, of course, but she couldn't resist going back, again and again, to Queenie, usually just before Christmas, and saying, 'Come on, Queen, you can spare it and I ought to buy something nice for the kid, the poor boy has little enough. Bad enough that you didn't want him, now you're keeping him in penury, begrudging your sister the means to give him a good time once a year?'

Queenie always coughed up. Sometimes she ranted and shouted and said, '*This is the very last time*,' but of course it never was. It became Nora's habit to pay Queenie a pre-Christmas visit and then go back down to Brighton on the train with her pockets stuffed with cash.

It was just unfortunate that on the final time she did this, Queenie turned her down flat. Told her she could say what she wanted, *tell* whoever she wanted, it wasn't going to happen. This was going to *stop*. But this put Nora's back up. She decided to up the stakes.

She made her usual trip up to the Smoke to screw a few more quid out of her guilt-ridden sibling, but this time there was a difference. This time, she took Bruno with her. Let Queenie look him straight in the eye and *then* tell her no. When Queenie opened the front door and found Nora standing there with a dark-haired boy at her side, she felt her heart pound painfully in her chest. She saw the strawberry birthmark on his face and knew exactly who this was.

Oh Christ.

It was *him*.

She stared at Nora and the boy for a long, long time and then she managed to spit it out: 'Fuck you, Nora. What the *hell*? What the . . . what are you playing at? What are you doing, bringing him here?'

The boy was watching her with wide, dark blue eyes. They were like Max's eyes. And his hair – black and thick and wavy – exactly the same.

'I thought it was time you two met,' said Nora sourly. '*This* is what you've been turning down, Queen. This boy here.'

'This isn't convenient,' said Queenie, her chest hurting now, her breath coming hard and fast. Of all the mean tricks, showing up with the kid! She went to close the door. Nora stuck her foot in it.

'Oh no you don't,' she said primly, her mouth a tight angry line. She turned slightly, looked at the boy. 'You stay out here a mo, Bruno. We're going to have a talk.'

'You can't come in,' said Queenie, but Nora was barging through into the hallway, showing surprising strength despite her scrawny build. 'No!' hissed Queenie. 'You can't . . .'

But Nora surged ahead like a battleship, heading straight for the kitchen, taking off her coat, placing it neatly over the back of a chair.

Queenie felt like she was going to scream. Max had called in on her and he was upstairs right now, looking for some old documents. Jonjo, who'd come back with him, was out back, using the facilities. She had to get rid of Nora and the damned boy – quick!

★

Jonjo was busy having a slash outside in the lavvy when he heard female voices coming from indoors. His mum was kicking off at somebody. Screeching like a banshee, saying, '*No! You can't!*' Oh, she could do that, Mum. Best to clear out when that happened. He zipped up, pulled the chain, went out through the yard and back indoors. Max had come downstairs and was yanking on his coat in the hallway. Both him and Jonjo paused; they exchanged a look.

They both knew that *other* voice.

Aunt Nora.

That cow, she was up here scrounging again. After Nora left, Mum would be in a rotten mood. They'd all come to dread a visit from their God-bothering aunt. Even mild-tempered Eddie hated her. Both men paused, listening.

'Least you can do, isn't it. All things considered,' Nora was saying.

'I said, didn't I, right at the start, that there would be once and then no more,' Queenie said, her voice shrill with temper.

'Yeah, but I got expenses, Queen. You know that.'

'What the hell were you *thinking*, doing this?'

Jonjo's beefy face twisted in a sneer. He widened his eyes and looked at Max. Fuck's sake! The damned woman was on the cadge again. He followed Max into the kitchen.

Both women stopped talking as Max and Jonjo came in. Mum looked – what? – guilty? Like they'd caught her in the act of something she shouldn't be doing. Nora looked startled, but grim-faced.

'Oh! Max! Jonjo darlin', your aunt Nora's come to call,' said Queenie, trying to smile, but it didn't reach her eyes.

'You want her in here?' Jonjo asked, fastening his eyes on Nora, who shrank back. She knew about Jonjo and his hair-trigger temper.

'Oh, your auntie just needs a loan, that's all. I've given her a few quid. She's just off, aintcha, Nora?' Queenie looked nervous. *Go,* her eyes were saying to Nora. *Clear off, quick.*

Max stared at the two women. Queenie looked genuinely upset. He didn't like his aunt. And here she was, the bloodsucker, getting money out of Mum once again.

'Go,' he said.

'But I . . .' started Nora, looking between these two towering bulky blokes – her nephews – and her sister.

Jonjo reached out, grabbing Nora's coat off the back of a chair. He shoved it into Nora's arms so hard that she staggered back. 'You heard Max. Piss off out of it.'

Nora departed, leaving the front door open. Through the open window beside it, Max saw her talking to a dark-haired boy with an angry-looking mark on his face.

'Who's the kid?' he asked Queenie.

Max looked at his mother. She was clutching her chest, shaking her head. He pulled out a chair quickly and she sat down.

'Nobody,' she rasped out. 'Just one of her church strays she brought for a day out I shouldn't wonder.'

'She do this much then does she? Come up here asking you for money?' he asked.

Queenie's first impulse was to say no, not at all, but she was unnerved. God, that had been close! Max and Jonjo could have heard something they shouldn't, about her *other* son, the boy she'd given away. This was all getting too dangerous, far too close to home. She found herself nodding.

'All the bloody time, she's up here,' she said, wringing her hands.

It felt to Queenie like this would go on forever – Nora showing up, demanding money. It was money Queenie could easily afford nowadays, but she was forever aware that her secret son was something her three legitimate adult boys, respectably born and brought up, must never know about. And she had no way of guaranteeing that Nora wouldn't, one of these fine days, decide to just spill the beans. Jesus, she'd brought the boy here, right to their door!

Queenie shook with the queasy, gut-churning realisation of how close she had come to disaster. Nora was getting reckless. Nora was getting to be a bloody nuisance, and if she persisted, then the shit would fly and Queenie's repu-tation in the eyes of Max, Jonjo and Eddie and of all her neighbours and her friends and her relatives could be ruined. They would laugh at her, the once-revered Queenie Carter, and gossip behind her back. She would be a pariah. Steeped in shame. She would be *finished*.

Then Max said the magic words. 'It's OK. Calm down. Just take a breath. I'll take care of it,' he said, perturbed to see his mother so shaken up.

'What?' Queenie looked startled. 'Well – how?'

'Just leave it with me,' he said, and he went along the hall and out the front door, Jonjo following at his heels.

*

Once they were outside, Max saw that Nora and the kid were gone. He turned to his brother, grim-faced. 'Take a couple of days to let things settle,' he said. 'Then go down to Brighton and have a word. Mum's too bloody soft with her – that's obvious – so we're stepping in. She feels sorry for her, I suppose. But we don't want this to happen again, her getting shook up like this. She's not well. Make certain that Nora understands that. OK?'

'Sure, Max,' said Jonjo.

# 20

'That's him! There he is, *that's him!*' shrieked Annie, grabbing her cousin's arm.

'Ow! Ow! Ow!' protested Kath, yanking her arm free.

They were standing in the open shop doorway, and Kath had just popped in for a chat. The storekeeper was watching them from behind his bacon slicer with a sort of weary contempt. Bloody shop workers. You hired in a pretty girl like Annie, you were *nice* to her, paid her pretty well, and what of it? She wouldn't even let you give her a poke in the stockroom when the missus was out.

The two girls stood in the doorway and watched the Mark X Jag glide past with the big man at the wheel, Max Carter in the back.

'God, he is so *gorgeous*,' sighed Annie while Kath stood there rubbing her arm. He was, too. He was the gangster prince who was soon to become a king.

'Dream on,' sniffed Kath.

But Annie *did* dream of him. At night in bed she conjured up visions of meeting him, actually *talking* to him.

'It's never going to happen,' Kath told her as a customer shoved past to get inside the shop.

'Customer!' yelled the storekeeper, who didn't see why he had to pay Annie ruddy Bailey and then serve customers himself.

'Coming,' said Annie, rolling her eyes and grinning at Kath. She watched the car out of sight, then turned back into the shop.

'I'm off then,' said Kath.

'Cheerio,' said Annie, pasting a bright smile on her face as she went behind the counter. 'What can I get you?' she asked the woman standing there.

But her mind was still on him, of course.

On Max Carter.

## 21

By the time he was fifteen, Bruno was a maestro with the knives. He'd picked up an old GPO leather tool holster at a church sale, complete with a broad, thick leather belt. The three stiletto knives fitted in there perfectly. He got a tool out of the garden shed and carefully punched another hole in the belt, which was intended to be worn on the waist, but he fitted it so that it slotted neatly around his chest, like a shoulder holster.

The holster lay snugly under his left armpit, the knives tucked inside it. Now, with the same intense application he'd shown on hitting targets accurately, he practised drawing the knives from the holster at speed, one after the other, *thwack, thwack, thwack* at the dartboard.

Truth was, he had nothing much else to do. No friends to see. School was over – not that he'd ever much bothered with it anyway, despite all Nora's nagging that he should. All he had around him were the smiley-faced tourists passing through – and Nora's scowling mush. Alone, he stayed in his room and practised drawing the blades, going faster and faster. He greased the inside of the holster and concentrated on perfecting his throws, listening to the satisfying *thunk* as each blade hit the dartboard. He honed the stilettos to razor sharpness on a whetstone, putting a good cutting edge on them.

He practised.

He got good.

# 22

Jonjo Carter had a strong urge to protect his mum and an even stronger one to win her approval. Oh, he knew he wasn't Max. He wasn't *the favourite*. It galled him when Max bought Mum flowers on Mother's Day, because he knew the bouquet *he* gave her would never be as nice or as expensive. He'd felt the hurt of being second fiddle all his life. Max was the head of the household and Eddie the adored baby, so where did that leave him? He was the middle son, the *nothing*. And he knew he wasn't the brightest knife in the drawer. He couldn't think quick, like Max.

But Jonjo knew he'd show them all, one of these days. He'd gamble big or play the stock market or *something*, and then Queenie would realise that he was in fact the best of her sons. He'd live on Jersey and own a private yacht, a big one. She would love him then, more than she did Max, and he would carry around the trophy of her adoration like a prize.

Maybe the first part of making that change happen was this, what he was doing now, taking the skeleton keys and unpicking the lock the way Max had taught him. Slowly, slowly. You couldn't rush it.

He was standing outside Aunt Nora's house in Brighton with Steve Taylor, Max's best mate and one of his most trusted men, addressing the tricky problem of the lock at gone two in the morning, just three days after Max had told him to sort this out.

'You're sure about this?' Steve asked him. 'This is what Max wanted?'

'Damn right I'm sure, what you think I'm fuckin' *stupid* or something?' Jonjo's temper flared.

Jonjo knew for sure that Nora was back in Brighton; they'd clocked her earlier, coming back from the local shops. He felt puffed up with pride and he didn't want Steve Taylor puncturing his mood. Max trusted him to do this. He knew he fucked up sometimes, but this was an opportunity to show that he could really be depended upon.

The tumblers fell and the lock gave a loud *click*. Jonjo pushed the door and it juddered open with a groan of ungreased hinges. By the light of the moon he saw Steve's teeth flash in a grin.

Jonjo eased the door open, flicked on his torch. There was a side table with tourist brochures stacked on it, a grandfather clock, a carpet swirling with reds and greens, patterns so violent they could make you dizzy. A long thin hallway, and a staircase. He led the way up there. No one had to tell him where Aunt Nora slept; he remembered that from their rare childhood visits to Brighton's stony seaside. She occupied the front room right at the top of the house.

He made his way up there, opened the door with Steve hot on his heels. The room was in darkness. He crossed it quickly, stealthily. A single bed. Yeah, that figured – dried-up old bat that she was.

Aunt Nora was stretched out on her back, snoring loudly. She was wearing a pale blue winceyette nightie, buttoned right to the neck. Her hair was rolled up in pink sponge curlers. Steve half-laughed and Jonjo elbowed him.

*Shut up, you tosser.*

Jonjo very gently placed one shovel-sized hand over his aunt's mouth. Her eyes flew open like a virgin feeling the icy touch of the vampire. A noise started in her throat.

'Aunt Nora, don't start shouting, everything's fine. Max wants a word with you, OK? Now don't shout, don't scream. I'm going to take my hand away, all right?'

Nora, her eyes wide with fright, nodded.

Jonjo removed his hand. Nora didn't scream. She gulped in a breath. 'Jonjo? What do you . . . ?' she started.

'That's it,' said Jonjo, ignoring her words. 'No need for any noise. Get yourself dressed. We're going to sort all this out so everyone's happy, all right?'

★

Jonjo and Steve waited outside Nora's bedroom door while she dressed. When she emerged, Jonjo took her arm and moved ahead of Steve.

Something, some peculiar *feeling*, made Steve turn and look back as he stood on the landing. The door opposite Nora's room was ever so slightly ajar. He turned his torch on the opening and the beam lit up a young man's face. He saw wide frightened blue eyes, a weird mark on one cheek. Steve stood there, hesitating. Then he flicked off the torch's beam and followed Jonjo and Nora down the stairs.

Jonjo was getting Nora into her shoes, holding out her coat. Then they left the house and got in the car: Steve at the wheel, Jonjo in the front passenger seat, Nora alone in the back.

'Where are we going?' she asked. 'Are we going to Queenie's place?'

'You don't need to concern yourself with that,' said Jonjo, turning to smile at her. 'Just relax there and don't worry.'

There was no more talking as Steve drove, only the roar of the engine and the soporific hum of the heater. It was a cold night, and Nora was glad of the warmth in here. But getting her up in the middle of the night, for the love of God. What were they thinking? Well at least now things would be properly sorted. Max would be reasonable, she was sure of that; he had been ever since he was a boy. People made mistakes and women got pregnant when they shouldn't. He would understand that, and once Bruno's existence was out in the open there could be a proper settlement made on him, so that she didn't have to embarrass herself going up to London begging for cash like she had been.

After all, she was keeping Queenie's child. Didn't she *deserve* some sort of proper recompense, when she'd covered up Queenie's 'mistake' for so long?

Then she stopped thinking about Queenie and all the wrongs her sister had visited upon her. The car had turned in, rolled over a stretch of tussocky grass – she could see it, vivid as emeralds in the headlights. She could hear the wind; it was loud here, it was strong.

*Where in the name of heaven were they?*

She leaned forward to ask Jonjo, but he was already getting out of the car, admitting a freezing gusty breeze that snatched at her breath. They were on the coast still. Nowhere near London then. Had Max come down here to speak to her? That must be it. Well she was going to get her point across. She was going to tell him all about his beloved mum and what she'd got up to with that travelling salesman, when she ought to have known better.

Steve got out from behind the wheel. Both front doors slammed shut. Then Jonjo came round to the back of the car and opened the door right beside her. Instantly her hair was blown into disarray. She reached up, realising she'd left one of her pink sponge curlers in the fringe. She pulled it out. What would Max think, her turning up in such disarray? Well she would tell him that he shouldn't rouse people in the middle of the night just to talk to him. It wasn't on.

Jonjo grabbed her arm – so roughly that a small cry escaped her. He was bruising her.

'Jonjo . . .' she started, but the force of the wind took all the breath away from her.

The two big men were hurrying over the grass, the wind battling at them like a boxer. Nora couldn't speak – the wind was too strong, they were moving too fast. She saw lights way ahead, winking, and a stretch of inky darkness.

The sea. She was looking at the sea. There were fishing boats out there, a long way out, their dim lights bobbing on the waves. The torch lit the way. She could see how the grass was flattened and tossed about in the squalling breeze.

Then abruptly it seemed that the grass ran out. The torch showed only blackness and those tiny bobbing lights stretched to a paler horizon. The wind screamed around them. Nora felt her bowels turn to liquid.

*She was looking at the sea and they were on a cliff.*

'No . . .' she started, but Jonjo caught her arms. Steve bent and grabbed her legs. They swung her once, twice, three times – and then they let her go.

Nora felt herself plummeting, falling like a stone. She didn't even have time to scream before she hit the rocks below.

# 23

Bruno often wondered how different his life might have been, if his mother – his *real* mother – had actually wanted him in her life. But Nora – that old witch – had told him he wasn't wanted, and it was a crying shame, but that was a fact. Queenie Carter didn't want him, because the knowledge of his very existence would embarrass her in front of her adult boys, her *real* sons. They would know that she'd been fucked by some travelling oik in her later years, and that he, Bruno, was the shameful result of an inappropriate joining together.

Then *it* happened.

He'd been in bed, asleep, and he'd heard noises at the front door and then to his horror there had been people coming up the stairs. He'd stayed under the covers for a long time, listening, waiting for someone to come bursting into his room and knife him or something awful. There were no tourists staying right now – and anyway what would they be doing skulking about in the middle of the night? Nobody would dare come in this late, not with Nora always laying down the law about lockouts if anyone dared try to enter the house after ten in the evening.

Bruno's heart was thundering in his chest as he lay there, waiting for trouble. But nobody came into his room. Somehow he plucked up the nerve to get out of bed and creep over to the door, opening it just a crack. People were moving about out there. Nora's voice was shrill, nervous. Then there was torchlight. He could make out big men, two of them. He drew back, watching, and then they were coming out of Nora's room across the hall, pulling the door closed behind them. The torchlight flickered, moving in a cold blue-white cone.

His gasp of surprise nearly shopped him. He slapped a hand over his own mouth. He knew one of the men. He'd seen him before, standing in Queenie Carter's hallway behind Max, easily visible because he was the taller, towering over his older brother.

*Jonjo Carter.*

What the fuck was Jonjo Carter doing here, creeping into Nora's bedroom in the middle of the night? He heard voices mumbling. Nora's was mixed in with Jonjo's. Then Jonjo and his accomplice came out onto the landing again and Bruno distinctly heard: 'You're sure about this?' from the dark-haired man, the one he didn't know.

'Direct orders from Max,' said Jonjo firmly.

Then to add to Bruno's confusion he saw Nora stepping out of her bedroom fully dressed. He nearly stepped forward, nearly asked her what the hell was going on – but he didn't. Some innate sense of self-preservation prevented him doing that. He'd already decided, on first sight of Jonjo, that this was bad news. Anything involving Jonjo, Bruno didn't want to know about. So he kept still, kept quiet.

Jonjo and Nora went off down the stairs, no doubt pausing at the rack to take down her coat. Maybe Jonjo Carter helped her into it, who knew? Bruno couldn't see that. Then, he was dazzled. Blinded by a torch's beam. He froze to the spot, unable to move. He saw the outline of the dark-haired man behind the torch. The light paused on Bruno's face and he blinked. What the hell . . . ?

Then the beam flicked off and the man went on down-stairs. His heart racketing in his chest, Bruno strained to listen, to hear them coming back up, to hear the dark-haired one telling Jonjo that they had a witness to whatever the hell they were up to.

But instead he heard the front door close. Bruno realised he'd been holding his breath, anticipating trouble. He let out a tremulous sigh. He was shaking. Sweating, too. Now all was quiet but for the wind coming bracing and fresh off the sea, buffeting the house as it always did on these long winter nights. Usually he liked the sound; it was comforting, made him feel warm and snug in bed while outside storms raged. Now, with the house empty but for him, the noise was eerie. Out in the road, a car door slammed and an engine revved and then sped away.

He never saw Nora again.

# 24

The big empty house loomed around him throughout the following days. He went round the shops, got himself a fish supper, carried on living. Why should he bother reporting Nora's disappearance to anyone? Of course her churchy mates called by on Sunday to collect her, but he just told them she was ill in bed and they fucked off. Actually, after a while, he rather liked having the house to himself. Nobody to fix his dinners or do his washing, but what the hell. He managed. And then the police came and a solemn female PC broke the news to him: Nora was dead. It was in the *Brighton Echo*: she'd chucked herself off Margate cliffs.

The police asked him questions. Was he Nora's son? He answered yes. He didn't know what else to say.

Then the social workers came and Bruno thought, watch out: they were going to sweep him up and plonk him in some charity doss house with a load of other unwanted kids. He'd already been dumped once. He wasn't having that, not again.

He had to formulate a plan. He went along the seafront, skimming pebbles into the tossing waves, and thought bitterly about his *real* family, the ones who didn't want him. What he thought had happened was this: Jonjo and his mate had done the business on Nora. She really wasn't the type to go chucking herself off anywhere. He was sure that she would consider suicide a mortal sin. Such a decisive act would be far too dramatic for the likes of her, anyhow.

Well, he was free of her now. He was free of everything and everybody. He was abandoned and alone, as always. He thought of that early memory, him in his soggy nappy, crying on the kitchen floor, only to be shouted at, chucked a bottle of cold tea and a bit of ham. Bruno decided that he had to get out of here before the authorities nabbed him.

He would go to London. He *also* decided that he was going to get a job while he was there. He was fifteen; he was old enough and chunky enough to be useful to one of the gangs. What about the one that Nora had mentioned, run by Davey Delaney? The ones who'd been causing his 'brother' Max trouble?

Yeah, the brother who didn't want to know him. The one who had Aunt Nora chucked off a cliff. The one whose mother – Queenie bloody Carter – had left him to be dragged up by Nora.

Davey Delaney, the king of Battersea. Now there was an idea. And once he was in London, he could spy out what the Carter boys were up to. They might not want him, but he couldn't deny that he was hotly, avidly curious about them. He was an outsider, a blow-by, but they were the real deal, the ones Nora had always told him about. Eddie and Jonjo and Max.

Eddie was a fruit, apparently.

Jonjo was a mouth-breather, a thug with a couple of brain cells rattling around in his head getting lonely.

Max, though. It was Max who most interested Bruno. Max was the boss, the eldest. Rich now, Nora had told him. She'd said you could see the power oozing out of him, and the intelligence. Even Nora had stepped carefully around the eldest Carter boy. She might not have liked him but she certainly treated him with respect. If Bruno got a job with the Delaneys, then he could watch Max Carter from close quarters, and plot how best to take his revenge on the bastard – *and* on his mother Queenie, the cold-hearted cow.

Bruno drew out cash from the bank account that Nora had helped him set up some time ago – leaving just a pound in the account to keep it open in case he decided to use it in the future. Then he packed his bags and headed for the railway station to get his ticket to the Smoke.

He didn't tell a single soul goodbye.

# 25

Max wasn't in the best of moods. The Delaneys were – as always – a sharp pain in his arse, having knocked off a load of his goods coming down from Manchester to London. Davey obviously had never forgiven him for the stitch-up with the Newhaven watches, and it didn't look like he ever would. Mum was poorly – her heart. Max's plan was to get her away to the country at weekends, have her in the annexe relaxing, nothing to do, with Miss Arnott the housekeeper taking the weight off.

And now here was Jonjo, standing in the Palermo Lounge's foyer, nobody in here for the moment except the cleaners in the main bar, Steve Taylor in the bogs, and Jonjo and Max and Tone, who was peacefully sitting just inside the main door reading the day's paper. Jonjo was saying . . . for Christ's sake! *What* was he saying?

It was days after Jonjo and Steve's Brighton visit to Aunt Nora. Max had almost forgotten about it, he was so tied up with the business and his worries over Mum's health. He'd got her private doctors, the best, Harley Street and everything, but they'd only told him what the NHS lot already had. There was a weakness; she had to be careful. But then he'd remembered Jonjo's Brighton trip, and said, how did it go?

'It went fucking fantastic,' said Jonjo. 'We won't get no more trouble off her.'

Max frowned. Jonjo could be heavy-handed. 'You took it easy on her, I hope? Spelled it out?'

'Spelled it out in block capitals,' said Jonjo with a grin. 'Chucked the old mare off Margate cliffs.'

'You what?' Max said blankly. He couldn't have heard right.

'Picked the lock and got in, told her you wanted a word and she came quiet as a mouse. Got her in the car and drove her straight there. She went over without a murmur.'

Max stared at Jonjo. 'You mean that?' he said. Jonjo made daft jokes, all the time. Maybe this was one of them. It wasn't very bloody funny, though.

'Sure I mean it,' said Jonjo, starting to look surly as he always did when Max questioned him about anything. 'We . . .'

He didn't finish the sentence. Max flew at him, got his elbow across Jonjo's throat and shoved the bigger man back against the wall. Jonjo found himself unable to breathe. His eyes bulged and he pawed at Max's arm, trying to gulp in air. Max pushed hard, harder, infuriated, *royally* pissed off, dimly aware that Tone had come to his feet, dropping the paper to the floor, and was approaching fast. Max shoved harder, red rage blurring his vision, intent on his aim – which was, right now, to throttle this stupid fucker, his brother, to death.

'You did *what?*' Max roared. 'You stupid cunt, what did you go and do that for? I said *have a word.*'

Jonjo wheezed. His face was red, then purple, as Max applied more pressure. Max could feel someone tapping at his shoulder but he was too enraged to pay any attention.

Jonjo's eyes were starting to close. They flickered, lost focus. On the edge of his fading vision, he could see Steve Taylor coming out from the main body of the club, see what was happening, and being quite unable – the *bastard* – to stifle a smirk at Jonjo's expense.

'Boss,' said Tone close by Max's ear. 'That's enough now. He can't breathe.'

Tone's voice seemed to penetrate the fog of fury. Max stepped back and Jonjo sagged, collapsing to the floor, fighting for air. Max walked away before he gave in to the strong desire to kick Jonjo in his fat head. He paced the lobby, dragging a hand through his hair, looking down at his crumpled brother in disbelief.

'What the fuck?' he shouted. 'I said *have a word*. That's exactly what I meant. She might have been a bitch, we all know that, but she was *family*. You don't do that to one of your own.'

The colour was coming back into Jonjo's face as he sat gasping in air. He glared up at Max and pushed himself to his feet, using the wall as a crutch. He sagged there, hauling in breath after breath. He looked at Max, then at Steve Taylor standing back there still trying – and failing – to suppress a smile, then at Tone, who went back to his seat by the door, picking up his paper and starting to read, as if nothing untoward had just happened.

'I misunderstood,' panted Jonjo. 'All right? I didn't get it right, I admit that, but . . .'

'Get it *right*?' Max stabbed a finger at Jonjo. 'You *cunt*. You better not have brought trouble to our door with this. You went on your own? Wait a minute. No. You didn't. You said "we".'

'I took *him* with me.' Jonjo nodded toward Steve. Jonjo's face was brick-red and sullen now. He was rubbing at his throat. 'Damn, you fucking near killed me.'

Max felt a twinge of relief. Steve was sound – silent as the grave. But he was still furious. 'In future, you tosser, you listen to what I say. You don't improvise. You don't kick off and do little old ladies. It's not on. I won't fucking have it and believe me I'm not lying. The *next* time you do anything like this, brother or no, I will fucking *finish* the job. You got me? I will *eat* you between two slices of bread, you stupid *cunt*.'

Jonjo was silent, eyes downcast. Max thought that the big lug hadn't looked any different when he was ten and get-ting a walloping off Mum for some foolish misdemeanour or other. Jonjo's trouble was . . . well, Max didn't have the time or feel like putting in the effort to fathom exactly what Jonjo's trouble was. All he knew was that if his brother'd had half a brain, he'd be extremely bloody dangerous.

'Get out of my sight,' he said, very low.

Jonjo needed no second telling. Brushing past his older brother, he went.

# 26

The police turned up at Queenie Carter's house one day, a man and a woman. Queenie felt her faltering heart give a painful jolt as she opened the door to find them standing on the step. A visit from the Old Bill was never welcome. Her sons were *good* boys, of course they were, and she wouldn't hear a word to the contrary, but they'd had trouble with the Bill over the years. The Yard were always bothering them, asking about their business when they had no right to.

'Mrs Queenie Carter?' asked the policewoman.

'Yes. Why?'

'Can we come in please?' the policeman asked.

'I asked you why.' Queenie was instantly agitated, ready for a brawl, to defend her sons to the last.

'We've bad news, Mrs Carter.' The policeman turned to his companion. 'Go in and stick the kettle on, eh, luv?' The policewoman brushed past Queenie. The policeman took Queenie's arm. 'Come along now, missus, let's get you sat down.'

Queenie found herself hustled along the hall and plonked into one of her own kitchen chairs while the policewoman filled the kettle.

'What's this about?' she asked weakly. Her heart was beating an unsteady tattoo in her chest. She felt dizzy, full of dread.

The policeman, a big plump man of middle years, sat himself down beside her and patted her hand. When the police start being kind to you, you know you're looking at trouble, she thought.

'God's sake,' she gasped out. 'What is it?' Nightmare images were playing through her mind. Max, run over, hurt, dead. Jonjo getting into fights and being knocked over, banging his head on a pavement. Little Eddie, being picked on, getting knifed.

'It's about your sister, Mrs Dawkins,' said the policeman as the policewoman found cups and tea and milk and the kettle started to roar away on the hob. 'We're sorry to have to tell you, but she died, Mrs Carter.'

'She . . .' Queenie's mouth dropped open. 'What do you mean? She's fit as a fiddle, Nora. You must be mistaken. Died? Died how?'

Someone was turning a key in the front door lock. They all froze, waiting for the new entrant to show him or herself. Max came in, strode along the hall, took in the sight of the policewoman making tea, the policeman sitting there with his hand on Queenie's.

'What?' he asked.

The policeman's eyes hardened. Max bloody Carter! Half the Met would love to get this flash bastard for something. But he was slippery as an eel – there was just no catching him.

The policewoman placed the filled teacups on the table.

'We had some bad news for your mother, Mr Carter,' said the policeman smoothly. 'Her sister has died and as the only known next of kin, we had to inform her of the fact.'

Max said nothing. He looked at Queenie's bleached-white face and felt his guts churn with guilt. This was *his* fault, landing a shock like this on her. It was him who had entrusted that thick fucker Jonjo with the job of warning Nora off. It was *his* responsibility – and just look how it had turned out.

'How did she die?' Queenie asked, thinking of her own painfully thumping heartbeat. She'd been to all the doctors – so many of them – and been told over and over that there was a weakness there, the result of that old infection – but maybe this was a *family* thing, this trouble. 'Was it her heart?' she asked. She thought of the boy then – Bruno. Her dirty secret. The police hadn't mentioned him, and she certainly wasn't going to.

'I am afraid she committed suicide,' said the policeman. 'I'm sorry.'

'She *what?*' Queenie said faintly.

'Off Margate cliffs,' said the copper, and then seemed to think more was required. 'I'm sorry for your loss.'

Max moved forward and placed both hands on his mother's shoulders. He felt them start to shake.

*His fault.*

Queenie was weeping now, in shock and grief. She and Nora had never been close, but they were blood. Sisters. This was *awful*.

'But Nora would never do a thing like that,' Queenie was saying between sobs. 'She was a churchgoer. Keen as anything on all that, she was. She said when she went, she would leave all she had to the church. Not that I cared, of course. It was her business what she did with her money. But . . . she would think it a sin, killing herself. She wouldn't do it.'

'Nevertheless, she did.' The copper gave Queenie's hand one last pat and then stood up. He looked at Max and pulled a sheet of paper from his pocket. 'This is the Brighton undertaker's details. Perhaps we can leave this with you now, sir?'

'Yeah. Of course,' said Max, taking the piece of paper. His innards twisted with guilt. Fucking Jonjo, leaving a mess like this behind, acting the bloody giddy goat and screwing everything up – as usual.

But no. He couldn't blame all this mess on Jonjo. He should have made himself clearer. He was head of the family, head of the firm. The buck stopped with him. This was *his* fault.

'I'll have to organise the funeral,' said Queenie, thinking frantically. She would have to go down to Brighton and she wasn't well enough to go alone. So Max would have to take her. And then he would be confronted by Bruno, who must still be at Nora's house.

Queenie's brain was spinning. She doubted Nora would have made provision for the boy. The church and lining her own pockets, those things had always come first for her. First and last. Bruno was an inconvenience, as Nora had never stopped telling her sister. Bruno was *Queenie's* mess, not hers.

Now it was all going to blow up in Queenie's face.

Max would find out.

He would be disgusted with her.

Her heart gave a hard spasm in her chest as she thought of that. If her secret came out, that was it – she couldn't live with the shame. She thought of Nora, hurtling over a chalk-white cliff to her doom. How low would you have to feel, before that seemed like a sensible option? She knew Nora was a low-key sort of woman – she always had been – but *this*? Suicide? A sin against God?

The police were going. They hadn't even drunk their tea. Max saw them to the door and then came back into the kitchen and gazed at his mother. She looked sick, almost jaundiced. He remembered her in years past as hearty, healthy, strong; now, she was a shadow of her former self.

'Tell you what,' he said, sitting down next to her, tucking the piece of paper into his jacket pocket. 'I'll go down there tomorrow and fix up the funeral. No need for you to be troubled with all that.' He paused. 'I'll give her a good send-off. I promise. Do you think you'll want to attend?'

Queenie shook her head. Her chest felt tight, vice-like. She was going to be found out. Max would stumble across Bruno down there in Brighton and her secret, her shame, would be revealed. She felt fatalistic all of a sudden. Well, let it happen then. She couldn't fight this any longer. She was too old; too sick.

Max took her hand in his. 'Look. Don't worry,' he said. 'I'll see to everything. And this weekend you can go down to the Surrey place. Tone'll take you. The weather's going to be good. You can rest up there. How's that?'

# 27

Bruno went to 'their' places – the Delaney streets, the ones around Battersea power station. He loitered outside their scrapyard, drank in the pubs he knew they owned. He got himself settled in a derelict place nearby and squatted there with two alkies, elderly old soldier sorts with the red-veined noses and bad teeth of the permanently intoxicated. They stoked up a little fire, sat around and drank and told Bruno tales of improbable past glories.

'You know the Delaneys?' Bruno asked them. They were all right, these two: harmless.

'Everyone knows them around these parts,' said the one called Peter, swigging from his bottle and then belching mildly. 'You don't want to go mixing with them sorts, boy.'

Bruno ignored that. He *did* want to mix with the Delaneys. They hated the Carter mob. They were just the ones he wanted to get the inside track on Carter dealings and to work out his best plan of attack.

Peter and Ben shared the food they scrounged with Bruno, offered him drink. This must be what it was like to have friends, he thought – people who watched your back. He chipped in with his cash from the Brighton bank and began to trust these two. Then he got back to the squat one afternoon and found that Peter and Ben were gone and two youngsters of around his own age were occupying the place instead, shooting up beside Peter and Ben's old brazier. They stiffened, wild-eyed as feral dogs, when Bruno came in.

Bruno stood there, staring at these incomers. He had in his hand a carrier bag full of beer cans, chocolate biscuits, bread and a hunk of cheese, which was going to have been supper for him and his companions.

'Where's Peter?' he asked these two. 'Where's Ben?'

One of them was heroin-skinny, the other chunkier, evil-eyed. They looked at Bruno and started to smile.

'Gone,' said the thin one. 'They decided to leave. Didn't they?' He smirked at his pal.

So they'd scared off the old soldiers. Bruno watched them warily.

'What's in the bag?' asked the fatter one.

'Food. Drink,' said Bruno.

'Give it here then.'

'No,' said Bruno.

'Listen to it! Thinks it's tough,' said the skinny one, his eyes rolling in his head. 'Hand the bag over, pal. Got any money on you?'

'No.'

'Lies through his teeth too,' said Skinny. 'Get the bag, Dean. Go on.'

Dean started toward Bruno. Bruno dropped the carrier bag out of his right hand and with snakelike speed reached under his jacket and snatched the knives one by one out of the holster under his left arm.

*Thwack! Thwack! Thwack!*

The first one sank itself into Dean's right forearm, the second into his left, the third into his right leg, just above the knee.

'*Jesus!*' Dean shrieked, crumpling to the floor.

Bruno strode up to Dean and snatched the blades out one by one, yanking them free of his arms and his leg. He wiped them clean on Dean's shirt and slotted them back into the holster. Then he turned on the skinny one, who was cowering back, expecting mayhem.

'Get out, arse-wipe,' he said. 'And take your big friend with you.' He smiled coldly. 'I think he might need a doctor.'

★

After that, Bruno had no more trouble with interlopers, but he never saw Peter or Ben again. Once again, he was alone. He waited and watched the Delaney mob moving around the town, doing business. He saw Davey the old man, and Tory who was starting to take over the reins, and Pat. There was a set of twins, a man and a woman: Redmond and Orla. They were staggeringly beautiful, the pair of them. Flame-haired and green-eyed and as perfect as carved alabaster.

Bruno admired flawless beauty in others. The birthmark on his face embarrassed him. People stared at it. He had never attended school if it could be avoided – and mostly it could – but whenever he did turn up, the kids there had gawped at him, called him Strawberry. Made fun of him. He hadn't made friends but his years spent with the cheerless Nora had made him tough. So he stayed on alone in the squat, washed himself in pub toilets, and said loudly in all the Delaney places that he was Max Carter's enemy and that he wanted to hurt the Carter clan – but no one seemed to take any notice.

Then, suddenly, someone did.

# 28

He was walking out of the Blind Bear one night when two big blokes grabbed him. They hefted him easily off his feet and bundled him into a car. It roared through the night-time streets until he had no idea where he was, none at all. Any slight resistance from him was met with a painful poke in the ribs from a knife. They searched his pockets, opened his jacket and found the holster with the stiletto blades.

'Look at this! Fancy, innit?'

They took both the holster and the blades off him. Oh shit. He was in trouble.

'What's this you been saying, birthmark boy?' the knife man asked him, breathing ale fumes all over his face. 'You saying you're against Max Carter? You got it in for him? That tosser?'

Bruno had to swallow hard before he could force words out. 'It's true,' he said.

There was a flash of a grin, lit by strobing street lights as the car barrelled along through the night.

'Tell it to Tory, yeah? See what *he* makes of it.'

★

The car stopped at last and they hauled him out of the back of it and bundled him inside a snooker hall.

'You little bastard, you been asking for this, giving us all that shit about Carter,' said the knife man as he was hustled inside.

Bruno was gripped by terror. He had come to London with high hopes; no way had he expected that his intention to sign on with the Delaney gang and wreak some overdue vengeance on the Carters would land him in trouble.

The Delaneys were the sworn enemies of the Carters. They had a big scrapyard in the shadow of the power station that covered a multitude of sins every day. He'd been outside; he'd seen it with his own eyes. Hot cars and vans used in robberies and even assassinations came in there and were pulverised. He'd heard all the tales. The high gates and guard dogs and security men pacing around the yard always scared off the curious. If the police got too interested, they were paid off. If they didn't accept payment, other Delaney connections within the force would see to it that they were demoted and moved quietly away.

Beside the scrapyard, the Delaneys owned pubs, gym clubs and snooker halls like this one, and all the other businesses on Delaney turf paid them protection.

Bruno had tried in the gyms first, said he was looking for work with the Delaney crew, but that drew silence and suspicious looks. Giving up on that, he'd proceeded to the pubs and asked the landlords how he could get in touch with Davey Delaney. Or could he speak to Tory the eldest son, or Pat, if not to their dad?

Blank looks.

Nobody wanted to say a word to him.

He'd stayed on. Fed himself on fish suppers, palled up with Peter and Ben. Loitered around the edges of the Carter patch, sometimes. Saw bulky Jonjo. And sometimes there was a dark-haired man with him, one he recognised. It was the one who had been there on the night of Nora's death. The one with the flashlight, who had looked straight back at him then decided to leave him alone. Nora's killing had been a direct order from Max. Hadn't Jonjo said so, when he stood there on the landing at Nora's Brighton boarding house, just about to commit a murder? He had.

Once or twice, Bruno had caught a glimpse of Max Carter himself. His brother, the one that mattered. Strange thought. He had seen the way Max looked at him when he'd stood out there on the pavement. He'd heard Max's words.

*Who's the kid?*

*Just one of her church strays.*

Of course, he could blow the whole damned comfy Carter world apart, couldn't he, if he wanted to. Could break it to the three *legitimate*, the three *wanted* sons of Queenie Carter that their mum was a slag and he was the result of her fooling around, outraging all sense of decency, at a time of life when she really ought to have learned how to behave.

He hugged that thought to him, when he lay alone at night in his ratty little squat. The bright red neons from the strip club opposite flickered and disturbed his sleep for most of the night. He didn't care. He had a plan and that plan was revenge, on the mother who'd abandoned him and on the favoured son, Max – who had everything *he* should have had.

Bruno was a strong young man in his prime, but these men were hauling him about as if he weighed less than a feather. Inside the hall there was thick smoke from a hundred cigarettes, low long oblong lights pooling on green baize. There were ten snooker tables set out under the lights, and men turned and looked as the two carried Bruno in; but no one objected. No one seemed even slightly interested. A couple of the men looked up, then went back to their game.

Bruno struggled and writhed, but he was helpless.

A few paces and then he was *slapped* down onto one of the green baize tables, so hard that all the breath was driven out of him in a loud, painful *whoop*. Balls of all colours scattered. Men moved around the table, making way.

'Hold him,' said one of them who'd carried him in here.

# 29

Someone grabbed Bruno's legs. He kicked out, but it was useless. They were too damned strong. Suddenly he was sprawled out, helpless on the table, his shoulders rammed agonisingly against one of the pockets, his legs spread wide, and he could see one of the men – the one with the hat, one of those who'd carried him in here – holding a snooker cue across the baize from where he lay pinioned. The hatted one picked up a white billiard ball and placed it on the baize, took aim with the cue – and sent the ball scudding hard and fast straight into Bruno's bollocks.

Bruno let out a shriek. Oh Christ, that *hurt.*

The men around the table laughed.

'What you been doing, asking around for Davey Delaney?' asked one of them.

Bruno, writhing, said nothing. He thought he was about to be sick, he was in so much pain. 'What's this crap you been spouting about being Max Carter's enemy?'

'Speak up, arsehole, or the red one's going in your nuts next,' said the hatted one. His eyes rested on Bruno's pain-twisted features. 'No? Right then.'

The one in the hat picked up a red ball and took aim.

*Oh Christ oh no, please . . .*

Bruno tensed and writhed. His balls throbbed. He was aware of them all watching around the table, laughing at his anguish. The one with the hat was taking aim. He was going to do it.

'No!' Bruno screamed, trying to escape but unable to.

'What the feck's this?' asked a deep male voice.

Bruno dared to look.

Another man had approached the table. He snatched the cue off the man in the hat.

'What's going on?' he asked.

'Just a bit of fun. This nipper's been asking around for Pa, Tory. Thought he might need teaching a lesson.'

The one called Tory leaned in with the cue and poked Bruno in the chest with the tip.

'What you asking about Pa for, boy?' he asked in a deep Irish lilt.

Bruno couldn't speak past the agony in his scrotum. Tears were cascading down his face.

'Let him go,' said Tory to the men who were restraining him. They let go of his legs and Bruno sat up on the table, clutching at his crotch.

'I asked you a question,' Tory reminded him.

'I just wanted a job, that's all. I can do anything,' Bruno gasped out, his face a mask of anguish. 'I can be useful.'

Tory stared at the boy with the black waving hair and blue, blue eyes. A shame about the mark on his cheek, because otherwise this could be – without doubt – the most beautiful boy in the world. Like a Roman coin, the boy's profile showed a hook of a nose, a stubborn chin. A noble profile. He looked to be as tall as Tory himself, but thinner, leaner, narrower across the shoulders. The boy looked as if he'd known hard times – he was pale, and there were shadows under those startling blue eyes – and his expression was wary, like a much-kicked animal.

What sort of harm could a cringing kid like this do to the Delaney clan? None whatsoever. Pat and his heavy-handed cronies had no finesse. No eye for beauty. They had just felt like giving the kid a kicking. Morons.

'Get him off there,' said Tory, and many hands hustled Bruno off the table. He stood there cringing, clutching at his balls, watching them all with eyes streaming with tears.

'He's been saying he hates Max Carter,' said Pat.

'Has he now? Well, don't we all, Pat.'

'He was carrying these.' Pat held up the holster with the stilettoes tucked inside.

Tory looked at Bruno with interest as he stood there shivering with fright. Such a gorgeous boy, but for that one little flaw. Such a pity. 'Give him his knives back,' he said to Pat, then, to Bruno: 'All right. You can sweep up in here, sort the toilets out. The cleaner's off sick and the place is turning into a fucking midden, so it is.' Tory glared around. He didn't want to show how much the boy's beauty had jolted him: you never showed weakness of any kind, not when you were boss of the crew – which he was, now that his dad had more or less handed over the reins. 'Now, you load of bog-trotting tossers? You leave the bloody boy alone . . . You got that?'

They understood. They nudged each other, moved away, smirking but careful not to let Tory *see* them doing it.

They knew which way Tory's interests lay. His last paramour had run out on him just weeks ago, and it looked like the next one was just about to take his place.

# 30

The trouble with Ruthie Bailey's sister, Annie, was this: she always knew *exactly* what she wanted. She'd been just eleven years old and starting at big school when she'd first become aware of Max Carter, being driven around town. Everyone seemed nervous of him; here was a man with power, wealth – and good God, his looks.

Max Carter was a handsome man, not overly tall but compact and muscular, always moving with athletic ease. Women turned to look at him when he passed them by. His hair was thick, waving, black. His skin was swarthy, golden; his eyes a dense dark navy blue; his mouth sensual beneath that piratical hook of a nose. Annie reckoned he could do you physical damage in an instant, if he wanted to.

Of course, he was older than her. But he was young to have so much clout around the area. She'd heard tell of him winding up the Delaney gang, and that was impressive. They were tough bastards.

'He'd never look twice at you,' Kath told her scathingly. 'I've seen him up Carnaby Street with models, *fabulous* girls.'

But Annie wasn't put off. She dreamed of him at night in her single solitary bed, dreamed of him kissing her. Sometimes she would wake, shuddering with a strange pleasure, having dreamed of him holding her, touching her. She didn't mention how she felt about Max Carter to Ruthie, who still shared a bedroom with her, and she swore Kath to secrecy over the matter. She was afraid that Ruthie, being older and probably a lot wiser too, would scoff at the idea and destroy the dream, which she hugged to herself night after night.

Max was always there, just out of reach, an unattainable prize that she coveted so much it made her ache with longing. He owned three nightclubs, and she was jealous as hell when Ruthie got a job behind the coat counter in one of them. Damn! Why hadn't *she* thought of that, instead of wasting her life in that mangy corner shop? But, however, it gave Annie a chance to show up at the club, get past the doormen, chat to her sister and maybe even get to see Max himself, close-up.

Connie was a drunk – everyone knew it – but even during her more lucid spells she was unnecessarily sharp with Annie, never giving her so much as a word of praise. Annie'd got all Ruthie's hand-me-down clothes to wear, nothing new, nothing special, and she got used to that treatment; she got used to being strong. The one light in her dreary life was Max Carter, her dream man. She didn't care that he was dodgy. Everyone said that and it didn't sway her, not in the least. He was the only one she had ever wanted.

Then Ruthie came home one day and said to her half-sozzled mother and her astonished sister that she was engaged.

'To who then?' Annie laughed, because Ruthie was a shy girl. She didn't think Ruthie even knew the facts of life. Those hot, heavy, *unsatisfying* dreams Annie had were, she was sure, quite beyond Ruthie. They were both virgins, both innocent where men were concerned. How could quiet, polite, *dull* Ruthie be 'engaged'?

'To Max Carter,' said Ruthie, her soft eyes shining.

Annie stared open-mouthed at her big sister while Connie started screaming and shouting with excitement.

'You . . . *who*?' Annie asked. This wasn't possible.

'Max Carter. He owns nightclubs and I got a job at the Blue Parrot, you remember, and then I moved to the Palermo Lounge . . . ?'

Annie was nodding impatiently. 'Yes. Yes! I know that. You told me. But how . . . ?'

'We just got talking,' said Ruthie, beaming. 'You know, he's really nice. We've been out on dates. He's been the perfect gentleman.'

Connie was nearly dancing around the room. 'You *what*?' she yelled happily, pound signs lighting up her bloodshot eyes. 'Max bloody Carter? This calls for a drink! You clever, clever girl,' she said and swooped in to kiss Ruthie's flushed cheek. Then she looked at Annie who was standing there, poleaxed. 'Aintcha going to congratulate your sister then?' she snapped.

Annie could barely speak, she was so shocked. Ruthie – plain, cow-eyed, mousy-haired little Ruthie – had bagged a job at Max's club and now she had bagged Max! It was a horror story. It just couldn't be. And, Annie thought, why hadn't *she* had the sense to get a job in one of his clubs? If she had, she would have made damned sure that there would be a wedding ring on her finger before very long. She *loved* Max Carter. She always had. And somewhere at the back of her mind there had always been the firm belief that one day he would be hers.

And now?

That wasn't going to happen.

She looked at Ruthie, smiling, and at Mum, embracing her. All those years, she'd craved him like a drug, and now he was going to marry her sister, the sister who always got *everything*. Bitterness stirred in her gut, uncoiling like a snake ready to spit venom. She couldn't believe it. She *wouldn't* believe it. Of course she loved Ruthie. They were blood, and blood counted. But now Annie looked at her sweet, beloved sister as if she was a stranger, and all she felt in that moment was a chilly, all-enveloping rage.

Annie had never asked for anything. She had taken it as read that she was the youngest, the least important, the rebellious child who'd get a thick ear rather than a cuddle. She had accepted Mum's scorn and ridicule. Learned to live with it, relished it almost, because it was attention of sorts and God knows she got little enough of that.

But *this*.

Her sister, getting Max Carter, the one man Annie had coveted all her young life?

No.

This couldn't happen.

She wouldn't let it.

# 31

One evening, Tone dropped Max off at the Palermo Lounge. He went inside, nodding to the doormen, who respectfully nodded back. Max was pleased to hear the happy hubbub of chattering voices that told him the club was packed with punters. The scent of booze and cigarettes was strong in the air, a sure sign everyone was having a good time. Ahead he could see women in glittering jewels, furs tossed over the backs of their chairs, men in dinner jackets lighting cigars and drinking whisky from crystal glasses. Max could hear 'Mona Lisa' – the Nat King Cole song – being played by the band. He was never going to forget that song – he just didn't know it yet.

At the cloakroom station there was a dark-haired girl bending over, leaning both elbows on the counter. She was chatting, her face turned upward and smiling, to someone out of sight inside the cloakroom. Max took one look and thought *gorgeous*. He stopped just inside the door, taking off his own coat, his eyes arrested by the girl's legs, which seemed to go on forever. She was wearing long white plastic PVC boots and a black miniskirt that should have been against the law, it was so short. Her top half was covered in a clingy V-necked white blouse, frilled and low at the neckline like the ones P J Proby wore.

Max stood there a moment longer, taking in the view. The girl's hair was a long cloud of darkness, backcombed into an exuberant bouffant. He couldn't see her face, but she was chatting animatedly to someone on the other side of the counter. He stepped forward, laid his coat on the counter beside the girl, and saw Ruthie in there for the first time, wearing her staid little cloakroom attendant's uniform, Ruthie who had recently transferred from the Blue Parrot to here. Her eyes lit up when she saw him.

'Oh!' Ruthie turned her warm smile on him. 'You two haven't met, have you? Max – this is Annie, my sister.'

The girl straightened. She was taller than he had supposed – hence those heart-stopping legs! And she was arrestingly beautiful. She had a perfectly shaped oval face, a straight no-nonsense nose, full pouting lips made pale by pan-stick, and her eyes were a dark green. Like tourmalines, he thought. They sparkled with bold intelligence and a hint of laughter. He felt that somehow she *knew* she'd already knocked him sideways.

Now he saw her close up, he realised he had seen her before around his manor and watched her with interest, the way any man would, without having a single clue that she was Ruthie's sister. She'd been hanging around with one of his workers who did the milk run, Billy Black. Those legs, that was what he remembered. Yes, she was fantastic. And without a doubt, she was trouble. Hadn't his dad always summed it up, before he left them all and headed off for sunnier pastures?

'Avoid the lookers. Marry a plain woman, son,' he'd told his eldest boy. 'Keep her well fucked and poorly shod and she'll never leave you.'

Somehow, Max realised, he had absorbed the old bastard's advice and yes – he was going to marry Ruthie. Who was plain. Homely. The type that would never give you trouble. Not like *this* one. Ruthie was a little brown hen beside this exuberant bird of paradise.

Annie Bailey was holding out a hand. 'Hello,' she said in a soft, husky voice.

*The sort of woman whose hand you kissed,* he thought. He didn't kiss it though. He took it in his, shook it lightly. Her grasp was cool, slim-fingered, the skin soft. He quickly reined in thoughts of what the *rest* of her skin might be like to the touch. He let her hand drop, feeling that cool as it was, still the contact had somehow scorched him.

'Hello. Nice to meet you,' he said.

'And you,' she said.

Afterwards, he couldn't even remember what they had talked about. Ruthie had taken his coat, and then had busied herself with more patrons coming into the club. He had made conversation with Annie Bailey; maybe he'd talked about the weather, the club. Maybe he'd asked where she worked, what she did, but for the life of him as he later went on into the main body of the club, he couldn't remember. All he could think about was her eyes, gleaming with bright knowing humour. Whatever they'd talked about, he knew that her eyes and his had been having an entirely *different* type of conversation.

*Let it go,* he told himself.

He had everything neatly worked out. He had the clubs now. He had Mum well looked after. No more skivvying for her, thank God. Eddie was a wild child, always off with various boyfriends, and Jonjo was an idiot; that went without saying. He had Ruthie who would take care of his home life over the future years, see that everything ran smoothly. Entertain, stuff like that. Ruthie was a sweet girl.

Annie was . . . something else.

*Mistress material.*

Yeah, that was it. But not *his* mistress. No way. That would be entirely too close to home.

# 32

Max was at the Palermo again, leaving Queenie at home packing up a weekend bag. She'd have a rest down in the country. Miss Arnott would make a fuss of her, see that she was well looked after. Ruthie was in the club working, and he had a word with her, then went on in, thinking of how well Ruthie and Queenie got on. Thinking that yes, Ruthie was one of his better decisions. It was quite something, to earn Queenie's approval – and sweet, biddable Ruthie had achieved that with ease.

All the usual faces were in and one of the new singers, a pretty blonde in a red dress, was up on the stage, fronting a four-piece band. Some couples were out on the small circular floor, smooching along to the number she was singing.

Max went to his usual table – the best in the house – near the front of the stage. On the way he paused to shake hands, kiss an upraised cheek, chat and laugh. He took in the happy punters, the red and gold drapes behind the stage, the gold MC placed prominently at the top. He waved to a couple of his mates and was content, after the pig of a day he'd had, to see that here at least, in business, everything was running just as it should.

Jonjo was already at their table, smoking a Dunhill and sipping whisky. He looked warily across as Max sat down.

It was days since they'd had the ruck over Nora, but Jonjo hadn't forgotten it.

'No Eddie?' asked Max.

'Off somewhere,' said Jonjo with a huff of disgust. 'You can guess doing what.'

Max had no interest in Eddie's sexual appetites – that was *his* business.

'You got a face like the wrath of God, mate,' said Jonjo with an uneasy grin. 'What's up?'

'Did I tell you the busies called round?' said Max. A hostess came over, put his usual Chivas Regal down on the table. He nodded his thanks. Took a sip.

'What for?' Jonjo's grin vanished.

Max stared at his brother, cold-eyed. 'What for? What the fuck do you think for? To tell Mum that Aunt Nora took a dive off a cliff and wound up dead.'

'Shit.'

'That was bound to happen, don't you think?'

'How'd she take it?'

'How'd you think? It hit her like a ton of bricks, the poor cow.'

Jonjo opened his mouth to speak and then thought better of it. Max's face was very still, but underneath that composure there was still a snapping dragon, thunderous in its rage. Best keep quiet. Then a tiny dainty blonde in a pink lace dress came over – Tansy Driver, the eighteen-year-old daughter of one of Max's close business associates.

'Going to dance with me, Mr Carter?' she asked Max.

Jonjo was sitting there with his tongue hanging out. He liked young blondes in the bedroom department. Max didn't; all his past girlfriends had been brunettes – and anyway Tansy was *way* too young. She was here tonight with her parents; her father was a large-scale and very influential property developer who'd put business Max's way, and Max was aware that he had to keep Tansy's daddy sweet. He stood up, moved onto the dance floor with her, chatted to her, made her laugh. He didn't feel like it, not in the least, but sometimes you just had things to do.

'Can I cut in?' asked a low female voice.

'Sure,' said Tansy, pouting a little but standing aside as the song ended. Then the band struck up a sultry new song and the singer joined in. Tansy drew away, still pouting, and went back to her parents' table. Max was left standing there, face to face with Annie Bailey.

He didn't want to dance with her. But she was right here and he wasn't about to make any sort of scene by refusing, not right in the middle of the club and with Ruthie on the premises. Annie moved into his arms, her dark green knowing eyes on his. Her long dark hair tickled his hand as it slid across the back of her cream silk blouse.

'So how are the wedding plans going?' she asked him in that low husky voice as they danced. That voice had haunted his dreams, and he had been waiting – dreading but somehow *wanting* – to hear it again, for real.

'Fine, so far as I know,' he said. She smelled disturbingly sweet, of vanilla and musk. He found himself wanting to grab a handful of that cloudy dark hair, to inhale it. And more. Much more.

'You don't know?' asked Annie.

'Not my department,' he said.

They moved together, the singer pouring out her heart, a song of love and loss and deep, dark desire.

'What's that aftershave?' asked Annie. Scenting him, just as he was scenting her, he realised.

'I dunno. Trumper's Lemon? I use that sometimes.'

'It's nice.'

She put her head against his shoulder as they smooched around with the other couples on the dance floor. Max could feel her breasts tight against his chest, her thighs moving against his. He hoped to God he wasn't going to get a hard-on. After a little while, Annie said: 'You're making a mistake.'

Max drew his head back, looked into her eyes. She was close, far too close. He had only to dip his head a tiny bit and his lips would touch hers. 'What?'

'I said . . .'

'I heard what you said. What do you mean?'

'Ruthie's not the woman for you,' said Annie.

'Why would you say that? Don't you want your sister to be happy?'

'But she won't be, will she? Not with you. You're too strong for her. She's a Virgo you know. That's a mutable sign. What are you?'

'That's such bollocks,' said Max.

'Scorpio. Am I right?'

She was. Max nodded. 'So?'

'That's a fixed sign. I'm a fixed sign too. Taurus. I'd be strong enough for you. Maybe even a little *too* strong.'

'I expect I'd manage to slap you down if you needed it,' said Max with a tight half-smile. Christ, she was irritating. And sexy as hell. Queenie approved of Ruthie, but *this* one? She'd throw a fit at the very idea. She was used to ruling the roost and would not tolerate another headstrong woman in the family. She would hate Annie. And Annie, he was perfectly sure, would hate Queenie right back.

'There are other ways to get want you want, Max, and they don't involve slapping,' she said.

Her face was right there, inches away, her lips inviting. He had a sudden and shocking image in his mind: him on a bed with her beneath him, both of them naked, her long legs twined around him, her cries of passion frantic as he pushed into her, again and again and again.

Then the song ended and everyone applauded. Max stepped back, away from her. She was still smiling straight into his eyes. She leaned in and said, very distinctly: 'Coward.'

*Coward?*

If any man called him that, he'd knock him clean across the room. But this damned girl? He didn't know what to make of her, with her fearless eyes and her angel's body.

Then she walked away. He watched her go back to the foyer. Billy Black was there and she paused there, talked to him. Then she went to the hat-check station where Ruthie was working and grabbed her coat. Then she was out of sight: gone.

Max went back to his table and sat down.

'Who's the tart?' Jonjo asked.

'Her? That's Ruthie's sister.' Max gulped down his whisky.

'Hot stuff by the look of her.'

'I wouldn't know,' said Max. And he wasn't *going* to know, either.

# 33

Max knew he shouldn't go there. He wasn't an impetuous type of man. Usually, he could control himself in any situation, without a shred of difficulty. He was the exact opposite of Jonjo, who was impulsive, quick to anger, who had big fantasies of private islands and yachts and all the pussy he could eat – and no brains to back these daydreams up. Max knew that big dreams had to be worked for, and he did the grunt work, the daily grind, to achieve them. Jonjo, you had to keep on a leash. He was the *complete* opposite of Eddie, who these days could only get excited by pretty boys, floral shirts and the latest haircut and who – unlike Jonjo, unlike Max himself – didn't have an aggressive bone in his entire body.

But . . . there she was, time and again, *the girl*, around town, in The Grapes, on the streets, and right there in the club, leaning on the counter chatting to her sister. And then she would look up and their eyes would meet, and time would slow down.

*Mistress material.*

She was an itch he dared not scratch. You didn't shit on your own doorstep and you *certainly* didn't jump into bed with the woman who was going to be your sister-in-law. Plans for the wedding were already well under way. Ruthie was in a state of excitement; her obvious joy as touching as a child's. She was a sweet girl and she would make a lovely wife. And of course Connie, her mother, scrawny old drunk that she was, well, she was over the moon. She was ordering new net curtains, putting fancy new furniture on tick, having – probably for the first time in her life – anything she wanted, because Ruthie would talk to Max about it and Max would pay.

He didn't mind that. Fair enough, he was marrying the girl, she would soon be solely his responsibility and he could tolerate Connie although he would never like her. He despised drunks; they reminded him of his father. Max had it all reasoned out. Ruthie would make a great wife. Connie could be kept out of the picture as much as possible. But . . . there was a fly in the ointment wasn't there: Annie. That damned *girl*.

One day he was walking along the street in Bow and there she was. Again. He suspected she was following him around, anticipating where he'd be, where she was likely to bump into him. She turned from a shop window stuffed with miniskirted mannequins and saw him coming. Her cousin Kath was with her, nudging her in the ribs, grinning. Kath and her mother Maureen, Connie's sister, lived right next door to Connie and her daughters. He'd met them.

'Oh! Hi, Max,' Annie said, smiling – shoving Kath, giving her a *shut the fuck up* look.

'Hello. Ruthie not with you then?' he asked. Reminding her – and himself – that there was Ruthie.

'This is my cousin Kath,' said Annie.

'I know. We've met before,' said Max, and then, not even intending to do it, he did it. 'Look Kath – give us a minute, will you?'

'Yeah, OK.' Kath went off into the shop to eye up the dresses.

'Did you want to talk to me about something?' Annie asked, very wide-eyed and innocent, like she wasn't fully aware of the fact that she was driving him crazy.

'Yeah, I did. Are you following me around?' he asked, very direct, giving her the hard stare that made grown men grovel. It didn't have the slightest effect on her.

'*Following* you?' Annie said. 'Why would I do that?'

'It's just that you seem to pop up everywhere I go. That's all.'

'Coincidence.' She shrugged. 'Still happy with Ruthie then?'

'Why wouldn't I be?'

Damn this girl and the way she distracted him. He had business matters, *important* matters, to attend to. The Delaneys were always at his throat, always making trouble, kicking off at venues who paid up to Max's mob, upsetting the owners, calling Max's influence into question. And he couldn't have that. He had good men at his back, and that helped. Steve Taylor was worth his weight in solid gold. Tone was a diamond. And there were many others. He couldn't manage it all without them. Of course, Jonjo was good when someone needed slapping down, but for anything that required thinking, working stuff out? Forget it.

'You're both still sure of this, are you? The wedding? Marriage? All that?' Annie was asking him. Her eyes were suddenly serious, not laughing anymore.

'Date's set,' he said.

'Dates can be unset,' she pointed out.

Max narrowed his eyes. 'You want your sister's wedding called off? You think Ruthie deserves that, do you?'

Annie said nothing. She shrugged and suddenly found the pavement very interesting. All around them people passed, some of them nodding to Max. He barely saw them, barely saw any of it. The air was fizzing between him and this damned girl, he felt the charge of her, the crackling electric *pull* of her, like he'd shoved his fingers into a light socket. Cars roared by in the road and a big black Jag pulled sharply into the kerb, the man at the wheel instantly killing the engine.

Max drew in closer to Annie and spoke, low and clear.

'Look. It isn't going to happen, all right?'

'What isn't?' she asked, gazing up at him.

'This. Us. Whatever you want to call it. Get it out of your bloody head, will you?'

Annie's eyes were steady on his. Steady and green and *extremely* seductive. What was she going to do now? Shout? Cry? No. Neither of those things. Instead, she shocked him. She drew in closer. And then she said: 'Can you get it out of yours?'

Then Kath came out of the shop clutching a bag and she said: 'Bought a dress for Saturday night down the Palais. You getting anything?'

Max and Annie stood there, eyes locked. Annie dropped her gaze.

'Nah, think I'll skip it,' she said, and she took Kath's arm and walked away.

Tone got out of the Jag, looking after the two girls. Max looked too. Jesus God. Those *legs*.

'She looks like trouble, that one,' Tone remarked.

'Who asked you?' snapped Max. He got in the car. 'Just bloody drive, will you? Let's get over to the Parrot.'

Tone, grinning, got back behind the wheel, started the engine, and drove.

# 34

Bruno was settling into the Delaney firm. He'd progressed from cleaning out snooker hall bogs and was put on the milk run, collecting monies all around the Delaney manor.

'And be straight about it, boyo,' Tory warned him. 'Or you'll get trouble.'

Bruno wasn't stupid enough to try and fiddle the Delaneys. He did his job and – even better – he grew steadily aware that there was a special place in Tory Delaney's cold gangster heart for a good-looking boy like himself.

Bruno started to do nicely for himself. He didn't miss Brighton; he loved the Smoke. He didn't miss poor old Nora either. He felt free, he was getting paid OK and soon he was trusted with even more of the firm's work. He went out collecting debts, banging on doors, scaring punters who were late paying up with his stylish trio of stiletto blades.

'What you got against Max Carter then?' Tory asked him.

Bruno didn't say that they were related and he'd been dumped by the family. 'He did my old lady. I'd like to settle the score, that's all.'

Tory liked Bruno very much. He took him down Savile Row and got him measured up for a couple of suits. Took him into Holland and Sherry and bought him a vicuña coat.

'Cashmere is ten times warmer than wool and vicuña is ten times warmer than cashmere,' Tory told him. 'It's extremely expensive. Vicuñas live in the Andes – they're like alpacas but they're wild and can only be caught to be shorn every three years. The Incas declared it against the law for anyone except royalty to wear vicuña. It's so fine, it's like touching a cloud.'

Bruno ran his hand over the coat, turning back and forth in front of the full-length mirror in the shop. It was exquisite. And Tory was right – it was *amazingly* soft.

'I love it,' he said.

'It's yours,' said Tory.

Tory also bought Bruno four Gieves and Hawkes shirts and a pair of gold cufflinks with lucky horseshoes engraved on them. Tory frowned over Bruno's well-worn cheap plastic shoes and took him into Jones the Bootmaker to kit him out properly. He got Bruno's thick unruly hair properly cut and tamed at Trumper's and agreed to Bruno's request that it be dyed blond.

Bruno looked *great* as a blond and he kind of liked the fact that he looked different, not like the lonely dark-haired kid he'd once been. With his sharp suits and his sunglasses – he wore them indoors and out; he knew he looked ultra-cool in them – he was edgy, trendy, eye-catching. He started to feel good about himself, and he had never felt like that before. Tory dabbed pan-stick on the birthmark on Bruno's cheek, showing him how easily it could be hidden.

'But it's OK uncovered,' Tory told him, scrubbing the make-up off afterwards. He held tight to Bruno's shoulders and their eyes met in the mirror. 'It gives you a tough look. It's distinctive.'

Bruno looked in the mirror and knew that Tory was telling the truth. He did look eye-catching now. So much better, and he was grateful.

'You're bloody beautiful,' said Tory roughly. 'And you know it.'

Then he kissed Bruno's neck – just once, very hard, and Bruno shivered with a mixture of lust and alarm.

Tory took him to an apartment he kept at Dolphin Court in Pimlico to attend a party. Bruno couldn't believe what he was seeing. There were peers of the realm, Lord Boothby and others, gang leaders too, the Kray twins among them. Ronnie put his hand on Bruno's thigh and Tory didn't like that. These were people Bruno had only ever seen in the newspaper or heard about on the radio, all here drinking gin and snorting cocaine. High church people were romping with fabulous boys and stunning girls in the bedrooms. And then Bruno looked at Tory, and saw himself for what he truly was, at last. By coming here, by accepting Tory's gifts, he had given permission for Tory to make him one of *them* – the glamorous young creatures these grown men liked to have around, the ones they liked to screw.

He didn't know if he was up for that. Deprived of affection from an early age, he knew he had no real moral compass and he had no particular physical liking for women. Nora'd had absolutely no idea what to do with a child; she'd adopted him like a stray animal and then found him troublesome, moody, not what she had expected at all. So he'd grown up detached, solitary, remote. Still – women liked him, stared at him, flirted with him, and he'd even had a girlfriend or two, nothing serious.

Up to now, he'd brushed aside Tory's overtures in that direction – the squeeze of the shoulder, the touch of a wayward hand on his backside – fending him off for a long while, which only seemed to make Tory keener. They swam together in the basement pool at Dolphin Court, and Bruno was well in now, *far* in with Tory Delaney. He could have anything he liked, anything at all. Life was just *grand*.

'Why not come to bed with me,' said Tory while they paused at one end of the pool. 'Come on. You'll like it. I won't hurt you.'

Finally, thinking that this would be the way to comfort, riches, to living in style and safety – just as any ambitious girl would think – Bruno agreed.

It was a revelation. The pot of Vaseline on the side table alongside the line of coke and the bottle of Bushmills and the two lead crystal glasses. The caressing, the touching, the harsh thickness of Tory's mane of red hair under Bruno's fingers, the final hard push of Tory's prodigious cock inside him, the unexpected, *shocking* spasm of pleasure and pain and the shuddering, screaming jolt of absolute desire, finally and so unexpectedly fulfilled.

They lay together afterwards, arms wrapped around each other, the gangster and his boy. Bruno had never felt so close to another human being. He was in thrall to Tory Delaney. He didn't like to think about love, but maybe this was what it felt like.

Maybe.

He really didn't know.

He understood hate all right and when he thought of hate he thought of Queenie Carter and her little darling Max.

But love? He didn't know a damned thing about that. How would he?

# 35

Everything in Bruno's life was going well. He was a strong lad, a maestro with the knives, and the Delaney boys were only too happy to make full use of him.

Tory taught him all about avoiding attracting the interest of the authorities. Easy for Bruno really; he didn't even have a birth certificate, he'd never been registered – to all intents and purposes, he simply didn't exist.

'Keep your money close. No accounts. In a safe, yeah? Or keep it in a deposit box out of sight,' Tory told him. 'You'll learn.'

Bruno thought of that account Nora had opened with him in his youth, but dismissed it with a shrug – there was fuck-all in there, anyway. She'd cobbled together some fake ID for him, which the bank had easily accepted.

Tory Delaney soon trusted him enough to send him off on bigger jobs. Bruno went to Newmarket racecourse with another couple of the lads, one of whom was a skilled telephone engineer. There was a big race going on, and it was going to be fixed. It had all been arranged and would net the Delaneys nearly half a million in bets. One of the iffy Newmarket bookmakers was in on the deal, getting a cut; a mediocre French horse was quietly replaced by a better one. Some of the off-course bookmakers suspected betting patterns and tried to raise the alarm, but that was where the telecoms boy came in – he'd already cut the lines.

After he'd proved himself with that success, Bruno took part in shop and bank raids and the Irish boys clued him up on the way to conduct himself throughout. Like the rest of them, he learned to wear heavy coats, hats and industrial-grade face masks for the smother-up. Like the others, he was armed with pickaxe handles with taped ends to improve the grip.

After nearly shitting himself with fear during the first heavy job, he soon got in the swing of things and piled in with the rest of the mob. Then when the Guildford job came up and he was offered a place on it, he jumped at the chance. Tory had it all planned out. The stuff the gang would nick from some stupid posho's house would be fenced to reliable contacts and each of the lads taking part would earn a ten per cent share of the take. It was a good deal and Bruno was determined that he was not going to let Tory down.

Pat Delaney drove them there in the big van and they parked a long way up the road, pulling into a wood and edging in close to the trees so that no passing motorist or curious plod would see the van there and raise the alarm.

Five of them trudged along the lane in the cold frosty night air and up to the house.

'Pile of loot this lot cost,' said Tory, taking in the moonlit building, vast and beautiful.

'All the sweeter then,' said Pat with a wolfish grin. 'Cost the bastard dear, why not?'

Bruno was focused on the job, feeling both apprehensive and excited as they trailed up the long sweeping drive. The country night was as still as could be, only an owl hooting way off in the distance to disturb the peace of it. How, Bruno wondered, did people get to afford gaffs like this?

They crept around to the back of the place. There was a smaller building here, an annexe. Tory'd had the place scouted out in advance and it had been decided that they would do the annexe first, then the main house. When they'd got all the goods together, Pat would go back for the van and they would load up and be off.

Pat got his picks out and applied them to the lock on the annexe's main door. While he worked, the rest of them stood around, their breath pluming like smoke in the frosty air, thumping their middles with their arms to keep warm. Picking a lock took skill and it took patience – you couldn't hurry it. So no one asked Pat how it was going. They waited. And soon Pat straightened and grinned around at them, putting his picks back in his overcoat pocket.

'And we're in,' he said, flicking on his torch.

He shoved the door open with his shoulder and aimed the pencil-thin beam of the partially taped torch inside. It was like Aladdin's cave; straight away they could see gilded furniture, vast mirrors, costly ornaments. Grinning, they followed Pat's lead.

# 36

Queenie Carter woke with a start, wondering what had jolted her from sleep. As usual, sudden wakefulness brought all manner of woes down upon her beleaguered brain. Nora was dead. Max had sorted out the funeral, seen her decently buried. He'd made no mention of Bruno being at the Brighton house, so Queenie knew she'd dodged a bullet there. She wondered where Bruno had gone, felt guilt over the boy's troubles, but what could she do? She just hoped that she never, ever saw him again. Clive – oh God, Clive! – was gone forever, but he was still alive in her memory, so sweet, seductive, handsome. And her health was declining; that scared her so much. Her boys! How would they manage when she was gone?

Her chest was pounding and she was going to have to take some of those pills the doctor had prescribed. This old place creaked like a ship in a gale at night, particularly if it had been a warm day; she ought to know that. The joists in the roof, cracking as they cooled, must have woken her.

Max had been so pleased to give her this bolthole, this sanctuary from town worries – so pleased that she still didn't know how to tell him she hated it. She hated the country silence; she detested Miss Arnott the housekeeper who looked down her nose at cockney Queenie with her rough London accent. Queenie was a city woman and she hated it here. But how to tell Max that? He was her precious boy and she loved him like mad, too much to hurt him by telling him she didn't want to be in this place.

When he'd said Tone would drive her down, she'd thought Tone might stay. Or that Max might come too. But no. She was on her own here with that poisonous cow Arnott who had the cottage further out in the grounds. So there was really no one to talk to, nothing to even bloody do because Arnott cooked all the meals and dished them up in the annexe dining room. Arnott was always starchily polite, while Queenie wished she'd take that stick out of her arse and try to be a bit more friendly.

*Noises.*

She could hear noises downstairs. She wasn't imagining it. This wasn't the rafters, crackling. This was someone *moving about*. Her racketing heartbeat accelerated still more as she realised that the noises she was hearing couldn't possibly be the housekeeper, not at this hour – and the sounds were too loud, anyway. It wasn't just one set of footsteps she could hear, it was many. And they were male, she thought, not light enough to be female.

Moaning in dawning terror, she reached out a shaking hand and flicked on the bedside light. The clock said two-thirty in the morning. She didn't have a telephone up here in her bedroom. There was one downstairs in the hall. She listened, alert as a hunted deer. Heard a crash.

'*Careful, you bastard!*' snapped a man's voice.

*What to do, what to do?*

Queenie sat up and swung her legs to the floor, staggered to her feet. She thought of opening the window, shouting for help. Would Arnott hear her though? She doubted it. And anyway what could *she* do? There was a marauding army downstairs; one scrawny feeble woman wasn't going to have any effect on them.

She tottered across the room and reached the door that led out onto the landing. She took down her thick velvet dressing gown from the hook there and hurriedly slipped it on. As she did so, a huge pain tore through her chest and she gasped and took a few faltering steps back. She *had* to take her pills. Had to sit down.

But now there were heavy huge footsteps, coming up the stairs.

Queenie sank back down onto the bed, sick with fear.

*The handle was turning.*

Her eyes fastened to it in horror.

Slowly, slowly, the door opened and the light from the bedroom illuminated a man padded out in overcoat, mask and hat. He was holding a pickaxe.

A wailing scream escaped Queenie as she saw him.

'Help, you've got to help me,' she groaned, her hands clutched to her chest.

The man just stood there, looking in at her. The noises from downstairs were louder now, but this one was apart from all that. He stood there, frozen. And then slowly, oh so slowly, he lifted a hand and pulled the mask down from his face. She saw the mark. She saw *him*.

It was Bruno, her unwanted son. He was standing there like a waking nightmare, like she was being haunted for all her past sins. And maybe she was. Maybe she *deserved* to be.

The sight of his face was enough. The pain was too big for her to bear. She keeled off the bed and crashed to the floor.

# 37

The first Max knew about the break-in at the Surrey place was a telephone call to his flat over the Palermo at gone four in the morning. He woke up and was on full alert instantly as he snatched up the receiver.

'Hello?'

'Mr Carter?' It was Miss Arnott's voice, but somehow not. The pitch was very high, verging on hysteria.

'What's wrong?' he asked, sitting up.

'I'm so sorry. It was . . . men. Horrible big thuggish *men*. They broke in. They broke into the annexe.'

Max felt everything freeze inside him. 'Are they still there? Have you called the police?'

'They're gone now. I didn't . . . it woke me up when the van came up to the door of the annexe. I couldn't go over there, I didn't dare. They were loading things into the van. They didn't go into the main house although I thought they would. I was *sure* they would. I thought they'd started on the annexe but that they would finish up in the main house. But they didn't. They just left and by that time I'd called the police and then your mother . . .' Her voice tailed away.

'Is she all right?' asked Max. For God's sake! Queenie had been there all alone. He felt his innards twist into a knot of horror.

'I'm so sorry, Mr Carter,' said Miss Arnott.

# 38

Queenie Carter's funeral took place on a dreary rain-lashed April day. Everyone in the East End turned out for the occasion, lining the streets as if an empress was passing by. Men doffed their caps, women bowed their heads as the funeral cortege – a huge fleet of black Daimlers – wound its way through the streets to the church. A man in sombre black stepped ahead of the hearse and the pace was stately. Everyone gawped at the pink-flower-covered coffin within. Bouquets were stacked all around it, and along both sides MUM was spelled out in pink and white carnations.

The church was packed for the ceremony, Queenie's three sons dressed in black up at the front. The vicar spoke eloquently of what a valued member of their community Queenie had been, what a good woman, such a firm friend to everyone who lived and worked around her. Then – at last – it was over and Queenie Carter was laid to rest in the churchyard.

Back at the house in Bow, all the women who lived down Queenie's street put on a tremendous spread and The Grapes' landlord sent over casks of ale and twenty bottles of his best whisky. Max stayed for an hour or so, then he left Eddie and Jonjo to it and went and sat by the grave. The men had already filled it in and laid the flowers all over the clay-coloured earth. Tonight those flowers would be frosted, browning, dead.

Max sat there for an hour, in the rain. Then Tone turned up, and Steve.

'Need some company, boss?' asked Tone.

'No,' said Max.

They piled onto the bench beside him, unworried by his cold rejection.

'Wondered where you'd got to,' said Steve, and slapped him on the shoulder. 'I was the same when my old lady went. Couldn't take it in. Seemed *wrong*, somehow. We guessed you'd be here. Do you think heaven exists? Because if so, I reckon Queenie Carter's already up there.'

'Just fuck off, would you?' said Max.

'Can't leave you here, boss,' said Tone, shaking his head. 'Wouldn't be right.'

So they all got into the car and Tone dropped Max off at his flat over the club. Max proceeded to get himself as drunk as he possibly could, to blot it all out. He lay on the bed and thought, *They did this.* The post-mortem report had said her heart had given out. It was *due* to give out, but why had it given out right then? Because she'd been scared to bloody death. Scared witless by a gang of men rampaging around in the house and there had been no one there to help her, no one to turn to.

Of course it was the fucking Delaneys. Miss Arnott had shown him the small green paper shamrock left on the door-mat in the annexe. Their calling card. He thought that the reason they hadn't moved on to the main house was because they'd disturbed Mum and she'd dropped dead with the fright of it. So, they'd wrapped up the job early and scarpered. But they hadn't been able to resist one last taunt aimed straight at Max and at no one else. The shamrock.

'You tell no one else about this,' he'd told Miss Arnott, pocketing the thing.

Miss Arnott took one look at his face and nodded. 'Of course. I never would.'

'Make sure you don't.'

The Delaneys had scared his mother so much she'd died.

Max fulminated about it, spent too much time alone, repulsed all efforts to prise him out of his foul, brooding mood. Once Max got into one of his dark moods, there was no shifting him and everyone around him knew it.

There would be trouble – they all said it.

And soon, of course, there was.

# 39

Finally it was the night before Ruthie and Max's wedding. Annie Bailey felt physically sick. She'd coped with everything – with her mum hating her, with her dad leaving, with being shit-poor all the time. But here at last was the straw that was going to break the camel's back. Ruthie and Max were going to be married tomorrow.

There had been all sorts of trouble, rumours flying about, in the weeks leading up to the wedding. Something about Queenie Carter's death earlier in the year, happening during a botched robbery. There had been the massive funeral, people lining the streets. She and Ruthie had stood out there, and Connie – although of course Mum had been reeling drunk. But Annie didn't really pay much attention to any of it.

She wondered about *him*, of course. Wondered how badly he'd taken his mother's death. He'd been raised as a little prince, the favourite of Queenie Carter's three sons, the eldest. The closest to Queenie, without a doubt.

The night before Ruthie and Max's wedding, Annie was wandering the streets with her tranny tucked in the pocket of her cream PVC raincoat, listening to Ruby and the Romantics singing 'Our Day Will Come'. But that was bullshit. Her day was *never* coming. Her chance at happiness was going to vanish, tomorrow. Ruthie would be Mrs Max Carter, and her? She would be nothing. An afterthought. Just like always.

All her young life, she had coveted Max Carter. Max was rich, immensely charismatic, handsome as a pirate with his thick waving black hair, hard dark blue eyes and aggressive hook of a nose. She had only to think of him to melt. He was so dangerous, so alluring, with his many legitimate businesses – among them the profitable, always busy trio of clubs – the Palermo Lounge, the Shalimar and the Blue Parrot – but he also ran a big well-organised gang, just like the Richardsons, the Krays and his arch-enemies the Delaneys, taking protection money from the shops, arcades, massage parlours and snooker halls all around Bow and into Limehouse.

*He was going to be her brother-in-law.*

She couldn't stand the thought of that.

Ruthie wasn't working tonight – she was getting ready for her big day tomorrow, after which her life would change completely. She'd have a posh place in town, a big house in the country, she'd have *Max Carter*. And Connie, their mum? For her, this was like winning the Pools. No more hiding from the rent man. Ruthie hadn't even married him yet, but already Connie was living it large with new furniture, a fridge for God's sake, and even a TV.

For Annie, standing there in the drizzling rain, her long boots leaking water, her feet frozen, tomorrow was going to be the end of it all. On her tranny Roy Orbison was now carolling 'In Dreams I Walk With You' and his words were all about her, about her rotten life, which was just about to go from bad to worse.

Tomorrow, Ruthie would walk down the aisle on Uncle Tom's arm – and Max Carter would be waiting for her at the altar. Annie looked at the big red billboard up outside the Palermo Lounge; the star turn tonight was Heinz and there was a picture of him there, white-blond hair and a bland boy-ish face.

People, dressed up to the nines, were going into the club. She stood there in the shadows, watching them. Then she realised she wasn't the only one loitering. She saw Billy Black across the road. Billy was one of Max's boys and she'd known him for years.

'Hi, Billy,' she said.

The long-faced man in the deerstalker hat and long cream mac turned and looked at her with solemn brown eyes. Billy often did the milk run – collecting money from the businesses who paid up to Max's firm. He was a bit simple, but he was harmless. He clutched a briefcase to his chest; he always carried it around with him. He probably slept with the damned thing.

Annie indicated the club door, brightly lit with red neon, the bulky doormen wearing evening dress. 'Not going in?' she asked.

'No,' said Billy. He wasn't a great one for small talk. Or any talk, come to that.

Annie stared at the club doorway. Music was drifting out from there into the rain-soaked night. Inside, all would be luxury and warmth. *Max* would be in there. She had seen him go in, earlier. It was freezing out here, and the rain was starting to come down harder.

Suddenly she made her decision.

'I want you to take me into the club,' she told Billy.

Billy looked startled. He gave it some thought, then he said: 'All right.'

'Come on then,' said Annie, her heart thwacking away against her ribs at the shock of her own audacity.

Annie tucked her hand into the crook of his arm and they walked over to the club.

'Billy,' said the bruiser on the door.

'Phil,' said Billy.

Phil, twenty meaty ugly stones of solid muscle, stood politely aside. Billy and Annie went in. Billy kept his coat on – and his hat – but Annie handed her raincoat over to the girl at the counter. Then they moved into the main body of the club.

The supporting act was on, a red-haired woman in a green velvet dress giving a husky rendition of 'Mad About the Boy' to a piano accompaniment.

Annie's stomach clenched as she saw Max there, sitting at one of the candle-lit tables near the stage, his brother Jonjo with him. She didn't like Jonjo, who was well known for kicking off at nothing and treating a procession of blonde women like dishrags. Max looked over at her and she felt a jolt, hard as a punch, as their eyes met. He said something to Jonjo, who looked over too, and grinned. Max stood up and came over to where she stood, Billy at her side.

'Billy,' said Max. 'Go and get yourself a drink. On me.'

Billy wandered off, leaving Annie standing there alone with Max. Her mouth was dust-dry and her heart was beating hard. She felt like maybe she needed a drink too. Only she rarely touched alcohol, didn't like the taste. Being raised by Connie was enough to put you off drink for life.

'You want a drink?' asked Max.

*No. I want you.*

Annie shook her head. Standing this close to him was torture. She could smell that same lemony cologne on him, fresh and faintly acidic with that underlying note of sandalwood.

'You want to come over to the table and join us?' he said, having to lean in close to make himself heard, his breath tickling her ear.

She shook her head again. She didn't know *what* she wanted. Maybe to stop time. Roll it back, to that moment just before Ruthie had broken her heart by telling her she was going to marry him.

He was staring into her eyes and she saw something in his that touched her. Pain. She thought of all that he was, all that she'd heard about him. About his mother's death. He was hurting – she could see that. Determined not to show it, but hurting nevertheless. And if she was reckless, she thought that tonight he was reckless too. Throwing his fate to the winds and not caring about the shitstorm that would surely follow.

She ought to be afraid of him.

But she wasn't.

The air between them was crackling with a strange electric *something* that took all her breath away.

'Big day, tomorrow,' he said.

Annie nodded. She was surprised to find herself close to tears. She never cried. *Dig deep and stand alone* – that was her motto. She was tough. But not tough enough to take this. She wanted to say, don't do it, please don't. But now she'd come in here, and she'd actually got this far, she found she couldn't say a word.

Time had stopped. They stood there, close together, eyes locked.

'I'm going upstairs,' he said, leaning in again, speaking against her cheek, sending shivers down her spine. He moved back, held her eyes for another long moment, then leaned in once more. She felt her skin prickle, her nipples harden, every nerve ending in her body responding to his nearness. 'Come up in a bit. If you want to.'

And having said that, he moved past her, out into the lobby. She turned and watched him lift the little rope barrier with PRIVATE, STAFF ONLY on it, replace it, then go up the stairs.

The woman on the stage stopped singing and the audience applauded her warmly. Annie could feel the blood whooshing in her ears; she felt so light-headed that she wondered if she might faint.

She hesitated.

*Oh God. Ruthie . . . ?*

But she loved Max Carter. She'd always loved him. She always would.

Annie went over and lifted the rope barrier. Stepped through. Replaced it.

She went up the stairs.

# 40

This, Max Carter told himself, was not love. It was lust. He had lusted after his fiancée's sister and now here they were, naked in bed together. He'd made love to her very thoroughly and she was exquisite, responsive – yes, mistress material. He enjoyed her as he didn't think he'd enjoyed any other woman, ever. And now she was asking him if he'd minded that she'd been a virgin.

Now he had to say it, quickly, knock this whole damned insane thing on the head before the trouble *really* started.

'No. It doesn't matter a bit. Because this is a one-off.'

He saw the satisfied smile freeze on her face. 'What?'

'This shouldn't have happened, and we both know it. But now it's done, and finished.'

There was nothing else he could do. Tomorrow he was walking up the aisle with her sister Ruthie, who was a lovely girl, plain and homely and destined to be a perfect wife, for God's sake! The whole thing was happening now, the wedding was set, everything was ready for it. He couldn't let this go on. It would be cruel, and it would be stupid, to do that.

Annie shrank back from him.

Well, that was good. Let her.

But then she frowned and said: 'But, Max . . .'

He grabbed her chin and stared into her eyes.

'No buts,' he said. 'This is it. Finished and forgotten.' He drew back, patted her cheek. 'Good girl.'

★

*Good girl?*

Annie couldn't believe he'd said that. She felt rage rip through her, replacing all those tender, deeply erotic feelings she had just experienced for the very first time. After heat came cold. Now she felt frozen and in utter despair. What they'd shared here tonight had been bliss, total rapture. For her, anyway. She'd melted in his arms, marvelling at the hard texture of his golden skin, sinking her fingers into those silky black curls, feeling the full extent of wonder at the strength and the beauty of him, the musky scent of him, the sensation of him – at last – moving inside her, becoming part of her.

But now? He was dismissing her. Telling her in no uncertain terms that what she had believed to be the start of their love affair was in fact the ending.

Yes, there was guilt. Of *course* there was guilt, because she loved Ruthie so much. Ruthie was sweet; Ruthie would *never* do anything like this to Annie. But – just as she had all through their young lives – Ruthie had won again.

Ruthie *always* won.

Ruthie got first dibs on clothes, on affection from Mum, and now she got Max.

It was all so bloody unfair.

And this time? Annie wasn't having it.

# PART TWO

# 41

Bruno was at the Pimlico apartment when he heard the news. He'd stayed overnight and Tory had gone out yesterday evening; he'd said he was meeting up with a business associate at the Tudor Club in Stoke Newington.

'Want me to come along?' Bruno had asked him.

'Nah, precious.' Tory had fastened his tie, shrugged on his raincoat, and dropped a kiss onto Bruno's cheek. 'You'd be bored to tears. I'll be back by about one, OK?'

But Tory hadn't come back. Bruno drank a bit too much and fell asleep on the sofa and then suddenly it was seven o'clock in the morning. He jolted awake, looked around him. Still no Tory. And someone was ringing the buzzer, leaning on it, wanting to be let in. Bruno crawled, yawning and holding his aching head, from the sofa. He was wearing the expensive black-trimmed red silk dressing gown that Tory had bought him last Christmas. He slipped his feet into the matching mules with the gothic-style B embroidered on the front of them – another gift from Tory – then went and pressed the intercom.

'Yeah?'

'Let me up, boyo,' said Pat Delaney's voice.

Frowning, Bruno pressed the door release. A minute later, Pat came blundering in.

'You heard?' he said, looking at his brother's 'paramour' with the distaste he reserved for all 'weirdos'. If you weren't a hard-nosed straight heterosexual bruiser like him, Pat Delaney had no time for you. Everyone knew that.

'What?' asked Bruno.

'About Tory,' said Pat.

'What about him? Where is he?'

'Where'd he tell you he was going?'

'What is this? He said he was going out to the Tudor.'

Pat was shaking his head like a wounded bear. He swiped a hand over his brow and stared at Bruno.

'You'll have to clear out,' he said.

'*What?*' Bruno stared right back at Pat. He knew Pat had never liked him, but what fresh hell was this? 'Where is Tory?' he asked more urgently. 'Tell me.'

'Tory's in the city morgue,' said Pat harshly.

Bruno's mouth dropped open. He couldn't utter a word.

Pat was nodding. 'Someone jumped him in the car park outside the club.'

'Jumped him? What . . . ?'

'Shot him. Three times in the chest, once right through the head. He's dead. I've just been and identified the body.'

Bruno stood there, speechless.

'And so,' Pat went on remorselessly, 'the family want you to clear out of here. *I* want you out. I'm in charge now, you got that? I don't want Ma or Pa getting wind of any of this ruddy to-do. He was their eldest boy. They'll want to bury him decent. They wouldn't want any of *this* known about.'

Bruno felt the room sway around him. Tory, dead?

'Who . . . who do they think did it then?' he managed to croak out.

'Nobody bloody knows, but I know who *I* think did it. Max fucking Carter, that's who. That Guildford job you did with us where the old girl died? That was his mother.'

So the thing had come back to haunt him at last. He'd been there, he'd confronted Queenie – and she'd died. Now, Max had achieved revenge; Tory, head of the Delaney mob, was dead. And Bruno's protector was gone.

'But why . . . ?' Bruno started.

Pat moved towards him and gave him a vicious shove. Bruno fell back, startled, down onto the sofa.

'Stop with the questions, you fecking shirt lifter,' he snarled. 'Show a bit of bloody decency. Get packed up and get out. We don't want you here. I'll give you an hour, all right? Then you be out or I'll be back to chuck you through that fucking window. You got that?'

Bruno nodded.

He got it.

Once again, he was alone, and unwanted.

And once again it was all bloody Max's fault.

The *bastard*.

# 42

After the explosion – inevitably – came the fallout. Annie Bailey had succeeded in her aim to get Max into bed with her. She had been stupidly happy about that, thinking in her girlish way that Max would realise marrying Ruthie was a mistake, that he wanted her – Annie – and that he would call the whole thing off and they would run off together, down to St Tropez or somewhere equally exotic, and it would all work out OK.

But somehow everything after that had not gone to plan. Annie'd got home from work a few days after Max and Ruthie's wedding to find her suitcase packed up and waiting for her at the bottom of the stairs. Then she found out that Ruthie had been on the phone to Connie, saying she knew Annie had slept with Max. Annie had let Ruthie know on the day of the wedding that the whole marriage was a bloody farce – and now Ruthie couldn't see how she was going to go on with it.

Annie was still desperately – maybe foolishly – hurt that Max had gone ahead with the wedding, furious that he hadn't fallen in with her dream of elopement, of a happy future for the two of them. She threw it all in Connie's face, admitted everything, apologised – as was her way – for absolutely nothing.

Connie chucked Annie out of the house. And, not knowing what else to do, Annie went across town to Aunt Celia's

Limehouse abode, which she had always believed to be a safe place to stay, being as Celia was Dad's sister, not Mum's. But what did she know?

Her first discovery about Aunt Celia's home was that it was inside Delaney territory, right on the Carter borderline, and that Celia paid protection to the Delaney clan. Her second discovery was that her chic, suited, dark-haired and button-bright-eyed aunt with her red-painted nails and her ivory cigarette holder was in business. Annie thought she knew *what* business, too. Mum had spoken of it, said Celia ran a 'massage parlour', which everyone knew was a fancy way of saying a whorehouse. After meeting the girls who worked there, Dolly, Aretha, Ellie – and Darren, who attended to the gentlemen who preferred boys – Annie knew that it was all true.

It didn't bother her. Anywhere right now was better than home.

And there was a third discovery – a bad one. The Delaney gang, the one Celia paid protection to, were in deep mourning, because someone – maybe, no *probably* Max Carter – had shot Tory Delaney dead.

# 43

Bruno attended Tory's funeral. Well, he didn't *attend*, exactly. He suspected that if he made himself too visible, Pat would be on him like a madman. Instead he loitered in the background, standing just inside the church doors during the long-drawn-out Catholic service, then slipping out early and standing by the lychgate in the rain to watch the Delaney family and the priest gather around the open grave in the distance. The parents looked old now. Davey Delaney was no longer the big strapping Irishman he had been, and his wife Molly was thin, white-haired, decimated by grief.

Bruno saw Pat take hold of his father's arm more than once, to steady him. The other one was there too – Kieron, who was an artist, everyone said. Bruno had never met him face to face, and he thought grimly that now he never would. The Delaneys didn't want him anywhere near them.

The twins were there, Redmond and Orla, standing tall and slender and elegant in black. And there was *another* set of twins, two big hard-eyed red-haired male cousins he hadn't seen before. They'd probably come over from the auld country to see Tory properly buried.

Pat, Redmond and the strapping pair of male twins lowered the coffin into the ground while the priest intoned the final words that would see Tory – Bruno's lover – laid to rest in the soil of England.

Bruno supposed he ought to feel sorry over Tory's death. Regretful. But he knew himself now; inside and out. He was a loveless child who had become a stone-cold adult. Not his fault. He struggled with emotion, on any level. And about the means of Tory's death? He knew everyone believed Max Carter was the one responsible. He believed it too.

When the mourners started to disperse, Bruno went to make himself scarce. He didn't want Pat catching sight of him and giving him a hiding. But to his surprise he was called back by Redmond.

'Bruno?' said Redmond, coming down onto the pathway, the two heavy-duty male twins trailing him, one on either side.

Bruno turned amid the surging crowd of departing mourners and looked Redmond in the eye. He'd heard the rumours that were flying around, and they had contained a big surprise. Pat, the eldest remaining Delaney child, was apparently not in charge of operations: *this* one was, along with his twin Orla. Bruno wondered how Pat was taking this state of affairs. Maybe it had been old Davey's wish that Redmond take the helm. Who knew? Bruno knew little about Redmond but looking into his grape-green eyes and seeing his cool hard expression, you had to think that here was a chilly customer, an analytical thinker, one who would slap even a hard nut like Pat into place if he should need to do it.

'Yes?' Bruno saw Pat looming near and kept his eyes downcast. But to his surprise Pat gave him a wide berth. Pat moved past, out into the road, away.

'A sad day,' said Redmond.

'Yes,' said Bruno, thinking that Redmond didn't look sad, not at all.

'These are my cousins – Cormac and Seamus.'

Bruno nodded to the two hulking men. They looked dangerous, he thought. Lean and hard-eyed, hawkish and red-haired. You wouldn't mess with them. These were re-inforcements, plain and simple. Tory had been chopped down in his prime, and Redmond wasn't looking to follow in his footsteps anytime soon. And if Pat *did* cut up rough about not being the boss now, if Cormac and Seamus were firmly on Redmond's side – as it seemed they were – they would come in very handy.

'They've come over for the occasion,' said Redmond. 'You were close to Tory, I believe?'

Bruno shrugged. There was no way he was going to unveil the true nature of his relationship with Tory Delaney. He'd been threatened by Pat already, and he had no idea what Redmond's take on the situation might be, or even if he was aware of it. He felt a shudder of apprehension. Also – worse – Bruno thought of his own ties to Max Carter. He was *related* to Max and everyone believed absolutely, without question, that Max had killed Tory. Bruno could find himself in serious trouble if ever his connection to Max should come to light.

'Tory valued you,' said Redmond.

'I suppose so.'

Valued? As a lover, maybe. Tory hadn't used Bruno's skills too much in other directions. Occasionally, yes. Most often, no. Bruno knew he'd walked down wicked ways with Tory, but Tory had adored him; Bruno had never had that before, and he missed it.

All his life Bruno felt he'd been looking, *searching* for something, only he didn't know what that something might be. Maybe it had been Tory. Or maybe it would be when he finally came up against Max Carter and had a stiletto to his

throat. After all, he'd come to London for that express purpose, to find Max, to take revenge for all the shitty things that
had ever happened to him. First there had been Nora, now
there was Tory to add to the list of grievances. But somehow
Bruno had become distracted; he'd never fulfilled his original
goal.

Not *yet*, anyway.

'Tory liked you as a useful man to have around. Sharp,'
Redmond elaborated.

'Good. That's good to hear.'

'If I should call on you, would you be equally useful to
me?'

Bruno looked at that long pale face. Tried to see further,
into the workings of Redmond's mind. Couldn't. But Redmond seemed to be offering him a way to stay within the
organisation, and he needed a job now he wasn't going to be
Tory Delaney's pet any longer.

'Of course,' he said.

'Good. I'm pleased,' said Redmond, not looking pleased
at all.

Bruno nodded and walked away, feeling like he'd opened
the door of a freezer and the temperature all around him had
just plummeted to sub-zero. Bruno had never been up close
to Redmond before now; had never felt the full blast of that
chilly personality. But so what? With Tory gone, he would
have been out on the streets, fending for himself. Now, he
was part of the firm again. All he had to do was keep Redmond happy and keep out of Pat's way. Neither of which
should be too difficult.

# 44

Over the time that followed, Bruno learned things about Redmond. Things that made him pity him almost. And fear him too. Because he recognised a kindred spirit in him. Redmond was dead inside, just like he was. *Worse* than he was. Bruno came to know that Tory was nowhere near as dangerous as Redmond. Redmond could flay the skin from a shrieking body and laugh while he did it. Tory had been positively gentle by comparison. Redmond could literally *break* people, shatter them into a million pieces.

There was a girl Bruno knew of – Mira Cooper was her name – and she'd worked as one of the upmarket call girls at the bordello that high-powered Annie Bailey had established for herself in Mayfair, after leaving her Aunt Celia's Limehouse place for richer pastures.

Annie Bailey had done very nicely for herself after a while, it seemed. Redmond had put up some of the funding to get her started in her new venture, and it had all been rolling along nicely. The girl was clever. She was in tight with Redmond while also, at much the same time, getting in deeper and deeper with Max Carter. Word on the street was, she'd become Max's mistress. Seeing her swanning around town, Bruno thought *lucky old Max.* You'd have to be doing very well for yourself to be able to afford a woman like that. But Bruno hoped she realised the tightrope she was walking.

Annie's Mayfair abode was a big, perfect penthouse apartment set in a gorgeous block on the corner of Oxford Street and Park Street. The Ritz was a step away in Piccadilly and Buck House was just up the road, and the Houses of Parliament too. There was a private balcony, porterage, lifts, beautiful marbled bathrooms, fabulous bedrooms – the whole of it done out in luxurious golds and pale blues.

The girls that Annie had working there were not run-of-the-mill brasses; they were exquisite, groomed, top of the range. And Mira had been top of the top with her thick long treacle-streaked blonde hair, huge lamp-like blue eyes, flawless skin. She could have been a model or anything she damned well pleased. To see her and Annie Bailey swaggering down Bond Street with their fur coats and their sunglasses and their thigh-high boots was truly something to behold.

Bruno spent one blissful night there with Mira. It cost him a small fortune, but what the hell, he was working and for once he could afford it.

'So,' she said, smiling into his eyes as she led him into one of the superb bedrooms. 'What do you like, Bruno? What can I do for you?'

She was dazzling. He was almost breathless with lust.

'Kiss me. Kiss me everywhere,' he said. He meant 'make me feel loved', but he couldn't say anything as lame as that.

Mira kissed him, caressed him, peeled his clothes away, sat him down naked on the bed. Then she stripped, slowly, pressed the whole length of her fantastic body against his, made love to him. They fell asleep twined together, and woke in the morning still wrapped in each other's arms.

Oh, she'd been so sweet, so sensual. He'd been so struck by her, so enraptured.

Then somehow Mira got hooked up with Redmond. She fell in love with him or some shit like that, Bruno supposed. She'd been out at Clevedon House with some lord or other and met up with Redmond and all had seemed lovely for about five minutes flat, then Mira started having trouble sleeping. There were rumours she'd lost a kid. Redmond got her drugs. *Powerful* drugs, and it seemed after that there was no way back for the poor bitch. Later, Bruno heard that she'd died in a clinic somewhere, a hopeless junkie.

So Bruno learned early on in his association with Redmond that you had to step very carefully around him. For a while Bruno had lived in dread that Redmond might share Tory's tastes and fancy a pretty boy like him, but that never happened and he was grateful. It was clear to him that Redmond might be cool and controlled and in charge in everyday life, but behind closed doors he felt that Redmond could turn out to be sadistic – and he didn't want any of *that*.

# 45

Bruno remained fascinated by the Carter boys and it gave him a sort of thrill to know that he held a secret power over them – that he *could* act, at any moment, and they didn't even know he was hanging over them, a constant threat. He often saw them around town and watched them. Well, it was more than that, sometimes. Sometimes he *followed* them. Spied on them. Thought how easy it would be to pick them off, one by one. Maybe Eddie the fruit first, then big gormless Jonjo – and then Max.

Ah yes.

Max. The cool one. The hard, muscular, arrogant one. The head of the clan. The one who hadn't given a stuff, who hadn't wanted to know when his own aunt came to his mum's house, cap in hand. The one who had coldly, with no thought to Bruno, no thought to family loyalty, ordered Nora's death. The one who had killed Tory, the only person who had ever treated Bruno well.

When he thought about that – and he thought about it a lot – Bruno knew that Max was the one who was fully responsible for Nora. There was no way Jonjo would ever have acted without Max's say-so. Poor old Nora, tossed off a cliff.

*Brutal.*

And Tory. His lover, shot through the chest, then in the head. That strong body, the body he'd come to know so well, reduced to nothing but mouldering flesh and bone.

Bruno toyed with ideas, ways to end Max, while he practised, over and over and over again, with his three stiletto blades. He dreamed with an almost erotic pleasure of the ways he would finally put a finish to Max Carter. Maybe – yes – with the knives, or maybe he'd get a gun – easy, when you were in tight with the Delaney gang – and shoot Max in a symbolic way, an echo of Tory's death, three shots to the chest, one to the head, his death matching Tory's, the one cancelling the other out. Or maybe he'd get Pat and some of the boyos round, catch Max unawares, toss *him* off a cliff – just like Nora.

★

In the February of nineteen-seventy, when *Hair* was playing at London's Shaftesbury Theatre, Mick Jagger had been fined two hundred pounds for possession of cannabis and the first jumbo jet had landed at Heathrow airport, Bruno followed Max and Annie Bailey – who was now Annie Carter, Max's wife – out to Majorca. Things had been happening with Max and this 'Annie' woman. Word on the street was that Max had finished his non-starter of a first marriage to Ruthie Bailey, divorced her and married this woman, her sister. And he'd heard that Ruthie had forgiven her sister for snatching her man away.

The Carters had a child with them, a little girl. *Their* child, Layla. Bruno saw the lovely place Max owned there on the island, set high above the crashing sea and felt fresh bitterness, fresh envy and hatred, grip him. Max had everything, didn't he. The perfect life, the perfect family.

But then had come, totally out of the blue, the blowing up of the Carters' perfect dream. Bruno was shocked to his soul by it. And as if he'd *wished* it into being, he'd seen Max – Max, the one Bruno would really like to be, if he was honest – thrown down onto the rocks below the finca by a marauding gang.

The irony of it wasn't lost on him. This was a mirror image of Aunt Nora's terrible death, and maybe Max Carter deserved to end the same way. Poetic justice.

Max *had* to be dead.

Bruno tried to forget it. Chalk it up to fate. After all, hadn't *he* played with the idea, almost luxuriated in the many possible ways Max's death could happen, for years?

He had.

But . . . Bruno found that he couldn't leave it there.

When the people who'd attacked Max in his Majorcan love nest had gone at last, taking the child with them – Max's child – Bruno sat for a long time in the concealment of the trees that surrounded the finca, wondering what to do.

He reasoned with himself over it. Max was clearly dead and gone. And he ought to be glad about that. It was the end of the story, the conclusion Max Carter richly deserved. He'd killed Nora and he'd killed Tory, and by doing so he'd twice taken away the only supports Bruno ever had. What Bruno knew he should do now was get a plane back to England and forget all about the Carter family.

He wanted – so much – to do that.

But they were *his* family. Like it or not, they were. And much as he'd hated Max, he had also admired him. He didn't want to, but he did. Several times Bruno passed a goatherd boy coming up the track that led to Max's finca. The boy nodded hello, raised a hand in greeting.

'You got money, mister?' he asked, bright-eyed, holding out a hand. 'You got pesetas, yes?'

Bruno noted the threadbare lime green T-shirt the boy wore, the thin shorts hitched up around his skinny waist with a length of rope, the dust-covered and worn-out sandals on his dirty feet.

Bruno almost said yes, so long as there was a favour done in return.

'What's your name?' he asked.

'Jaime.' The boy beamed.

'No pesetas,' said Bruno, turning his palms up, empty.

The boy's smile vanished and with a shrug he walked on. Bruno watched him take his flock down onto the rocky escarpment below. Would the boy find Max's dead body down there somewhere, impaled on rocks – or had Max ended up in the sea far below, to be taken by the tide, to be swept away to God knew where?

Bruno couldn't leave it.

He knew he *ought* to. He *wanted* to. Max deserved to die, especially after Tory. But – and this infuriated Bruno – he couldn't let the matter drop. He just *couldn't*.

The day after he'd seen the men hurl Max over the edge, when the women had gone from inside the finca and the place was empty, he met the goat boy on the path again.

'Pesetas?' asked Jaime hopefully.

Bruno gave in and gave him money. There would be more, he told him, if he found the man somewhere down there below the finca and got him help. Jaime had a smattering of English, enough to understand what Bruno was asking of him. And Jaime agreed that he would find the man, if he could, but he was probably dead. The cliff was steep, too steep to survive on, Jaime warned Bruno.

'What is his name?' Jaime asked.

'It doesn't matter,' said Bruno. 'Meet me back here tomorrow. That will give you time, yes?'

'Yes,' said Jaime greedily, pocketing his pesetas. 'But he will be dead.'

'That needn't concern you either. I want to know, either way. That's all. When I see you here, tomorrow at exactly this time, if you have found him – dead or alive – I will give you the second payment. All right?'

'All right.' Jaime shrugged. Then he looked at Bruno uncertainly, suspecting a trick, some kind of deception. 'You know him then, this man?'

'I'm his brother,' came out of Bruno's mouth.

He instantly wished he could snatch the words back. But it didn't matter, he reassured himself. The boy was a nobody, a peasant.

Then matters conspired against him and he couldn't be around to make the second payment and to find out whether Max had lived or died. Bruno had to get back to England in a hurry. Redmond had summoned him home: there was big trouble and the Delaneys were in the frame for something, Bruno didn't know what.

The minute he stepped off the plane at Heathrow, he was arrested.

He was just seventeen years old.

# 46

'Show me that trick again,' Redmond would say, long before Bruno was arrested, and Bruno would perform like a circus monkey, throwing his trio of blades, *thwack, thwack, thwack,* into whatever – and yes, *whoever* – Redmond wanted him to.

'And again,' Redmond would say, when he held one of his 'parties'. At these parties there would always be someone to be punished, to be made a fool of. Someone would have crossed Redmond, offended him in some way, and so punishment would be meted out as entertainment, and everyone would laugh and applaud while some poor helpless fucker was held down and put through agony. The first time Bruno was instructed by Redmond to try out his skills on a living target, he almost refused – until he looked in Redmond's eyes and realised that his refusal would land him in deep shit.

So – he did it.

The poor bloke had cheated someone down the snooker hall and for his pains he got three knives, thrown one after the other, into his hands. He'd never play snooker again.

After that first time, it was true what they said about these things – it got easier. Bruno performed his tricks for Redmond's cruel amusement and became a favourite of his. Bruno, in fact, became quite the stylish assassin with his dyed blond hair and his snappy dress sense and his fearsome stiletto blades.

He became harder, tougher. Deaf to pleas, deaf to screams. He was Redmond's toy; he was a weapon, to be used. Him and the Irish cousins Cormac and Seamus targeted – on Redmond's instructions – Roy Beamer, a financier who had tried to twist Redmond on a bullion deal. Big mistake. Roy ended up in the sea, wrapped in chicken wire and weighted down with iron and rocks.

Unfortunately a fishing boat then reclaimed Roy from the ocean's chill embrace, pulling him in with the nets, and investigation by the police led to Cormac's little yacht *Susie*, which he kept moored up on the Thames near one of Redmond's warehouses.

For once, Redmond wasn't laughing.

'You see how it is,' he told Bruno when the police investigations were getting uncomfortably hot for the Delaney mob and he'd called Bruno back from Majorca. Redmond visited Bruno in jail where he was under arrest, in custody, awaiting trial.

'I do, boss,' said Bruno.

'Poor Bruno.' Redmond gazed at him. 'Borderline illiterate, aren't you, poor thing? Not that clever. You're my sharp instrument, aren't you, my little knifeman?'

'Yes, boss.'

'Good. And you see also that this mustn't touch the firm? You do see that?'

'I do,' said Bruno, feeling uneasy.

'We'll look after you in the nick, don't worry. You'll be fine.'

Bruno stared, horrified. 'What . . . ?' He didn't want to do time.

'You do understand that, don't you?' said Redmond silkily. 'The firm is never mentioned. You take the blame, you alone. Or – inside or out – things could go wrong for you. Because we can always get to you. Never doubt that. So! You take the sentence and then we get you out pronto. All right?'

*All right?*

Bruno stared at his boss's cool, untroubled face. If he said no . . . then he was done for. He knew that. The Delaneys would get him and cut his throat. No honour among thieves, ever. He *knew* that.

But here was the stark reality of it.

He was going to do time. He was trapped. No way out.

'How long?' he asked, dry-mouthed.

'Oh – ten, maybe? Out in seven?'

*Seven years?*

'All right,' he said, because he could say nothing else.

'Good, good,' said Redmond, pleased.

But it was twenty years, not ten and certainly not seven.

Twenty long, long years.

# 47

You got used to life as a con. Mostly, Bruno kept his head down and tried not to get involved in the tricks and wheezes that the other prisoners pulled on the long-suffering guards. His only aim was to get his sentence shortened if he could, to avoid the punishment block, to get out early on good behaviour.

So he didn't soak the workshop thermometer in a bucket of cold water and then complain it was too cold to work. He wore the prison uniform and didn't set light to it as some of the other cons did. He didn't plot elaborate escapes although some did and mostly came unstuck. He kept his distance from trouble when it broke out, which it often did. Not only the prisoners but also the screws were living on a knife-edge half the time, and it was inevitable that there would be challenges issued to someone who had worked for one of the major London gangs.

The day came when Bruno was assigned work in the prison kitchens. He didn't mind the work, actually. It was almost hypnotic, sitting there peeling huge mounds of potatoes, then washing and preparing the greens, cutting the poor-quality meat into chunks.

It was OK until one of the big gay cons, Fat Barry, fancied a crack at Bruno and was rejected. Bruno was at ease these days with his own bisexuality. He fancied beautiful women, but his time with Tory had taught him that handsome men held a certain appeal too. Handsome men were great. But big fat ugly men? Not so much.

Fat Barry didn't take Bruno's rejection kindly. One day when they were working together in the prison kitchens, with 'Melting Pot' by Blue Mink blaring out of the radio over the sink, Fat Barry yanked Bruno's hand over a hot plate and then calmly walked away. Bruno yelled out and everyone in the kitchen very carefully looked anywhere but at Fat Barry or Bruno, not wishing to incur Barry's wrath themselves.

Bruno didn't even think. His hand afire with pain, he snatched up a kitchen knife, lightning fast, and *thwacked* it into Fat Barry's vast wobbling right buttock. Then he grabbed another and struck again. Then again. Fat Barry went down with a howl of anguish and there were titters from the other cons, quickly suppressed. Three knife handles sticking out of his arse, Barry went down onto his knees. Whimpering, puce in the face, he clawed at his backside, trying to reach the blades, and couldn't.

Some of the other cons hauled Fat Barry to his feet and hustled him away, his rear end bristling like a porcupine's, out of the kitchen. All the screws were laughing. One of them came over to Bruno and said: 'Where'd you learn to throw knives like that then?'

'Self-taught,' said Bruno, wincing, his hand aching. He went over to the cold tap and ran it hard over his shrinking flesh.

'Self-taught? You ought to get a job in a bloody circus. That was good.'

Bruno thought bitterly that the screw was right. He *should* have joined the circus, years ago; he should never have gone to London, should never have sought out the Delaneys or planned revenge on the Carter crew. It was all bloody non-sense when you sat right down and thought about it, and he'd had plenty of time to do that.

After that, Fat Barry never troubled Bruno again, fear-ful of repercussions. Time passed so slowly in prison. They moved you about, treated you like dirt, but you did your time and you didn't make a fuss. That was the only way you could handle a long stretch and stay sane.

# 48

After a while nobody bothered Bruno at all. All around the nick, it became known that you didn't touch Bruno Dawkins because he had the protection of the Delaney gang and woe betide anybody who forgot that. Also, he was in for murder, and the story was that the man in the chicken wire-and-stones suit that they'd fished out of the sea had crossed Bruno on a deal. Bruno got the nickname 'Knifer' after his kitchen incident with Fat Barry; added to his starry status as a pro hit man for the Delaneys, no one felt they could have a go at him, and that suited him just fine.

He kept his head down, did his time. Prayed for early release and never got it. His blond hair grew out and turned black again. He had no visitors, except for the rare times when he got desperate and sent out a VO – a Visiting Order – to Redmond, but it wasn't Redmond who usually showed up, it was always one or other of the twins. It was on one of their very early visits that he learned that his 'brother' Max Carter had survived the Majorcan attempt on his life. One of the locals had spotted him down on the cliffs and called for the brothers in the monastery nearby. For two years, Max had been laid up there, out of it.

'And then when he gets back to civilisation, guess what?' Cormac crowed.

Bruno shook his head. He couldn't guess. Somehow – shamefully – he felt sort of glad that Max had survived and that he, Bruno, had been instrumental in that.

'His old lady'd moved on. Took up with a Yank.' Cormac was laughing as he said it.

Bruno heard about the outside world on the radio and the TV, but it was like hearing chatter from an alien planet; it meant nothing to him, it was garbage. Vietnam blew up and then was over; Princess Anne got married; the country got its first female leader in Thatcher; Curry won Olympic gold. There was a new thing called the space shuttle, Elvis was dead and so was Maria Callas. Time moved on, relentless.

Bruno finished work in the kitchens and moved on to the library, which was boring because he didn't read too well. But it was OK.

Time ceased to have any meaning.

★

Near the end of his sentence, as the eighties came to an end, he was given his F75, his assessment for suitability for release. Then Cormac came to visit, and Cormac told him that Redmond had been in an accident.

Bruno didn't, by this stage, care if Redmond was dead and buried, but he could see that Cormac was shocked so, curious, he asked what happened.

'The Carter lot are Mafia-linked. They had one of theirs holed up on a loch side in Scotland. Redmond knew the bloke who'd been responsible for his sister Orla's death – it was years ago, a terrible tragedy – was there and he set out to finish the bastard. But the Carters were there too, and it all went wrong. The boss fell.'

*Is he dead?* Wondered Bruno hopefully.

'He was hurt bad,' said Cormac. 'Very bad.'

'But he's . . . ?'

'He's alive. Just. And he's bloody mad. Fucking *fuming*.'

'So what now?'

'We're going to sort it out,' said Cormac. 'We're going to get them.'

# 49

Montauk, Long Island USA, 1996

Annie Carter, still stunning in her early fifties, was walking along the white sandy beach in front of her house, trying – and failing – to clear her troubled mind. To her left the sea roared and thrashed. To her right, above the dunes and the clumps of marram grass that tossed and danced in the stiff breeze, stood her beautiful New-England-style clapboard house, big and duck-egg blue, its delicately sculpted eaves painted sparkling white. Hers, now – but once the house had belonged to Constantine Barolli, the all-powerful Mafia don she'd been married to when she had believed Max Carter to be dead. Then – briefly, following Constantine's 'death' – it had passed to his deeply corrupt eldest son, Lucco, then on to his youngest, Alberto; and Alberto – bless him – had gifted it to her.

Annie loved the house and she liked it down here on the shoreline – it was peaceful, cleansing, even with the crash of the waves and the high, eerie cries of the gulls circling and wheeling overhead. Dressed in old frayed denim jeans and a cream angora pullover, she was picking up shells washed in by the fierce Atlantic tides, looking at them, dropping them back onto the sand. She couldn't think today, couldn't even begin to concentrate on anything, because . . .

Because of *that*.

Her hand folded again over the scrap of paper in her pocket.

Just this morning, someone had dropped *that* through her door – a tiny piece of paper with numbers on it. When she'd picked it up off the doormat, unfolded it, seen the numbers listed there, her heart had all but stopped with shock. She'd looked at it, put it aside. Once. Twice. Three times. In fact, it had taken a full hour for her to persuade herself that she had to decipher it, whether she wanted to or not. Alberto her stepson could be in trouble. Layla – who was with him – could be ill.

Annie was happy that they were together, those two, but it was a happiness tinged with regret. She had always hoped that Layla would find some nice, straight man to love and cherish her, but Layla had instead fastened upon Alberto, Constantine's son by his first marriage, and the two of them had become close. Alberto was Mafia and he was wanted by the FBI, so Layla had to live her life with him on the run.

And so . . . *anything* could have happened.

She *had* to decipher the damned thing.

Annie had taken the paper into the study, sat at the desk and applied the code break. 'A' was one, plus three, and so on, all through the alphabet. When she'd done her work, she knew it wasn't from Alberto. It wasn't from a ghost – Constantine – either, although when she'd first seen it, in shock, she had almost thought that.

After that, feeling shaken, she'd come down onto the beach to try and gather herself. Now she took the *pizzino* out of her pocket. Looked at it again. The wind gusted, trying to whip the little scrap of paper from her hand. Really, she would happily let that happen, just let it float away into the ether as if she had never seen it, never read it at all. Why not? Her eyes lingered over the numbers. Caesar's code – the one that Constantine had taught her long ago. It was so basic that the genius minds at Bletchley could have cracked it in ten minutes or less. It was over two thousand years old. This *pizzino* said: *We must talk. Call me. The usual place. Majorca. Max.*

Max had never sent her a *pizzino* before. It was hardly his style. He had, however, been phoning her over the past week and she had been ignoring his calls. He'd phoned at her New York apartment, then at the club, then at this house, and she had blanked him. Refused to engage with him. Why not? After all, he'd done the same to her when he'd walked out on her a year ago.

It hurt her to even think about that. Mostly she tried to draw a veil over it. But now, the damned note had stirred everything up again and she remembered it all – the weeks when he'd coldly withdrawn from her, and then the final, damning confrontation when he said he'd tried but he couldn't get over her deceptions, still couldn't see past her moving on from him to Constantine as she had, and that he'd had enough. She'd been so horrified at the time, so completely shocked, that she hadn't uttered a word in her own defence. She'd lurched from disbelief to agony to dev-astation. She'd phoned her sister and told her everything.

'I think he had a difficult relationship with his mother,' said Ruthie.

Dear, sweet Ruthie. Always so understanding, so good, so *forgiving*. Ruthie had forgiven her wayward sister so many things, over the years. Taking Max off her, for one. And lots more. Annie could never forget how Ruthie had shielded her from their mother's worst drunken excesses, made excuses for her, held her hand when she was upset.

Annie *still* felt like shit when she thought of how she'd repaid Ruthie's kindness: stealing Max away from her. But that was love, wasn't it? There were no rules. Gradually, oh so slowly, the two sisters had made their peace with each other and now they could talk, could be friends again.

'*So?*' Annie demanded.

'So he has trust issues with women and I think you've overstepped a boundary somehow. She was powerful – Queenie. Dominating. Loud. Ferocious. It was always going to be hard, you and him. Well, him and *any* woman, so far as I could tell.'

After all that had happened up in Scotland, all the angst and rubbish involving Constantine, Max had turned cold on her. Then he'd said that they were over. Max had remained at their place in Barbados – alone – and he'd made it perfectly clear that they were finished – *done*. Bewildered, *destroyed*, Annie had come to Montauk to lick her wounds, to try to learn to be alone again, and single, and strong.

Only silence followed.

A whole year of it.

Then – just last week – the phone calls started. Like she wanted to talk to him! And now, *this*. A *pizzino*. A device he'd never ever used before. And what the hell was he doing in Majorca of all places? She knew what he was referring to when he said 'the usual place'. Of course she did. It was the discreet sun-baked hotel they had stayed at sometimes in Illetas. The one they had always thought of as *their* place. He wanted her to contact him there.

She wasn't going to.

As usual – as always – *he* was setting the agenda. Calling the shots.

*Well, not this time, Buster.*

She carried on walking, trudging through the powder-white sand, stuffing the paper back in her pocket.

No. She'd ignored his calls and she was going to ignore this, too.

She had plenty to keep her busy, things she had to attend to. At her Times Square club, *Annie's*, her manager Sonny Gilbert – a tall thin powerhouse of a man with a bald freckled dome of a head and thick red-rimmed glasses that he wore on a matching chain – had unexpectedly walked out of his job last week, saying he was stressed and needed to 'find' himself and that he was, as of now, taking a sabbatical to 'free up some head space'.

Annie wished she could do the same. Instead, she was up to her arse in work. All week she'd been interviewing new candidates at her Central Park apartment. Nobody was quite fitting the bill and she was thinking now of flying out Julian, the ruthlessly efficient general manager of Max's three London nightclubs, to sort it out for her.

This trip out to Montauk was a brief break, that was all. Tomorrow, she'd be back in the city, attending to club business. The New York club was a success, but the overheads were a killer and staff turnover was a nightmare. In the club's favour, there was no fighting inside it. She'd found that punters were much better behaved in New York than in London, for the simple reason that nobody was very likely to shoot you in London if you started a ruckus. In New York, however, where 'carrying' was the norm, you'd have to be mental to start a fight and risk getting killed into the bargain.

Today had been – until she'd picked the note off the doormat – a welcome break from all the madness. She'd come to Montauk to gather her thoughts, to rest. Now she paused, troubled, confused, staring up at the house – *her* house – with the wind buffeting her back. The house was pristine; you'd have no idea that tragedy had happened within its walls, and joy, and lots of other things in between.

She remembered Constantine Barolli, could almost see him out on the deck there, hands on the rail, gazing imperiously out at the ocean, king of all he surveyed. Constantine – the silver fox. She remembered the very first time they'd met. Nineteen-seventy. That awful year, when she'd lost Max, lost her daughter. She had gone to Constantine the Mafia boss in desperation to raise money in return for Layla's freedom.

It had been the day of Constantine's daughter Cara's wedding, and Annie had sat on the front step of his London house – just one of his many properties – begging to see him, exhausted, playing out, needing help.

And Constantine had given that help – for a price. Her body for his money. But somehow her rage at the cold-bloodedness of the deal had dissipated over time, and with Max gone she had sadly, reluctantly, moved on with her life, and Constantine had become close to her. Oh, he wasn't the love of her life – who else but Max could ever be that? But still – they'd shared good times together. And for a while with him she'd been almost happy, until Max – defying all the odds – had come storming, shockingly, back into her life.

She walked on with a sharp sigh. Max bloody Carter. His note in her pocket seemed to burn her flesh, right through the thin fabric of her jeans. His coded words fizzed in her brain. It annoyed the hell out of her that she was spending even so much as a second of her precious free time thinking about *him*. She was here to rest, right? And yet her brain was tormenting her, making that impossible. After all, it had been *his* decision to bail out, and now here he was, riling her up again. Sonny had fielded some of his calls at the club, John her Montauk maintenance man or Martha his wife who was housekeeper here had told Max – on her instruction – that she was busy, engaged, elsewhere. But still, Max had disturbed her. Dragged it all back up for her. The arguments. The cold silences. The final devastating breakdown of their tempestuous union.

'At least you can't accuse me of conducting an affair with my stepson anymore,' she had yelled at him on that awful last day. Alberto Barolli – Constantine's son, Annie's stepson – was down in the Caribbean somewhere with their now pregnant daughter, Layla. Out of reach, out of touch.

Max hadn't even bothered to reply. So she'd packed a bag and gone. And that was the last she'd seen of him. A whole year and not one bloody word. Then the calls. And now, the note.

So here she was. The breeze was rippling through her cocoa-brown shoulder-length hair and making her eyes water. She was just walking along in her comfy old sandals, picking up shells and thinking that there was *no way* she was going to be calling the hotel in Illetas. He could forget that. And she wouldn't allow herself to think of the lazy, sun-soaked times they'd shared there. She *wouldn't*.

Annie stopped walking. She swore and took out the *pizzino* again, thought: *Oh you bastard, why don't you go away? Why don't you leave me alone?*

She'd spent all her life in thrall to him. Grown up adoring him. Given herself to him as a virgin, wrecking her relationship with her own sister just to have him. And for *what*?

The weather was changing, the sky darkening to a brooding blanket of matt-charcoal grey. A storm was coming in. Usually she loved the storms here, loved the drama of them, loved to sit indoors all warm and cosy and look out while the weather raged and spat salty spume at the old clapboard house's firm, untroubled frontage. But the note had upset her, made her angry, made her sad. She knew she wouldn't have a good day today. Not after this.

She stuffed it back into her pocket again. She wasn't going to call him. She couldn't.

Then she looked around and was jolted back to reality when she realised that her minder wasn't down here with her. He had said he was going to follow her down from the house, and he was about as slow as a wet weekend, granted, but where the fuck was he?

'You're a wealthy woman and that could make you a target,' Ellie Brown, her old London mate – once cleaner, once call girl, now co-manager of the Shalimar, one of the Carter clubs – was always telling her.

Annie knew that Ellie was right. Once, of course, Annie had been so poor that all her clothes had been second-hand cast-offs from Ruthie. Now Annie wore designer, she possessed jewels, she had property and she had dual citizenship; she was no longer 'just' British. She was a woman of means, a woman of substance.

*Yeah, you're a big noise,* she told herself mockingly. *So tough that a bit of paper can scramble your brains!*

With Ellie's warning in mind, just months ago she had interviewed heavies and had selected a moustachioed ex-bouncer type built like a barn door out of the dozens she had seen. He'd interviewed well, been all bright-eyed and bushy-tailed and eager. He'd worked at the Times Square club for a while, doing the doors and evicting the druggies. He seemed to fit the bill.

But that was then, and this was now. And now she was thinking: *Uh-oh, wrong choice.*

The truth was, the man was lazy. He was supposed to watch her while she walked. She had *told* him she was going out onto the beach for a walk and he had said he would follow on, so where the fuck was he?

*He was nowhere in sight.*

'God Almighty,' she muttered in irritation and walked on, heading for the steps that would take her back up to the house. The wind was rising, the freshening effect of it starting to turn cold. Her skin prickled as upswept sand blasted it with stinging force. Her eyes started to stream tears.

Best get indoors.

She paused near the base of the steps.

The *pizzino* in her pocket taunted her.

'Fuck you, Max,' she muttered.

She took the damned thing out and with one decisive movement she shredded it into bits and held her hand up, opening her fingers, watching the pieces as they spiralled away, the wind sending them soaring out along the beach then out to sea, to be lost and forgotten.

That was it.

She would forget she'd ever received the note. She wouldn't call him.

She was living the single life here, getting on with business and losing herself in that. And it did have its compensations. No man trying to be the boss of her – that was the best part. And if she drank a bottle of wine alone some nights and was then too dizzy to crawl up to bed, so what? She wasn't a great drinker, never had been. Alcohol went straight to her head. But that was her business, her decision, no one else's.

Yes, she was *fine* on her own.

You could depend on yourself. Start depending on a man, and you were up shit creek.

Then she saw movement out of the corner of her eye. Ah, *there* he was. About fifty yards behind her. Maybe she was wrong about her minder after all. Maybe he was going to come good. But there was no fire in his eyes, no determination, no *spark*. It had all been there in the interview, of course – the job paid well – but she hadn't seen any suggestion of it since.

Annie turned. She opened her mouth to speak, to shout out something – probably something abusive, the note had put her in that sort of mood – and then she stopped.

That *wasn't* her bodyguard.

# 50

The man who was approaching was tall, angular, somewhere in his forties. Sandy-coloured hair peppering into white. A hawkish face. Mean sunken eyes set too close together. Maybe the sort of man she *should* have hired, instead of the languid tub of lard she had. She frowned at him as he came on, hurrying now. No one ever walked on this beach, except her and – when he could be arsed – her 'minder'.

*Christ! He was starting to run toward her.*

Annie felt her heart literally *jump* into her mouth. A lightning bolt of fear shot up from her toes right to the top of her head. Frozen rigid for one brief, shocked moment, she then snapped back to reality and spun around and ran, flat-out, for the steps. Panting, she raced up them and in horror she felt the vibrations go through the tall wooden structure as her pursuer hit the bottom of the flight and charged up, moving much faster than she could.

At the top she sprinted back toward the house, gasping with terror, fearing at any moment the impact that would take her down. She shot through the French doors and tried to slam them shut. But the white voile drapes caught in them, jamming them ajar.

No time to even try and rectify the situation and lock them. And he'd just break the glass, wouldn't he, and get in anyway.

Annie stepped back and stood, panting hard, flattening herself against the wall to the left of the doors. Maybe he wouldn't come in. But then – slowly, inch by inch, one of the doors was pushed open. The brisk sea wind caught it, billowing out the curtains with a fresh, chilling gust. Then *he* appeared – a big purposeful shape bringing with him a powerful blast of cold Atlantic air. The drapes moved around him as he came forward, cautious, watchful.

Annie saw the gun first, held firmly in his hand as he eased himself into the room. Then she saw his face, side-on. And then . . .

*His head was starting to turn toward her.*

She slipped the kiyoga she always carried with her out of her jeans pocket. The sprung metal ball leapt out as she swung it. The kiyoga was a martial-arts weapon, ideal for women as it increased their hitting power tenfold. She'd been carrying it around with her for years, and now she was glad of it.

The kiyoga struck the man's temple with amplified force and he shot sideways, the gun spinning out of his hand. As he hit the floor, Annie stepped in and hit him again, hard.

*Get them down and keep them down,* sprang into her head. Max again. Max always said that. Don't give them a chance to get up and finish what they started. Don't piss about. Strike hard and strike fast.

She drew back, panting like she'd just run for her life, which she suspected she had. She was shaking. She kicked the gun aside but she thought he wasn't going to be reaching for it anytime soon. He looked spark out, unconscious.

Then a bulky shape appeared in the open door that led to the hallway. Her minder came into the sitting room and looked first at the man on the floor, then at her.

'What the fuck?' he asked past a mouthful of food. He was eating pastrami on rye.

John and Martha came crowding into the doorway behind him.

'Mrs Carter? What's happened?' asked John, alarmed.

'Bring some rope, John, will you? Let's tie this bastard up.' She drew in a breath and pocketed the kiyoga. Then she addressed her minder.

'Oh, and by the way?' she gasped out. 'You're a useless arsehole.' She dragged in another breath and felt the room start to sway around her as shock set in, turning her legs to water. She sat down hard before she *fell* down. 'And you're fired,' she finished up.

Then the man on the floor started to move.

'Watch out!' she yelled.

The lean stranger came staggering to his feet. He was bleeding from two cuts on his head where the kiyoga had struck him and he reeled, dizzy. A shout went up from John, who lunged forward and grabbed the gun and fired, chipping a chunk out of the plasterwork on the ceiling. The noise nearly deafened them all. The man turned back to the French doors, shoved through the voile curtains – and was gone.

# 51

While Annie was fighting off an attack in Montauk, Max was busy reliving a bad memory. He was at his now unused finca, which was set high above a rocky bay not far from Palma, in the upmarket west of Majorca. Hands stuffed in jeans pockets, he was peering over the low wall at the edge of his property where it sheared off into a steep jagged drop, tumbling all the way down to the sea. He looked down at the depths below. The sun was hot on the back of his neck above the collar of his white shirt, but the sweat that sprang up there had nothing to do with the heat and everything to do with coming back to this place – and to the memories it stirred.

Far below, he could see the turquoise sea sucking and rushing at the pink-toned rocks. Once, sparrows had drunk at the edge of the pool right behind him. But the pool was dry now, empty of water, empty of everything but a few dusty yellowing palm fronds. No sparrows. No swimmers. Nothing. Nobody came here anymore.

He drew back a little, feeling hot, feeling in truth a little giddy, then with a supreme effort of will he forced himself to look again, over the great yawning depths to the rocks below. Suspiciously, he glanced behind him. Lightning never struck twice, but still – best to be careful. The cicadas hummed, a drowsy noise. The place was deserted. He looked back, down at the cliff, at the spume thundering against the rocks, while the gulls swept and wheeled above the pounding waters way down there.

The last time . . .

His mind flinched away from it, but he made himself go there. To dig the muck out, to pull it into the open.

It had been the early Nineteen-Seventies – what, twenty-odd years ago? He was in his fifties now. That was when he had been here. He couldn't remember the exact year. Probably he'd blanked it. Some men had thrown him over the edge of this cliff and their intention had been to kill him. But he had survived.

He let out a puff of air, shook his head.

*Christ.*

What he *did* remember – very clearly – was the fear. And after the horrific impact of the fall, the agony. The months in hospital, his mind empty and his body shattered. So this was the last place in the world he had ever wanted to return to or even consider. He hadn't sold it. He ought to, but in truth he hadn't even wanted to *think* about the place, not really. Nobody tended it. Weeds flourished everywhere, pushing up through gaps in the paving. The finca had an air of deep disuse, of buried secrets. It just sat here, a crumbling epitaph to a Seventies disaster in which he had been maimed, his wife and daughter had gone missing, his servants – Rufio and Inez – had been killed. Christ, so long ago.

*And his brother.*

Jonjo.

He looked at the empty pool. Jonjo – Max could freely admit – had been a fool, but he'd been *Max's* fool, his *brother*, and if anyone else ever said so, they'd be in trouble. Jonjo Carter had died in that pool. Annie had told Max that, a long time ago. She had thought Jonjo was Max; she had told him that too. She had swum out and found that she was mistaken. And had been relieved, of course. Annie had always hated Jonjo – and it had been mutual. Jonjo had hated her right back.

*So what the hell am I doing here?* Max wondered.

*Looking for a ghost,* came back the answer. Going back, when everyone knew you should *never* go back. All it ever gave you was regrets. But he couldn't help it. The past was haunting him, calling to him. He was trying to make sense of something that made no bloody sense at all. He'd had a phone call from his old pal Benito, which had mystified him – some bollocks about somebody paying, and a brother. What with the bad line and Benito's heavily accented voice, he'd had no chance to fully understand what Benito was getting at.

The old monk had mentioned Annie, Annie having answers. It was a jumble, undecipherable. So – here he was. He'd tried to contact her but – of course, the stubborn cow – she wasn't playing ball. He'd got a message to her through some old American mob contacts, telling her to get in touch with him at the Illetas hotel they had often, back in the past, visited together, stayed in together.

Into his mind came images, tormenting him. Him and her together, sun-dazed and warm on a private terrace, eating together in the evening, then bed. There was *always* bed, with him and Annie. They'd divorced in nineteen-eighty, then drifted back together. But then other things had happened and he'd admitted to himself that he couldn't go on with it, couldn't leave their past behind, couldn't forgive her for her evasions and her entanglement with Constantine Barolli; he couldn't trust her anymore.

This past year they'd been apart, not communicating at all. Her in America, him in Barbados. But now he knew they had to talk and that was dangerous because he knew he almost *wanted* that. To speak to her again, to see her, to – yes, he knew it – fall into bed with her, and if he did that then maybe he would even be stupid enough to pick up where they'd left off.

*No.*

He had good intentions, but the road to hell, he reminded himself, was paved with those fuckers. Good intentions had got him on the road to crime all those years back, his only intention being to help Mum crawl out of the hole of poverty; but crime, and his war with the Delaneys, had killed her.

So, get back with Annie? That wasn't going to happen. He wasn't going through that, not again. But talk? Yes. They *had* to talk because she had been here at the Majorcan finca, right on the spot on the day that Benito was alluding to. Maybe *she* would have answers. Himself? He had none.

Max turned away from the precipitous edge and went around the empty pool and over the sun-baked terrace to the door of the finca. He unlocked it – and stepped inside. Time for some shut-eye before he made the trip up to the monastery tonight. Then, one way or another, he was going to find out what this was all about.

# 52

Bruno Dawkins was sitting, his newly dyed brassy blond head bowed, in the front pew of a London church. Twenty long hard years he'd been inside, and he was no longer Tory Delaney's beautiful boy. Prison had hardened him; made a man of him. He was thirty-seven years old.

Just a week ago he'd walked out of Wandsworth – Cormac and Seamus had collected him from outside the prison gates – and he'd come home, to Battersea. Inside, he'd kept his nose clean – apart from the Fat Barry incident, of course – and mostly he'd been a model prisoner. Coming out, the warder who'd handed him back his belongings had wished him well.

Of course, the Delaneys were going to look after him. The Irish twin cousins took him to a flat, let him settle in, then they took him out for a slap-up meal and provided him with a very nice girl for the night. A boy if he preferred, but Bruno said no, the girl would do.

The day *after* he'd been released, Bruno had sauntered around town, not even recognising much about it, finding the traffic hectic, the people jostling him on the crowded pavements a worry: things had moved on, but he hadn't. It was going to take a while for him to catch up, get his bearings.

When he'd seen the church he felt relieved and walked in. He sat down in the echoing silence of the place and thought about everything in the chilly, peaceful air of the interior. He thought about what he'd just been through – all those years! Yes, it was true – Redmond *had* looked after him in jail, but only so no dirt would touch his own family name. Now Bruno was considering his cold, empty upbringing with the miserable God-bothering cow who'd dragged him up from infancy to adulthood. Poor old Nora. Long gone now. He thought about the Carters, and his long-ago threats of revenge upon them, most particularly on Max for Nora's death, and Tory's too.

Tory had loved him, hadn't he? He couldn't imagine that Tory would have treated him as Redmond had, but what could you do? Redmond was head of the Delaneys and so he was Bruno's boss. Bruno looked back now on his times with Tory at Dolphin Court as the best. But there was no more Tory, not now. All that was over with.

'Can I help you, my son?' asked a voice over his head.

Bruno looked up with bright blue, black-lashed eyes, and the young vicar who stared down at him was reminded, fancifully, just for a moment, of Michelangelo's *David*. A pity, of course, about the strawberry birthmark on the cheek, though; it spoiled the illusion of perfection.

'No,' said Bruno.

'Well – I'm here. If you need me,' said the vicar, and walked on up the aisle. He turned right in front of the altar and vanished inside the vestry.

As if anybody could help him! Bruno scrubbed a weary hand over his face and stood up. Things were in motion again now, with *him*, that wicked spiderlike bastard Redmond, pulling all their strings. Bruno shuddered, staring up at the cross behind the altar. Redmond had been in a terrible accident, but he had survived.

'He's changed,' Cormac had told Bruno. 'Be prepared for that.'

Prepared for *what* exactly? Bruno wondered.

'We've adapted the house in the yard,' Cormac went on. 'Hoists to heave him out of bed and into his chair, a sit-down shower, night and day nurses . . .'

Bruno turned, shivering, and left the church. He'd been summoned by Redmond – or what was left of him, anyway – and he was running late.

# 53

Redmond Delaney's Scottish 'accident' should have been fatal; everyone agreed on that. But it wasn't. After it happened, there had been a private hospital outside Edinburgh, the best of care, the most cutting of cutting-edge recovery programmes, but it had been touch and go, the Delaney cousins told Bruno, and the last rites had twice been spoken over Redmond's pulverised body.

That should have been *that*, but somehow not the surgeons, the doctors, the nurses, nor even the priest who'd twice attended him, had banked on the Irishman's ferocious, *furious* will to survive.

Still, everyone expected each new day to be Redmond Delaney's last. His injuries were horrific, life-changing. But the surgeons operated. The doctors circled. The nurses attended, and the man breathed on. Battered, shattered, all but destroyed – still, he *lived*. Quality of life didn't matter to him. He *had* to survive, no matter how bitter and loathsome that survival might be.

He needed revenge – against those Mafia bastards the Barolli family, and against Annie Carter, but most of all against the one who'd been a pus-weeping thorn in his side for as long as he could remember. *Max fucking Carter.*

Redmond Delaney lived for that – and that alone.

★

Bruno had never cared for Redmond. Truthfully, that cold fish had always given him the creeps and he was just relieved that Redmond didn't share his brother Tory's tastes. It had always been strictly business between them, and Bruno liked it that way. All had been fairly smooth – bearable, anyway – until Redmond took that high dive out of a castle window up north and into an ice-cold loch below.

He *ought* to have died.

Bruno wished he had.

Then he could have walked away from London and all the stuff he'd been through. Forgotten the cursed Delaneys in their Battersea bastion, forgotten the Carters too. Got the stink of prison off him. Grabbed his cash, taken off for somewhere warm and sunny.

But now, fuck it.

Redmond had gone head to head against the Mafia and the Carter clan and he'd lost. But now he was recovering – and asking for Bruno.

So Bruno knew it must be true – the devil really *did* look after his own.

# 54

Bruno went to the Delaney scrapyard and Seamus met him inside the office at the front of the house there. Together, they stepped through, into the lift. Seamus yanked the metal doors closed behind them, shutting them into its tomblike embrace. Seamus pressed the button. Clanking, straining, the lift descended one floor and then juddered to a halt. Seamus pulled back the lift doors and stepped out, Bruno following into pitch darkness.

Suddenly a light came on, illuminating a big square box of a room, white-painted and lit by a single hundred-watt bulb at the centre of it. And there was Redmond, seated in his wheelchair, a twisted smile on his face. Bruno's tongue was stuck to the roof of his mouth; he couldn't get an ounce of spit in there. His heart was beating a tattoo inside his chest.

Here was the reality of Redmond, then.

Bruno's boss was wearing a thin purple pullover and a pair of black trousers. His face . . . oh Jesus, Bruno really didn't want to look at his face. The impact when he fell must have caught him on the left-hand side, because that side of his face was wreathed in angry red scars. One eye – the right – blazed out, green, bright. The other – the left – was gone, a puckering empty hole all that was left of it.

'It's a bit shocking at first,' Redmond said, reading Bruno's expression. Redmond's head dipped and he was looking at his legs. Or where his legs should have been. The trousers ended mid-thigh on the right side, higher still on the left. Below that, his legs were gone. 'You see, there was simply too much damage to save these,' Redmond was going on, while Bruno fought down the bile that had risen in his throat. 'Constantine Barolli knifed me in my right thigh. Max Carter shot me in my left and hit me in the head with his gun. Brutal people, yes? Don't you think? *Terrible* people.'

*Or maybe just fighting fire with fire,* thought Bruno.

There was a big oblong table behind the ruin that was Redmond, and a hulking male nurse in a white uniform was filling a syringe. There were other things there too. Surgical instruments. The nurse turned, approached Redmond, rolled up his sleeve. Redmond looked up, sent that twisted, awful grin at Bruno again.

'Morphine,' he explained. 'I need quite a lot of this.'

Bruno said nothing – he *couldn't*.

'I'm going to deal with them, all of them,' said Redmond as the nurse drew back. 'Max Carter, let me see. I've attacked his businesses. His friends. His wife's slippery but I haven't given up on causing her pain, not yet. His daughter, too. I am going to let Max Carter feel the full measure of despair, just like I have over these past dreadful months. He's going to suffer, like I've suffered. And when he's suffered enough, I am going to kill him.'

Bruno swallowed. He felt sick.

'Now – Bruno! Good boy. I have something I want you to do for me.'

# 55

The Majorcan monastery was set high above and beyond Max Carter's finca, way up in the Tramuntana range of mountains. Hawks circled and called overhead, lifted by huge warm updraughts that spun, whirlpools of shifting air, at the edges of the mountains. The vast old monastery building dated from the twelfth century and it stood in solid isolation above the crashing Mediterranean sea so far below, its pink-and-sand tinted stone walls heated by the harsh summer sun. Thick fronds of scarlet bougainvillea, red as bloodstains, flowed over and around its entrance, thin straggling cork oak forests clustered around its perimeter. If you wanted to escape the troubles of the world, this was exactly the place to do it.

Max drove his hire car up to the gates and started to grin as he saw his old friend Benito standing there waiting for him, looking older now than when they'd last met. His tonsured hair was greying and he was leaning on a stick, but there was that same roguish twinkle of humour in the old soldier's eye as he waved a greeting.

Max stopped the car and climbed out. Even late in the day, the heat was like a furnace; it was crushing, oppressive, throwing up a shimmering haze through the clouds of pink dust churned up by the car. Lizards scuttled. The hum and rattle of the cicadas was almost deafening. Benito came

forward and the two men hugged, slapping each other heart-
ily on the back, laughing.

'My friend! How are you?' asked Benito in his broken
English.

'Fine. You?' asked Max.

'As you see. A little older, a little lamer – but still eighteen—' he tapped his brow '—in here.'

'You look pretty good on it,' said Max.

'I am fine. You have time for dinner? I still have whisky. None
of that raw rubbish. A twenty-year-old single malt. The best.'

'Lead me to it. And then you can tell me what this is all
about.'

Benito's ready smile dropped from his weather-beaten
face. His dark eyes were suddenly serious. 'Come in, my
friend. Come in.'

★

Most of the monks ate their dinner in the refectory, but
instead of joining them Benito led Max into a small ante-
room where they could have their dinner and their conversation in private.

Once they were seated, one of the younger monks –
Andreu, Benito called him, a bent young man with a humped
back – brought their food in to them, a surprisingly lavish
spread of Ramallet tomatoes, Grimalt cheese and *cocarrois* –
small pasties filled with ham, vegetables and garlic.

Benito talked about world affairs, then he asked after
Annie.

Max hadn't yet told Benito that he and Annie had parted
company. It wasn't a subject he felt he wanted to discuss with
anyone, not even one of his oldest friends.

'She's fine,' he said.

'Ah. And your girl? Layla?'

'Abroad. People travel far and wide these days, don't they.'

Benito nodded and the next course came in. *Tumbet* this time – a vegetarian dish – and salt cod and paella.

The hours passed and the daylight faded into night-time. Andreu lit candles on the table and on the dresser nearby, creating a glow that moths fluttered around in a crazy dance of death.

'God alive, you'll have to hoist me from this table with a crane.' Max laughed. They ate in silence for a while, but he was getting impatient to hear the real purpose of this meeting, this thing that was too sensitive – Benito had claimed – to be properly discussed over the phone.

But Benito shook his head when Max touched on the subject.

'Later, my friend. Let's not spoil our dinner.'

'It's bad, then? Whatever this thing is?'

Benito shook his head, not being drawn. 'Later,' he said more firmly. Then a man appeared in the alcove leading to their little dining room and Benito said: 'Ah,' and stood up.

The man moved forward. He looked a typical Majorcan – slight of build, black-haired, tawny-skinned. He was handsome and he was wearing a clean pair of dark jeans and a pale yellow short-sleeved shirt that revealed firm muscular arms. Somehow Max found him familiar.

'Come in, come in,' said Benito, beckoning, pulling around a chair. He turned and smiled at Max. 'Look, my friend. You remember? This is Jaime.'

# 56

Max was staring at the younger man as Jaime slid into the chair Benito offered. Noting the dark-skinned brow, the soft, chestnut-brown eyes. The slightly crooked nose. The broad mouth, that had smiled once with pleasure but now did not.

'*Jaime*?' Max echoed. He remembered that day, so long ago. Lying on a tiny ledge that had broken his fall down onto the rocks and into the ocean, convinced he was going to die. Thinking that no one would come; that no one could. He'd been broken and bloodied. The rocks were treacherous. And then a miracle occurred, in the shape of this man who had then been a small boy, out herding his goats. 'Jaime?' Max grinned and reached across the table. Jaime held out a hand and Max took it, grasped it. 'Good God! After all this time.'

'How are you?' asked Jaime in passable English.

'Thanks to you? I'm good.' Max's grin faded as he looked between Benito and Jaime. 'Is anyone going to tell me what this is all about?'

'Let's get some more wine,' said Benito, and gestured to the hunchbacked young monk who was loitering in the alcove. 'Another bottle, Andreu,' he said, and the youngster vanished.

'Now come on,' said Max. 'Tell me what's going on.'

He looked at Benito, who seemed to be examining the pristine tablecloth. Then at Jaime.

'Who's going to say it?' asked Max.

'I am,' said Jaime suddenly.

Benito looked at Max. He sighed. 'Jaime confided in me. And I felt I had to tell you. That's why you are here, tonight. That's why Jaime is here too.'

Jaime nodded, his eyes holding Max's gaze. Finally, he spoke.

'I was paid to find you. I didn't just stumble across you when you lay injured on the rocks. Someone paid me to look for you. Someone who knew you fell – that you were *thrown* – down from the finca and onto the rocks below.'

Max was dimly aware of Andreu coming back with the wine, bustling around the table in his simple brown habit made of homespun, putting a glass in front of Jaime, filling it with the rich red liquid, then topping up Benito's glass, and his own. He tried to take in what Jaime had said. He stared at the younger man. Nervously Jaime took a mouthful of wine, set his glass down.

'If I found you – and I did – this person was supposed to have paid me more. Lots of money.' Jaime swallowed, downed more wine. 'But he didn't show up. I never saw him again.'

Max looked at Benito, who nodded. 'He swears it's the truth,' he said.

'What, was this one of the people who tossed me over there in the first place? They were the only ones who knew I could be down there. Why would they do that?' asked Max, frowning.

'I'm sorry. I don't know who he was. He was young, not much older than I was. Blond. There was a mark on his cheek, right here. All this has troubled me, you know. For years, it's troubled me.'

'Annie always said that at the time she didn't know where to look for me,' said Max. 'And anyway she thought it would be pointless. The kidnappers told her I was dead and gone. And they were putting pressure on her to get back to London, to raise cash for Layla. She had to put that first.'

Jaime put a hand to his throat. He gulped. Sweat was breaking out on his forehead.

'Jaime?' Benito laid a hand on the younger man's arm. 'Are you all right? You mustn't worry. Just tell the truth and all will be well.'

'Yes! The truth. You're right.'

'You're among friends here,' said Max.

'No, I . . .' Jaime was coughing; he couldn't seem to get words out.

*Poor bloke's nervous,* thought Max.

He stared at Jaime. Hot colour was flooding the younger man's face and he was gasping. He seemed to be fighting for air. Max looked at the three glasses of wine on the table. His and Benito's, topped up from a fresh bottle, were as yet untouched. Jaime's glass was nearly empty. Benito was picking up his own glass absent-mindedly, lifting it to his lips, then pausing, his eyes resting with concern on Jaime. Max looked up at Andreu – but it *wasn't* Andreu the hunchback; this man was older, sly-eyed and straight-backed. Max lunged across the table and struck the glass out of Benito's hand. It fell onto the flagstoned floor and shattered.

'*What* . . . ?' Benito started, but Max's attention was fastened on the one who'd poured the wine. Seeing Max's intent, the man bolted off through the alcove and out, disappearing down the passageway.

Jaime slumped sideways, his eyes turning up in his head. He hit the floor and lay there, immobile, gasping hard; trying to suck in air and failing.

Max got down on his knees beside Jaime while Benito hurried off, stick at the ready, after the man who'd brought the wine.

'Jaime?' Max said, cradling his head. 'Can you hear me? Who paid you? Can you tell me who?'

He looked down at the man in anguish. This man had saved his life. But it was perfectly obvious that there was no way to save *his*. Max could smell a bitter-almond scent with each tortured breath Jaime struggled to take.

*Cyanide.*

'*Who paid you, Jaime?*' Max persisted.

Jaime's jaw was slack. He was dying. There was no way to stop it. A feeling of deep, soul-wrenching regret surged through Max. Whatever the means or the motivation, this man had saved him. He owed Jaime his life.

'Jaime?' he said faintly. It was no good.

Max looked up to see Benito surge red-faced back into the alcove. Benito shook his head. He hadn't caught the man.

'I don't know who he was,' he gasped out, his eyes desperate as they rested on Jaime. 'Is he . . . ?'

Max shook his head.

'I found Andreu. Poor Andreu! His head's caved in; he's lying in the wine cellar. It's a nasty wound, but I think he'll be all right. I've sent someone down there to tend to him.' Benito stepped forward. 'My God!' He crossed himself. 'This poor boy. Is there anything we can do?'

Max didn't think so. That stuff worked fast.

'Jaime?' he said. Jaime was weakening, his breathing growing shallow.

'Broth . . .' he gasped out.

'What? Jaime, what?' asked Max.

Benito came and knelt by Jaime. He started to pray, absolving Jaime of all his sins. The last rites. Max felt choked all of a sudden. A young man in the prime of his life, and he was dying because of something that involved *him*.

'Brother,' said Jaime huskily.

'Whose brother?' asked Max.

'Yours,' said Jaime.

# 57

Max and Benito sat up into the early hours, drinking whisky and talking over the awful events of the previous evening. Max wondered out loud if they should call the police, but Benito shook his head.

'No, no. We will find our dear friend Jaime a resting place in the catacombs here. He had no family, you know; his parents are long dead and he has no wife, no children. We do not want the police here, disrupting everything.'

Max stared at his old friend.

'Benito,' he said, 'you don't seem to understand. Jaime was poisoned because someone wanted him kept quiet. It's a criminal matter. God knows I'm not a great fan of the police, but there's a time and place for them, and I think this could be it.'

Benito shook his head. 'But I do understand. I understand only too well.'

'How is Andreu?'

'Shocked. Hurt. But the brothers are tending him and he will be fine.' Benito gave a dry smile. 'We know how to keep quiet, Max. And that is what we will do.'

Max was silent for a long moment, then he said: 'I'm sorry. I brought trouble to your door.'

'Not your fault.'

'Still . . . if there's anything I can do to help you, tell me.'

Benito was staring at Max's face. 'What Jaime said. About your brother paying him to search for you.'

'I'm as puzzled by that as you are. I told you, didn't I? Both my brothers are dead.'

'And . . . you are sure of that?'

A pang of long-buried grief caught Max square in the midriff. He swallowed another mouthful of whisky and let out a sigh.

'My youngest brother, Eddie – I was with him when he died. There was no mistaking it.'

'I'm sorry. And the other one?'

'Jonjo?' Max took another swallow. Memories swirled through his brain. Nineteen-seventy. Christ! That day. What should have been a carefree day, him and Annie and Layla, Jonjo and one of his blondes. All of them enjoying the early spring sunshine on the Majorcan finca's warm terrace, unaware that disaster was about to befall them. 'This is good stuff,' he said.

Benito poured them both another. 'Ardbeg. From a little Scottish island called Islay.'

He clinked his glass against Max's, and they both drank.

'This Jonjo. Your brother. You saw him die too?' asked Benito after a pause.

The candlelight flickered and the night was deep and dense all around them. It was so late now that most of the brothers were in bed. First, they had moved Jaime's body down to the cellars, and Andreu was being tended to in their hospital section. All was quiet. Secrets could be told at such a time, memories could come flooding back.

'I didn't see it happen, no,' said Max.

'But someone else did?'

'Yes. Annie did. There was an explosion. I was grabbed, thrown over the side of the cliff, landed on the rocks. I was out of it. But Annie was there. The pool house blast knocked her out cold and when she came round she saw a dark-haired man in the pool, face-down. She thought it was me. She dived in, swam out, but it was Jonjo.'

'And he was dead.'

'Shot between the eyes, she said. She also said that when the next morning came, his body was gone.'

'So these people thought they'd killed you that day.'

'But they hadn't. Thanks to Jaime. Poor bastard.'

'Why would they remove your brother's body?'

Max shrugged. 'Who knows? They snatched Layla too, poor kid. Annie had no idea I was so close by. She was in a panic, getting messages off the kidnappers about Layla. She had to go back to London to raise money fast. She didn't have time to stop and search for me.'

Max heard himself say that. *She didn't have time.*

And that was true, wasn't it? Annie had been under extreme pressure and she had done what she could to save their child. She'd had to prioritise, to put Layla first. And it had all gone to hell at that point, hadn't it: Annie had flown back to London believing him dead, she had contacted Constantine Barolli the Mafia boss for help, and it had set her down a new path. By the time Max had recovered, two long years had passed – and Annie had adapted to a new way of life, become involved with a new man.

That was where everything had gone wrong. That moment when the explosion had ripped through the Majorcan finca's pool house was precisely the point at which their worlds had been torn apart. Slowly, slowly, they had reassembled themselves – but after that? Truthfully, for him, nothing had ever been quite the same.

Max had tried – God, how he'd tried! – but he knew he had never been able to forgive her for her actions, for her remaining links to Constantine Barolli. The memory of it all had blighted their relationship and now he didn't know if it would ever be possible to rebuild any part of it.

Benito was biting his lip and staring out of the window. Dawn was coming soon; already there were thin ivory and tangerine streaks of colour looping across the lightening eastern sky. The birds were starting to sing. It was going to be another bright beautiful day on this sun-kissed isle, and Jaime wasn't going to see it. Anger and grief raged in him. Because of *him*, Jaime was dead.

'You're going to have to talk to Annie about all this,' said Benito. 'She was there, on the spot.'

'I know that. I've been phoning her in the US. I sent her a note. She's not playing ball.'

Truthfully, Max didn't know how he felt about the prospect of meeting up with Annie again.

He'd decided that they were over, and he wasn't about to go back on that decision. However he tried to reason it out, to find excuses for her behaviour, he couldn't forgive it. Realising that, he'd had to call it a day. He'd been brutal about it, he knew, but he had to cut the thing dead. He couldn't stand long-winded discussions about right or wrong, getting her to justify what she'd done. Giving up on him. Marrying another man. Then the deceptions. The *lies*.

She would have all the arguments ready to hand of course.

Omertà. The Mafia code of silence which she – as Constantine's wife – had been obliged to abide by.

'What Jaime said makes no sense. Not if both your brothers are truly dead,' Benito was saying.

'Of course they are. Look, as you say, Annie was there. She had a front-row seat for the whole damned mess.'

He didn't want to talk to Annie. He didn't want to see her. He couldn't go there all over again, delve into all her deceptions, hear all over again about all the Mafia crap she kept banging on about. But he knew he was going to have to bite the bullet and see her again. Talk to her. But he was dreading it. He hadn't seen her for a whole year and he liked it that way; he'd acknowledged to himself that their mad, impetuous relationship was over. Let her live her own life in the States, and he would carry on with his in Barbados.

Maybe there would be new people in both their lives. Or maybe not. Perhaps Annie was – had in fact *never* been – the right woman for him. She was altogether too strong, too forceful. She could act independently without a moment's hesitation, never questioning her own decisions. She was – he hated to admit it, but it was true – actually like him, in a lot of ways. Like his poor old mum, too. Gutsy. Fearless.

'I'll talk to her,' said Max. Like it or not, he was going to have to.

'That would be good. Maybe she has answers that we do not.'

'Maybe,' said Max, thinking that Annie always had answers – mostly to questions that you wished you never had to ask. 'Look, Benito – me and her? We're not on the best of terms right now.'

'I gathered that. Why?'

Max shrugged and after a moment he began to talk, working back over the explosion at the finca all that long time ago and everything that had gone on since.

'I thought I could let it all go. What she'd done, what she became when I wasn't there. But after what happened in Scotland last year I realised I couldn't. And when I realised that, I left her.'

Benito eyed Max's downcast face. 'My friend, you have to speak to her.'

Max gave a bitter little smile. 'You know what? I think I'm afraid to. Me! I've had one year on my own, and how will I feel if I see her again? I haven't a clue. She's caused me more pain in my life than any other woman, ever. I'm not in a hurry to get back to all that.'

He looked at Benito, whose face said it all.

'Yeah, all right.' Max sighed. 'I'll do it.'

# 58

It was an easy enough job. At five one morning, Bruno took the keys of one of the Delaney scrapyard lorries with no number plates. He drove it across town to the place, as instructed, and pulled up outside. He sat there a moment, listening to Queen and Bowie pounding out 'Under Pressure'. He stared at the unlit neon sign over the red double doors, the beautiful windows, the images of fantastically attractive girls.

People were moving all around the city, even at this early hour, but Bruno wasn't bothered, not even when he saw one man passing in the street pause and watch what he was doing.

Bruno drove the lorry out across the road, then slammed the thing into reverse. With a scream of the accelerator the lorry shot backwards. The impact of it hitting the front of the club was deafening. Glass flew out in a crystalline shower, glossy images shattered, the frontage collapsed.

The onlooker stood there, mouth open, astonished.

Bruno threw the lorry into gear and sped away.

# 59

Chris Brown had been getting earache off his old lady about there being no clean napkins in the place. He was the co-manager of the Shalimar nightclub in London and he ran the show with Ellie, his wife, who was an old friend of Annie Carter's from her knocking shop days. Ellie was a bit of a stickler for detail. She was enormously proud of the club with its golden angels and cherubs, its tiger-striped seating, its luxe gold-leafed wall décor and tobacco-brown carpeting, and just one little thing like the wrong napkins could send her into a tailspin.

'What, serviettes, like that, you mean?' Chris asked her, wondering why this mattered at all.

'We don't call them serviettes. The proper term is *napkins*. We need our napkins back because we're serving food and no way am I doing paper napkins. Fresh white linen – that's the ticket. The ones with the Shalimar embroidered on the corner in gold.'

'You've phoned the laundry place?'

Starburst Laundry always handled their cleaning.

'They say they're short-staffed.' Ellie was irritably polishing glasses.

'Then the answer's simple, no? Get another company.'

So Ellie got another company. All was well – except for the fact that Starburst Laundry didn't seem to much like the idea of being kicked to the kerb. Their MD phoned the general manager, Julian Prothero, who oversaw the running of all three of Max Carter's clubs – the Palermo Lounge, the Shalimar and the Blue Parrot – and offered Julian a sizeable bung to get the business back.

'Sorry, no can do,' said Julian, who had been getting grief off Ellie Brown over marks on the towels, late deliveries. The game was up; the love affair was over. He declined Starburst's bung politely and moved on.

Then at five one morning – three days after Julian had turned down Starburst's offer – Ellie and Chris, who lived over the shop in their very nice flat, were awakened from sleep by all hell breaking loose. The noise was so loud that Ellie fell off the bed. Chris shot upright and grabbed the baseball bat he always kept to hand when they slept. He staggered around, more asleep than awake, and finally composed himself sufficiently to grab the door key and go downstairs in his pyjamas to see what was happening.

It was cold down there; that was the first thing he noticed. But then he realised why. There was glass crunching under his feet and he could see cars passing outside, which normally he could not, because usually there were big plate-glass windows, heavily tinted and covered in images of beautiful girls, obscuring the view out onto the street. He swiftly came to the conclusion that someone had smashed in the tinted and lavishly adorned windows all along the front of the club.

He went to the big red double doors and unlocked them, swinging them wide. Instantly a man, standing slack-jawed outside on the pavement said: 'Christ, you see that?'

'No. What happened?' asked Chris. He had stepped on glass and was vaguely aware that his naked toes were bleeding and that the – no doubt innocent – passing pedestrian was eyeing the baseball bat in his right hand with trepidation.

'Some blond-haired bloke smashed a lorry right into your bloody windows. Hell of a mess innit? Then he just drove off.'

'Did you get the number plate?'

'It didn't have none.'

By lunchtime the damage had been assessed and the insurance company contacted. Julian had turned up and told Chris and Ellie about the bung offer and said this had to be Starburst. The place was turning into fucking Chicago, mobs moving in – for God's sake! – on laundry and refuse companies. What the hell was the world coming to? He hated to do it – it choked him, made him sick to his stomach – but Julian was straight on the blower giving Starburst their contract back.

When Ellie phoned Annie Carter, which she did most weeks, she told her about the windows, and that the club would be closed all this week and next, and that the damage was costly both in terms of replacing windows and also replacing the massive promo photos and lost revenue. It was a bitch and she was never again going to mess with the laundry company.

'You think *you* got problems?' Annie told her about Sonny Gilbert running for the hills and about the man chasing her up the beach and into the house.

'Jesus! What happened then? You call the police?' Ellie was genuinely alarmed.

'He ran off. I was going to tie him up and ask questions, but he was gone too soon.'

'I thought you had a minder.'

'I did. Now I haven't. I fired him.'

'Get another one. One of those hard-arsed ex-SAS types. Don't piss about.'

'I was thinking of Steve Taylor, wondered if he'd like the travelling though. He's taken up with that new woman, hasn't he? Kirsty?' asked Annie.

Steve Taylor had been one of Max's chief enforcers for a lot of years. Steve had done well out of being Max's personal attack dog and he'd done a bit of minding for Annie too, off and on. She liked Steve, very much.

'I don't think it's serious, him and this "Kirsty". For his sake I hope not. Chris doesn't think it is. So yeah – ask Steve. I would,' said Ellie.

'I will,' said Annie.

But the best-laid plans, and all that.

# 60

There were worse things to do that smash up nightclubs, far worse. Bruno discovered this when Seamus and Cormac called upon him to assist them one dark summer night.

'Teach the fecker a lesson,' Seamus – or was it Cormac? – muttered as they all piled into one of the scrapyard vans.

They were spookily alike, the twins. Side by side, Bruno found them almost impossible to tell apart.

'My dick's bigger than his,' Cormac always joked.

'Yeah, but so's his gob,' Seamus would shoot back.

Both Delaney cousins were grinning, like kids out on a spree. Bruno kept quiet. He'd just do his job, then he'd fuck off back home to bed. He'd learned not to be curious; it was safer that way. He did what he had to do, and took no interest in it. He found that worked out fine for him.

He took no notice of Seamus's angry head wounds. The twins got into scrapes all the time, and it was best never to enquire closely about what they got up to. When Cormac parked the van up, Bruno looked out to see mist rising off water – they were by the canal. The silent boats and the bridges lent the scene a Victorian air, like Jack the Ripper was about to come sweeping through, his cloak spread out like the wings of a dark angel.

But there was nothing fanciful about all this. The doors opened, the interior light came on, and Bruno found himself looking at an unconscious man, thick-set, dark-haired, dressed in a camel-hair coat and expensive – new, judging from the unmarked soles – shoes.

The twins hauled the man out.

'He's feckin' heavy,' complained one.

'Bring the rope,' the other one snapped at Bruno.

They dragged the man free of the van.

'I'll give him a top-up,' said Cormac, grinning, pulling out a hypodermic syringe from his pocket.

Seamus shone a torch on the back of the man's head while Cormac injected the stuff into the man's thickly muscled neck, just under the hairline.

'Morphine,' said Cormac, seeing Bruno staring.

'Could do with a shot of it myself, right now,' said Seamus, indicating his wounded head. 'Bitch hit me hard.'

'Letting a feckin' woman best you? Pah,' scoffed his twin.

'Ah shaddup.'

The three of them dragged the unconscious man toward the bridge. They were all gasping and panting under his weight. They got the rope around his neck once they were on the bridge, tied it securely to one of the bridge's stanchions. Slowly, inch by inch, they let the man drop until he was hanging there, suspended by the rope biting into his neck.

'All done,' said Cormac.

Through the swirling mist he was staring at the dim outline of a long red narrowboat, its deck bristling with pots full of flowers. Nearby was another boat, a shelf full of books left out on its deck. The damp would ruin them.

'All right?' said Seamus.

'Thought I saw someone move over there,' said Cormac.

Seamus looked. 'Nah. Nothing moving now.'

Cormac didn't look convinced. Still, they piled back into the van and Bruno was glad that was over. But there was worse to come of course. There was *always* worse to come when you worked for the devil himself. There was no end to it. He was – just as the twins were – Redmond's toy, to do with as he wished. If Bruno protested, there was every chance that he would wind up just like the hanging man on the canal. He could run, he supposed – but to where? He felt, in his soul, that wherever he fled to, Redmond Delaney, all-seeing with his spies all over the city, all over the *country*, would always track him down and dole out punishment.

But . . . maybe there *was* an end. The end would be Max Carter, Redmond's sworn enemy, dead like the man on the bridge. Max had shot Tory, who'd adored Bruno, who had shown him warmth, friendship. Max had given the order to kill Nora. But then – Bruno had never really cared for Nora anyway. He'd never loved her – how could you love anyone so cold?

Still, there was no doubt in his mind that Max was Redmond's ultimate target. And now, after all this time, did Bruno *really* want to be a part of that? Did he truly want to kill Max Carter – his *brother*?

Yes.

Of course he did.

He would be revenged at last.

He told himself that, over and over.

# 61

DCI Hunter and DS Nolan were alerted to the finding of the corpse, found hanging from a footbridge over one of the quieter stretches of the London canal system, early in the day. By the time they arrived at the scene, the SOCO team were already there in force. It was high summer now, but down by the canal, shadowed as its chill waters were by tall graffiti-marked buildings, the heat of the day was a long time coming.

Hunter could see Draycott emerging from his Range Rover, neat and smiling as always. He went round to the back of the car and opened the boot, started pulling out white coveralls. He looked up as Hunter and Nolan approached. Philip Draycott was a small, precise man with a jovial air about him. He always wore colourful bow ties, sometimes adorned with snow scenes at Christmas, musical notes when it was the last night of the Proms, baby chicks at Easter. His small stab at levity, in the grimmest of jobs.

'Hunter,' he said.

'Hello.'

Draycott pointed. 'Down there.'

Hunter walked over to where the POLICE – DO NOT CROSS tapes were strung up at the south side of the bridge, blocking the towpath from curious onlookers. A uniformed PC was standing guard there and both Hunter and Nolan flashed their IDs. He lifted the tape, let them through. Hunter could feel the cold coming off the sludgy waters even though the sun was beginning to climb in the sky.

A man was hanging by his neck from the bridge, the rope digging deep into his flesh. His mud-brown eyes were half-open and filmy, his dark hair moving a little in the breeze. He was wearing an expensive-looking camel-coloured coat and nice shoes, Italian leather. A decent dark grey suit too, the lapels of which appeared to be hand-stitched, bespoke. The police photographer was taking his picture for posterity. When the photographer was finished, he nodded to the two burly coppers who were standing waiting patiently on the towpath. One of them came past Hunter and reappeared up on the bridge. From up there, he started to saw through the rope holding the cadaver with a knife. Two more uniforms came down the steps and they took the weight of the corpse as the rope gave way. They laid the man out on the towpath and stepped out of the way so that Draycott could approach.

SOCO were still laying out markers. The photographer hovered, snapping away, getting every detail down. There was little room here, so Hunter went up onto the bridge and stood there watching over the parapet while Draycott did his thing. Something about the hanging man looked familiar.

When the van arrived, they got the corpse into a black body bag and into the back of it, Draycott came up to Hunter.

'Suicide?' Hunter asked.

'Maybe. Stones in the overcoat pockets.'

'So we think he topped himself?'

'Wait until I get him on the slab.'

'ID?' Hunter asked.

Draycott held up a plastic evidence pouch with a wallet inside. 'Over a thousand pounds in there in cash. And a lot of debit and credit cards. And – yes – ID.'

'Who is he?'

'A Mr Steven Taylor.' Draycott pulled out a photograph. A pretty dark-haired woman, too much make-up, pouting at the camera with overinflated lips, a promise in her eyes. 'He's got a note in here naming her as his next of kin. Kirsty Allen.'

Hunter's mouth had dropped open.

'What?' asked Draycott.

'I thought he looked familiar,' said Hunter. 'I know him.'

'Not a personal friend, I hope?'

'No. Far from it.'

Steve Taylor had once been a lynchpin of the criminal underworld. These days he ran a legit operation, a security firm, while still working for the Carter lot.

'I'll get our boy to the lab and see what we can find out,' said Draycott, and walked back to his car.

'Steven Taylor?' asked DS Nolan, curious. He was pretty new, not yet familiar with the area.

'I'll show you the file,' said Hunter.

'Big one?'

'Massive. But slick as shit, as you'd expect with that lot. The Carters used to run a stretch of Bow and part of Limehouse, back in the day.'

'Run?' asked Nolan.

'Big criminal gang. Like the Richardsons and the Frasers held the south, the Regans the west, the Nashes had The Angel, the Delaneys had Battersea and a bit of Limehouse down by the docks until the Carters snatched it off them. The Krays had Bethnal Green. The Carters held Bow. Unlike the Kray twins, however, they never got caught. Never. Not once.

The Carters are an old Cockney family, East End born and bred. Queenie was the mother, scary old tart she was by all accounts. Strong woman. Fiery. Very old-school. Brought her three boys up hard. And Max was the eldest. The hardest.'

Nolan was watching his boss's face. 'What's the story on her, then? She still alive?'

'Nope,' said Hunter, frowning. 'She died in strange circumstances, actually – a robbery, I heard. She just happened to be there, and it did for her. Dicky heart. Before that, the Delaneys and the Carters were at loggerheads. After Queenie's death, things took on a whole new level of nastiness.'

'Like?'

'Shootings. Contract killings. What I'd have given to have tied that slippery bastard Carter down on one single charge. Never succeeded, though.'

Hunter fell silent. The Carter clan were a legend in the East End. When he'd been a rookie cop, still wet behind the ears, he'd learned of them, of Max the leader, of Jonjo, Eddie, and their mother, Queenie. Better men than him had tried to get the Carter boys put away, but then – did that even work? The biggest and best of the crims always managed to carry on their business, even when they were tucked safely away inside, and he knew Max Carter would have been no exception.

But all that was in the past, wasn't it?

So far as he knew, Max Carter was more or less straight now.

More or less.

And as for Max's wife Annie, well, Hunter hadn't seen her around town for a long, long while. He thought back, to times when she'd crossed his path. Dazzling woman. Bent as fuck. Tough as nails.

He had to shake himself then. The Carters were the past. Or at least he had thought so, until Taylor had shown up dead. Taylor had been with Max Carter since they were boys. He was Max's right hand.

*Never go back,* thought Hunter.

But to sort this mess out? He was afraid he might have to.

# 62

Bruno was just doing his job, following orders, smashing a thing or two to smithereens, collecting monies from around the manor, throwing scares into late-payers, administering a slap or two where necessary.

'Boss wants a word,' one of the twins said to Bruno. 'Over at the yard.'

There was a guard on the gate this time, a Dobermann Pinscher dog on a lead snarling, whippet-thin, at his side.

'All right?' the man said, letting Bruno and the twins through and locking the gates behind them.

The three men crossed the graveyard of vehicles, then walked on into a small office at the front of the house. The twins led the way to the old-type lift complete with its black wrought-iron doors. Bruno stepped in behind them and they yanked the cage shut. They stepped out again at the bottom into pitch blackness.

Suddenly the light came on. Bruno blinked. There sitting in his wheelchair in the centre of the room beneath the single overhead bulb was Redmond. This time, Bruno didn't look *at* him, exactly. He kept his gaze a little off to the side; that way, maybe he could cope with this and not get the horrors too much.

'Ah – Bruno. Did I ever tell you this? For quite a while – you won't believe this, but it's true – I turned to the church, just as you do, Bruno.' Redmond smiled. Or tried to. His face seemed all wrong, twisted, sneering. His empty eye socket was blank, blackened. 'Ah yes, that surprises you, I can see. I know you go to the church, Bruno. I'm always watching, never forget that. Yes, I turned to God, but I'm afraid that sometimes He has let me down.'

Bruno said nothing. His skin was crawling. Again he remembered the night by the canal, the twins injecting the bulky man just under the hairline – killing him – then hanging him up like a puppet on a chain.

'The thing is, Bruno, have I made all this clear? I am going to torment him.'

'Torment who?' asked Bruno, but of course he knew.

'Max Carter. Who else? I attack his businesses. His friends. His wife, did I mention her? Ex-wife now of course, but that flame always did burn brightly and I suspect it still does. His daughter too. You know what my plan is, Bruno?'

Bruno shook his head.

'I take it all from him, bit by bit, nice and slow. It's time he paid, and paid in full, for all the years he's crossed me and my family. And then, dear Bruno – I will kill him. I promise you that.' Redmond glanced back at the table. Surgical stuff there still. Hammers, saws, scalpels, retractors. 'Painfully. Slowly. Giving him plenty of time to consider the error of his ways.'

Bruno could say nothing. Wasn't that what *he'd* wanted, all along?

But if that was so, why did his flesh creep, why did he look at Redmond and feel nothing but revulsion?

'Now, Bruno. Good boy! I have something else I want you to do for me . . .'

# 63

DCI Hunter and DS Nolan went to Steve Taylor's house in Hampstead.

'Nice gaff,' said Nolan as they walked up to the front door of the high-gabled Victorian house on Parliament Hill. It was beautiful, elegant and set close to where you could walk through and admire the rolling acres of green Heath, bathe in the ponds, view the city's spellbinding skyline. 'And they say crime don't pay.'

'Yeah,' agreed Hunter, thinking that the place had obviously cost a stack of money but that it wouldn't do Steve Taylor any good now. 'But then – Steve Taylor hasn't committed crime for a long while, has he? He's gone straight. Runs a business for his mate Max – Carter Securities. Does nicely out of it too. Hires out bodyguards for celebs and aristos. It's spread all the way out to Essex and down into the Home Counties.'

Hunter rang the bell, and presently a tiny Malaysian woman in a black dress and white frilled pinafore came and peered out at them from around the half-closed door.

Hunter and Nolan held up their IDs.

'Police,' said Hunter. 'Can we speak to Kirsty Allen please?'

'Who is it, Latipa?' asked a high, strident female voice from somewhere back in the house.

The door swung wider as the woman looked back. Hurrying across the hall, fake dark tresses and large artificial boobs bouncing, came a woman wearing a lime-green bikini, a matching brief kimono and twinkly high-heeled silver sandals that beat out a rapid tattoo on the cream-coloured travertine marble hall floor. 'Is it the police? Well about time. I said the day before yesterday that I was worried but nobody came, and now he's been out all night.'

The woman charged up to the door, pushing the smaller woman out of the way. She glared out at the two cops.

'So you've pulled your fucking finger out at last,' she snapped at Hunter. 'When are you people going to take this seriously? My boyfriend's gone missing. No explanation. No nothing. And all you do is take notes and . . .'

'You are Kirsty Allen, yes?'

'Yes! Of course I am.'

'Can we come in?' said Hunter. 'We need to sit down and talk.'

★

They broke the news. She cried. Latipa stood in the doorway, listening, looking, while in the background D:Ream were singing 'Things Can Only Get Better'. When that stopped, an overexcited DJ moved on to a track by Boyzone.

'Perhaps you could get Miss Allen a cup of tea?' suggested Hunter.

Latipa snorted, turned away.

Kirsty paused in the midst of her tears and scowled. 'That cow! She's never liked me, you know. You know what her name means? It means someone who's gentle and kind. Can you believe that? Well I can't, the chippy little whore. She worked for Steve. Not me. And now he's bloody gone . . .'

The crying started again. 'What the fuck am I going to do now?' she sobbed.

Neither of the detectives could answer that.

'We believe Mr Taylor was in the security business.'

She nodded. 'That's right. He worked for the Carter family. Did well out of it. That's his BMW out front, top of the range. He liked nice things. Treated me like a lady. You know.'

Hunter didn't know. Neither did Nolan. But he knew the Carters all right and he knew they always ran a profitable operation.

Latipa was back. She stood in the doorway again, her arms folded, her face grimly satisfied. No teacups anywhere in sight.

'You'll have to get out!' she said loudly. Then, more loudly: 'Out! Out! His peoples will get this place and you will have to go back to whatever you were doing before in those dirty clubs. Shaking your arse, yes?'

Kirsty surged to her feet. 'Shut the fuck up!' she yelled.

'You treat me bad, you expect nice? Well, lady, you got shock coming. Good times over.'

Latipa turned and was gone again.

Sobbing, Kirsty sank back down. 'Oh Christ, oh Christ,' she moaned.

'What was your occupation?' asked DS Nolan. 'Before you moved in with Mr Taylor?'

'None of your bloody business,' she snapped tearfully.

'But it is our business, Miss Allen,' Hunter pointed out. 'This could turn out to be a murder investigation.'

She stared at the pair of them. 'Well don't look at me! You said he was found hanging from a footbridge. I thought . . . well I thought you meant he'd done himself in. You didn't say a damned thing about murder.'

'Did you notice that Mr Taylor was in a low mood?' asked DS Nolan. 'Was he maybe getting treatment for depression? Was there ever anything like that?'

She was shaking her head. 'No! What, Steve? He was rock-steady. Never turned a hair. If the roof caved in, he wouldn't even blink.' She gulped. 'I liked that about Steve. You felt safe with him.'

'And your occupation, miss?' persisted Nolan. 'Can you tell us that please?'

'Dancer,' she sniffed.

From the hallway there came a loud snort of laughter. Latipa sashayed by, grinning, wielding a wet mop.

'Exotic dancer,' Kirsty elaborated.

'Stripper!' shouted Latipa from the hallway. 'She take her clothes off, is disgusting!'

Kirsty was on her feet again. 'I told you – you shut the fuck up!' she bellowed.

The detectives took note of Kirsty's last place of employment, then decided it was time to leave.

★

After Hunter and Nolan had gone, Kirsty felt the need to see a friendly face. She phoned the man she'd been seeing on the quiet and asked him to come over.

'Sure,' said Bruno. 'I'll be right there.'

As Bruno put the phone down, Redmond, who was sitting right beside him getting another morphine dose off his male nurse, said: 'That her?'

Bruno nodded.

'Good,' said Redmond. 'Off you go.'

Bruno picked up his jacket, put it on, swiped a hand through his blond hair to tidy it, and left.

# 64

Before he went to see Kirsty, who he had been hanging around with – on Redmond's instructions – since he came out of prison, Bruno went and sat in the church for a while. It reminded him, being in here, of Nora and her goody-goody mates, of Sunday school and harvest festival, none of which were fond memories really. But slowly, sitting there in the cavernous building, looking at the cross behind the altar, he began to feel steadier. The inner tremor that any meeting with Redmond Delaney induced in him was starting to recede.

'Can I help you, my son?'

It was the same vicar – too plump, too young, his eyes so wide and innocent. Bruno had *never* felt innocent. Or young. He had never even felt happy, except perhaps when he was *thunking* his knives into the dartboard, honing his skills, forgetting everything else.

*And then, dear Bruno – I will kill him.*

After making him suffer the torments of hell, losing his livelihood, his friends, his wife, his child, then Redmond was going to do it at last. He was going to kill Max.

Bruno thought of the surgical instruments, laid out ready on the table in the cellar. Bruno could feel the road he was on forking; he could take one path or the other. But which? Truth was, he *admired* Max Carter. Didn't want to, *hated* to, but he did. He feared twisted, hideous Redmond. But . . . the Delaneys had looked after him, hadn't they? Max's lot never had. And they'd taken Nora from him. Worse – they'd taken Tory.

But . . . all those years inside he'd done for the Delaney mob. Years that he would never get back. Was that 'looking after' him? Really? And now they'd used him again, placed him in the Shalimar spying out the land, which was where he'd met Kirsty, who was an attractive girl and an OK shag and tied up with the Carter business.

'My son?' The vicar was still there, looking down at the bowed blond head of Bruno. 'Can I help?'

'No,' said Bruno, standing up. 'I don't think anyone can.'

# 65

Annie phoned Ellie Brown in London from her Montauk house. She was due back shortly in New York to carry on with interviews for Sonny's position. Time was tight, but this was important. She didn't have Steve's number to ask him about resolving her security problem, but she was sure Ellie would.

Annie was still shaken from what had happened with the man chasing her up from the beach. She found herself waking in the night, sweating, anxious, thinking someone was in the room with her, knowing that nobody was. For the sake of her own sanity she needed to get this sorted out, and Steve was just the man to do it. She explained the situation to Ellie and asked for Steve's number.

Ellie was silent.

'Ellie? You there?' Annie asked.

'You mean nobody's told you?'

'Told me what?'

'Oh God.' Ellie's sigh shuddered down the line. 'What else could happen? It's just one damned thing after another. We had all this business with the front of the club being knocked in, and then, look, we had real bad news. Terrible news.'

'*What?*' The front of the club? What the hell? 'What terrible news?' she asked.

More silence.

'Ellie? What's going on?'

'News about Steve. Steve Taylor.'

'What about him?'

'He's dead.'

Annie looked at the phone. 'You what?'

'They found him hanging off one of the canal bridges.'

'Wait, I . . . just hold on. What are you saying? You mean Steve killed himself? Our Steve? That's not possible.'

'Annie! I'm telling you, he's in the morgue. The police are crawling all over the canal. His young bit of stuff, you know her, Kirsty? She told me. She's just left here weeping and wailing. I'm telling you, it's happened.'

'My God,' said Annie, shocked.

'I know, I know.'

Annie couldn't take it in. 'Do you really think he'd kill himself?'

'Steve? I'd have sworn not. I didn't think he had a frayed nerve in his entire body. But there it is – they found him like that.'

'God, that's awful.'

Annie stood there looking out at the ocean, wondering what the hell to say next, trying to take it in and failing. Steve had been with the Carters all through the years, a steady, reassuring presence. All the security issues she'd been confronted with would have been solved in an instant with Steve on the job.

'What about Tone? Does Tone know?' she asked.

'Chris broke the news to him. He's as shocked as the rest of us. They been mates for years, him and Steve and Max, you know they have. It's bloody tragic.'

'Is Max due back in London, with all this kicking off?'

'Tomorrow I think. I'm not sure. You're coming over, aintcha?'

'What? No, I'm up to my arse here in work . . .' Warning bells were ringing in Annie's brain. There was no way she was going to come face to face with Max. She'd got his damned note and she'd ripped it up. She'd blocked all his calls. Get in touch with him like he'd asked? After a year of utter silence? No. He could go fuck himself.

'Come on, you have to! There'll be the funeral. Kirsty's going to arrange it,' she said, 'because apparently he didn't have anyone even close. Not unless some long-distant cousin can be tracked down by the solicitors, which of course Kirsty is praying don't happen. Steve never talked about his family, did he? Anyway, Kirsty's still living at Steve's place, taken up squatter's rights. But she might yet have to shift her arse out of there. We'll see, won't we. But you'll want to be here for the funeral won't you? Christ, don't say you won't be here. You have to be. This is *Steve*.'

Annie closed her eyes. Fuck it. 'No,' she said.

'Oh come on . . .'

'I said no.'

'For God's sake,' said Ellie, and started to cry. 'Oh, this is awful! We're losing everyone, aren't we? First Dolly in the shooting at the Palermo, and now Steve. Come on, Annie. For pity's sake, *please* say you'll be there. I don't know how I'm going to cope if you're not.'

Annie stared at the phone.

She thought again of the note Max had sent her. The *pizzino*. Well fuck that. Fuck *him*. She wouldn't have to see Max at all, except maybe briefly, at the funeral. And she could make a quick exit from that. Ellie was right – she ought to attend. Steve had been a major part of her life, of *all* their lives, for a long time. And Ellie clearly needed her there. She had to at least show her face, pay her respects.

'Yeah. All right. I'll be there,' she said, and put down the phone.

# 66

'He wasn't exactly squeaky clean was he?' observed DS Nolan, tossing Steve Taylor's file on Hunter's desk and throwing himself into a chair. 'You read that?'

'Many, many times,' said Hunter grimly.

Nolan thought that his boss was just *made* for grim. Hunter had dark hair, dark eyes, a long lugubrious face and a turned-down trap of a mouth that really belonged in an undertaker's parlour, not a cop shop. Nolan had only been working with Hunter for a little while, but already he respected him enormously. Hunter was a true detective, digging out truth the way an anteater digs out termites. He never gave up, never gave in. He was implacable, thorough, and for that reason, he was fearsome. Nolan hoped that one day he would be even half as good a detective as Hunter was.

'Years ago . . .' said Nolan.

'Yes, I know. Years ago he was just a heavy working for Max Carter. Well, he still works for Carter, and he appears to have done bloody well out of it. The place on Parliament Hill, for instance. But you see, Nolan? In the end, crime really does not pay, and if Steve Taylor was alive and sitting right where you are sitting now, he would admit that's true.'

'But he isn't,' said Nolan.

'No, he's not. He's in the morgue across town.'

Hunter stood up and slipped on his suit jacket. Black, of course, and Nolan briefly wondered if Hunter actually *worked* that undertaker vibe, used it as a handy tool to intimidate wrongdoers. It sure as crap intimidated *him*.

'Which is where we are going right now,' said Hunter, sweeping towards the door. 'Come on, Nolan. Chop chop.'

★

The city morgue at Westminster was just about the last place in the world Nolan wanted to visit. He guessed that Hunter felt very much the same, but if you wanted to speak to the pathologist and to look over a body, that was where you had to go to do it.

As soon as they were in the autopsy room and Draycott had Steve Taylor laid out ready on the steel table, in they went. Hunter took a seat by the sink. Nolan stood beside him, no keener than his boss to venture too close to the centre of the action.

'So what do you think?' asked Hunter as soon as they were settled. 'Any possibility of suicide?'

'Well – the hyoid cartilage is broken, clearly from the pressure of the rope. But those stones in his pockets? I think they were placed there by someone else, someone wearing gloves.'

'Murder then?'

Draycott nodded. 'Yes, but not by hanging. He died from *this*. Take a look.'

The pathologist was beckoning them over to the table. They went, reluctantly. Neither wanted a grandstand view of death, of the big Y incision the pathologist had already made in Steve Taylor's earthly remains, of the red-raw marks around the corpse's neck. The pathologist lifted the dark hair just behind Taylor's ear.

'Look. You see? He was injected just under the hairline here. Morphine. Huge dose, knocked him right out fast. Then all his assailants had to do was string him up.' Phil gazed down at the face of Steve Taylor. 'A message to someone maybe? It's a shame. He was a good-looking man.'

Both detectives looked down at the dead man on the slab. It was true that Steve Taylor was impressive. But then he would be – once, he had been part of a crime lord's arsenal, the Carters' attack dog. Taylor's corpse was big, muscular rather than fat, solid as a tank. The mud-brown eyes were half-open, filming over, but the face in repose was strong, serene. In life, you'd find him intimidating. Now, in death, he had the air of a fallen gladiator; a fighter felled not by a sword but by a tiny little needle.

'Prime of life,' sighed the pathologist. 'But killed, no doubt about it.'

'Killed for what reason? He upset someone on behalf of the Carter lot? But then – I thought they were all straight now? Model citizens?'

Draycott placed the sheet back over the corpse's face and smiled gently at the two policemen. 'That, gentlemen, is your problem, I am glad to say. Not mine.'

# 67

Later that same day, Hunter and Nolan stood looking up at a modest business frontage tucked into a corner of an industrial estate. *Carter Security* was picked out in gold on black over the entrance. The bell on the door announced their arrival and they stepped inside. There was purple deep-plush carpet on the floor, two empty desks. A blonde girl of about nineteen was sitting behind a third, the furthest from the door, crying into a tissue. She jerked upright, sniffing, blinking back tears, as the two men came in. Hunter flourished his ID; so did Nolan.

'Police, miss. And you are . . . ?'

'Julie. Julie Adams.' She tucked her crumpled tissue up her sleeve. Her mascara was smudged all over her face. 'Are you here about Mr Taylor?' she asked, then started to cry again. 'Sorry,' she wailed. 'It's so awful. I mean, he was so *nice*. So polite. And then to do that! To hang himself. Why would he do that?'

Neither Hunter nor Nolan said that Steve Taylor had not hanged himself. It was obvious that passing on the news that Taylor's death had not been suicide but murder would shock her to the core.

'I let myself in this morning,' Julie was going on. 'I've worked here for almost two years and that's what I do, every morning. Mr Taylor gave me a key and I open up for him.

But after hearing the news yesterday, I just didn't know what to do. So I thought I'd better carry on, be here ready to take any calls. Did I do wrong?'

'Not at all. In fact I would say your conduct has been exemplary,' said Hunter. 'When did you last see Mr Taylor?' he asked, sitting down on the other side of her desk.

'The day before yesterday. He was in early . . .'

'How early?' asked DS Nolan, whipping out his note-book.

'Nine-thirty. He said he had some business – Romford, I think it was – and that he'd be out for the rest of the day.'

'He didn't say who he was meeting?'

'No.'

'He kept a business diary?'

'Oh, that.' She gave a tiny, tearful smile. 'He had one but he never used it. Used to drive us all spare. Clients would ring and we wouldn't have a clue where he was.'

'Who else works in this office?' asked Nolan.

'Terry Foreman and Jimmy Iles. They'll be in at ten.'

'Late start,' said Nolan, taking note of the names.

'Well, they work on into the evening pretty often.'

'Where is the diary?' asked Hunter, hoping against hope that just this once Steve Taylor had broken the habit of a lifetime and put a name, address or telephone number in there.

'In his office. Back there.'

'You keep busy, do you?' asked Nolan, looking around. The place looked innocuous, like a dentist's waiting room.

'Very busy. We cover celebrities and everything.'

'I'll just . . .' said Hunter and went off into the inner office with Nolan at his heels.

★

Julie was right. There was nothing in the diary. Nothing of any interest in the office at all, really, except for a few signed and framed pictures of Steve Taylor grinning with his arms wrapped around a number of high-profile celebs. Hunter and Nolan bagged up everything that seemed useful and took their leave of Carter Security, asking that Julie and her workmates would come down the cop shop when they had a free moment today and make statements. Julie, sweetly and still in tears, told them that they would, and she thanked the policemen for their help.

'It's so sad,' she said as a parting shot, starting to cry all over again.

'Yes. It is,' said Hunter.

# 68

The first thing Max Carter did when he got back to London from Majorca was go to his late mum Queenie's place, which he kept and maintained more for sentimental reasons than for anything else. The second thing he did was to turn on the TV news and when he did that he got the shock of his life. The female newscaster was talking about a man identified as Steven Taylor who had been found hanging off a London canal bridge. But it couldn't be the Steve Taylor he knew. That wasn't possible. Was it?

Max turned the TV off and phoned Chris Brown and said had he seen the news.

Chris had.

'It's not *our* Steve, is it?' asked Max.

'Yeah. I'm sorry as hell to have to tell you this, but it is. What a fuck-up,' said Chris. 'Whoever would have thought that Steve would do a thing like that? Topping his bloody self?'

*Not me for one,* thought Max. A crippling spasm of loss coursed through him. He'd been hoping Chris would say it was a mistake, that this was a Steve Taylor none of them knew. But it was *their* Steve, the same Steve who had been in Max's life just about forever, who'd grown up with him, worked for him, been a firm ally and a close friend. Now, he was dead.

'You're OK?' he asked Chris. 'You and Ellie?'

'Not really. Some joker rammed the front.'

'What?' Staggered by what had happened in Majorca, reeling from the news about Steve, Max felt like he'd just had the wind punched out of him all over again. 'For Chrissakes, why the hell would anyone do that?'

'Think it was something to do with the laundry company. The arseholes. We can't prove it. Just have to soak it up and carry on. They took it out with a lorry. Lot of damage, but no one hurt.'

'Sort it out with the insurance.'

'Yeah sure. Leave it with me. I'm so bloody sorry to hear about Steve. I really am. I know you and him have been tight for a long time.'

When Max got off the phone after speaking to Chris he put a call through to the US, to Annie's Montauk place. John the maintenance man picked up and told Max that his ex-wife was not there.

'So where is she?' asked Max.

John was apologetic. 'She's been back in the city for the past few days, but she phoned to let me know she was leaving the country yesterday. She flew out of JFK on Concorde headed for London. Before she left she spoke to Ellie Brown over there in England and Ellie told her there'd been a death – most unfortunate.'

So Annie knew about Steve. And Concorde? That shaved hours off a flight across the pond.

'Right,' said Max.

'Um – Mr Carter?'

'Yeah, what?'

'We have had some trouble here.'

'What trouble?'

'Mrs Carter said not to tell anyone, but in all conscience ...'

John told him about the man chasing Annie along the beach and up into the house.

'And that was why she contacted Ellie Brown, asking about Steve Taylor, wanting to get his contact details. She wondered if he'd come over as she wasn't happy with her security, and Ellie told her the bad news.'

Max was staring at the phone. Annie'd had trouble in Montauk. Chris and Ellie'd had trouble in London. *He'd* had trouble in Majorca, poor bloody Jaime getting done like that and all that peculiar nonsense he'd spouted before he died, about a brother. He still couldn't make sense of that. And Steve Taylor found hanging – the biggest shock of all. He said goodbye to John and went upstairs to shower and dress in clean clothes.

Coming back down, he went into the tiny lounge and stood there looking at the picture hanging over the gas fire. It was a portrait of Queenie, his mother; he'd commissioned it years ago, engaged a professional artist. Max thought it captured Queenie's forthright personality perfectly – but he knew Queenie had never liked it.

He left the house and hailed a cab at the end of the road.

# 69

The house Max went to was quiet that evening, the soft summer half-light draped around it like a cloak. The motion sensor porch light came on when Max put his key in the lock and went in, noting that the house alarm was set so that an intruder in the downstairs portion of the house would trigger it, while upstairs the occupants could move around freely. Wondering if she'd changed it, hoping she hadn't – he tapped in the code to switch the alarm off.

Once inside he paused and looked around him in the dim light. Here was another remnant of that other life – the life she'd had not with him but with Constantine Barolli, the Mafia don. It was a grand house and the hallway announced that, loud and clear. There were chequered black and white marble tiles on the floor, massive chandeliers overhead, priceless side tables holding lavish floral displays and a deep-buttoned porter's chair was tucked into a corner, covered in soft tan leather.

Max went up the stairs and, as he reached the top, he felt a movement. Something *swooshed* past his head, so close that he could feel the air stir. He sidestepped quickly, reached out and grabbed his attacker, spun him around so that his back *smacked* up against the wall. He heard a gasp. Then he realised a pair of breasts were pressing into his chest, and that the form was light. He was holding a woman.

'Quick reactions,' he said. 'But not necessary. It's me.'

'Oh for God's sake,' said Annie angrily. 'What are you doing, skulking about in the night? Where the hell did you spring from? How come you've still got a key?'

'I've just got back from Majorca. I was coming to talk to you.'

'What? Why?'

'What do you mean, why? I've been trying to get in touch with you. You know I have. All you ever do is block me.'

'There's a reason for that.'

'Oh? What is it?'

'I don't bloody well want to talk to you.'

'And that damned note I sent you, did you get that? Of course you did, you just ignored it. So don't ask me why I've come in here unannounced. If I'd knocked on that door downstairs you wouldn't have answered. I thought that if I sent you one of those damned coded notes you might take notice. But of course you didn't.'

'No. I shredded it and chucked it in the ocean. And no, I wouldn't have answered the door to you. Why would I? Look – just hand that damned key over, will you?' she spat out.

'Take it off me,' invited Max, starting to get pretty mad himself.

'The buzzer by the bed went off. It lets me know when the front door opens. I thought you were *him* again.'

Max reached out and flicked the light switch on. And there she was. His ex-wife. She was glaring at him, holding a four-inch stiletto-heeled shoe in her right hand. She was wearing an apricot silk chemise. She looked sexy as hell, and mad enough to spit.

'Who's him?' he asked. 'The bloke who chased you up the beach in Montauk?'

She grew still. 'How do you know about that?'

'John told me.'

'Well he had no right to.'

'Take it up with him.'

'Can you let go of my wrist? You're crushing it.'

Max let Annie go. She dropped the shoe and went over to the door into the master suite and vanished inside. Max followed and found her sitting on the disordered bed, clutching at her chest, gulping down breaths.

'Jesus! You nearly gave me a heart attack,' she complained. 'Don't *ever* creep up on me like that.'

Max went over there and sat down too. 'Tell me about what happened in Montauk.'

'Do I have to, right now? There's not much to tell. A man chased me up from the beach and into the house. I whacked him with the kiyoga and he legged it. That's about it, really.'

'You didn't report it?'

'You joking? That was Constantine's house. I still get drive-bys from the fuzz once a week, like I'm carrying on all the old traditions or something. I don't think they'd rush to my rescue, should anything unforeseen happen.'

And there it was again. Him. *Constantine.* That old bastard had stood between them for years. Max had tried, but he really wasn't the forgiving type; he had never been able to forget her relationship with that man.

When he'd suffered that near-fatal accident in Majorca back in the Seventies, he'd not only been physically injured but mentally, too. Two long years had passed. And by then? It was already too late. She'd made another life, a new life – with Constantine Barolli, the Mafia godfather. She'd breezed right on, forgotten him.

Would *he* have done the same, in her shoes?

No. Never.

All the baggage from her life with the Mafia don lingered. And then there had been that business up in Scotland. And she still had all the accoutrements of a Mafia queen so how could he forget all the shit that had gone before? She still had this house, the Montauk place, the *Annie's* club in Times Square, the Central Park apartment. All of it had been Constantine's – and now it was hers. Day after day, Max's nose had been rubbed in it. He *wanted* to forget all that had gone on between her and the don. He had even sworn to himself – and to her – that he would let it go, let it rest. But he couldn't. It just wasn't possible.

'I'm tired,' said Annie. 'Jet lag's a bitch, even on Concorde. Can we talk about this in the morning?'

'Yeah. Sure. If you can spare the time.'

'Don't push it,' she snapped.

'Where's Rosa? She here?'

Rosa was Annie's old maid, usually a fixture in the house.

'Over at her sister's,' said Annie. 'Peckham. No point her being here when the place is empty, and I haven't had much of a chance to let her know about my change of plan yet.'

'You don't have any physical security here? Only the alarm and that bloody buzzer?'

'No. I don't. And I'll want that key back, Max. I mean it.'

He stood up. 'We'll talk in the morning,' he said. 'I'll take one of the spare rooms.'

'If you want to.' She shrugged.

'Will you stop with the attitude? I'm too tired for all this,' he said.

'Yes? Well so am I. So why don't you fuck off, Max?' she said angrily.

'Delighted to,' said Max, and left the room.

# 70

Next morning, Annie got up, washed, dressed, took a quick call from DCI Hunter in the study downstairs, then – shaken by what the detective had told her – she stepped outside. The summer weather had turned and now it was raining. She took a cab across town and alighted at the entrance to the Shalimar, where the rain and the wind was blowing in through the open double red doors at the front of the building. Chris Brown was there, sweeping up huge piles of shattered glass. Ellie was trying to vacuum bits out of the carpet – without, it seemed, much success. Workmen were in, boarding up the shattered frontage. Ellie switched off the Hoover, puffed out her cheeks and glared at her old friend as she came in.

'How's it going?' asked Annie, stepping gingerly, glass crunching underfoot.

'How does it look?' Ellie shot back. 'Can you believe this? Some bastard stove in the windows. Don't ask me why.'

'Why?' said Chris loudly. Now it was his turn to give Annie the evil eye, which he then turned on Ellie. 'You *know* why. You started farting about with the supplier and the supplier didn't like it. Hence the broken glass. Hence the shit we're in, thank you so very much, *dearest*.'

'Shall we . . . ?' Annie said, indicating to Ellie that they ought to go through to the bar and leave Chris to it, before this developed into a *real* slanging match.

'Yeah, let's,' said Ellie, happily abandoning the Hoover to lead the way to where it was quieter and warmer. 'Drink?' she offered Annie, stepping behind the bar, snapping on the radio. Seal was singing 'Kiss From A Rose'.

Annie looked at her watch. 'It's half past nine.'

'Oh I was forgetting. You can't hold your drink, can you. One sherry and you're out.' She sent a grim smile Annie's way. 'Well *I'm* having one. Need it, all this crap going on.' She went to the optics and poured herself a brandy. She gulped down a mouthful and slapped the glass on the bar. 'Whoever thinks it's a good idea to get married, let me tell you, they are fucking crazy,' she pointed out.

'Chris is a diamond,' said Annie.

'What, compared to Max?' Ellie gave a smirk and took another long sip of the brandy and looked at Annie's face. 'Last time we spoke, you and him hadn't spoken in a year.'

Annie gave a sharp sigh. 'He turned up at my place last night.'

'And?' Ellie's dark eyes were alight with interest. 'How's it going?'

'How's what going?'

'*You* know. You and him.'

'We slept in separate rooms.'

'His choice or yours?'

'I didn't exactly lay out the red carpet. Why would I?'

'Never go to bed mad,' said Ellie.

'What, stay up and keep arguing?' Annie gave a rueful smile. It had shaken her, Max's sudden appearance. So much for avoiding him. He'd cut straight through that, showing up unannounced, walking in on her as if he had every right to do so – which he didn't. He'd given up that right a year ago.

'This is bad, this news about Steve,' she said.

'Yeah.' Ellie drained her glass. 'Bloody sad. Hung hisself, yeah?'

'I talked to the Bill this morning.'

'Poor old Steve. He was always flash, wasn't he. Liked his Rolex and his fancy cars and his young bits of stuff. She's been in here, the latest one, Kirsty. Sobbing and yelling. Crocodile tears, I reckon. She worked here for a while and she was a bit of a one for the barmen, I know that for a fact. He liked to put the whole display out on show, our Steve, didn't he.' Ellie's eyes misted. 'Bless him. And really, where was the harm? So long as he was happy.'

'I don't think the police have got anything to go on, yet,' said Annie. She pondered over her next sentence and decided to go ahead anyway, even if it *did* upset Ellie. With things like this going on, it was better to be aware, surely? 'The police don't think it's suicide, Ells. Hunter told me it was murder.'

Ellie's face froze. Not saying a word, she went back to the optic and shot another inch of amber fluid into the glass. She turned back to Annie, took a sip. Then she quickly downed the rest.

'You're bloody serious,' she said at last.

Annie told Ellie what Hunter had told her. Ellie listened. Then she blurted out: 'Hold on. Hold *on*. This is . . . God, what the hell . . . ?'

'Frightening,' said Annie.

'Yes! Does Max know about this?'

'Not yet. At least, I don't think so.'

'Someone had a go at you over in the States.'

'That's why I phoned you. I was going to get Steve to come over and sort out my security.'

'Wait on. We just had our frontage smashed in. We thought it was the laundry people. What if it wasn't? What if this is someone having a pop at the Carter firm?' Ellie paused. 'You. Steve. This place. It could all be connected.'

Annie didn't want to think that. She *was* thinking it, had been thinking it since she'd arrived back in London. She was going to have to speak to Max about this. Only . . . they weren't speaking. Currently, they were snarling at each other, at best.

'Ellie, keep calm,' she said.

'Keep *calm*?' Ellie blew out her cheeks. 'Is that all you got? Keep fucking *calm*?'

Annie picked up her bag from the bar. 'At the moment?' she said. 'Yeah, it is.'

And she left the club.

## 71

'Where the fuck have you been?' asked Max when Annie got back to Holland Park.

She found him sitting behind the desk in the office, with its old-colonial-style furnishings – tan leather chesterfields, gold banker's lamp on the desk, priceless Aubusson rugs on the brightly polished hardwood floor. All this had been Constantine's choice of décor, and she had never got around to changing it. It suited the house, so why bother?

'And a very good morning to you, too,' said Annie, throwing her bag onto the couch and herself after it. She let out a breath, closed her eyes. Hoped – briefly – that when she opened them, he'd be gone. Anywhere, just not in her face. Back to Barbados, maybe. That would be good.

'So,' she said, opening her eyes. He was still there. Annoying. 'What's been going on?'

Max heaved a sharp sigh. 'I got a call from Benito.'

'Benito? What did he want?'

'He had something to tell me.'

'Like what?' Annie'd met Benito. He was an old soldier who long ago had turned to God, devoting himself to His service in the monastery up in the mountains. Benito had saved Max, been a friend to him when he had no others.

Max stood up and moved around the desk. He came and sat down on the couch opposite her, the coffee table and about a hundred miles – she felt – between them. But there was still that old stirring, she acknowledged, and was irritated by it. Max was so damned *macho*. Sitting there, leaning forward with his elbows on his knees and wearing jeans and a plain white shirt, he still had a way of knocking the breath out of her. His shirt sleeves were rolled up to show darkly tanned and muscular arms lightly furred with black hair. His eyes were that dense, dark blue, boring into hers. Max radiated power; he always seemed on the point of movement and he was always in control of any situation. And whether he made her furious or not – and mostly, he did – she still always felt that irritating *hit* of his maleness, his acute physicality, whenever she was near him. And right now she really, really wished she didn't.

'I wasn't pissing about with the phone calls and the note. I have to talk to you,' said Max. 'About what happened out at the finca in nineteen-seventy.'

Annie hadn't been expecting *that*. And she wasn't pleased by it, either. That had been one of the worst times in her entire life. Losing him. Losing Layla. Thinking that she would never, ever get either of them back again. Fighting to survive, to somehow make something workable out of the most God-awful mess.

'Why would you want to talk about that?' she asked faintly.

'Because when I went up to the monastery last week Benito had someone there to meet me, a face from the past. It was the boy who found me back then.'

Annie sat up straight. 'Jaime?'

Max nodded. 'Yes, Jaime.' There was a flicker of pain in his eyes, there and then quickly gone.

'What?' Now Annie was alarmed. Whatever this was, it was something bad. 'What happened?'

Max told her. He left nothing out, not even Jaime's awful death. Not even what the poor bastard had said with his final struggling breath.

'Your *brother*?' Annie echoed. 'But . . .'

'But Eddie's dead. Long dead, years ago. He couldn't have been talking about Eddie.'

'But . . . Jonjo's dead too,' said Annie.

'But there it is,' said Max. 'Jaime said *my brother* had paid him to search for me, to find me.' He stared hard at her. 'Look. I wasn't there, I didn't see Jonjo's body. But you did. So tell me. Don't leave any small detail out, OK? Tell me what you saw that day.'

'He was *dead*,' said Annie. 'Shot through the head. There was a bullet hole *here*.' She pointed to the space between her brows. 'Right here. There was blood in the water. I saw his body floating in the pool when I came round. I thought it was you. I dived in, swam out, turned him over and then I realised it was Jonjo.'

Annie thought about that. She had always disliked Jonjo; he was a mouth-breather, thick and aggressive and he treated all women badly, like useful commodities he could pick up and put down on a whim. She remembered him all too well, him and his endless procession of blondes, his obsession with Marilyn Monroe. He'd always hated Annie because she was bright, brunette, absolutely not a bit of fluff to be picked up and then discarded. She was her own woman. She had her own mind. Jonjo hated that.

'And what then?' asked Max, his face grim.

'Then?' Annie dragged her hands through her hair. This was weird. Just *ludicrous*. There was no way Max's brother could have paid Jaime the goat boy to search for Max. She was *certain* Jonjo had been dead in the pool. 'Then . . . well, nothing. He had the girl with him, didn't he. One of his blondes. Jean? No, Jeanette. That was her name.'

'And?'

'We'd both been drugged. Rufio and Inez . . . oh Christ, I've told you what happened to them. We were shaken up. Jeanette was hysterical – I had to calm her down. Then the phone calls started, saying you were dead and that if I ever wanted to see Layla alive again, I was going to have to find half a million pounds. Jeanette and I stayed the night, locked inside the finca. I got the shotgun down out of the loft, thinking whoever'd done the hit and snatched you and Layla could come back overnight. They didn't. And next morning when I looked out, Jonjo's body was gone.'

Max got up and paced around the room. 'So you believed Jonjo was dead.'

'I did. Of *course* I did.' Annie gave a long, drawn-out sigh. 'Everything started going wrong from that point onwards, didn't it. Because of what happened that day, I had to get help.'

Max stopped pacing and stared at her. 'Yeah. From Constantine fucking Barolli.'

Annie returned his stare. 'You owe him your daughter's life. And mine.'

'I know what I owe him. I know everything about that cunt now, don't I. *And* about you. I wish I bloody didn't.'

Annie veered off that subject. They were here, speaking, which was something of a miracle in itself, but push it too far on that topic of conversation and they would both start saying things they wished they hadn't.

'Jaime has to be mistaken,' she said. 'There's no way Jonjo could have survived.'

Max started walking again. 'I think someone killed Jaime to stop him telling me what he did. They were a little too late, though. He managed to say that my brother paid him to find me.'

'No, Max. No! It's just not possible.'

'And then there's all this other strange shit going on. Steve getting done for God's sake.'

'Hunter says it was murder for sure,' said Annie. 'He phoned me this morning. Told me.'

Max was silent for a long, long while. Then he said: 'The lorry through the front of the club. And you, someone was after you.'

'Jaime was mistaken,' said Annie firmly.

'Or you were,' said Max, stopping in front of her.

'What?'

'You could have been wrong about Jonjo being dead. You could have been, admit it.'

'*What?*' Annie shook her head vehemently. 'Max, I saw the damage. I was *this close* . . .'

She held up a hand, inches away from her face.

Max looked down at her. 'No. I think you're wrong. Somehow – God knows how – I think Jonjo's alive.'

# 72

'That's ridiculous,' said Annie flatly. 'It's just plain crazy. If Jonjo was alive, why wouldn't he make himself known to you? It's been years, years in which you've had no contact from him whatsoever. Wouldn't he try to get in touch? Of course he would.'

'That day at the finca,' Max persisted. 'You were in shock. You must have been. The pool house was blown up. You'd been drugged. You woke up and there's a dead body floating in the pool. You said yourself that you panicked. Dived in, swam out. You must have been half out of your mind at that point. You *could* be mistaken.'

'No. I know what I saw. There was blood in the pool.'

'Red dye?'

'Oh sure,' said Annie sarkily. 'That makes perfect sense! And how do you explain the bullet hole? And the fact that he wasn't breathing?'

'Shit, *I* don't know. Maybe it was make-up. Maybe he was holding his breath.'

'For what purpose? Look. Say the wound was make-up and the blood was dye. Say he was holding his breath. Well, why? To fake his death? In that case, why was he doing that? And as I said before, why hasn't he been in touch? Did he fake his death to maybe just drop out of sight? Was he in trouble at that time with the authorities?'

'Jonjo was *always* skating too close to the edge – you know that.' Max stared at her. 'You didn't like him.'

Annie got the message, loud and clear. She stood up. 'You're right. I didn't like him. The man was an arsehole. But if you think I'd cook up some tall tale about him being dead, you're crazy. Why the hell would I do that? He *was* dead. I saw it.'

'You might *think* you saw it.'

'Or maybe I'm lying? Is that what you're driving at?'

Max was very still, staring at her. 'Are you?' he said.

Annie snatched up her bag and surged toward the door.

'That's it. I'm done talking to you. You don't trust me. That's the truth of the matter, isn't it?'

'Hey! Hold on.' Max hurried to block her way. 'Look – you haven't given me any cause to trust you. What have I ever had off you over the years but half-truths?'

Annie stopped, staring at him. Slowly, she started to nod. 'This is really about Constantine. Isn't it? This is *always* about Constantine.'

'No it isn't. But since you raise the subject, all right, let's get on it.'

'Right,' snapped Annie, although she didn't want to. Not now, not ever. 'Let's.'

'Oh and don't take on that wounded tone of voice. Fact is, I was off the scene in the Seventies for two years and in that time – *two bloody years* – you just moved right on. And then that business in Scotland, for God's sake . . .'

'How many more times? I thought you were dead. I *believed* you were dead.'

'I wasn't.'

'Christ! Just get out of my bloody way, Max. I've had enough.'

Annie went to barge past him. He caught her arm, held her there. They glared at each other, nose to nose.

'We have to talk about this,' said Max.

'I've said all I've got to say.' Annie looked down at his hand on her arm.

Max let go. Annie went to the door and walked out into the hallway.

She was halfway across it when the doorbell rang. Still boiling with anger, she went over and flung the front door open.

'*What*?' she barked out.

It was Hunter and his young sidekick.

'Time for a chat, Mrs Carter?' asked DCI Hunter.

'Not really.'

'Won't take long,' he said, stepping briskly inside, DS Nolan following at his heels. 'Is Mr Carter here?'

'Yes,' said Max, who had followed Annie out into the hall. 'He's here.'

Thinking bitterly that this day was just getting better and better all the time, Annie led the way into the drawing room and they all sat down.

'So . . . ?' Annie asked Hunter.

'I wanted to talk to you both,' he said, looking pointedly at Max, 'about your employee, Mr Carter – Mr Steven Taylor.'

'OK,' said Max.

'You've heard the tragic news? Mrs Carter has told you?'

'I've heard it.'

'Mr Taylor worked the security arm of your business, didn't he? Carter Securities?'

Max nodded.

'And the business was in good order?'

'It was making a tidy profit. We covered London and Essex. Steve was hoping to expand out even further soon, and I saw no reason not to.'

'Did Mr Taylor have enemies, Mr Carter?' asked Nolan.

'We all have those,' said Max. 'But no. Nobody I can think of offhand.'

'And yet someone hung him off a bridge,' said Hunter with a dry grimace of a smile. 'You didn't fall out with him at all then? He wasn't dipping into the profits?'

Max eyed Hunter steadily. 'Steve wouldn't do that. He's been a mate of mine ever since we were kids. He was straight with me.'

'And with others?'

'If he had any trouble, I didn't know about it.'

'The woman he was living with, this Kirsty Allen,' said Hunter, turning his attention to Annie. 'Did you know her, Mrs Carter?'

'I know she worked at the Shalimar before she took up with Steve,' said Annie.

'And after . . . ?'

'She gave up work, so far as I know. Steve kept her.'

'She's a lot younger than him,' said Nolan.

'That's true. And that's Steve's business,' said Annie sharply. They all knew Steve had been a flash git with a taste for the young honeys, God bless him. It was just *him*. Just Steve.

'Sadly we can't ask him about their relationship – as he's been murdered.'

'You're absolutely certain it's that then? It can't be suicide?' asked Max.

'We are certain.'

'Yeah? How?' shot back Max.

'The post-mortem showed that he in fact died from a lethal injection, *before* he was hung.'

'Christ,' murmured Annie.

The doorbell rang.

'I'm sorry, are you expecting visitors?' said Hunter.

'No. I'm not. I'll just be a moment,' said Annie, and left the room.

# 73

When Annie opened the door, Layla was standing there.

'Hiya . . . *Mum?*' she said and stepped past her into the hall. She dumped a holdall on the floor, swept her hair back and stared at her mother.

'What are you . . . ?' They both said at the same time.

'I thought you were in Barbados with Dad,' said Layla, staring at her mother in confusion.

'I thought *you* were with Alberto,' said Annie. 'And . . .'

The baby! The last time Annie had talked to Alberto – in Scotland, when they had been confronting the threat that was Redmond Delaney – he had told her that Layla was pregnant.

She swept a quick assessing gaze over Layla. Her daughter was wearing a sky-blue cheesecloth blouse and faded jeans. Her Chanel sunnies were perched on top of her head, dragging back her sun-streaked brown hair, accentuating her sharply defined cheekbones. She was thinner – much thinner than when Annie had last seen her. She was darkly tanned and the tan made her green eyes shine with a feline light. There was a brittle look to her, as if she might shatter like glass if you touched her. She *definitely* didn't look pregnant.

'Don't ask,' said Layla, then she spotted Max standing there through the open drawing room door. She headed straight in there.

'Dad!' Layla literally threw herself into Max's arms.

'Honey.' He hugged her tight. Kissed her brow. 'This is a surprise.'

Hunter and Nolan had got to their feet and were taking in this father and child reunion. Layla detached herself from Max, her eyes glittering with the start of emotional tears. Annie came into the room, looked at her husband and her daughter, reflected briefly that Layla had brushed straight past *her* but had piled into Max's arms like a bird fleeing a storm. Same old, same old.

Layla had always been Max's girl, and that had intensified after her parents' divorce in nineteen-eighty. Layla – a teen-ager at the time – had blamed Annie for the split and had put her mother through hell as payment for the destruction of their family unit.

Resolutely, Layla had favoured her dad Max more and more, spending months with him in Barbados and snubbing her mother. But time passed and slowly Layla's attitude had softened. Still, Annie knew damned well that – even now – for Layla, Max would always come first.

Annie turned her attention to Hunter. 'Sorry for the inter-ruption. This is our daughter Layla.'

'Yeah, sorry,' said Layla, turning toward them. 'Barging in like this.' She held out a hand to Hunter. 'Hello.'

Hunter shook her hand. 'I'm DCI Hunter; this is DS Nolan.'

'Oh. Hello,' said Layla, turning to DS Nolan. 'Sorry.' She turned to Annie, her eyes anxious. She knew her parents. She knew that a police visit was never good news. 'I'll go on upstairs, get unpacked. You carry on.'

Layla left the room. Annie closed the door after her.

'Now,' she said. 'Where were we?'

★

Hunter and Nolan left the Holland Park house half an hour later. After Annie had closed the door on them and as they went down the steps, Hunter, who never missed a damned thing, said to Nolan: 'Don't even think about it.'

'What?' Nolan turned innocent eyes on his boss.

'The girl.' Hunter had seen that punch-in-the-solar-plexus reaction to a woman before. Christ, he'd felt it *himself*, with the girl's mother. He had acknowledged to himself long ago that there was something special, some sort of weird relationship, between him and Annie Carter. Maybe because he'd saved her life, once back in the dim distant past. Maybe because they both knew there was an attraction there, but circumstances had conspired against them and so it would simply never happen. 'Trust me, that girl's the sort of trouble you would never, ever want. Not unless you want to end up in a similar situation to our corpse Mr Taylor.'

'I have no idea what you mean,' said Nolan, although he did. When Layla Carter had turned toward him and said *hello* he'd felt three things: his stomach had caved in, his pupils had dilated and his cock had stirred hungrily. He knew *exactly* what Hunter meant.

'She's Mafia connected.'

'*What?*'

'Don't go there. Seriously.'

'Mafia? Really?'

'Really.' Hunter glanced back over his shoulder. 'You see that house?'

Nolan nodded.

'Once owned by Constantine Barolli – a very dangerous man. And his son's the same. Everyone wants him. The FBI for instance. And that's just for starters. The son – Alberto – is God knows where, but he's in tight with the girl Layla, everyone knows it, so at any moment she could be scooped up by the CIA and taken off for interrogation. Also, Max Carter would rip you a new one if you stepped within an inch of his daughter. So seriously – spare yourself a world of pain. Don't fuck around with that lot.'

'Wasn't intending to,' said Nolan.

'Yeah. I could tell.'

'So where now?' asked Nolan, that glinting green-eyed stare, that slender figure, that long hank of sun-tossed cocoa-brown hair all replaying itself in his mind. *Layla Carter.*

'Witnesses,' said Hunter. 'We're looking for witnesses and we've got fuck-all chance of finding any, is my guess. But we'll try. Or at any rate *you* will. Get uniform on door-to-door within a couple miles' radius of the spot where Taylor was found. Trawl the whole length of the canal if you have to. And the boatyards. The companies that hire out pleasure craft. Has anyone reported any suspicious activity near that bridge? Seen something that doesn't add up? You know the drill. You drive,' he said, and tossed Nolan the keys.

# 74

'So,' said Annie, coming into the bedroom across the hall from hers, the one that was always thought of as 'Layla's'. She closed the door after her. The police were gone. Max had gone too, saying he had something pressing and that tonight he'd take Layla out to dinner, be ready for eight.

'You can come too, if you want,' said Max to Annie, like she was an unfortunate afterthought.

'Oh gee – thanks,' she'd said in return, her voice dripping sarcasm.

'So what?' asked Layla, avoiding her mother's eyes, yanking creased items out of her holdall and tossing them into the wardrobe.

'Leave those out and I'll send them to the laundry,' said Annie.

Layla slammed the wardrobe door shut. It was as if she hadn't heard Annie at all.

'You all right?' asked Annie.

'I need a bath. I've been travelling for *days*,' said Layla.

'Layla,' said Annie sharply.

'What?'

'The last time I saw you, you were on your way to meet up with Alberto somewhere down by the Florida Keys. You looked like you'd won the sweepstake. And the last time I saw Alberto, he told me you were expecting a baby. Now . . .' She shrugged.

'I don't want to discuss it,' said Layla, and crossed to the en suite and went in there, closing the door pointedly behind her.

'Welcome home,' said Annie under her breath. She went back downstairs to the kitchen and fixed herself a coffee. Then she took it to the drawing room, settled down, and waited.

★

Layla came down over an hour later. She was wearing one of Annie's summer dresses, black with a tiny yellow sprigged flower pattern.

'Sorry, I thought you wouldn't mind,' said Layla, crashing onto the couch opposite Annie and indicating the dress.

'I don't. That's OK. Get you a coffee?'

'No, I'm fine. Where's Dad taking us tonight?'

'No idea.'

'Just so long as they don't put anything *fishy* on my plate, that's all.' Layla hated fish. The smell, the taste, the texture.

'Layla,' said Annie.

'Hm?'

Annie watched her daughter. Layla's eyes were avoiding Annie's. She was rubbing her thumbs over and over against her index fingers – a self-comforting gesture. Annie's eyes were drawn to the missing little finger on Layla's left hand – a stark reminder of that awful time back in the Seventies when she'd been snatched away as a small child and Max had disappeared. A horrible time. Sometimes, Annie wondered how they'd all got through it. They had, somehow – but those days had left their mark. The past had a way of doing that. You thought you were through it, done with it – but you weren't. It had a way of *haunting* you.

She thought of Max, questioning her about Jonjo's death. Jonjo *had* been dead. Hadn't he?

'Layla, what's happened?' Annie asked her daughter, very gently.

Layla was looking all round the room, and Annie saw the suggestion of tears in her eyes.

'Oh – nothing much, really,' she said, gulping. She wrapped her arms around herself as if she was cold and trying to generate some warmth.

'This doesn't look like nothing much to me. What happened with the baby?'

Layla gave a tiny, tight smile. A tear trickled down over her cheek and she swiped it angrily away.

'What is it, sweetheart?' Annie asked again.

'I lost it. Miscarried. And I've left him,' Layla blurted out. 'Alberto. It's finished.'

Annie was silent for a beat. Then she said: 'Honey, I'm so sorry. Where is Alberto now?'

Layla managed a bitter little laugh and wiped at her eyes. 'We don't ask that question, Mum. You know that. Walls have ears! All you need to know is that I've left him, it's over. I couldn't go on that way. I just couldn't. Living on that damned boat, cruising around. It was just *aimless,* just *awful.* I'm not that kind of person. I need stability in my life. I need routine. I'm a fucking *accountant.* I just couldn't do it anymore. And then I got sick and I lost the baby. And he didn't even *talk* to me, the bastard. He shut me out. So I just couldn't go on with it all.'

Annie was squinting at her daughter, trying to take this all in. She was shocked. She had never imagined for one minute that the red-hot romance between Alberto and Layla would come to such an abrupt end.

Layla shrugged hopelessly, her face a mask of misery.

'You can't imagine what it's like, living on the run. Everyone thinks it's a pirate's life – sun, sand, blue seas – and yes I do see that people might make that mistake, might see it as an adventure, exciting . . . but it isn't. It's a pain in the neck. You're always looking over your shoulder. Always scared. Always worrying about someone saying the game's up. Anyway!' She heaved a heavy sigh. 'It's done. I had to bail out. I've left him.'

'I'm sorry,' said Annie. She loved them both, her stepson and her daughter. She had never wanted this to be the outcome of their affair. She had always hoped for a happy ending, for them as a family, living their best life.

'Yeah, well. It happened. It's over. And really – I'm glad I'm out of it now.'

'You discussed leaving him then? You talked to him about it?'

'No. It would have been too painful. I lost the baby and that drew a line under everything, for me. I just left.'

Layla dissolved in tears then, sobbing her heart out. Annie went over to her and hugged her tight.

'It'll be all right,' she said firmly, smoothing back Layla's hair, kissing her brow. 'You're home. That's all that matters. Everything else? We can sort it out.'

But Annie thought of Max's recent trip to Majorca, and his questions, and Jaime's death. And Steve – Steve Taylor of all people, tough as fuck and afraid of nothing – found dead, hanging from a bridge, and she wondered if this *could* be sorted.

# 75

Early next morning, before either Max or Layla had risen to greet the day, Annie got up, dressed, and went out to flag down a black cab in Kensington High Street. While the cab wove its way through rush-hour traffic, she sat back and thought about all that had happened.

Last night's dinner – Max had taken them to the Connaught – had not been a success. Before dinner, Annie had broken the news to Max about the loss of their grandchild. *During* dinner, Max mentioned his new venture – another club, the Ventura up west, but even the excitement of a new project couldn't lift the mood. Max had broken the news to Layla about Steve before they went out, and she'd been terribly upset. Devastated. After that, Layla had been silent, Max had been edgy, and Annie herself had not felt in the mood for small talk. They were all relieved to get home, to retire to their rooms, to no longer feel the need to 'chat'.

But now it was morning, and as her cab pulled into Parliament Hill she saw Steve's lovely house there and felt sadness flood over her again. He'd been so proud of it, throwing barbecue parties in the back garden, inviting all the old gang over, showing off, enjoying the fact that he had a maid running around the place and a glamorous young woman on his arm. Poor bastard.

Annie paid the driver and walked up the path and knocked at the door.

No answer.

She knocked again.

She was on the point of turning away, going back out into the road to hail another cab when the door opened. Kirsty Allen stood there, bleary-eyed, pulling a pink robe across her bosom.

'What the hell time do you call this?' she asked.

'Nine-fifteen,' said Annie, turning back and stepping up to the door. Kirsty half-closed it. Annie stuck her foot inside and applied her shoulder. Kirsty staggered back, her unmade-up eyes widening in outrage. 'Hey! You can't do that.'

'Just did,' said Annie, stepping inside, shoving the door shut behind her. 'Why don't you get the maid to make us a coffee?'

Kirsty snorted. 'I would if she was bloody well here. Got pissed off with her droning on about I'd have to get out, out, out! Such a *bitch*. I'm having to do every damned thing myself.'

'Right,' said Annie. She remembered the kitchen from her past visits here. She opened a door off the hall and went in and put the kettle on to boil. Hunting through the cupboards, she found coffee and whitener and cups. She set everything out on the worktop, found a spoon, and made the drinks.

'You seem to know your way around here pretty well,' said Kirsty, flicking on the radio. 'Lady in Red' poured out.

'Been here before. I think it was the girl *before* you I met – Sylvie? The Swedish one? – at one of Steve's parties.' Annie led the way into the sitting room, put the coffees down on the occasional table and went and drew back the curtains at the big bay window. Then she sat down. Kirsty slumped down too, yawning.

'God, I'm tired,' she complained.

Annie smiled at that.

'I don't know whether Steve had any family,' Kirsty said. 'Would you know? He never mentioned them.'

'He could have left all this to you,' said Annie, seeing clearly that Kirsty's mind was on the money. 'I don't know anything about Steve having family anywhere. But if he left you everything, that's an A1 motive for murder. I suppose you do realise that?'

Kirsty choked on her coffee. When she stopped coughing, she blurted out: 'How could I have done that? He was hanging off a bridge. You saw Steve; you knew him. He was a big bloke. He weighed a ton. How could *I* have done that?'

'With help you could.'

'Help from who?'

Annie shrugged. 'A boyfriend? Relatives?'

'What are you trying to say?'

'Just trying to establish the facts.' Annie drank her coffee. 'When did you last see Steve?'

'Last Sunday morning. We'd had a bit of a row. He went out – said he was going to the pub and *fuck* you – charming, yes? – and he didn't come back. I thought he was sulking. Turned out he was bloody *dead*.' Kirsty's lower lip quivered at that.

Annie watched her. Maybe the girl *had* had real feelings for Steve. Were relationships ever really worth the bother, though? Annie thought of Layla and Alberto breaking up. Now this from Kirsty about her and Steve.

*And what about me and Max?*

Annie flinched away from that thought. The trouble was, she was used to making her own decisions, being free and easy. Max would always interpret that as 'free to get laid by some other man', and he would be wrong. She didn't want any other man. She knew she'd kept things from him. She'd *had* to. And she definitely didn't want all the tedious baggage from their shared and separate pasts dragged up again.

Then she heard footfall overhead. She looked across at Kirsty, who stiffened.

'You got someone here?' asked Annie.

'So what if I have? It's a free country.'

Annie took in once again Kirsty's rumpled appearance. Of course. She had a man up there. Steve was still warm, and the girl was here – in Steve's house – fucking someone else. She drank down the last of her coffee and stood up. 'So – you going to introduce me?'

'No I'm bloody not.' Kirsty was on her feet too now. 'Listen, what I do with my life is *my* business. Nothing to do with the high and mighty bloody Carters, you got that?'

'Loud and clear,' said Annie, heading out into the hall.

She was confronted by a man of about Kirsty's age just coming down the stairs, buttoning a pale blue shirt. He was tall and his close-cropped blond hair looked too yellow against his pink-toned skin to be natural – but it suited him, gave him a louche, stylish look. He was angular, lightly muscled, very attractive. Piercing dark blue eyes. Black lashes, black brows. There was a penny-sized birthmark on his left cheek. Somewhere at the back of her mind, a bell rang; had she seen him before? She couldn't recall. He looked at Annie, then at Kirsty who was following close behind her.

'Hi,' said Annie. 'I'm an old friend of Steve Taylor's. Annie Carter.' She held out a hand as he got to the bottom of the staircase. 'And you are?'

His expression uncertain, he took Annie's hand, shook it briefly.

'Bruno Dawkins,' he said. 'Sorry, I didn't know Kirsty was expecting anyone.'

'Neither did she. Bye, Bruno,' she said, and went to the door and was gone, leaving the pair of them gawping after her.

# 76

Annie went to Ellie's.

'Now what?' said her mate, standing in the kitchen, still in her dressing gown, bleary-eyed and barely awake. 'Tea? Coffee?'

'Do you know a bloke called Bruno Dawkins?'

Ellie shrugged and yawned. 'I think so, yeah. He worked here once, about the same time as that tart Steve took up with, that Kirsty woman. So what?'

'Would you still have the CCTV recordings from the bar at around that time?'

'Maybe. But it might have been recorded over. Why the interest?'

'No particular reason. I'd like a look, that's all.'

'I'll see what I can do.'

After leaving the Shalimar, Annie called in at the police station and asked for Hunter. He came to the front desk, saw her standing there and beckoned her through. They went into his office and sat down.

'What can I do for you?' he asked.

'Kirsty Allen, Steve Taylor's girlfriend,' said Annie.

'What about her?'

'She's got a new squeeze. He answers to the name of Bruno Dawkins and he just stayed overnight with her at Steve's place. Do you know anything about him?'

Hunter pulled a pad toward him and made a note. He shook his head.

'No,' he said. 'Do you have a description?'

'Tall, blond – the hair's dyed, I think – strawberry birth-mark on left cheek. Youngish, six-pack.'

'Have you any reason to believe that Kirsty Allen is impli-cated in Mr Taylor's death?'

'No. None at all.'

'Then . . . ?'

'Just fishing.'

'Mrs Carter.'

'Hm?'

'We've had this conversation before.'

'Is this the conversation that goes, keep your nose out, Mrs Carter?'

'That's the one.'

'Steve was a good friend to me, over a lot of years.' *And something about Bruno Dawkins worries me.*

'I don't doubt it. One of Mr Carter's original "associates", I believe.'

'Do you believe that?'

'Yes. I do.'

Was he *flirting* with her? She'd often wondered, whenever they talked. Another time, another place, something could have happened. But not now.

'Seriously, Mrs Carter, watch yourself. Someone in your social circle has just been found dead. Don't let's add to the tally, all right?'

'Yep. Got the message,' said Annie.

'Good,' said Hunter, doubting it. 'Now, if there's nothing else . . . ?'

★

Annie went back to the Holland Park house. She put her key in the door to find Max and Layla out in the hall. They both turned to the door when she entered and stared at her.

'What?' she said, freezing.

'Where the hell have you *been*?' asked Layla.

'What the fuck?' said Max.

Annie looked at them both. 'What? I woke up early so I went over to Steve's place to talk to Kirsty, then back to Ellie's then down to the station to talk to Hunter. Then I came back here.'

'We were worried,' said Layla. 'Mum, we didn't know where you were. We were concerned. That's all.'

'No that's not all,' said Max sharply. 'With something like this business with Steve kicking off, you *don't* go wandering off on your own. It's bloody stupid. We've got enough to think about without going apeshit thinking you're the next one to be found hanging off a bridge.'

Annie eyed him coldly.

'Thank you for your concern,' she said. 'But – as you can see – I'm fine.'

She went on up the stairs and into the master suite. Presently, Max followed and closed the door behind him.

'Seriously,' he said. 'Don't bloody do that.'

Annie kicked off her heels and stared at him. 'Seriously? I think you'll find I can do whatever I want.'

'Is this about me giving you a hard time about Jonjo?'

'I don't know what you mean.'

'You are the most pig-headed bitch,' he said.

'And you're a bastard. I think we're square. I went to the station to tell Hunter that Kirsty's got another man.'

'Oh?' Max frowned. 'And when did we start helping the Bill?'

'When someone strung one of our mates up off a bridge. If he can find them, I'll help him in any way I can.'

'I'd rather you didn't.'

'Noted. And tough.'

'It's not wise. And it's not safe.'

'In your opinion.'

'Yes. In my opinion.'

'Well thank you for your input. Now, if you don't mind . . . ?' She indicated the door.

'I've told Layla to take over at the Ventura,' said Max.

'Oh?' This was news. 'Is she interested in that then?'

'I thought it might be something to interest her and she's going to give it a go. I've put one of the boys at her disposal. Don't want *her* wandering about on her own too.'

Annie gave him a sour smile but didn't rise to the bait.

'It'll take her mind off things,' said Max. 'Losing the baby. And Golden Boy. Although I don't think he's much of a loss. In fact, she'll be a damned sight better off without him.'

'In your opinion.'

'Yeah,' said Max, and went.

Annie got changed. Then she went back downstairs and out the front door. Tone was standing at the pavement's edge beside a long black Mercedes. He straightened when she emerged. Tone was eighteen stone of meaty muscle, bald as a coot and with gold crucifixes dangling from each cauliflower ear. He wore an immaculate black suit, white shirt and black tie.

'Tone! Nice to see you. You waiting for Max?'

'Nope. I'm waiting for you, Mrs C,' said Tone, opening the door for her.

Annie stared at him. Then the penny dropped. 'Max phoned you?'

'He did, yes. Said I was to make the car and myself available to take you wherever you wanted to go.'

'Is that all he said?'

'No, Mrs C. He said you was going mental and I was to keep an eye on you, because you was a "mad bitch", pardon my French. So where do you want to go?' Tone asked.

Well, it would save on taxi fares, Annie told herself. And Tone was a useful guy to have about in a tight corner.

She told him.

Tone took a step back. '*That* place?'

'Yep, that's the one,' she said, and stepped inside the car.

# 77

'What are we looking for? Exactly?' asked Tone.

They'd driven across town after stopping off at a florist's. Then Tone had parked up the car and now they were walking along by the canal's greenish waters. In the distance, they could see the place where *it* had happened, and they were moving toward it steadily, seeing it highlighted in the drizzly murk by the vivid ribbons of crime scene tape. They were being passed on the towpath by bikers, joggers. Narrowboats were moored here and there. Someone was frying bacon on one of the boats, its scent mingling with the cold musty smell of the canal. A small sandy-coloured dog raced around on top of another boat, barking its head off. A grizzled grey-haired man of about eighty came up on the deck of the *Mary Anne*, which was painted scarlet red and decked out with a shockingly vivid array of flowers in too many pots to count.

'Morning,' said Annie. She stopped walking. So did Tone.

The man grunted, sat down by the tiller with his mug of steaming tea in his hand.

'Tragic, that,' said Annie, indicating the bridge and the crime scene tapes. 'You heard about it? The bloke they found there?'

'I heard about it. Everyone did.'

'Were you moored up here when it happened?'

'Nah, I move about. Rolling stone, me. Gather no moss.'

Annie and Tone walked on. 'When did you last see Steve?' Annie asked him.

'That would be last Sunday. We met in The Grapes, had a pint or two. He seemed all right.' Tone squinted at her. Up above, the sun was trying to shine faintly through the low grey clouds. It was chilly down here by the water, even if it was supposed to be summer. 'That's what bothers me, you know,' Tone went on. 'He was the same old Steve. Unshakable. You know how he was. And then that night, *that* happened? It still don't seem possible.'

They were getting closer to the crime scene. No police here today, just the tapes under the bridge, warning people not to cross. Another boat was chugging towards them, painted emerald green and gold with a large sign on the deck saying SANDWICHES/BAGUETTES 99p. COFFEE/TEA £1. Over on the other side of the canal, there was a black boat tricked out as an artist's studio; there were paintings for sale, good ones, spread out all across the deck.

'Look at that,' said Annie.

'There's a library boat too. I've seen it. Look, it's moored up there, a bit further on.'

They were standing alongside the crime scene now. The chill off the water seemed deeper here, colder. No flowers had been left yet. Annie took the cellophane-wrapped red roses and laid them just by the tapes, thinking that this was too bloody sad for words. She hadn't written a note; there was nothing to say. What *could* you say to someone who had stood by you for so many years? More than once, Steve Taylor had yanked her arse out of trouble. Max's too. They had debts to Steve that could never be repaid. And now it was too late to try. He was gone.

They paused there, looking at the grimy water but thinking of Steve. Annie let out a sigh. Then they walked on.

'Did Steve say on Sunday what he was going to be doing that afternoon, that night or Monday?' Annie asked Tone.

'Nah, not a word.'

'Kirsty said they had a row Sunday morning. Steve said he was off to the pub, and he was, wasn't he. To see you.'

Tone nodded.

'But then he didn't go back home or into the office and there was nothing in his work diary, no appointments. I can't place him after that. Sunday's the cut-off point.'

'He didn't say anything about what he was planning to do,' said Tone. 'Mostly he was moaning on about that girl Kirsty, and I said to him, "Steve my old mate, what you doing to yourself? The girl's too bloody young for you. Why put in so much effort? Get yourself a proper woman, someone who speaks your language. Kick that bolshie little tart to the kerb."'

'Sound advice,' said Annie.

'Yeah, but I don't think he listened.'

They were approaching the bookshop. A Swampy-type youth who was wearing many glittery nose ornaments, thick sludge-coloured knitwear and a fistful of corn-yellow dreadlocks on top of his bony head was moving about the deck of the narrowboat, laying out big cardboard sales notices with HARDBACKS 99p/PAPERBACKS 50p scrawled on them in red paint. He looked up as they came alongside, laid out the gangplank, indicated the open doors leading down into the main body of the boat. Inside, Annie could see shelves stacked with books.

'All right?' he said, smiling. 'Shop's open.'

'You moor up here often do you?' said Annie. 'Do much trade?'

'Ah, so-so,' he said, making a see-saw motion with pale long-fingered hands.

'Heard about what happened under the bridge there?' Annie indicated the crime scene tapes.

'Yeah, who didn't? Nasty, uh?'

'You weren't moored here then? On Sunday? Or Monday maybe?'

'Me? Nah. No way. The filth asked me the same question.'

Annie looked around them. The old grey-haired man on the red boat was still out on deck, sipping his tea and watching them. 'What about him, then? You know him? See him here often?'

'He's here all the time,' said Swampy.

'Oh. Right,' said Annie. That wasn't what they'd been told. 'You sure you weren't here Sunday or Monday?'

'What?' Swampy was looking awkward. 'No. I said so, didn't I?'

'You said he was here all the time, that old man over there. Was he here then, on either of those days? Were you?'

'No bloody comment,' he said and went down into the main body of the boat and slammed the double doors shut behind him.

'Well that's annoying,' said Annie. She looked back along the towpath, to where the old guy sat on his boat, still watching them and pretending not to. 'Go and offer the old chap some money for information,' she said, slipping Tone a twenty.

'Will do. What if he don't have any?'

Annie shrugged. 'Then we're out of pocket. It's worth a try.'

★

Tone reported back to Annie within minutes. The old man had turned down the money, saying he knew nothing about what had gone on, and what were they, plain-clothes police or something? Tone had assured him they were not and left a contact number, just in case.

'I could rough him up,' said Tone helpfully. 'If you want.'

'Nah. Let it sit for a bit.'

Tone drove her on over to the Shalimar, where progress was being made. All the broken glass had been piled into a skip and the workmen were there now, measuring up for replacement windows.

'Only trouble is, it's going to take time, all this. We'll be out of commission for a fortnight,' Ellie told her, leading the way upstairs.

'Chris said that Layla's back,' Ellie told her.

'Keep that to yourself,' said Annie sharply.

'Of course I will,' said Ellie, looking hurt.

'I mean it, Ellie. Not a word. Tell Chris to button it too.'

'Yeah. Sure. I know it's tricky for her. Being as she's with *him*,' Ellie hissed in a loud theatrical whisper.

'Ellie – keep quiet will you? I don't want any trouble for her. She won't be staying long, anyway.' That was probably a lie, but Annie was thinking of covering Layla's tracks – the more dust she kicked up, the better.

'Of course. I get it. I won't say a word.'

*What, and break the habit of a lifetime?* wondered Annie.

'Well, there's some good news,' said Ellie.

'Oh?'

Ellie reached down by her chair and rummaged in her handbag. She pulled out a DVD in a plain white folder.

'Found the CCTV that shows Kirsty and Bruno Dawkins standing together at the bar. Lucky it wasn't wiped. It's there, nice and clear.'

'Good. Thanks.' Annie pocketed the DVD. 'Anything else?'

'Nope.'

Annie finished her tea and left.

# 78

*At least Dad could have given me a glamorous bodyguard,* thought Layla as Paul – unsmiling, unspeaking and dull-as-ditch-water middle-aged Paul – drove her over to the Ventura. On the way, they passed the Shaftesbury Theatre where *Tommy* by Pete Townshend was playing to packed-out houses and rave reviews. Layla hadn't seen it. She'd lost touch with the modern world; sailing around the Caribbean for months on end could do that to a person.

The Ventura, after the sparkle and razzamatazz of Shaftesbury Avenue, was a let-down. The front of the club was dull red brick, and it was covered with a vast exoskeleton of scaffolding. Inside, it was even worse. A wreck of mouldering plaster, bustling workmen throwing swear words at each other, roaring machines and the blare of radio one.

Max's general manager, Julian, a selection of architect's drawings under his arm, was there and he tried to hide his annoyance at this new arrangement – Layla being in charge of operations and not him – as best he could. He shook her hand and gave her a smile that was distinctly chilly.

'It's a mess,' he said, before she could get the words out.

'Yeah,' agreed Layla, while Paul loitered, looking bored in the background.

'Come back here and have a look at the plans,' said Julian. 'It's important that the Carter corporate image is carried through here in exactly the same way as in the three other clubs.'

*You don't say,* thought Layla.

Still, she followed him back to a dusty table and took an interest as he spread out the drawings and showed her what was what.

*What am I doing here?* she wondered trying to stay focused on what he was saying. An image rose in her mind. Sundrenched beaches, the yacht, and oh God him, yes, Alberto, his blond hair bleached, his muscles tanned . . .

'So what do you think?' asked Julian.

'What?' Layla was thrown, jerked back to the here and now. *What* had he just said?

'The plans. I thought gold leaf over the bar area – no cutting corners, so . . .'

Layla was already moving away. Paul fell into step with her. Well trained, obviously – and probably very frightened of her father.

'Whatever you think best,' she said to Julian. 'Carry on, OK?'

She was almost racing for the door. Once outside, she gulped down dust-free air and paused there, Paul loitering close by.

'Anything wrong?' he asked her.

'Nothing,' she said.

'Where to now?' he asked, and then there was a commotion above them.

Paul looked up. So did Layla.

A piece of metal scaffolding was falling down from above, heading right for her.

# 79

'Somebody,' said Nolan, coming into Hunter's office and closing the door behind him, 'has been down by the canal asking questions. There's been a complaint. Bloke feeling intimidated.'

'Well that didn't take long,' said Hunter with a sigh. 'Let me guess. Tall dark-haired woman, accompanied by a thug. Which one? Now let me see . . . well, one's in the city morgue, so it has to be the other one. Big boxer type, bald, gold crucifixes in his ears?'

'That's the one,' said Nolan, slumping down in a chair.

'You ever need a getaway driver, he's your man,' said Hunter with a dry smile. 'Once head jockey for the Carter mob. Can do handbrake turns, skid a car sideways into a parking space you'd swear was too small for it, anything you like. Can make anything that runs on four wheels sing, damned near. And can break your bones with lethal efficiency.'

'Impressive.'

'So what's he done?'

'He just sort of leaned into this Halliday guy and offered him cash for information about our hanged man. Bloke was scared shitless.'

'He's right to be. But we can't have that, now can we? I'll have a word with his handler.'

'Want me to go over?' asked Nolan.

'I do not. We have had no luck with witnesses. I am not happy. I want you to do precisely what these two have been doing. Get your arse down there again and talk to everyone and anyone, and please assure our frightened old guy that words will be exchanged with the offending people about his "intimidation" and that it will not, under any circumstances, happen again.'

'Wouldn't take a moment to just pop in on the Carters,' offered Nolan helpfully.

'What did I say to you?' asked Hunter.

'In reference to what, sir?'

'Keep clear. People are taking a keen interest in their movements right now and I don't want you getting caught in any crossfire, lawful or otherwise.'

To Nolan, that sounded interesting.

'Nolan,' said Hunter firmly. 'I know you think of yourself as something of a hit with the ladies . . .'

'Not at all, sir,' objected Nolan. Although he did.

'But this time, take me at my word: you don't want to go there. All right?'

'Right,' said Nolan, but he was thinking otherwise.

# 80

Maybe Paul wasn't so dull and middle-aged as she'd thought. While Layla stood there staring upward in amazement, Paul shoved her back inside the doorway and fell through it after her. She heard the metal scaffolding pole hit the pavement outside with a resounding *thwack* that coursed right through her, seemed to travel all the way up from her toes right to the top of her head.

*That would have hit me,* she thought, dazed.

She was sitting up, winded, shocked, and Paul was already on his feet, stepping back outside, peering up, then coming back into the club, stepping over Layla and running to Julian and the workmen.

'Who you got up on the roof?' he was asking.

'Nobody. What . . .' Julian said, and Paul was grabbing one of the workmen. 'Show me up there. Julian, stay with Layla.'

And he was gone.

'What the hell happened?' asked Julian.

Layla nodded at the metal pole lying out there on the pavement – where she had a few seconds ago been standing. She was starting to shake. Julian took off his coat and draped it around her shoulders. 'Come on, let's get you sat down . . .'

Five minutes later, Paul was back. 'Couldn't see anyone up there,' he told her.

'It probably just came loose somehow,' said Julian.

'Yeah. Maybe. Yeah, probably that was it.' Paul looked at Layla, sitting there, shivering despite the warmth of Julian's coat. 'Come on, let's get you home.'

★

She told Annie and Max about the accident at the Ventura as soon as she got home.

'Paul pushed me out of the way. Then he went up on the roof to see if there was anyone up there, but he couldn't find anyone. It probably just came loose – that's what everyone thought.'

'For God's sake,' said Max.

'And he's sure there was no one up there?' said Annie, worried.

'I said so, didn't I?' snapped Layla. Then she dragged a hand through her hair. 'Sorry. Look. I've had a think. It's good of you to offer, Dad, but I don't think what I need right now is to take on the Ventura. Julian's got it all in hand, best leave it to him. He'll do a far better job than I ever could and I appreciate it, I really do – you trying to distract me from everything – but all I need really is to be left alone, to just have some space to myself to work everything out. OK?'

'Of course,' said Max. 'If that's what you want.'

'It is,' said Layla, and went upstairs.

Annie and Max exchanged looks.

'*Was* it an accident?' Annie pondered aloud.

Max was shaking his head. 'Who knows. But there's too much going on for my liking. *Far* too bloody much.'

## 81

Next day, Layla visited the florist and then went down by the canal bridge where Steve had breathed his last. She laid her little tribute there, next to Annie's roses. She couldn't believe that he was gone, her 'uncle' Steve. He'd been such a regular feature of her childhood, dandling her on his knee, always looking out for her.

*All right, squirt?*

That was what he'd always called her when she was little, tipping her upside down until she shrieked with laughter. As she laid down the flowers, she looked at her left hand. One little finger, missing. When she'd been snatched as a child, Steve had been instrumental in bringing her safely home. She owed him a lot. To think of him dead was too painful. Unbearable, when she was already at such a low ebb.

She looked around her. There were several boats moored up here. One with paintings spread out and with people moving about on the deck, admiring them, asking about prices. There was an old guy on a red boat brimming with pots of flowers, sitting alone at the tiller. And another, where sandwiches and teas were out on sale. It was a regular centre of commerce down here. There was even a bookshop boat, advertising HARDBACKS 99p/PAPERBACKS 50p, which was moored closer than the others to the bridge. Always interested in books, Layla went up the gangplank to get a closer look, maybe distract herself from the sombre purpose of her visit.

There was nobody about.

She knocked on the closed double doors. No answer.

'Hello?' said a male voice right behind her.

She spun around.

'Sorry. Didn't mean to make you jump,' said Nolan. He fished out his warrant card. 'I'm DS Nolan, you remember? We met at your mother's place.'

Layla didn't remember him at all. She'd flown home in a state of anxiety and depression; she hadn't been up for noticing men. She still wasn't, but this time she did take in that DS Nolan was tall, with thick straight treacle-brown hair. She also noted that he had big velvet-grey eyes and prominent cheekbones and was wearing a pretty snazzy dark suit. He was one of those individuals who always seemed to look irritatingly *neat*, no matter what the occasion.

'Sorry, I just came down to lay some flowers,' said Layla.

'I'm here asking around, seeing what I can find out, whether anyone saw anything,' said Nolan, thinking that he hadn't been wrong; she was *gorgeous*.

'Well I can't help you there. Just back in the country.'

'From where? Somewhere nice?'

'Nowhere in particular,' said Layla guardedly. She looked at the bridge, still festooned with crime scene tapes. 'Do you think you'll catch whoever did it?' she asked.

'That's our intention,' said Nolan. 'You knew him well then? Our hanged man?'

'Yeah,' said Layla. She held a hand to her waist. 'Since I was *this* high. He worked for my dad.'

'Sorry. It's shocking.'

'It is.' Layla knocked again at the closed double doors. 'Not open for business, by the look of it,' she said, and moved up onto the deck where there were a couple of bookcases set out, packed with paperbacks. 'Maybe he left these out all night? Seems silly. The damp'll ruin them.'

'I'm not much of a reader,' said Nolan. 'You?'

'Love books. Books and sums.'

'Sums?'

'I'm an accountant. Or I was, anyway.'

'Not my scene at all,' said Nolan with a grin. 'Show me a spreadsheet and my brain gets up and leaves the room.'

'Well, we're all different,' said Layla, moving around so that she could see the books on the other side. A pair of swans drifted past, eyeing her hopefully. Maybe the bookseller fed them. They loitered, pristine white, beautiful, their feet paddling madly, clearly visible under the surface.

'Wish I had something to give them,' she said.

'You shouldn't give them bread,' said Nolan. 'People do, but they shouldn't. Very bad for them.'

Now Layla had to smile. 'You a twitcher?'

'Only on Sundays. They mate for life, you know. Cute, yes?'

Layla shrugged, the smile slipping from her face. Once, she had thought *she* would mate for life. Now? She was not so sure. The swans stayed, circling, and then when it was clear no treats were forthcoming, they paddled off, over to the other side of the canal, no doubt hopeful that the artist over there would be more generous.

Her eyes drifting away from the swans, Layla's attention was caught by something billowing out in the water by the anchor chain. She moved closer to take a look.

'Careful,' said Nolan. 'Deck's slippery up here.'

Layla peered over the rail and down into the water. 'Can you see? Is that something tangled up in the anchor chain?'

'Can't be,' said Nolan, moving forward. He looked over the edge of the boat. 'What . . . ?' he said aloud, and then he saw that there *was* something down there. She was right.

He moved to the winch and turned it to pull in the anchor. Creaking, groaning, the weed-covered chain started winding in, inch by inch.

'It's bloody heavy,' said Nolan.

Layla's eyes were fastened on what was coming up from the depths. Then she saw the dirty cornrow hair, the face that was blanched of all colour. Milk-white eyes that peered straight ahead and saw nothing.

'Jesus!' She clamped a hand over her mouth and jumped back from the prow of the boat.

Nolan stopped pulling on the chain. The people on the boat on the other side of the canal were looking. A woman over there dropped a painting and let out a shriek. Together, Nolan and Layla stared down at the boat's dripping book-loving owner who was hanging there, his hands tied to the chain.

He was, without a single doubt, dead.

# 82

Annie got down to the canal within a half hour of Nolan phoning her. She found police cars parked up there, blue lights flashing, cordons being set up, an ambulance. The place was alive with activity, with PCs herding interested onlookers away. There was a black body bag lying on the towpath, clearly with a body already tucked inside it. She looked around anxiously. Nolan had told her Layla was here, that she'd had a shock, and could she come? But she couldn't see Layla anywhere.

'There,' said Tone, just as she was starting to panic.

He was pointing to the flower-festooned red boat, which was moored further along from the bridge. She felt the tension flow out of her then. There sitting at the helm was the same old guy she'd seen before with his thick mop of grey hair, wearing a navy-coloured guernsey sweater – and there was Layla, sitting at his side, a blanket wrapped around her shoulders, a tin mug of tea clasped in both hands. It was warm today, but she was shivering.

'Layla!' Annie hurried along the towpath and up the gang-plank.

'Mum?' Layla called out, and then, instantly: 'Where's Dad?'

'I don't know.' Aware that she was second choice, that she would *always* be second choice to her daughter, Annie sat down and gave her a quick hug. 'What happened?'

'I just came down to lay some flowers for Uncle Steve,' said Layla with a shudder. 'I went on the book boat and then I saw something on the anchor chain. It was the book man. Someone tied him on there. He was *dead*.'

Annie was aware of the old man eyeing up the huge looming bulk of Tony, then looking at her.

'Thank you so much,' she said to him. 'For looking after her.'

'No problem. Only did what anyone else would do.'

'Did you see anything?' Of course, he would say no. He'd said it before, when she'd asked about Steve's murder, and he would – of course – say it again when she asked about *this* man's death.

'Nothing.' He shrugged, but Annie thought she could see the lie right there, in his eyes.

Tony moved in a little closer to the man, but Annie shook her head and he stilled – just as DCI Hunter came along the towpath and stood at the bottom of the gangplank and said: 'Mrs Carter. What a surprise, seeing you here again.'

Annie nodded to Nolan, who was standing at Hunter's side. 'Your DS phoned me, asked me to come. My daughter's had quite a shock.'

'You've taken Miss Carter's statement?' Hunter asked Nolan.

'Yes, boss.'

'Then if you and your daughter will excuse us, Mrs Carter? We have work to do here.'

Annie was watching a police photographer lining up shots, the flash firing faintly in the bright light of day, whirring as it recharged. A white-suited pathologist was moving around the body bag. 'Do you think this is connected to Steve's death?' she asked Hunter. 'Do you think the bookseller saw something, and somebody wanted him silenced?'

'That's a possibility,' said Hunter smoothly. 'Now, Mrs Carter, if you don't mind . . . ?'

★

Max was at the Holland Park house when they got home. Annie told him what Layla had discovered, down by the canal. He went straight to Layla.

'You OK, honey?'

'I'm fine,' said Layla. 'Really. No need to fuss. It was just . . . *horrible*. That's all. And after that scare I had at the club . . . it was a bit much.'

Max looked at Annie. 'You OK?'

'Fine,' said Annie.

'It was the bloke who sold the books? Dead?' Max queried.

'Someone tied him to the anchor chain and then let it drop,' said Annie. 'Layla, go up and take a bath. Just try to relax. OK?'

'I will,' said Layla, and went tiredly up the stairs.

'Wait,' said Max when Annie went to follow her. 'I want a word.'

He led the way into the study. Annie followed, closing the door behind her. 'So?' she asked, leaning against it.

'What do you think this book guy saw?' Max asked. 'Maybe something on the night Steve got done?'

'How would I know? Could be anything. Could be nothing. Maybe someone just *thought* the poor bloke saw something, and that was enough of a reason to finish him off. And what about the old guy in the red boat? The book man said he was always there; he saw him moored there all the time. He's the best bet for some info, wouldn't you think, now that the book man's been shut up once and for all?'

'Did you speak to the old guy?'

'Couldn't. The police were there.'

'Then I'll go down there. Wait until the police clear out, have a proper word.'

'Could take some time. They'll be guarding that crime scene overnight now, I reckon.' Annie felt uneasy. People were *dying* here. First Steve, now the book man. And she wasn't even counting poor Jaime, who'd perished in Majorca. And what about the bloke from the beach in Montauk? If he'd caught up with her, would he have killed her too? And Layla's accident. Was it an accident at all? Something awful, something deep and dark and dangerous was kicking off. It made her shiver.

'Maybe it's best to keep clear,' she said. 'If one of the Bill sees you pitching up there, they might think you're involved. That maybe you and Steve fell out and then you'd be in the frame for it.'

'Steve was my best mate,' said Max, stopping his restless pacing to stand in front of her.

'I know that. You know that. The Bill, however, will be looking to pin this on someone before the public start getting restless, and you don't want that someone to be you.'

'OK then. I'll send a couple of the boys when things are quieter.'

'To rough him up, you mean? Come on, go easy. He was good to Layla.'

'I'll get him a medal minted,' said Max sarcastically. 'If we have to mess him up a little to get answers, then we'll mess him up, whether he's a good Samaritan or not.'

'I don't approve of this,' said Annie.

'Noted,' said Max. 'I'll be taking the car tomorrow, and Tone. You stay put, OK?'

Not waiting for her answer, he went past her and out.

'Bastard,' murmured Annie.

But when Max showed up late next day, he gave her the news that the old man had vanished, and the red boat with him. He'd scarpered. Upped anchor and pissed off out of it.

★

'What do you mean, gone?' Hunter asked Nolan. They were in Hunter's office and Hunter was in a bad mood. Over the course of the afternoon he'd had a few high-level phone calls that had startled him out of his usual calm and could put him in a difficult position.

'Like I said, boss. Mr . . .' Nolan glanced at his notebook '. . . Mr *Halliday* has departed the scene. Pulled up the anchor and buggered off.'

Hunter, who had been sitting behind his desk, now stood up, all six foot six inches of him, and rammed a finger into the desktop. 'He *what*?'

'Sorry, sir,' said Nolan. As if any of this was *his* bloody fault.

'Nolan,' said Hunter loudly. 'I want that man and his boat found. Get me a map of the canal system. Get all points alerted. He's our only possible viable witness and I want him stopped.'

'Yes, sir,' said Nolan, and left the room.

# 83

While Layla stayed in bed and Max went out, Annie spent the next morning playing the CCTV in the drawing room, trawling through hours of boring rubbish, people jigging around on the dance floor, hostesses coming back and forth to the bar time after time with trays full of drinks, then empty trays, then more drinks.

She was yawning on the couch, almost comatose, when she saw Kirsty Allen come swaggering up to the bar – and there was Bruno, behind it. They both leaned on the counter, chatting, laughing. Something about him troubled Annie and she didn't know what the hell it was. He seemed – this was stupid and she knew it, but he seemed *familiar* somehow.

Stupid.

Until she'd seen him coming down the stairs at Steve's house, she was sure she had never seen him before, never met him. So why?

She looked at Bruno's image, there on the screen. Froze it. Stared some more.

Nothing. She didn't know the man. She was wasting her time.

★

Max was pleased to see the new plate-glass windows were in and the Shalimar was starting to look like its old self again. Ellie was pleased too.

'Chris has been going apeshit over all this, Mr Carter,' she told Max when he called in, after having first gone to the Ventura and talked to Julian about what had happened to Layla there.

'It was an accident,' Julian had told him.

And Max had thought *yeah, maybe*. Still, he was glad that Layla had backed away from this job, left it to Julian.

'Who's your contact at the laundry?' Max asked Ellie, and then got back in the car and directed Tone across town to the laundry company, which occupied the corner section of a large industrial unit south of the river. Max and Tone went inside and asked a sulky-looking girl who was standing at the front desk of the dry-cleaning department for Todd Benson, Ellie's contact.

'He's out back, he's busy,' said the girl.

'Fetch him,' said Max.

'I can't do that. He won't like it.'

'OK.' Max stepped around the end of the desk and went into the back room where the scent of perchloroethylene was nearly overpowering. People were folding sheets, hanging up curtains in plastic covers, steaming dresses. Aware of the front desk girl coming squawking after him, Max walked on, Tone following. People stopped what they were doing and looked, intrigued by this diversion from the dull routine.

'Todd Benson?' Max asked one of them. The man indicated a door at the back.

Max went there and pushed it open. Outside, leaning against the wall, was a short paunchy man with a thin fluff of ginger hair on his head and a drinker's angry red colouring.

He was wearing an ill-fitting suit and dragging deeply on a cigarette. As Max stepped out from the shop, he exhaled two long plumes of smoke and his eyes widened.

'What . . . ?' he asked.

'Todd Benson?' asked Max.

'Yeah,' he said. 'Who wants him?'

'Hit him,' Max said to Tone. Benson found himself lifted off his feet, staring into the dispassionate gaze of a bald man-mountain with a gold crucifix set in the lobe of each ear.

Benson let out a yell as Tone pulled back a massive fist.

'Wait! Wait, whatcha doin', man?' Benson squealed. His cigarette fell to the pavement.

Tone paused.

Max eyed the man coolly. 'There was an accident. At my club. You know it? The Shalimar? I'm the owner. Max Carter.'

'I know it. Sure I do,' he gasped out. Christ, and who *hadn't* heard of Max Carter?

'Good. Only I take a dim view of people crashing things through my front window, you got that?'

'What? I . . .'

'Because my manageress moved her laundry order to another firm.'

'Wait, I didn't. I wouldn't . . .'

'Go on, Tone. Get it done.'

Tone drew back his ham-like fist. Benson shut his eyes and flinched back against the brickwork.

'You still saying you didn't?' said Max.

'Listen,' panted out Benson. 'You could beat me black and blue and what could I tell you? My bosses wouldn't do a thing like that. What you think they are, bloody Mafia? Are we in ruddy Chicago or something? Jesus! I told your general manager – what's his name, bloody Julian? I told him and now I'm telling you, whatever happened, it had *nothing* to do with us.'

Tone sent a quizzical look to Max. Max considered, then nodded. Tony dropped Benson from a height and he staggered then regained his balance. Tone drew back. Then Max leaned in and his voice was low but forceful enough to send shivers up the spine. 'Listen. If I find your sticky prints – or your boss's – all over this and you've lied to me, you know what?'

'What?' gasped Benson.

'I am going to come back here. And I promise you – I am going to hang you up by your bollocks.'

# PART THREE

PART THREE

# 84

Seamus summoned Bruno to the yard.

'Boss wants a word,' he said.

The usual guard was on the big metal gate, the dog on its lead beside him.

'All right?' the guard said, locking the gate after Bruno had stepped through.

Bruno wasn't all right. He was shit-scared. But when Redmond called, you went. Seamus met him at the front of the house and together they stepped through into the full-sized lift, Seamus yanking the doors shut, enclosing them in the lift's tomblike embrace. The lift descended one full floor and then juddered to a halt. Seamus pulled back the doors and stepped out. Bruno, feeling his mouth dry, his underarms sweaty, followed into pitch darkness.

When the light was turned on, illuminating the big square box of a room, Redmond was waiting.

Hideous. Deformed. Better if he'd been dead, thought Bruno, and wished that was the case. Bruno could feel his heart trying to pummel its way out through his chest wall.

'Good boy,' said Redmond. 'Now – there's something I want you to do.'

And whatever it was, Bruno knew he was going to have to do it.

# 85

An hour after they left Starburst Laundry, Tone parked up the Jag and sat in it while Max took a stroll through the graveyard, stopping at a particular group of headstones. He stood there in front of them, looking, remembering. Beneath those headstones – and they were elaborate, grandiose, black marble and gold lettering, the best he could afford and he'd paid for each and every one of them – the deceased members of his family lay slumbering.

The grandparents. His mother – Queenie. Ah now, Queenie. She had been something else, something better; a strong woman and Max had loved her and then he had lost her in that robbery organised by the Delaney crew. He'd had his revenge for that, many times over. And of course he had *married* a strong woman, eventually. Married her – and divorced her too.

But first he had picked out Ruthie Bailey because she was sweet-natured, presentable – yes, perfect wife material. *Big* mistake. His second choice – Ruthie's sister – had been an even bigger one. Annie was a force of nature, just like his mum had been. Maybe that was even the whole essence of the attraction – maybe Annie reminded him of Queenie.

His eyes moved along the graves. There was, of course, no headstone for Jonjo his brother, because Jonjo had died in Majorca and his body had vanished. Max was still working through that whole subject in his mind. Annie was not a fanciful woman and she was *sure* she had seen Jonjo dead out there. But Jaime had said that *his brother* had paid him to search.

And there . . . ah, there was little Eddie.

Eddie had been his youngest brother. Gay as a fish, but what of it? He'd never frightened the horses, never given Max a moment's concern. Then – it hurt still, to think of it – he'd gone out one evening and strayed into Delaney territory.

Today Max had brought them all flowers, his departed family: pink roses for Queenie, pink for Eddie. He got rid of the old blooms, curled and brown as they were – it was some while since he had last been here – then put the fresh ones in water. That done, he stood staring at the stones, wondering what the fuck it was all about. You struggled through life, fought your way out of the slums, worked hard to achieve things, managed to rise above the crap and the bother, and then you died.

Other people were moving around the cemetery. A woman was weeping, on her knees. An elderly couple walked slowly between the rows of stones, pointing out verses. Max sighed. He had his own small family still alive, his ex-wife and his daughter. But one day they too would sink into the earth, cease to be. And so would he.

*Ah, what the fuck.*

He turned away from the graves and went back to Holland Park.

*

Annie was still watching the CCTV recording of the club's bar area over and over, winding, rewinding, back and forth.

Bruno behind the bar, Kirsty leaning over it. They were chatting, laughing.

It was maybe on the hundredth time of watching that she paused the thing and looked hard, really *hard*, at Bruno's face.

'I'll be damned,' she said faintly.

A bolt of excitement shot through her.

Forget the blond hair and the birthmark. Take that away, and the face you were looking at . . .

'*My God*!' she breathed.

Annie jumped up off the couch and paced about, her eyes still glued to the screen.

It couldn't be – could it? But it *was*.

That was *Max*, right there. Only it wasn't. It was *Bruno*. She thought of what Max had told her, about Benito's phone call, his weird claim that Max's 'brother' had paid Jaime to look for him.

And here was a possible answer, wasn't it? It hadn't been Jonjo. Jonjo was dead. But it could have been *this* man, couldn't it? It could have been Bruno Dawkins.

★

Annie was crossing the hall later when she saw the post on the mat. She went to the front door, bent and picked it up. Circulars. Bills. And a plain white envelope with READ ME scrawled across the front of it in red pen.

'What the . . . ?' she murmured, slipping a nail under the edge of the flap and yanking it open, just as Max's key turned in the door. He stepped in, saw her standing there, the envelope in her hand.

'Hi,' he said, then looked more closely at her face. 'What's up?'

Annie unfolded the sheet of paper. On it, in the same scrawling hand as was on the envelope, was written:

YOR NEXT

# 86

'Did the postman bring this?' snapped Max. 'Is it franked?'

'You just came in the door, did you see anyone?' asked Annie. She was holding the thing in her hand, staring at it.

YOR NEXT

Max swore and turned back, flinging the door open. He ran down the steps, looked left, looked right. Then he came back inside.

'Nothing,' he said, shutting the door firmly behind him.

'It's not franked,' said Annie. She turned over the envelope. 'Not even addressed. Just this, here: "READ ME".'

'But it came with the rest of the post?'

'Well, who knows? But it was here, with the rest of it.'

'What's going on?' asked Layla, coming out of the drawing room and crossing the hall. She looked at her mother's sheet-white face and took the piece of paper and the envelope from Annie's hand and read it.

'What the *hell*?' she burst out.

'What time does the postman come? Usually?' asked Max.

'About midday. Except when he's off and someone stands in, then it's later.'

'Is the usual one on now?'

'Yes. So far as I know, I think he is.'

'Where's the local depot? You got their number?'

'No of course I don't have their number. Why would I?' This barrage of questions, coming from a man who hadn't shown a single iota of care for her for over a whole damned year, was starting to irritate the shit out of her. 'And you needn't concern yourself, OK? It'll be some crank, that's all.'

'What, saying "you're next"?' Max stared at her like she'd gone insane. 'Jaime's dead. Steve's dead. That bookshop bloke down on the canal too. Layla – excuse us, will you?'

Layla nodded, frowning, and went upstairs.

'Time we had a talk,' said Max, and grabbed Annie by the elbow and marched her into the study.

# 87

'What the hell is wrong with you?' Max asked when he'd closed the study door behind them. He leaned against it, watching Annie as she moved over to one of the big gold-threaded Knoll sofas and sat down.

Annie tossed the note onto the coffee table and sat back.

*You,* she thought. *You are what's wrong with me. You've been wrong for me all my life, right from the first moment I started mooning over you like a lovesick calf. But you decided we were over, and that was . . . well no, it wasn't fine. It was far from fine, but it was the deal. I accepted it. And if I start to let you back into my life and it all goes wrong again, this time it will be truly, truly bad. It will break me clean in two; I know it.*

She shrugged, said nothing.

'Talk to me, will you? Dammit, why do you always do this, shut down this way?' demanded Max.

'I've got nothing to say,' said Annie, feeling that she had a *lot* to say, actually, only not to him, *never* to him.

Max came over and hauled her to her feet. She hadn't been expecting that. Angrily she shrugged off his grip and sat down again.

'Tell me *exactly* what happened at the Montauk house,' he said, his voice low, insistent. He shoved the note aside and sat down on the coffee table, so that he was on the same level, staring eye to eye with her.

Annie didn't meet his gaze. She couldn't. Max reached out, put a hand under her chin, *made* her look at him.

'You're a mad cow,' he said, and there was a thin thread of laughter in his voice. 'And you might not believe this, but I really don't want you to end up on a slab like Steve and Jaime and that other poor sod in the canal. So you had better start talking.'

'You want me to tell you what happened in Montauk? Really?' Annie stared at him, her eyes hostile. 'Max – for a whole year you haven't given a shit about me. You told me it was over between us. I accepted that. I even *understood* it. Nice and neat. Like cutting off a limb. So let's not start trying to sew the damned thing back on, OK? It's beyond repair, it's rotten, so let's leave it at that. I don't need you – out of some peculiar sense of *obligation* – to start poking your nose into my business all over again. All right?'

Max stared at her, long and hard. 'Of course I'm obligated to you. You're the mother of my child.'

'But you don't trust me. You don't believe me. You made all that very clear.'

'Can we just leave that to one side, for now?'

'Leave the whole damned thing, Max. I really don't care.'

'Don't you think I had good reason not to trust you? When you'd been lying to me for years?'

'Oh Christ. *Really?* You really want to do this, all over again?' Annie surged to her feet and started walking around the study.

'No.' Max stood up too. 'I don't. So let's just stick to the facts for now, OK? Tell me what happened in Montauk.'

'Fine.' Annie stopped pacing.

'So . . . ?' Max prompted.

Annie told him all about the man chasing her up the beach and into the house.

'You didn't have security with you?' asked Max.

'Yes.'

'On the beach?'

'No. Not on the beach.'

'Why not?'

'Oh fuck . . .'

'But at the house? You had security then?'

'Yes.'

'And what was your "security" doing while all this was kicking off?'

*Eating a pastrami on rye,* thought Annie, and a half-hysterical laugh nearly escaped her.

'He was useless. I've fired his arse. I was going to get in touch with Steve, get him out there. Then Ellie told me . . . it was awful, about Steve. I can't believe it, even now.'

Max was standing in front of her, his arms crossed over his chest, head down, thinking.

'This could all be connected, couldn't it. Steve. Jaime. The Montauk business. Now a possible witness to Steve's death, getting topped. And that business with Layla, an accident. Or was it?'

'The poor bloke may have witnessed nothing. Someone might just have *suspected* he did,' said Annie. Thoughts of Steve brought her mind to Kirsty Allen – and Bruno. If she told Max what she suspected about Bruno right now, would he believe her? She doubted it. She could hardly believe it herself. 'Max, do you know of a Bruno Dawkins? When I went over to Steve's place to see Kirsty, he was there, just coming down the stairs.'

'No. I don't, offhand. I'm not happy about that old bloke who helped Layla upping sticks and going. What had he seen? What might he know?'

'Hunter'll find him.'

'Maybe I'll find him first.' Max went over to the desk and reached for the phone.

Annie watched him walk; great economy of movement. A latent, restrained aura of power. As ever, Max oozed a sexual heat that could easily make a woman's head spin. But that was *not* going to happen with her. Not this time.

Then, just as he was about to snatch the phone up, it rang. He picked up. 'Yes?'

He listened. He said: 'All right. Keep calm.'

'Who is it?' asked Annie.

Max put the phone down. 'That was Kirsty. She says the police just phoned her and let her know the latest.'

Annie's stomach clenched. 'Which is?'

'They're releasing Steve's body for burial. I'm off over to his place, just a couple of calls to make first.'

'What? So soon?'

'That's what she just said.'

'And she's asked you to go over?' asked Annie.

'She's in bits.'

'Where's her boyfriend Bruno?'

'How should I know? You carry on, I'll just . . .' and he turned away from her, back to the phone.

'Max,' said Annie urgently. 'About him. About Bruno.'

'What about him?' he asked, pausing.

She told him.

'Don't be bloody stupid,' he said.

★

It was an easy enough job. At five o'clock one morning, as instructed, Bruno took the keys to one of the plateless scrapyard lorries and tried to clear his mind – but he couldn't. Cormac hadn't made a success of braining Layla Carter – and whenever Bruno thought about that, the near-miss she'd had – he found that he couldn't feel anything but relief that she was OK.

Still, he had a job to do. He drove the lorry over to the Blue Parrot and smashed it through the frontage. Then he threw the lorry into first, floored the accelerator, and sped off. He had a very full schedule. Redmond had another job lined up for him.

# 88

With Max busy and Layla not wanting company, Annie took herself off, accompanied by Tone, to see Ellie. As they sat upstairs in the flat over the club and Ellie poured out the tea, she told her old mate about the police releasing Steve's body and the fact that Kirsty had just phoned and spoken to Max, and he'd gone over there.

Ellie looked at Annie as if she'd gone completely mad.

'I wouldn't let Chris go within a mile of that woman. She's a bloody piranha and her diet is man-specific,' said Ellie. 'I reckon she's going to cash in here, you know. Scoop the jackpot, get every damned thing.'

'Well, she's already replaced Steve in bed,' said Annie, thinking of Bruno coming down the stairs. Bruno, with Max's face. Thinking of Kirsty, who had every reason to get Steve out of the way, collect the money and install Bruno where Steve had once been.

Ellie harrumphed. 'No surprises there. And you let Max go over there? Ha! So would I.'

'Ells,' said Annie in some irritation. Downstairs, someone cranked up the club's massive sound system and started stomping out Diana Ross's 'Chain Reaction'. 'What the fuck would that bother me for? We've been separated for a year. If he wants to start dancing the horizontal fandango with that tart, good luck to him.'

'You don't mean that.' They could hear the cleaner working and the phone was ringing on the bar downstairs. They
heard Chris's deep voice as he picked up and said hello.

'I bloody do.' Although Annie wondered about that. How
*would* she feel, if Max took up with someone new? Well, he
could have done that already. He could have moved some
dusky beauty in to his Bajan home and she would be none
the wiser. 'There's no possibility of me stopping Max doing
anything he really wants to do, anyway.'

'You know what? I think there's still something there.'

'I think you're dreaming,' said Annie, feeling weighted
down by sadness. Max bloody Carter! She'd loved him all
her life, and what had it ever brought her? Heartbreak. Fighting. Mad reunions – and *devastating* partings.

They heard the heavy thud of Chris's footsteps coming
up the stairs. He passed by the kitchen where they sat, then
retraced his steps and stood in the kitchen door. Distantly,
they could hear the Hoover still running and Diana still belt-
ing it out with the Bee Gees backing her up.

'You'll never guess,' he said.

'No, we won't,' said Ellie.

'Janice just called. Blue Parrot's had the front smashed in.
She was trying to reach Max but she can't. I'm going to call
him. Is he at yours?'

'He's at Steve's place with Kirsty,' said Annie.

'Jeez!' Chris's eyes widened. 'You think that's safe? Poor
bloke'll get carried out on a stretcher.'

'I told her,' said Ellie. 'That cunt Kirsty's got more war-
paint on her mush than Sitting Bull at Custer's last stand.
Tits always out on display. Ruddy great false eyelashes – you
seen them? And skirts up to here.'

Annie looked at Ellie. She looked at Chris. Both were smirking.

'What's so bloody funny about him going over there to help out?' she enquired.

'If you're happy with it . . .' said Chris innocently.

'I'm perfectly happy. Really, I don't give a shit.'

'Oh sure,' they said in chorus.

# 89

'The thing's vanished,' said Nolan, coming into Hunter's office and flopping down in a chair. 'Seriously, guv. We've had uniform going all up and down the length of the canals and it's just not there. No red boat stuffed with flowers anywhere. It's gone.'

'Boats,' said Hunter, 'do not vanish.'

'This one has.'

'This isn't the bloody Bermuda Triangle, Nolan. Do I have to repeat myself? That old chap's our only potential witness and we have to find him. Check the boat houses. Don't fuck about. Check *everything*.'

'Yes, sir.'

Hunter gave him a dead-eyed stare. 'So shift. Get out there and find the fucking thing.'

\*

Max was having the same problem as the police. He'd been on to all his street contacts, and nobody had so far turned up the old gent in the red boat. Putting that aside, he went on over to Parliament Hill, to Steve's place. Kirsty flung open the door to him, looking flustered.

'Oh! Mr Carter, thanks so much for coming,' she said, and burst into tears. 'It's all so awful.'

She led the way into the sitting room. Max followed, wondering if the tears were genuine. Kirsty might be in line to make a tidy profit out of Steve's death. But then – maybe he was seeing it wrong. His inbuilt and self-protective cynicism was working overdrive at the moment. If Kirsty *had* loved Steve and not just seen him as a meal ticket, then he had to pity the poor bitch. Love could cut you to ribbons. He knew that because he'd been in love too – the stupidest kind of love of all – with his own wife. Even the sight of Annie stirred the animal in him, and even after a year's separation, that feeling hadn't diminished. He wished it had, but it *hadn't*.

As soon as they got into the sitting room, the phone started ringing. Kirsty picked up and said hello. Then she held it out to Max.

'It's for you,' she said.

It was Chris, telling him about the Blue Parrot. More bad news. He told Chris he'd go over there soonest and put the phone down and then – as if on cue – Kirsty flung herself, sobbing, into his arms. Max let her stay there for a moment or two and then gently pushed her back, guided her down onto the sofa and took a seat opposite.

'So the police are releasing Steve's body,' he said.

She nodded. 'I can't believe he's dead,' she said, groping for a handkerchief, finding it, dabbing at her eyes.

'Do you need help dealing with the funeral arrangements?'

'That's so kind of you.' She gave a trembling smile.

'Steve was my mate.'

'I know. It's all so terrible.'

Was she really upset, or faking? Max was trying to decide and it was difficult when his mind was still reeling from what Annie had told him about this 'Bruno' character. She had shown him the CCTV from the Shalimar and – yes – he had to admit to himself that the man did look spookily like a younger version of himself.

But – his *brother*?

No. Surely not.

But then, there were things stirring in his memory. The impossibility of it being Jonjo who'd paid Jaime to look for him. And there was something else, wasn't there. Something from years ago.

He'd mulled it over several times and here it was again, staring him in the face, the thing he did not want to see: Queenie, his mum, taking off for Brighton and Aunt Nora's place, staying there for months and coming back subdued, somehow so different. He thought of what Annie had said about Bruno's age and – yes – that would fit.

He didn't want to think it, or even *consider* it, but the fact was this: Queenie could have dropped a kid while she was there in Brighton, the child of that flashy creep who'd been hanging around the house. What was his name? Clive? Yes. He'd never forget it. Bastard had got *right* up his nose. Queenie could have left the kid with Nora and – Christ, was *that* why Nora had taken to coming up to London with her begging bowl, wanting money: to support Queenie's kid?

He thought of how uneasy his mum had been whenever Nora visited, and – *shit* – there was a kid, he remembered, standing out on the pavement one day. Max remembered that clearly, and Mum had told him it was one of Nora's strays from the church.

But what if it wasn't?

What if the kid was an illegitimate shameful mistake, the result of her later-life fling with that greasy bastard Clive?

'My wife said you had company when she called on you the other day. Someone called Bruno Dawkins,' he said to Kirsty.

Kirsty stiffened. 'Company? Oh! Well that's right. I did. Bruno was staying over. He's a friend and I was so gutted about Steve, he didn't feel he could just leave me here on my own.'

'That was good of him,' said Max, remembering what Annie had said about her suspicions of Kirsty and this 'Bruno' romping in bed overnight – with Steve not even cold in his grave. Bruno – for God's sake! – who could well be his own damned brother.

'So he's not still here?'

'No he's not.' Max noted that – as if by magic – Kirsty's emotional tears had dried up.

'OK. Well . . . thanks so much again for coming,' said Kirsty.

'It's nothing,' said Max, and left.

Tone was waiting in the car. Max got in and he started the engine.

'You know a Bruno Dawkins?' Max asked him.

'Not offhand. You want me to ask around?'

'Yeah, do that.'

# 90

Tone drove Max over to the Blue Parrot. The manageress, Janice, was hopping mad.

'Happened this morning. Nobody saw a thing, of course. I was upstairs asleep and the whole front caved in. Lorry or something, I dunno. Just *look* at the bloody mess.'

Having calmed Janice down and seen that running repairs were in order, Max asked her if she knew anyone by the name of Bruno Dawkins.

'Who's he?'

'Do you know him?'

'Sorry, Mr Carter, I don't.'

Max then went over to the Palermo and warned the manager of what he might expect to happen next. They were under siege here, and his gut feeling was that Benson had been telling the truth and that this had absolutely nothing to do with Sunburst. Granted, Ellie had fallen out with them, but why so extreme a reaction?

The Palermo's manager said that he was going to step up overnight security, set up cameras outside, maybe catch the bastards in the act if he could. He also said how damned sad he was to hear about Steve Taylor.

'Steve organised the doors in here. He did a cracking job, you know,' said the manager.

'He was a top bloke,' said Max. Then he thought of Kirsty over there on Parliament Hill, about to scoop up everything Steve had ever worked for. 'Do you know a Bruno Dawkins?'

'Sorry, boss. I don't.'

Max went on over to the Shalimar and found Annie upstairs at the kitchen table with Ellie, drinking tea. As he ascended the stairs, he could hear the merry chatter of the dancers in their dressing room, which was down the hall from the kitchen. Chris was there in the kitchen with Ellie and Annie, leaning against the worktops eating a biscuit. He straightened as Max came in.

'All right, boss?' asked Chris.

'Yeah. Fine.' He was getting tired of asking it, but he asked it anyway. 'Chris, d'you know Bruno Dawkins?'

Chris looked blank.

'I do,' said Ellie. 'He worked here. Last year, it was. Only for a few months. Tending the bar.'

'Yeah, and this was where Kirsty met him,' said Annie, looking at Max. 'They were together in the bar CCTV like I showed you.'

'Yeah.' Ellie snorted. 'They were an item, for sure. Always at it in dark corners. That was before she met Steve and thought he'd be a safer bet. At which point, she dropped Bruno like a hot potato.'

'I don't think she dropped him at all,' said Annie. 'He was with her when I called over there. They looked very cosy.'

Max went off along the corridor to the office to make a phone call, passing the dancers' dressing room as he did so. Annie heard an outbreak of laughter, a flirtatious chorus of '*hiya, Max*'. Ellie sent Annie a smile. Annie sipped her tea and said nothing.

Presently they heard Max talking on the phone. Ellie poured out more tea. Chris took a second biscuit. Then Max came along the corridor and back into the kitchen.

'Just had a word with Steve's solicitor. He recently made a new will, favouring Kirsty. Guess who witnessed it?' he asked the assembled company.

'Surprise us,' said Annie.

'A Mr Bruno Dawkins and a Miss Latipa Dunne.'

'That's our boy,' said Chris. 'But Latipa Dunne? That don't ring any bells.'

'Yes it does.' Annie stood up.

Max looked at her.

'The cleaner at Steve's place. Her name was Latipa. Kirsty fired her. It was pretty obvious they hated each other.'

'Well she agreed to witness the will, whether she hated Kirsty or not. And that's not the only thing. It was rewritten just a month before Steve's death. Having no family, he'd planned to leave everything to the gym we used to attend in the East End. Then just a few weeks before he died, he switched it all over to Kirsty.'

'*What?*' said Annie sharply. 'We need a word with this Dawkins bloke. And Latipa Dunne.'

Max went back to the office. More greetings from the dancers; then he was back. 'Latipa's over at Carter Security right now. And why wouldn't she be? You know a good cleaner, you give her as much work as you can,' said Max. 'Let's get over there.'

## 91

Max and Annie went back to Holland Park first and left Tone with Layla.

'I don't need a bodyguard,' she protested.

'You've got one. You go out, Tone goes with you,' Max told her.

'Mum needs one more, surely?' Layla was still prepared to argue the point. 'She was the one who got that note – not me.'

'Your mother's with me,' said Max. 'She'll be OK.'

'Yeah, my hero,' said Annie, not without sarcasm.

With Tone installed in the porter's chair in the hall of the Holland Park house and Layla given her instructions, Max took the Jag and drove Annie over to the industrial estate where Carter Security was situated. They went into the building. Through a half-glassed wall at the back, they could see Latipa in Steve's office, working. They could hear the high whine of the vacuum cleaner and the scent of polish was wafting pleasantly in the air.

In the front office, the three desks were all occupied today, thin little Julie Adams at the back, Terry Foreman in the middle, Jimmy Iles at the front. All three were on the phone, taking bookings. Annie reflected grimly that Steve's death hadn't much stood in the way of commerce. When Julie finished her conversation she hung up, made a quick note and rose from her desk with a hesitant smile.

'Mr Carter. Can I help you?'

He gestured to the back office. 'We want a word with Latipa, that's all.'

Julie sat down while Max moved on, Annie following close behind. He went and opened the door into what had once been Steve's domain. 'Latipa?' he said loudly, to make himself heard over the noise of her machine.

Latipa turned and stared at the pair of them. She switched off the vacuum and silence descended. 'Yes?' she said.

Max gave her his most charming smile. 'Take a seat, Latipa. We want to have a chat.'

'What about?' She looked wary.

'Steve Taylor's will,' said Max.

It was as if all the colour, all the life, drained out of her face.

'Nothing to do with me,' she said quickly.

'What wasn't?'

'I witness it. They ask me to and I did.'

'You say "they". Who was that? Was it Steve himself?' asked Annie.

'Yeah, and Kirsty.'

'Was Steve under any pressure to do that? Change his will?' asked Max.

Annie could see Latipa wrestling with herself at this point. She hated Kirsty and would love to drop her in the shit. But, to Annie's surprise, honesty prevailed. 'I don't think.'

'Well, you were there. Was he or not?' persisted Max.

'No. Bruno witnessed too.'

'We know that and we'll be talking to Bruno soon.'

'Boyfriend of hers,' said Latipa. She sniffed. 'Used to come indoors when Mr Taylor was out.'

'Thanks for your help, Latipa,' said Max.

'It's nothing,' she said, looking unhappy.

'Anything else you want to tell us?' he asked.

'No! Nothing to do with me,' she said, turning her back to them, switching the vacuum on.

They went back into the outer office. Julie was watching them anxiously.

'Keeping busy then?' Annie asked her.

'Yeah. Business as usual. Which seems awful. I hate it, Mr Taylor not being here. Dying like that. It's so terrible.' Julie's eyes filled with tears.

'Any problems, give me a call. Phone through to any of the clubs,' said Max.

'Thanks,' said Julie.

They walked through to the front door and Annie opened it. Charming! Somehow he had a sweet and tender way with young girls, but with her? All he did was snarl at her. Bastard. There was a pop and a sharp *crack* and something hit the back wall. For a moment Annie thought it was Latipa, hauling the vacuum about, knocking against the desk, something like that. Then there was another popping noise and one of the photo frames on the wall above Julie's desk shattered, sending a waterfall of glass shards all over the place. Julie let out a shriek.

Annie started to turn and then she became aware that she was being grabbed, being *hurt*, actually. A piledriver knocked all the wind out of her. Within a couple of seconds she was flat on her back on the floor. She lay there, bewildered, hardly able to breathe because there was a crushing weight on her chest. Time seemed to stall. Julie was screaming. The vacuum cleaner had stopped and Latipa had decided to join in with the noise, letting out weird little shrieks. The two boys were shouting. A car was speeding away from the front of the building. Max's body was very heavy, very solid as it lay over hers. She could feel his heart, pounding. She tried to raise her head.

'*Keep down,*' he snapped in her ear.

Julie's screams had died to a whimper.

Annie stopped trying to get up.

# 92

He hadn't been supposed to kill them, of course. Bruno knew this. Redmond had been very specific in his instructions.

'Wound them. In the arms, the legs. You know the sort of thing. Don't shoot to kill. Just make them *suffer*.'

Only – he hadn't. He'd pulled up in front of Carter Security and started shooting, just as instructed, but he'd shot the walls, the ceiling. He'd seen the glass at the front of the building shatter, had seen Max Carter push his ex-wife to the floor. None of the bullets touched Annie and Max, or any of the others. He made sure of it.

Bruno drove off, parked up a mile away. He sat there behind the wheel, shaking, wondering *why* he hadn't been able to do it. He hated Max Carter, after all, didn't he? The killer of Nora. The killer of Tory, who'd loved him, the first person *ever* to treat him well. So why did he feel unable to finally do what was needed, carry out Redmond's instructions and in so doing take his own revenge too?

He didn't know.

He slammed his fists into the steering wheel over and over again, trying to reason it out. But he couldn't.

He would tell Redmond the gun had misfired.

What else could he do?

# 93

It was barely two hours since they'd been shot at in Steve's office. The police had been summoned there by Julie. First SOCO and uniform had pitched up, then Hunter and his sidekick. A policewoman had sat a hysterical Latipa down, and Julie and her two male co-workers. She made them all tea, reassured them, took statements from them and then sent them all home.

Hunter and Nolan questioned Annie and Max. They had nothing much to tell. They were here, in Max's place of business, in the office that Steve Taylor had run on behalf of the Carter family, and the next thing they knew, someone had fired shots. Two. Ballistics were there, digging bullets out of the wall so they could check the calibre and find any tell-tale striations that could help them identify the weapon.

'You got any enemies, Mrs Carter?' Nolan asked Annie.

'Too many to count,' said Annie.

'You?' He turned his attention to Max.

'None whatsoever.'

'Got no idea why anybody would shoot at this office? At the two of you? At any of the people who work here?'

'No,' said Max.

'All right. You can go,' said Hunter, watching Max the way a desert mouse would watch a scorpion. 'We may want to question you further, though.'

'Fair enough,' said Max.

They went.

When they got back to the Holland Park house, Max said to Annie: 'Pack a bag. We're getting out of here.'

'You what?'

'You heard. People putting notes through the letterbox, people taking pot shots at us? We're going somewhere under better cover.' Max was speaking coldly, but mostly because he was annoyed with himself, with his own weakness. In that split second when the bullets had started flying around, his first – his only – instinct had been to protect Annie, and that annoyed the hell out of him.

'Like where?' Annie asked. She was still feeling shaky and he was talking to her like a bloody field marshal, barking out orders. The last thing – the *very* last thing – that she needed was him coming in here telling her what to do.

Max glanced around the room. 'You ever have this place swept for bugs?'

'Never. I'm not paranoid, like you.'

'Well, if you haven't, I'll tell you once we're outside. Get packed up. I'll get a message to Layla.'

'Yes, sir,' said Annie sarkily.

'You got any better ideas?'

'No I haven't. Why don't you go fuck yourself, Max?' asked Annie, and went off upstairs to pack a bag.

★

Having left Hunter still poking around the crime scene at Carter Security, Nolan carried on with his search for the elusive canal boat. Uniform were on alert and were scouring the length of the whole system, looking upcountry, everywhere.

Nolan was looking along the London canals and coming up empty on Mr Halliday and his narrowboat. He was in the process of checking storage sheds, asking around boat-yards. He had only been called off it by Hunter's summons to the Carter offices. He didn't fancy going back to Hunter and telling him yet again that the Halliday boat couldn't be found; he didn't particularly want his arse kicked up between his shoulder blades, and these days Hunter seemed in just the mood to do it.

Painstakingly Nolan was working his way up from the Isle of Dogs past Limehouse Cut, the Lee Navigation canal, Regent's Park, through the Camden Locks to Little Venice, all the way down to Bull's Bridge Junction and Hanwell Locks. Try as he might, he couldn't magic up a boat and its owner just because he wanted to. Late in the afternoon, he gave it up for the day. He went back to Hunter and received the bollock-ing he knew he was due.

'Tomorrow's Steve Taylor's funeral,' said Hunter when he'd finished laying into Nolan. 'We'll both be there. All right?'

'Sure, boss,' said Nolan, thinking that at least it would make a change from combing the waterways for something that was bloody impossible to find.

Then it hit him, all at once.

If the boat couldn't be found, there had to be an explana-tion. And Nolan thought that he *had* that explanation, right now. But OK. Hunter was tired, it was late in the day, his boss wasn't in the mood for wild speculation.

'Well actually – if you could spare me tomorrow? There's another thing I'm looking at,' said Nolan.

'All right. Just get on with it, will you? I'm up to my arse here.'

Nolan thought that yes, his idea *was* pretty wild. But it just might be right. If you eliminate the possible, what's left? The fucking *im*possible, that's what.

Get the funeral out of the way and then he'd tell Hunter all about it.

Or – hold on – no. He wouldn't. He would go ahead and find what he was looking for first. Make some calls. Take a few days if needs be. And *then* he would spring it on Hunter and get a pat on the back and be told what a clever DS he really was.

Good plan.

He *liked* that plan.

# 94

'You've got to be fucking kidding me,' said Annie.

They were standing in front of a tiny terrace house in a noisy street in Bow, bags in hand. Annie was looking up at the place's frontage like she was having a nightmare.

'Nope. Not kidding,' said Max, putting a key in the door and going inside.

'This is . . .' Annie was still out there on the front step. 'This was your mum's old place, wasn't it. It's Queenie's.'

'Come on in,' said Max.

'What, we're stopping *here*?' Annie was still on the doorstep.

'Yep. You never met Mum, did you?'

Annie snorted. 'I heard reports.'

She stepped into the gloomy little hall, pushed the front door closed. The place looked clean, at least. It was old and unloved, but the floors had been polished and there was a pleasant scent of air freshener; and it felt warm – the heating had been running.

Max led the way into the kitchen. 'What does that mean?' he asked, dropping his overnight bag.

Annie pulled out a chair at the table and sat down. 'It means that Ruthie – my sister, you remember her, the woman you married and did the dirty on with me?'

'I remember Ruthie,' said Max, not rising to the bait.

'It means that Ruthie told me about Queenie. That she was a queen in every way. That she was a bitch. Dominating. Forceful. Oh – and a pain in the backside, I distinctly remember Ruthie saying that.'

'Ruthie got on with Mum OK.'

'She was scared to death of her. Ruthie was much too mild to cope with your mother.'

'They seemed to get on.'

'Bullshit. Queenie liked Ruthie because she could keep her under the thumb. How long have we got to stay in this rat hole?'

'Until we figure out who's trying to kill us,' said Max. 'There's food in the freezer. It will do.'

'Right.' Already she was missing her creature comforts. She could feel the walls closing in on her.

Annie got up and wandered out of the room. She crossed the hall and opened a door into a small lounge, neatly furnished. And there, over the fireplace, was a head-and-shoulders portrait of Queenie Carter. This was Queenie as she had been in her later years, with her imperious expression, her hard little mouth, her sharp blue eyes, her white strictly coiffured hair billowing around her head like a cloud. Annie stood there looking up at the painting and felt a shiver go right through her. She knew Queenie would have hated her – and the feeling would have been entirely mutual.

And weren't there just two bedrooms here?

Max had followed her in.

'I'm not sleeping with you,' she said, just to make it clear.

'Why not wait until you're asked,' said Max, and went back out into the hall and into the kitchen.

'I don't give a shit whether you ask or not,' she shouted after him, following him out there. 'It's not going to happen.'

Max was filling the kettle at the sink. 'Tea?' he asked.

*Bastard.* 'Yes. How lovely. How fucking *civilised.*'

Max slapped the kettle onto the counter and switched it on. He turned to face her.

'You and Layla can take the double, I'll take the single. All right?'

'Perfect,' snapped Annie.

When Layla arrived, bringing Tone with her, Max sat them all down in the lounge and explained that they were all going to be careful for a while.

'For how long is "a while"?' asked Layla anxiously.

'Until we get to the bottom of whatever's happening.'

'Someone was taking pot shots at us when we were at Steve's office,' said Annie.

'*What*?' Layla was aghast.

Max gave Annie a look, which she swiftly interpreted as: *What did you have to go and tell her that for?*

'No harm done,' said Max. 'But that, and your mother being chased up the beach over in the US, and Steve going like he did, and then the bloke on the boat . . . well you know damned well what happened to him. Something bad's going on. And until we know exactly what, we keep close.'

At bedtime, Annie told Layla that they were sharing the double bedroom and that Max was going to take the single.

'What is going *on* with you two?' Layla moaned.

'Nothing is going on,' said Annie, and refused to discuss the matter any further.

Tone stayed downstairs, on the couch. Somehow, they all slept. And awoke next morning to a bright breezy day full of sunshine.

It was the day of Steve Taylor's funeral.

# 95

Hunter turned up for the Taylor funeral for the sole purpose of keeping his eyes on the mourners. Nolan was busy elsewhere, doing God knew what and Hunter was far too bloody tired to enquire, so he attended alone. He watched Kirsty Allen and her handsome blond escort up at the front of the church, watched the rest of the mourners. Some well-known crims were here in their Sunday best, including . . .

'Hello, Mrs Carter,' he said to Annie as she passed by looking indescribably hot in a black cartwheel hat, a figure-hugging black dress and high heels, red lipstick on her mouth, her eyes hidden by a large pair of Chanel sunglasses. Not far behind her came *him*. Max bloody Carter, elegantly and expensively turned out. Fucking gangster. And their daughter followed on at a distance with a ruddy great minder at her side. She was a stunner, he thought, just like her mother.

'Detective! Hello,' said Annie. 'Keeping an eye on us, are you?'

Before he could formulate an answer and pick his chin back off the floor, she gave him a thin taunting smile. God, the nerve on the woman! Yesterday she'd been shot at. Today she looked as cool as could be – and twice as fuckable.

Max passed them both and went and spoke to a couple of big men who were standing by the church doors.

'I didn't think you'd show up today,' Hunter said to Annie.

'It's the funeral of an old friend,' said Annie.

'I mean, after what happened yesterday.'

'Look around you, Detective,' said Annie.

Hunter looked. At six-foot intervals, hulking sharp-eyed men were stationed, watching the mourners but not interacting with them. They were also watching the perimeter of the graveyard, the traffic passing by in the road, the pedestrians, everything and anything.

'Impressive,' said Hunter. 'I hope none of those men are armed, Mrs Carter.'

'Of course not,' said Annie sweetly. 'I heard you lost one of your witnesses. The old chap in the red boat.'

Max's boys had been down there and they hadn't found him either. No one seemed to have a clue where he'd gone to. People had told them the police were looking for Mr Halliday. It was weird, but suddenly he was gone.

'Keep clear of all this, Mrs Carter,' said Hunter.

'Of course,' said Annie, and then there was no more time to talk because the hearse was arriving. Max came back down the path and said to Annie: 'Get inside now.'

She nodded and moved away, toward the big arched double doors of the church where the vicar was waiting to escort the departed up the aisle. Hunter followed but took a seat well away from all the action, right at the back.

He'd attended a lot of funerals, in his day. Personal ones and ones where he just hoped and prayed a killer would turn up, show themselves. This one was heavily attended in every way. He saw the three Carter Security workers sitting close by, Terry Foreman and Jimmy Iles and the girl, Julie Adams, who took one look at the men bringing her boss's coffin up the aisle and burst into tears. Foreman patted her shoulder awkwardly.

The vicar came stepping solemnly in his ceremonial robes up the aisle, the big gold cross held before him, and here came the six men bearing the coffin aloft on their shoulders – Max Carter on the right at the front, the Carter driver Tony on the left beside him, then four other men, all of whom Hunter knew to be in the pay of the Carter family.

The men laid the coffin – bare of flowers as had been the deceased's wish, as stated by his partner Kirsty – on the dais at the top of the aisle, and then they sat down. The funeral ceremony began. There were speeches and hymns and a eulogy read by Kirsty, who broke down in pretty tears midway and had to be escorted back to her seat, sobbing, by Bruno Dawkins.

Hunter watched Kirsty with a cynical eye. According to Annie Carter, Kirsty had lost no time in jumping into bed with this new man after Steve's unfortunate demise. Hunter tuned out the rest of the ceremony, and soon it was over. They carried the coffin back outside, and Hunter'd had enough; he didn't wait for them to plant Steve Taylor in the ground. He left.

## 96

Of course there was a wake. They all had to stand around and eat cucumber sandwiches at Steve's house on Parliament Hill, sign the book of remembrance in the hall – and Annie had to remind herself, the house wasn't Steve's anymore. Now it was destined to be Kirsty's. And Kirsty seemed more than willing to share the place with her fake-blond boyfriend.

As the mourners stood in the conservatory, sipping drinks and helping themselves from the buffet table, the roar of chatter and the odd burst of irreverent laughter filled the sun-filled room. Annie was watching the lean, long man with Kirsty, mapping his face with her eyes and then looking over to Max.

Brothers?

She was annoyed to find herself thinking that Max was the hottest man in this entire room. Women responded warmly to him. One was chatting to him right now, a thirtyish and very well maintained blonde. Her face was animated, slightly flushed, her focus totally on him.

Layla had decided she was not coming to the wake, so she'd gone back to Queenie's old house with Tone in close attendance. Annie was glad of that, really. She didn't want to have to put on a cheerful face for Layla when she was so agitated over Max and so sad over Steve. Three of Max's minders were in the room, watching her, watching him – and, of course, watching everyone else for signs of untoward movement.

'Can I get you a drink? I'm Simeon,' said a tall aristocratic man with a sweep of light brown hair and a long, smiling face. *Old money,* she thought. He held out a slender, languid, long-fingered hand.

Annie shook it. 'Annie,' she said. 'Thanks, but I'm fine.'

'How do you know Kirsty?' Simeon asked.

'I don't, really. I was a friend of Steve's. How do *you* know Kirsty?' It seemed an unlikely pairing, this elegant aristo and Kirsty.

'Oh, just friends you know. Acquaintances.' He looked uncomfortable at the question and Annie thought that maybe he'd been a *client* of Kirsty's. A lot of the dancers she knew did cash in hand for a quick leg-over out the back of the clubs.

'Sad business. Terribly sad,' he said, swiftly changing the subject.

'Yes. Steve worked for my ex-husband.'

'Who's right here,' said Max, appearing at her elbow so silently that Annie felt her innards clench with surprise. Max held out a hand. 'Max Carter. And you are . . . ?'

Simeon introduced himself and then scarpered across the room to chat up the blonde Max had previously been talking to.

'You didn't have to give the poor bloke the death stare,' said Annie, almost amused.

'The what?'

'You know exactly what I mean. That look. If *you* don't want the goods, don't begrudge them to someone else.'

Max turned and faced her full-on. 'Who said I didn't want them?' he asked. 'They're mine, after all.'

'Yours? I don't think so. We divorced, remember? In nine-teen-eighty.' She held up her left hand. 'See? No rings. Which means I'm a free agent, so enough with the alpha male crap.'

Max smiled. 'He's not your type anyway.'

'And what is my type? Exactly?'

'I think we both know the answer to *that* one.'

'Oh, you must mean Constantine.' Now she was goading him deliberately. Suddenly, she couldn't help it. He wanted a fight, did he? Well, let him have one.

'Actually I didn't mean him. I meant me.'

'Don't flatter yourself.'

'But now you mention it, after me, you *did* take up with him.'

'He was a very handsome man. Powerful. That's a turn-on, you know. Power.'

'I know it is for you,' said Max, his face suddenly grim.

'The fact that you'd been missing for two years after what happened in Majorca, did you forget that? *Two bloody years.* Things changed. Time healed. I moved on.'

'In double quick time, yes.' They were nose to nose now, biting out words, snarling at each other. 'I should have known you were a tart. Didn't you do that, once upon a time? Run a knocking shop? Should have been a warning for me, really.'

'Tarts charge,' Annie snapped out. 'I never charged Constantine. And as I recall, I never charged *you*.'

'Bitch,' rapped out Max.

Bruno passed by, nodding to her as he went. Annie frowned. She was sick of arguing the toss with Max. She was sick of feeling fearful and on edge. She shivered despite the heat and crush of the room. 'And what are we going to do about *him*?' she wondered out loud.

'Christ knows. I've been putting feelers out.'

'You think it's possible then? You think he really could be your brother?'

'Yes I think it's possible. But he's been spotted going in and out of the old Delaney scrapyard over in Battersea. I don't like that.'

Annie stiffened at the mention of the Delaneys.

'Well at least that bastard Redmond's out of it now, dead and gone,' she said, shivering suddenly despite the warmth of the room. She'd *seen* him, thrown from a high window in Scotland. And thank God for it. 'I hate these things. Funerals. Wakes. I've been to too many.'

'So what do you want to do now?'

Annie gave Max a cool look. 'I want to go home. To Holland Park. But if that's off the cards, then back to Queenie's place. If I must.'

'OK. Let's go then.'

'It would be interesting, don't you think, to have one of your boys watching *this* place? Seeing who comes, who goes?'

'What are you thinking?'

'I don't know. I'd just like to know an awful lot more about Kirsty and her boyfriend.'

'We can do that. Have someone outside in a car, taking a few photos. Why not?'

They found Kirsty to say their farewells. She was in a huddle in a corner of the sitting room with Bruno standing over her. They were whispering, laughing. Annie thought of Kirsty's tears in the church. Being led sobbing back to her seat by Bruno. Crocodile tears, probably. Now, Kirsty looked almost high, but as Annie and Max approached she quickly sobered up.

'Time we were off,' said Max, eyeing Bruno with both intense curiosity and deep suspicion. Yes – it was possible that Bruno was Queenie's kid. Somehow Max couldn't make himself believe it, though: maybe he just didn't want to.

'Oh. OK,' said Kirsty. 'Thanks for coming, both of you.' She sent a flirtatious smile Max's way, but her eyes were frost-cold as they turned on Annie.

'Thanks,' said Annie.

'My pleasure,' said Kirsty.

When Annie followed Max out into the hall, she glanced back. Bruno and Kirsty were still there in their corner – and they were laughing again.

When they got outside, Annie showed Max the page she'd torn out of the book of remembrance in the hallway. Max looked at the signature she was pointing to – that of Bruno Dawkins. She opened her handbag and produced the YOR NEXT note.

'Look. It's the same writing,' she said.

Max gave her his glinting pirate's smile. 'Clever girl,' he said.

'Have you made up your mind yet? About him?' she asked.

'Nope,' said Max.

'You think he really could be the one? The mystery brother?'

Max thought of Queenie's long-ago absence, her months-long visit to Nora's place. Yes. It was possible. Fuck it. He *knew* it was. He also knew that Queenie would have sacrificed without a qualm her sanity, her health, *anything* – but never her spotless reputation as the mother of the head of the Carter clan.

'We'll see,' he said.

# 97

Bruno couldn't believe he'd come *this close* to Max at Taylor's wake. As always when he caught sight of his 'brother', he felt overwhelmed. Max had a way about him; you felt like you were in the presence of something special whenever he appeared. Max was, Bruno knew, everything that he himself had always longed to be. Elegant. Cool. Powerful. To stand within a couple of feet of Max Carter was awesome. And yet, Bruno still felt painfully conflicted. This was the man who'd topped Tory Delaney – Tory, who had treated Bruno so well, shown him there was more to life than hardship and loneliness.

But this was *also* the man who'd given the order to toss poor old Nora to her death. Whatever Bruno personally thought of Nora, he knew he owed her. Without her, he could have ended up in the care system, passed from pillar to post like so many other unwanted kids. And Max – through Jonjo – had killed her.

Bruno would never forget seeing Jonjo lumbering through Nora's house, escorting her from the premises. Him and that other one, the one he now knew was Steve Taylor. He'd never seen Nora again, after that. And then that time in Majorca, before he'd been banged up for that Delaney murder business. Max had been in trouble. Serious trouble; dying. And Bruno should have been pleased about that. After all, Queenie

Carter had rejected *him*, but she had adored Max. But again – the turmoil within himself, it screwed him up.

He'd felt compelled to pay the boy Jaime to find Max. He had in effect saved Max Carter's life. He'd blurted out to Jaime – not meaning to – about being Max's brother, but of course that would have gone no further.

'You OK, sweetheart?' Kirsty was asking him after Annie and Max Carter had taken their leave.

'Why wouldn't I be?' He shrugged.

'Never mind them,' said Kirsty, her eyes following them as they crossed the room, heading for the front door. 'Looking down their noses at us. Well who's the winner now, eh? I'm going to get all this – I'm sure of it.'

Show Kirsty enough money and she'd be happy as a clam. If she was right and she was going to inherit Steve's wealth, she'd be delighted. But Bruno had other concerns. The way Nora had raised him meant that he'd grown up hard. While she'd given attention to her guests at the boarding house, her approach to his childcare had been nothing but an afterthought. He had often been so very alone, so cold, so hungry and in desperate need of affection. Nora wasn't capable of that. And Queenie his real mother'd had no desire to give it to him.

He thought about that, sometimes. About the cold spinster sister and the one who was a good-time girl having flings into her middle years. He disliked them both. He disliked, most of all, what their legacy had done to him because he knew that he was cold, in his turn, towards the women who entered his life.

Bruno knew that he had never been in love, not once – not even with Tory Delaney. So maybe he was cold to men, too. But he still had this *weakness* around Max. And that conflicted with his work for Redmond Delaney. Yes, he hated Max. He was sure he did. But maybe now he hated Redmond

even more. Redmond had used him cruelly, coldly. Max – at
least – had never done that. Bruno knew that Eddie Carter
was dead, Jonjo too, and he had yet to shed a single tear over
either of them. But Max . . . ah, Max was different. He didn't
like the thought of anything happening to Max, not anymore.
Max – and this was ironic – reminded him of Tory. He had
that same powerful vibe going on, drawing people towards
him.

When all the mourners departed later in the day, Bruno and
Kirsty lay in the big copper bath upstairs together, sipping
champagne. Apart from the obvious financial benefits, there
were other advantages to hooking up with Kirsty. Bruno was
appreciating two of them right now; Kirsty's big fake boobs
were bobbing around atop the soap suds, her nipples – naked
but for two gold hoop piercings, one in each teat – standing
out hard as organ stops. He felt himself getting hard too, just
looking at her. She was *delicious*. A gold-digging little tart, of
course, but gorgeous for all that.

And Bruno wondered what Kirsty's reaction would be if
she knew, in all her money-grubbing innocence, that he had
been there, helping out, on the night Steve died? Would she
even care?

'Do you know someone ripped a sheet out of the book of
remembrance?' Kirsty was saying.

'No. Did they?' And who cared?

'Rough lot,' sniffed Kirsty.

'Time for bed,' he said, standing up.

'So I see.' Kirsty smiled, staring admiringly at his engorged
cock.

Bruno reached down and grabbed her, hauling her out of
the bath. She shrieked, laughing, as he carried her in a fire-
man's lift, over his shoulder, dripping, into the bedroom.

They didn't reach the bed.

It was only after they'd had sex that Bruno thought about the book of remembrance and the note he'd put through the door at the Holland Park house – and wondered.

*

Colin, one of Max's boys, got set up early next morning in a grey nondescript little car that would attract no attention. He parked up out in the road so that he could easily see the comings and goings at the house on Parliament Hill. He had his camera at the ready, egg and cress sandwiches, a flask of strong black coffee and a bottle to pee in. At twelve, one of the other boys on Max's payroll would take over. Until then, Colin was settled in and started work. He recorded the arrival of the milkman, then the postman. Took some shots of both. A blond youngish man came out of the house at ten-thirty. He snapped him, too. Then the glam young piece that Steve Taylor had taken up with, Kirsty, she came out an hour later, all dolled up, skirt up to here. She hailed a taxi and departed.

Nothing else happened.

Max's boy ate his sandwiches, drank his coffee, and then it was twelve and his replacement arrived, so he could go and let Max know what he'd found. Which was precisely fuck-all. But never mind. It was a job, and it had to be done right. Tomorrow, he would do it all over again.

# 98

The day after Steve's burial, Nolan came into Hunter's office, found him knee-deep in paperwork and said: 'Got something to show you, guv.'

'Don't call me guv.' Hunter didn't look up. He was signing letters, writing reports, shuffling invoices. He hated paperwork. 'This isn't the bloody *Sweeney*.'

'Sorry, sir.' Nolan stood there, waiting, almost bursting with the need to say what he had to say.

Finally, Hunter looked up at him. 'Can't it wait?'

'No, it can't. Seriously, you are going to be pleased with this.'

'Well – where is it?'

'You'll need to put your coat on for this one.'

Hunter stood up, stretching. 'If you're wasting my bloody time . . .'

Nolan had to suppress a triumphant grin. He led the way out of the office and down into the car park.

★

'The thing is,' said Nolan later as he was walking with Hunter along the canal towpath. 'What I was puzzling over was, where do you hide a boat? You can't find the thing, so where the hell is it? I thought maybe Halliday could have gone off upcountry using the canal system, maybe in the Birmingham direction, but our dead book man said that Halliday was *always* there, he didn't move around much. But there he was – apparently gone.'

'Quite. So . . . ?' prompted Hunter.

Ahead, men in dayglo jackets were fiddling with hooks and chains, attaching them to a crane. A crowd was gathering on the opposite side of the canal, and there were police cars there, policemen moving people on, telling them there was nothing to see here and to go on about their business. What did they think this was, a ruddy circus?

'So how to hide a boat?' said Nolan. 'How would you do that?'

'In a boatshed?' suggested Hunter.

'Tried that. Came up with nothing.'

'What then?' The crane was powering up. The chains leading down into the water were tautening, taking up a weight.

'Well, what you do is this,' said Nolan. 'You *sink* it. You pull out the plug and you flood the thing and it goes to the bottom of the canal – and that's why we haven't been able to find it.'

Hunter was looking at Nolan, open-mouthed.

'I got the police chopper up yesterday while you were at the Taylor funeral,' Nolan rushed on. 'I told them to go the whole length of the canals here. From above, you'd be able to see what you couldn't from the ground, right? And they spotted something right here. Thirty feet long, under the water. Something *red*.'

The crane was engaging, the motor roaring into life. The chains creaked and groaned and the men in dayglo jackets moved around, talking, pointing, watching as something started to come up out of the water. Weed and water were streaming off the huge shape as it breached, whale-like, above the surface.

It was big, and it was red.

It was Halliday's narrowboat.

All the remaining pots of bright blooms slid off as it tilted and came up. Water gushed off the hull in a cascade. And there at the cabin window, his white hair floating like a mermaid's in the water, his hands up and seeming almost to wave to them as he stared out at them with dead, glazed eyes, was Mr Halliday.

Nolan had found the damned thing. *And* its owner.

# 99

There was nothing wrong with a cop buying a woman a cup of coffee. After his triumphant day down by the canal, Nolan was feeling pumped and he couldn't deny that Layla Carter was definitely a person of interest as far as he was concerned – and not in a bad way. They'd found the boat, and more. He was the hero of the hour. That wouldn't last, but he was basking in his boss's approval for a change, and he liked it. He wanted to celebrate it. A good excuse, really, he told himself, to get up and personal with that fascinating girl.

Forbidden fruit, really. But all the more exciting for that.

The Carters had moved out of Holland Park and into a small house in Bow, and it was to that address that he went, ostensibly to tell Layla Carter of his discovery. Really, though? To just stare into those beautiful eyes of hers, to be close to her for a while. He'd been overwhelmed by her at first sight, and he had never in his life felt like that before with a woman.

*Dangerous.*

Yes, he knew that.

But did he care? He did not.

He was a bit taken aback when the door was opened not by Layla herself – he knew very well that her parents were elsewhere – but by a massive besuited man with a bald head and gold earrings.

Confronted by what was almost certainly Tone, the Carter mob's driver, Nolan decided the formal route was the best way to go. He showed his warrant card.

'I need to speak to Miss Layla Carter. Is she in?' He pocketed the card.

Tone looked at the young man on the doorstep. He nodded once and opened the door wide. He led the way, almost blocking out the light, up the hall and rapped on a closed door. He opened it.

'Police for you,' he said, and let Nolan into a tiny lounge.

Layla was sitting on a sofa reading the day's paper. As Nolan came in, she stood up.

'Hello, DS Nolan,' she said.

Tone was staring at Nolan, but he addressed Layla. 'You want me to stay?'

'No. Thanks, Tone.'

'I'll be in the kitchen if you want me,' said Tone, and went out, closing the door behind him.

'What can I do for you?' Layla asked Nolan.

*Just let me stand here and look at you,* Nolan thought.

'We found Mr Halliday's boat,' he said.

'Oh.'

'Someone pulled the plug. Sank it. Small wonder it couldn't be found.'

Layla's eyes were deadly serious. 'Why would anyone do that?'

Nolan pursed his lips. 'I'm sorry to have to tell you, we found Mr Halliday dead inside the cabin compartment. The pathology people are saying a blow to the head.'

Layla stood there, staring. 'God, how awful. Not . . . are you saying someone hit him? Killed him?'

'I'm afraid it looks that way. The full path reports aren't in yet, but they soon will be.'

Layla sat down. 'I couldn't really face the funeral . . .' she said, veering off of the subject of poor Halliday's death. Suddenly her eyes filled with tears. 'Well, I went to the church. But not the wake. I hate those things. Steve Taylor was like a favourite uncle to me. I loved him. And all this other stuff. The book boat owner, finding him like that. And now Mr Halliday. That's so awful. He was so sweet to me.'

'Sudden death's hard to cope with for those left behind,' said Nolan, hating that he'd made her sad. 'Look, can we get out of here? Can I take you for a drink or something?'

'Not possible right now,' said Layla, blinking back her tears. 'My father would go apeshit if I set foot outside without Tone – even if I *was* with a policeman.'

'I'd buy Tone a coffee too,' said Nolan, half-smiling. He walked around the sofa and sat down beside her. 'If it was absolutely necessary. Although he's really not my type.'

Somehow Layla forced a smile. 'No. Sorry. No can do. I can *make* you a coffee here, if you like?'

'No, I'm fine.'

'Well then . . .'

Silence fell between them.

'I'm just wondering how long I can wait before I pluck up the courage to kiss you,' said Nolan all of a sudden.

Layla's eyes widened with surprise. '*What*?'

'Sorry.' Nolan stood up abruptly. 'Shouldn't have said it. But the truth is, ever since I first saw you, I've thought . . . you're fantastic. Look, I'll go. I've made a bloody fool of myself, haven't I.'

Layla stood up too. 'Wait! Just hold on a second, will you?' She was half-smiling now, her eyes holding his. He was quite fiery. Quick moving. Impulsive. *Very* attractive. Nothing like Alberto, who was much more calm and commanding.

Whenever she thought of Alberto, there was still longing, still pain. But he was far away, and this was happening right here, right now. 'I don't think a kiss would be so terrible, do you?'

'I don't want to force you into anything,' said Nolan, thinking he had totally misplayed this. Cut to the chase *far* too soon, because he was used to his smiling boyish charm making life easy, making *women* easy.

But to his surprise Layla stepped in close to him. She lowered her voice almost to a whisper. 'Just kiss me, DS Nolan, and we'll see how we go, shall we?'

Nolan bent his head and very gently placed his lips on her, inhaling the sweet female scent of her, feeling her warmth, her softness.

He lifted his head and stared into her eyes.

'Harder,' she said.

Nolan followed her instructions and soon they were both gasping, their mouths hungrily caressing. Layla found herself having to pull free, step away.

'Sorry, did I hurt you?' Nolan was instantly apologetic.

'No. Not at all. You just took me by surprise, that's all.'

Her voice trailed away. It was like a soothing balm, being kissed again, feeling adored. Even if it was by this handsome stranger and not . . .

*Not by the man she loved?*

But she'd split from Alberto. Lost his baby and left him. And he hadn't come after her. She had half-expected that he would. She had even *hoped* for that, and then perhaps they would talk, they would thrash out their differences, try to at least. Truth was, she loathed the constant travelling, the fear of being hunted – while Alberto clearly relished danger and hated standing still. But he hadn't pursued her. He'd let her go. He hadn't cared enough to do otherwise.

Now she was looking at boyish, handsome, ebullient Nolan and thinking that there were other men in the world, less complex men, less *difficult* men, than Alberto Barolli with his Mafia legacy and his dangerous allure.

'Are you trying to tell me it's a long time since anyone kissed you? I find that hard to believe.'

'I'm not saying that.'

'Look, can I buy you dinner tonight? Bring Tone, OK?'

Layla almost laughed at that. It felt so long since she'd smiled or had anything to even smile about. And if she took Tone with her, how could Dad object?

'OK,' she said.

# 100

Layla was out and Annie was in a foul mood, feeling confined, closeted, overwhelmed by Max being here with her. If he was in the kitchen, she was in the lounge; if he was in the lounge, she was upstairs in the bedroom she and Layla were sharing. She was anywhere he was not.

Max was also nearly tearing the walls down. His mate was dead. His ex-wife was snarling at him. And his daughter was on a date – he couldn't believe this, but apparently it was true – with a copper.

So, when they passed on the stairs he grabbed Annie's arm and said: 'For Christ's sake, can't we at least behave like adults?'

Annie pulled her arm away, said nothing. She went on downstairs, into the kitchen, filled the kettle and slapped it on. Max followed.

'I'm going back to Holland Park in the morning,' she told him.

'You bloody well are not,' he said.

Annie's temper snapped. 'Listen. You may think you were able to tell me what to do when we were married – and you were mistaken in that, by the way – but now I do what I want, *when* I want. You suggested this but I'm suffocating here. So I'm going. First thing.'

'No,' said Max, as the kettle started to boil.

'No?' Annie was laughing in his face. 'Screw you, Max. I'm going.'

'I wish that fucking place would burn to the ground.'

Annie stared at him in surprise. 'What? Holland Park?'

'And it could be arranged. You do know that?'

'You'd burn down my *house*?' The tea she'd been about to make was forgotten.

'D'you know how it feels, you living there, in *his* house?' Max asked her.

'It's my house now.'

'It's his house. It's Constantine's. That bastard.'

Annie felt her temper stoking up. 'Are you really going down that road? Again?'

'Why not?' Max snarled, coming in close to her. 'Come on, tell me. What was so fucking marvellous about Constantine Barolli?'

Annie glared at him. 'You really want to know?'

'I really do.'

'All right.'

'So?'

'He made me feel *safe*. And that's something you never, ever did. He loved me. He protected me. He got Layla back to me.' Annie felt tears prick her eyes and fiercely blinked them back. 'Do you know what? With him being so much older than me, I think it was like finding the father I'd lost so early on in life. Whenever Constantine was around, *nothing* could scare me.'

Max was staring at her face. 'And with me?' he prompted.

'With you?' She gave a bitter little laugh. 'I'm scared all the bloody time. I'm anxious. I'm worried.'

'About what?'

Annie took in a breath. 'About *you*. And you don't actually give a fuck, do you? Come on, tell me. After our first night together in the Palermo Lounge, that night before you married Ruthie, how many other women did you take upstairs to that flat of yours? A dozen? Two?'

'*What?*' Max said, very quietly.

'You heard.'

Max came closer. Annie found herself pinned against the worktop, his hands on either side of her. Annie stared into his eyes, refusing to be intimidated. And then she realised that he looked almost grey, almost on the point of exhaustion. And of course he was. He'd just lost his closest friend. He had feelings too. More than she had, probably. She was the calm one, the one who turned away. He was more emotional than she was, moodier; she knew that.

'Oh, so you want to know the truth about that?' he said, very low, very intense.

'Yes. Go on. Surprise me,' said Annie. 'You didn't have any trouble at all forgetting me, did you, filling your bed with a parade of eager women?'

'It probably will surprise you but the fact is, I never took another woman upstairs to that flat.'

Annie narrowed her eyes. 'What?'

Max shook his head. 'It's the truth.'

'Why?'

'Christ Almighty, you really have to ask? All I could do after that night was think about you. I was completely bloody *obsessed* with you. Do you know what I think? If you never feel a damned thing for anything in your life, you're lucky. Feelings kill you. *Love* kills you. My marriage to Ruthie was over before it even began, and I wasn't interested in any other woman except you. I never was and the truth is, I never really have been. So you asking me about other women in that flat? It's a damned *joke*.'

Annie stared at him in amazement. 'You've never said that before.'

'You've never asked.'

Annie felt rage boiling up again. 'But you turned your back on me! You *dumped* me.'

'Self-preservation. I couldn't get over you and Constantine. All that business after the Majorca hit, all that shit up in Scotland? It haunted me. And then after that, we were getting closer all the time. I was getting in too deep, all over again. So I bailed.'

Annie shoved her fists into his chest. It was like pushing against a brick wall.

'Just get away from me,' she ordered, furious.

'Make me,' invited Max.

'You bastard.'

'Bitch.'

Then they heard the key turning in the front door.

# 101

Layla came back from her dinner date with Nolan buoyed up, happy; he'd taken her to a humble little Italian, and she'd loved it. It wasn't the grandiose five-star scene she was used to with Alberto, but she'd had fun. Nolan was excellent company and didn't seem too bothered that Tone tagged along, sitting at a separate table and giving him the evil eye.

Then she got back to her grandmother's old house and let herself in with the key Max had given her, Tone dogging her heels, and her good mood evaporated at the sound of raised voices coming from the kitchen.

They were fighting again!

All her life, she'd listened to this. They were always yelling and then making up. How the hell could anyone live that way?

Tone peeled off into the lounge. 'Think I'll turn in,' he said to her, and then he was gone. He was used to them fighting too, and he never got in the way of it; he was too smart for that.

Layla, however, opened the kitchen door. The shouting stopped, abruptly.

She felt suddenly furious.

'For God's sake!' she burst out. 'Why don't you two actually *talk* to each other, instead of snarling at each other like mad dogs?'

'Your father is impossible,' said Annie.

'Really?' said Max, his body still pressed against hers.

'Yes really,' snapped Annie, breaking free of him.

'And where the hell have you been?' Max asked Layla.

'Out. To dinner with DS Nolan. Who is very nice. Tone drove me; I was perfectly safe. All right?'

'So we're eating out with coppers now, are we?' asked Max.

'*I* am. I don't expect you to. Oh – I didn't tell you. They found the red boat. Someone sank it. And Mr Halliday was inside. The poor man's dead.'

'Jesus,' said Annie, shooting a glance at Max. 'The police found it?'

'Nolan personally.' Layla nodded. 'He had the idea that the best place to hide a boat was under the water. And he was right. They sent a police chopper up and spotted it from the air. I was very sad to hear it. Mr Halliday was so nice to me.'

'So you've been dining out with this very impressive copper,' said Max, not without sarcasm. 'Where?'

'Tone can give you all the details. We had a very nice night. We might even do it again.'

So saying, she went back out of the kitchen, slamming the door hard behind her.

## 102

'She might have a point you know,' said Annie when Layla had vanished upstairs.

'What?' asked Max.

'We could talk to each other. We could actually listen.'

'Right.'

'But then – you wouldn't even be here in the same room as me if you hadn't had that call from Benito, would you. About your "brother". Then you *had* to see me, if only to check whether I was imagining things when I said I found Jonjo dead in the pool at the finca. Otherwise, you wouldn't have bothered. We'd just have carried on as we were, living separate lives.'

Max didn't deny that. 'You could have been in shock after the explosion. Also, you said they'd drugged you. That could have a weird effect. Made you see things that weren't really there.'

Annie gave that some consideration. 'No,' she said at last. 'I was fine. Jonjo *was* dead, shot straight between the eyes.' She frowned. 'But – just the same – Jaime said your brother paid him to look for you.'

'He did.'

'We both know that's not possible. Unless . . . Bruno was there. Unless he really is your brother.'

They were talking to each other. Not screaming and shout-ing. Working things out, or trying to anyway. Annie took advan-tage of the sudden calm that Layla had induced, and dived in.

'Why did you decide to dump me, Max? What made you do that?'

He looked taken aback. Then he shrugged, said nothing.

*Oh for God's sake . . .*

'I thought we were fine,' she went on. 'We'd got over the business with Constantine.'

'Well – *you* had.'

'How was I to know you'd been brooding about it all this time?' she demanded.

'You bloody abandoned me. Took up with him instead.'

'Yes! I did! But you know why I had to do that. I had to put Layla first, get help, and then – I told you – Constantine was dependable. Reliable. He made me feel *safe*.'

'And I never did,' said Max.

'No. You didn't.' Annie ran a hand through her hair in agi-tation. 'We were fine, I thought. We'd beaten the Delaneys. Redmond was dead. After Scotland, everything seemed as if it might be OK. We were back together. And then, right out of the blue . . . you just put me aside.' Annie shook her head. 'I was *devastated*.'

Max was staring at her face. '*You* were devastated?' He gave a scornful snort. 'Welcome to my bloody world.'

Annie stood up. Another couple of minutes and they'd be right back in the same place again. Yelling at each other. Sud-denly she felt tired to the point of exhaustion. But he'd given her something, hadn't he? He'd given her the knowledge that he could feel emotion, could feel pain. It was very little, but maybe, just maybe, it was a start.

'I'm going to bed,' she said, and left the room.

# 103

Nolan was busy going through all the witness statements on the Taylor case and feeling pretty pleased with himself after he'd wined and dined Layla Carter last night; she was a sweet girl. Beautiful. And he'd found the Halliday boat. But Hunter came in like a bear that had been bitten up the arse and asked what the hell was the progress on the Steve Taylor murder. *Was* there any?

Well, there wasn't, much. And now they had two more stiffs to add to the tally, things were really mounting up here. The book man, Cyrus Toynbee. And poor old Stan Halliday, sunk with his boat. So here Nolan was, trawling through the statements again. The two blokes and the girl who worked in the Carter security office. Nothing there. Nothing that smelled *wrong*, anyway. The Malaysian cleaner, Latipa Dunne. The girlfriend, Kirsty Allen. He had her details from Ellie Brown.

Penny to a pinch of shit, Kirsty was involved, somehow. Usually in these things, it was the nearest and dearest. Made you think, really. *And* she'd taken up with this new bloke, much younger than poor old Steve, and livelier in the bedroom department no doubt. *That* made you think, too, didn't it? Nolan also thought of the strength involved in hoisting a sixteen-stone bloke up on a rope on a bridge. Could one man alone do that? Really? No. Certainly not.

All right then. Kirsty's new young partner. Start there. How about him?

He went down the corridor and tapped at Hunter's door, entered, sat down in a chair and said: 'What details have we got on Kirsty Allen's new squeeze, boss? Anything?'

Hunter's phone was ringing. He snatched it up, tucked it into the crook of his shoulder and snapped out a hello. As he did so, he rifled through a pile of papers on one side of his desk, shoved one of the pieces toward Nolan, and went back to his call. Nolan left the office and went down the hall and sat at his desk and looked at the single sheet Hunter had given him.

Bruno Dawkins, he read. Met Kirsty while he was doing bar work in one of the Carter clubs, the Shalimar. Whether their relationship preceded or ran alongside Kirsty's relationship with Steve Taylor, who knew?

Nolan stood up, went back along the corridor, tapped, entered.

'What the fuck?' asked Hunter, looking up from his desk.

'Is this all we've got?' asked Nolan.

Hunter looked annoyed. 'That?' He puffed out a breath. 'Oh yeah, that. It's irritating. Puzzling too.'

'Why?'

'Well, look – up to a certain point he doesn't seem to exist. I've checked. No birth registered in the British Isles. No taxes paid. No London bank accounts. *But* he's done time. An uneducated little scrote, no real background. But twenty years for murder, nineteen-seventy to ninety. Nasty business. Some bloke buried at sea.'

'So you've checked just London, for the accounts?' Nolan asked.

'Yes! But check further will you? As per bloody usual, I'm up to my arse here.'

'This Bruno Dawkins, did you see him at Steve Taylor's funeral?' asked Nolan.

'He was there. Supporting the grieving partner, helping her back to her seat when she broke down giving the eulogy.'

'Have you interviewed him?' asked Nolan.

'Not yet. Listen, I've got multiple murdering bastards on my patch, and I've got some sort of peculiar high-level crisis going on upstairs. I'm not happy. So for Chrissakes why don't you go and do that?'

'OK,' said Nolan, and wisely left Hunter to it.

★

Before Nolan went to speak to Bruno, he detoured to the Shalimar and had a word with Ellie Brown.

'You used to employ Kirsty Allen, is that right?'

'That's correct. I can show you the records. They're in storage though. Might take me a little while to find them.'

'And around the same time, Bruno Dawkins was working on the bar?'

'Um, who?'

'Bruno Dawkins.'

Ellie chewed her lip. 'Maybe. I think so. On a casual basis, yes.'

'You have his records too?'

'No. As I said, it was just casual.'

'Which is not strictly legal, I'm sure you know that?'

'I do. Of course I know that.' Hot colour was climbing up Ellie's cheeks.

'All right. Thank you.'

Nolan sat downstairs in the empty club, nursing a coffee while Ellie Brown searched for Kirsty's stored records up in the office. She came down half an hour later and handed him photostats. Ellie thanked God he hadn't asked for the CCTV that showed Kirsty and Bruno together – Annie still had that. 'Is there anything else I can do for you, Detective?' she asked sweetly.

'No, that's fine. Thank you for your cooperation. Can I take these?'

'Absolutely.'

When Nolan had left the building, Ellie phoned Annie at Queenie's old house and told her what had just transpired.

⋆

Nolan took the paperwork with him on his way over to Parliament Hill. He sat outside in the car for a while, thumbing through Kirsty's employment records at the Shalimar and regretting that there was nothing to be had on the elusive Bruno. Bruno interested Nolan very much; he'd seen him going into church on several occasions, and that seemed out of character. But what did he know?

Up ahead, he noticed a man sitting in a shabby car, alone, taking shots of Steve Taylor's house. Intrigued, he watched. Every time someone went in or out of the property, the man snapped them.

*Interesting.*

Had Hunter put him here? But surely Hunter would have told Nolan if he had. Wouldn't he?

Maybe. Maybe not.

Nolan got out of the car, locked it. He walked along to where the man was parked up and – dammit – the man saw him coming in the side mirror and started the engine.

Nolan picked up pace. He yanked out his warrant card and reached for the man's car door.

'Police! Wait . . .'

The man swerved the car out into the road and shot away with a chirp of scorched rubber, leaving Nolan standing there on the pavement, thwarted. Nolan didn't even have time to clock the registration number, the guy was that fast.

'Shit,' he said.

He went over and banged on the door of the house. No answer. Nobody in.

He went back to the car and drove back to the cop shop. Went straight into Hunter's office.

'Boss, did you put someone outside the Taylor house taking photos of people coming and going there?' he asked.

Hunter shook his head. 'No. I'd have told you.'

'That's what I thought. Yet there was someone sitting outside in a car, taking snaps. Who would that be I wonder?'

'The Carter lot,' sniffed Hunter. 'I bet you. You talked to Bruno Dawkins?'

'Not yet.' Annoyingly, Bruno seemed to have dropped out of sight at the moment.

'You checked all the banks yet?'

'Been busy.'

'Well get the fuck on with it, will you?'

# 104

Annie was sick of Queenie's place and sick of arguments so – to hell with Max and his dire warnings, to hell with notes and living in fear – she got a taxi back to Holland Park. The weather was good, the pool out in the back garden was heated, things were neatly in place – what did she want to stay in a poxy little terrace for, when all that was available? She almost sighed with bliss when she got back through her own front door. She went upstairs to the master suite, fished out her bikini and sarong, grabbed a hairclip and a towel from the bathroom, and went out the back, pinning up her hair as she went.

Once down by the pool, she retracted the motorised cover and waded in. God, it was warm! Blissfully she sank into its silky embrace, relishing the weightlessness the water granted her. It was so lovely here at the back of the house, enclosed with trees and shrubs, utterly private. She swam an easy, untroubled five lengths and then stopped at the far end of the pool, enjoying the solitude, eyes closed, perfectly relaxed.

'What the fuck?' asked an angry male voice.

Her eyes flew open. And there he was, near the steps that led down into the pool.

'Hello to you too,' she said.

'Didn't we agree that . . .' started Max.

'We didn't agree anything. *You* did. I didn't. Who told you I was here?'

'Layla saw you leave in a taxi. And I thought you might come back here. You don't like Mum's house, do you.'

'What's to like? It's a shithole.'

'You ever thought you could be queen? You got the attitude just right.'

Annie shrugged. 'I like comfort – so shoot me. And incidentally I saw your watchers. One followed me from Queenie's house. Two more were waiting outside here trying to look discreet and failing. So I felt pretty safe.'

'Still, you took a risk.'

'Yep. I did. Coming in?'

'No.'

'Why not? It's lovely and warm.'

'Things might get out of hand,' he said.

'Out of hand how? I promise not to jump your bones. You're not *that* irresistible.'

Now he was grinning.

'Suit yourself,' said Annie, and concentrated on getting her lengths in.

It was soothing, counting the strokes, inhaling on every second one, breathing out under the water. She fell into a rhythm and the water supported her. She began to feel all the aches and strains of the past few weeks fading away. Finally she paused, breathing hard, at the far end of the pool, and nearly bumped into Max, who was in the water beside her.

'Couldn't resist, uh?' she asked. 'Hey – I hope you're not skinny-dipping.'

'Nope. Found a pair of my old bathers upstairs.' He swam away from her overarm, his powerful strokes cutting through the water. He turned at the step end and then came back.

'Watchers or not, that was stupid. Coming back here on your own,' he told her.

'So you don't care about me, but you followed me here. Why?' asked Annie sharply.

'If anything were to happen to you, do you think Layla would ever forgive me?' he asked, swiping a hand through his hair to push it back.

Annoying son of a bitch. And he looked so damned *good*, too. That was the worst thing, really, how hot he was. Her 'little Italian' his mother Queenie had called him, apparently. He was dark-skinned, Latin-looking. Wildly attractive, yes. She could see that, respond to that even now, after all he'd done to her.

'So you're here for Layla then. Not for me. Not because *you* were particularly bothered. Right?' she pressed. But hadn't he told her he'd been devastated when they'd parted last year? Yes. He *had* said that.

But now, he said nothing.

'What a bastard you really are,' said Annie, and surged away from him, swimming overarm toward the far end of the pool. When she got there, he was already there, clinging to the pool's edge, waiting for her.

'You seem to like bastards though,' he said smoothly. 'As I recall.'

'Oh fuck off, Max,' said Annie.

'Nope. Don't think I will.' He came closer, closer . . .

'What are you doing?' asked Annie, startled, in the moment before his mouth was on hers and she was consumed by heat, by the hard touch of his skin, by everything about him. She struggled hard to break free but couldn't. Finally, he let her go and she surged back, away from him, feeling hot, bewildered – feeling far more than she wanted to.

'Don't do that,' she snapped.

'What, you like Layla's solution then? Just stay apart? Let the whole damned thing go?'

'You decided to cut all ties. I didn't.'

'So you didn't like the idea?'

'It wasn't my suggestion. *I* didn't call a halt to anything.'

'Right.' He came closer again, slipped his arms around her. She felt the snap on her bikini top being worked loose.

'What are you doing?' she asked, dry-mouthed.

'Stripping you,' said Max, and his mouth was on hers again.

She felt the same old treacherous desire uncurling itself in her guts, felt him pull the top loose, toss it onto the side of the pool, felt his hand close with aching, unbearable pressure over her naked, aroused breast.

'I hate you,' she murmured.

'Hate away,' invited Max, and he was pulling the bottom half of her bikini down and she *needed* to stop him, but she couldn't. She didn't want to. That too went onto the side of the pool and then to her complete alarm she saw his swimming trunks follow.

Naked, they twined together, and Annie found that she wanted this, every bit as much as he clearly did. This time when he kissed her she parted her legs, linked them around his waist, inviting him in.

'Bitch,' he hissed against her mouth, but he was ready for her, hard as iron and slick as velvet, and he pushed up hungrily, his cock filling her.

Annie clutched at the pool's edge, clawed at his shoulder, demented with the sudden onset of a desire that was so familiar and yet so overwhelmingly strong that it frightened her.

Her orgasm tore through her, *raged* through her, the minute he came inside her. Her head was thrown back in abandon and she felt every thrust, every move he made, crying out with pleasure as the well-remembered sensations took possession of her all over again.

It couldn't last. It was too consuming, too raw. Max came, thrusting furiously, emptying himself into her, holding her, *hurting* her, he was grasping her so tightly. Then it was done and his grip released, his head drooping onto her shoulder, his mouth biting into her skin, making her shudder all over again.

Then he lifted his head and she was staring into his eyes. His mouth was on hers again, his tongue caressing hers. Then he drew back, smoothing his hands more gently over her shoulders, sliding them down and around, settling on her breasts.

'God alive,' he gasped.

Annie felt embarrassed at the sudden violence of her own arousal. 'It's been a year,' she said weakly.

'I know,' he said, and kissed her. 'And you were right,' he said, his mouth hovering over hers, his eyes holding hers.

'What?'

'You were right and I was wrong. This is how we should have sorted this whole mess out. Skin to skin. Face to face. We should have talked.'

'But you didn't talk. And, Max? *This* isn't talking.'

'I couldn't. I *had* to turn away.'

'Will you talk now?' Annie asked. She felt on the edge of tears, and she *never* cried. He was the love of her life. His rejection had crucified her. Didn't he know that?

'Maybe,' said Max, giving her that devil-may-care grin, slipping his hands down to her waist. Pulling away from her physically. And mentally, too. 'If I feel like it.'

He was still playing with her. Annie twitched away from him, hauled herself out of the pool and stood up.

'Fuck you, Max,' she said, and she grabbed her towel and was gone.

## 105

Two hours later, Annie and Max were back at Queenie's place and Colin Pickford, one of Max's boys, was waiting there for them with a fistful of photos.

'That cop Nolan nearly caught me out there on Parliament Hill yesterday,' said Colin. 'He was on his way over to have a chat when I took off.'

'Take a different car tomorrow. Park in a different spot. Tell Si to swap over too. But keep on it,' said Max.

'Will do.' Colin spread the pics out on the kitchen table. Nothing very exciting there, Annie thought. The milkman, the dustbin men, a window cleaner, a gardener pottering about among the big blowsy pink hydrangeas at the front of the house. A new young cleaner arriving for work, then leaving. And . . .

'Shit!' Annie exclaimed, clutching a hand to her throat.

'What?' asked Max.

One of the shots showed a man standing at the front door of the house; he was tall, sandy-haired, hawk-nosed. Looking all around him, like a foot soldier would. She knew that look, all too well. Then another shot – the door opening, the man stepping inside the building. Looking back, checking everything around him. Just like Max or one of his men would do. Annie picked up the photo. She stared hard at it.

'What is it? You know him?' asked Max.

'Yeah,' said Annie. 'I do.'

'How? From where?'

Annie gave a shudder as she stared at that long brutal face. Max was watching her with concern; she'd gone pale. Her hand was trembling.

'From the US,' she said at last.

'What did he do?'

'He chased me up the beach and into the Montauk house,' said Annie. 'That's *him*. He had a gun. I think he was going to kill me.'

## 106

'No,' said Annie. 'Wait.'

She was still staring at the picture, frowning.

'What?' asked Max.

Annie wrapped her arms around her body, put a hand over her mouth. Stared some more.

'Col,' said Max. 'You can go.'

Colin departed, leaving them alone in the kitchen.

'What is it?' he asked her.

'I don't understand this,' said Annie. She was shaking her head.

'What?'

'Less than a week ago I hit this bloke, *this same one*—' she stabbed the photo with her finger '—with the kiyoga. He was cut. Bleeding. I hit him twice.' She pointed. 'There. And there. Now will you please explain to me why his head's not bandaged? Not cut? There's not a damned thing wrong with him, is there. Not a mark on him. I don't understand.'

Max was silent, staring at her face. Finally he said: 'And you're sure it's him. Absolutely one hundred per cent sure?'

She nodded. 'I would never forget that face. It's him all right.' She gave a short, mirthless laugh. 'Unless he's got an identical twin.'

# 107

Nolan loved this part of the job – the digging. Some of the detectives hated it, but it was meat and drink to him. He loved burrowing around in the archives, tracking things down. Currently, he was looking for a non-existent man called Bruno Dawkins, contacting banks to find his accounts. But Bruno apparently had none.

'That's Bruno,' he said countless times over the phone. 'B.R.U.N.O.'

Always, the answer came up no.

He shared this with Hunter. 'No joy on a bank account for this character.'

'We've covered the London branches?'

Nolan nodded. 'Didn't think you'd want me spending too much time on it.'

'Well I do. Try . . .' Hunter leaned back in his chair and looked at the ceiling. 'Try east and west of the capital. Try south.'

'North?'

'Why not. Spread the net. Getting a funny feeling about this guy.'

Nothing came up. Nothing, nothing, nothing.

And then, late one muggy, rainy day when Nolan had given up all hope of ever finding an account for Bruno Dawkins, and was just off home for a TV dinner and a good kip, he got a call from a Brighton bank.

'DS Nolan?' said the woman at the other end. 'You were inquiring about an account for a Mr Dawkins?'

'Yes. I was.' It would be nothing. It was *always* nothing.

'We have an account.'

Nolan slapped his bag back down on his desk and slung his raincoat over the back of his chair. He snatched up a pen.

'Account number? Sort code?' he prompted, and she reeled it off.

'It's in the name of a Mr Bruno Dawkins. There's a pound sitting in it so it's not a dead account, just unused. The last time anything was withdrawn from it was in the Sixties.' She gave him the exact date and time. 'Mr Dawkins took out forty-nine pounds from it and then never touched it again.'

Nolan was nearly jumping up and down with excitement. He gulped down a breath and said, not hoping, just praying really: 'Do you have an address?'

'I do,' she said. 'But after all this time it's probably not current, I'm afraid.'

'I think I love you,' said Nolan, grinning from ear to ear.

She laughed. 'My husband won't approve of that. Here's the address.'

When Nolan came off the phone, he ran along the corridor and nearly fell through Hunter's open office door. 'Boss!' he said.

'What is it? Building on fire?'

'Got an address for Bruno Dawkins, found an account he took out as a teenager. Hasn't touched it since, but it's there.'

'What's the address?' Hunter had his pen in hand, at the ready.

'Brighton seafront. Marine Parade.'

'Let me make a call to clear it with the Brighton police. Then we'll take a look,' said Hunter. He tossed Nolan the keys. 'We'll take the A23 down through Crawley. You're driving.' He snatched up the phone. Looked at Nolan. 'Go on then. Start the engine. I'll be out ASAP.'

★

They reached Brighton at just gone 10 p.m. and checked in to a cheap hotel with two single rooms overnight. In the morning they dressed, breakfasted, and proceeded to Marine Parade, where Nolan parked up. Hunter unfolded his long body from the passenger seat and got out. Nolan followed and they stood there with the sea breeze gusting all around them, flattening the hair to their heads in an icy blast. The cry of the gulls was loud down here, the conditions wildly elemental. The sea was bashing itself furiously against the pebbles down on the beach, hissing with rage at being turned back. Down on the seafront they could see the distinctive turquoise railings, with some hardy souls walking their dogs on the beach while white-topped waves flung themselves up onto the shingle.

A spatter of salty rain hit Hunter's face as he stood there and looked up at the house. It was a tall cream-painted bow-fronted Georgian, set out over four floors. A grand elegant house, and these days probably a costly one too.

'Of course there's no chance that his relatives – or even he – could own it still,' said Hunter.

'None, I'm afraid,' agreed Nolan. 'Not judging by the state of that bank account, anyway. But the present owner could know something of him, I suppose. Did I tell you I've seen him going into church a couple of times?'

'No. That's interesting. Well let's see then. Shall we?'

Hunter went up the steps to the front door and rang the bell.

# 108

Redmond seemed to like it in the scrapyard cellar. Bruno thought he did, anyway. Like a spider scuttling in a corner, Redmond liked to loiter down here, plotting, planning – and dealing out death by proxy.

*This* day, Redmond had called Bruno here to the scrapyard. Bruno had gone to the office, stepped into the lift, which creaked and crawled its way down below ground.

There in the cellar was Redmond.

'The thing is,' said Redmond, 'I was angry that your gun misfired at first. Very angry. But now? Perhaps it was just as well. Because actually, I like to do it this way. A little at a time. To torment him, you see.'

'Torment who?' asked Bruno, but of course he knew.

'Max Carter. Who else? Poor dim little Bruno. I attack his businesses. His friends. His ex-wife. His daughter too – don't think I've forgotten her. I take it all, bit by bit, until there is nothing left. I let him feel the full measure of despair, just like I have over many years past. And then, dear Bruno – I kill him. Slowly. Painfully.' A snakelike smile flickered across those chilling, ghastly features. 'I give him plenty of time, you see, to consider the error of his ways. And then – when he's begging me for it – then, he dies.'

# 109

The police had a long wait and were almost about to go when the door was opened by a woman Hunter placed as somewhere in her eighties. She was grey-haired, thin, clearly frail. She clung onto the wall while she stood there at the door.

'Yes?' she asked in a crisp upper-class voice, not warmly. It had obviously cost her an effort, getting to the door, and that hadn't pleased her.

Hunter flashed his warrant card. 'Police, madam. Sorry to disturb you. We are looking for a man called Bruno Dawkins who we believe used to live here, along with a Mrs Nora Dawkins, who was the then owner of this property.'

'There's no one of that name here,' she said, and went to close the door.

'Just a moment, please. I apologise for the disturbance, but this is an important matter. You own this house? Are you Mrs Isaacs?'

She looked at him, her expression obstinate. 'Of course I do. And yes, I'm Jennifer Isaacs.'

'And for how long have you owned it?'

'Young man, if you know my name you probably also know the answer to that question.'

'Just checking details, Mrs Isaacs.'

She softened a bit. Told him the year she'd bought the place but couldn't really recall the details of the people she'd bought it from. 'It's too big for me now. All the stairs, you know. I've been here since the Seventies. I believe at one time it was run as a bed and breakfast, if that helps, but I couldn't be sure. Is that all?'

'Yes,' said Hunter. 'For the moment. Thank you.' He pulled out a card. 'If you think of anything else that could be of use to our investigations, could you give me a call?'

'Yes,' she said, taking the card.

Then Hunter said: 'The Bruno Dawkins we're looking for, we believe he's a churchgoer. Would that help ring any bells?'

'No. Not at all,' she said, and closed the door.

'Not helpful,' said Nolan.

Hunter looked left along the row of houses. 'You take that end; I'll take the right. There might be someone still living along this road who remembers Bruno Dawkins.'

A cold windswept and dreary hour passed with Nolan and Hunter asking questions all along Marine Parade, then, having had no luck at all, they went back to the car and sat there while the rain started to hammer harder on the roof. Nolan started the engine.

'Back to town then, sir?' he asked.

'Back to town.'

# 110

Nolan and Hunter parted company back at the station. The rain was setting in now, making the summer evening draw in quickly, and Nolan knew he'd be glad to get back home and take it easy. He hated it when they hit a dead end. But there was always tomorrow, wasn't there? He thought of Layla Carter, wondered if he ought to give her a bell. But truthfully, tonight, he was tired after the wild goose chase Hunter had insisted upon. Tomorrow, he would call her.

He had his key in the front door when someone grabbed him.

'Whoa!' shot out of his mouth as he spun around, wondering what the hell was going on. There was a large man in a dark coat to one side of him. Another taller man, equally soberly dressed, was on the other. He couldn't move and he was disconcerted to feel his feet leave the ground as they marched him back down the steps and onto the pavement.

'Who the fuck?' he blurted, and then he was shoved into the back of a long black car, landing with a thump that knocked the breath out of him on plush leather seats. The men got in the back too, one on either side of him. Their bulk crushed him. He looked ahead, blinking in the gloom of the car's interior light. There was a thin, soberly dressed man sitting facing him, and there was someone else up front, sitting silently behind the wheel. The motor was running.

'What the hell is this?' snapped out Nolan. 'I'm a police officer. What are you playing at?'

The thin man facing him gave a very thin smile. 'I know you are a police officer,' he said in an American accent.

Nolan could feel his heartbeat accelerating. The two hulking men were crowding in far too tightly; he was finding it hard to breathe. He could smell leather and sweet cologne and an almost overpowering miasma of wealth in here. 'My boss is expecting a call from me in . . .' Nolan glanced at his watch '. . . exactly five minutes.'

'That's probably a lie,' said the thin man. 'Is it a lie, DS Nolan?'

'It's a fact,' lied Nolan, wondering how the man knew his rank and his name.

'Well, in that case I'll be brief.' The thin man sat back, folded his hands over his elegantly clad stomach and observed DS Nolan as if he were an interesting new breed of bacteria found squirming about on a Petri dish. 'DS Nolan, things have come to our attention.'

'What things?'

The thin man shook his head and smiled again. 'I think you know precisely what things I'm talking about.'

'This is ridiculous,' said Nolan.

He was tired, exasperated and he was bloody *scared*, too. This was a whole new feeling for him. He'd been brave, even reckless, all his life, and he didn't like it. These people seemed cold. Dispassionate. All of a sudden he had a mental image of old gangster films, Edward G Robinson machine-gunning his enemies. Nolan looked at the thin man, and at the two thugs who had him hemmed in – and he could imagine them rubbing out a life without an iota of guilt or pity. He had never encountered this type of threat before. And he had no wish, ever, to repeat the experience.

'OK, let me paint you a clear picture,' said the thin man. 'Layla Carter.'

'What about her?' asked Nolan.

'Certain people don't want you near her. You understand me?'

'What certain people?'

The thin man smiled again, his cold eyes gleaming, his expression sweetly tolerant. 'Not your concern. All that need concern you is the fact that you must avoid contact with her in the future.'

Christ, he was being warned off. He'd scoffed at it, but now he vividly remembered Hunter's words about Mafia, about messages from 'on high' concerning the Carter girl.

'And if I don't?' asked Nolan. He had to gulp down a breath to get the words out.

'That would make my colleagues very sad and very angry,' said the thin man. 'You wouldn't want that. Suffice it to say, if we have to meet up with you again, the outcome could be distressing for you. I think we all want to avoid that, don't we.'

Nolan swallowed hard. He wanted to avoid it, certainly.

'So long as we understand one another,' said the thin man. 'Do we?'

'Yeah,' said Nolan. 'We do.'

'Then thank you for your time,' said the man, and the man to Nolan's right opened the car door and stepped out onto the pavement. Nolan followed. He was still standing there, wondering if he'd just dreamed the whole damned thing, when the car – a Bentley – pulled smoothly away, and then it was gone, purring into the night.

# III

Layla phoned Nolan from Queenie's place next day. He picked up at the police station, heard her voice, and was instantly on alert.

'Are you free for lunch?' said Layla. 'We could . . .'

'No, sorry. We're on a big case, can't take the time out,' he said quickly.

'Never mind. Tonight then? Let me buy you dinner.'

'I can't. Sorry. I've made arrangements.'

'Oh.'

He could hear the hurt in her voice. He didn't like it; but then, he didn't like the thought of what the men in the Bentley might do to him if he *didn't* hurt her. She was sweet, bright, beautiful. Everything he wanted in a woman. Maybe she could even be The One. But he couldn't have her. No way.

'Sorry,' he said.

'That's OK,' said Layla, and he could hear her puzzlement. 'Maybe some other time?'

'No. I don't think so.'

'Oh.' There was a moment's silence, then: 'I don't understand. I thought we got on.'

Nolan clutched at his head and said it. 'Look – your boyfriend wouldn't like it. He's already passed that message on to me. Loud and clear.'

'*What?*'

'I was minding my own business, just going in my own front door last night when four men picked me up in a car. They told me to leave you alone. They were scary people. I'm not easily spooked, but I have to tell you – they managed to do it.'

Layla was silent.

'You still there?' asked Nolan.

'I'm sorry. That had nothing to do with me.'

'Look, let's just call it off. OK?' snapped Nolan. He put the phone down with a bang. Then he said: '*Shit*!' very loudly. Hunter, just passing by, paused at Nolan's desk.

'Problems?' he asked.

'None that I can't handle,' said Nolan. He looked up at his boss. Let out a breath. 'I had a visit last night.'

'From who?'

'What you said, about the Carter girl's connections . . .'

Hunter's usually deadpan face registered concern. 'They called on you? The Barolli lot?'

Nolan nodded.

'What did they say?'

'Keep my hands off. In a nutshell.'

'I warned you about this. Didn't I.'

'You did.'

'And?' asked Hunter.

'She just phoned me. Asked me out to lunch. Or dinner. Or bed, I think. That was next.'

'Which you very sensibly refused?'

'Yeah. I did.'

Hunter stood there, looking down at his DS. 'You didn't want to though,' he guessed.

'No. I bloody didn't.'

'Nolan,' said Hunter.

'Yeah?'

'They did you a favour. Believe me, they did. Chalk it up to experience. And forget it.'

★

Layla put the phone down, bewildered. The fucking nerve of Alberto bloody Barolli, warning people off! Annie passed by her in Queenie's narrow hallway.

'Do you understand men?' she asked her mother.

Annie stopped in her tracks and gave her daughter a grim smile. 'You're asking *me* that? Me?'

Max was upstairs. They could hear the boards creaking as he moved about up there.

'DS Nolan just blew me out. He says Alberto's people paid him a visit.'

'What? Where?'

'Outside his house. They told him to keep away.'

'Did they.' Annie leaned back against the wall and stared at Layla.

'I thought he was nice. I thought he *liked* me. But he just cut me off. Cut me *dead.*'

'So Alberto knows you're here.'

'I wish he'd back off.'

'Do you? Really?'

'Yes, Mum. I do.'

'Layla,' said Annie, looking at her daughter with sceptical eyes, 'listen to me. Your father dumped me a year ago. No explanation, not even a kiss goodbye. Now he thinks he can barge back into my life, just like that. So please – don't ask me about men. They're a mystery. Also . . .' she smiled and patted her daughter's shoulder '. . . a pain in the arse.'

'Mum . . .'

But Annie shook her head. Layla's love life – or lack of it – was the very least of her concerns. Those pictures of Colin's had unveiled facts that troubled her deeply. The man in the photo had no marks on his head because he was clearly the twin of the man who'd attacked her in Montauk, not the man himself. And she knew that Max was thinking exactly what *she* was thinking: that there was a particular family who had a history of red-haired twins – the Delaneys. One of Max's watchers had clocked the pair of them going into the Delaney scrapyard – and incidentally Bruno had been spotted going in there, too. And what were these two? Delaney relatives? Almost certainly, they were.

'Layla,' she told her daughter firmly, 'I have absolutely nothing to add about your sodding love life, OK? Trust me – I can't even handle my own.'

# 112

Hunter got a call from a querulous old lady who told switchboard she was Jennifer Isaacs. Nolan was sitting on the opposite side of the desk, so Hunter put the call on speakerphone.

'Young man?' she said. 'Is that you?'

Young man! Nolan would have laughed at that, had he dared.

'I'm Mrs Isaacs. You called on me in Brighton.'

'Yes, Mrs Isaacs. What can I do for you?'

'You said to phone if I thought of anything.'

'I did, yes.'

'Well I have. You said this Bruno person you are looking for was a churchgoer. So I asked at my local church. I do the flowers there. The vicar – our current incumbent – hasn't been in the position very long, but he's such a helpful man. He said he'd look back in the records and see who was the incumbent at the time you mentioned, when this Dawkins person lived here.'

'Very good.' Hunter yanked a pad and pencil closer, poised to take notes. *And how the hell was this going to help?* he wondered with a sigh.

'The incumbent was a Reverend Payne.'

Hunter scrawled that down. 'And where would I find him?'

'In the graveyard, probably,' said Nolan in a whisper.

Hunter shot him a look.

'He's in a nursing home. Cholmondeley Lodge. Here's the address,' said Mrs Isaacs.

The call concluded, Hunter hung up.

'Another trip down to Brighton?' guessed Nolan, thinking it would be an utter waste of time.

'Why not?'

# 113

Always now, after leaving the scrapyard, Bruno went and sat in the church. It reminded him a bit, being inside the vast old building, of Nora and her church mates, of her sending him to Sunday school, which had bored him. In fact, the only enlivening bit of the whole experience had been collecting little stamps of Jesus and the disciples to stick in a book. He'd liked that.

Slowly, sitting there, looking at the cross behind the altar, he began to feel steadier; the inner tremor that the sight of Redmond Delaney always induced in him started to recede. And what Bruno had done while he was in the scrapyard this time had caused him no small amount of terror. Still, it was done.

'Can I help you?'

It was the same vicar, too plump, too young, his eyes wide and innocent. Bruno had never felt innocent, or young. He had never even felt happy, except perhaps when he was *thunking* his knives into the dartboard, honing his skills, forgetting everything else.

*And then, dear Bruno, I kill him.*

After making him suffer the torments of hell, losing his livelihood, his friends, his family, Redmond was going to do it. He was going to kill Max.

But Bruno *admired* Max Carter. He didn't want to, but he did. And . . . the Delaneys had looked after him. Hadn't they? Of course, if he *hadn't* played ball, confessed, taken the judge's sentence for a crime he hadn't committed, they'd have found a way to slit his throat open, so he really hadn't had much choice but to do the time. He'd done it, and he'd come out, thinking, *dreaming,* of freedom, a life without the sinister Delaneys hanging over him. But they'd been there, waiting for him, ready to reclaim him. He was their pawn, their puppet. And he hated that. He was starting to wonder – and this amazed him – whether Max Carter might actually need some help. He was also wondering if he could bring himself to give it, and what it might cost him if he did. But he was already partly committed to taking action. He was already in the shit, wasn't he?

'My son?' The vicar was still there, looking down at the bowed blond head. 'Can I help?'

'No,' said Bruno, standing up. 'But thank you.'

# 114

'Here he is!' the nurse announced loudly as she showed Hunter and Nolan into the large, airy conservatory at the back of the Brighton nursing home.

The Reverend Payne was a blue-eyed old man with a brightly checked blanket draped over his lap. He was skinny as a newly hatched bird, a few wisps of hair clinging onto his scalp, his nose a big hook, his ears enormous. He looked up at the approaching detectives with a wide, shaky smile.

'Tea? Coffee?' asked the nurse brightly.

'No. Thank you,' said Hunter.

'You'd like some, wouldn't you Nigel?' she bellowed, alerting the detectives to the fact that the reverend was hard of hearing.

'No. Thank you,' said the reverend.

The nurse retreated and Hunter and Nolan sat down.

'Ghastly woman,' said Payne. 'Shrieking about the place. Not *deaf*, you know.'

A large hearing aid attached to his left ear suggested that this wasn't strictly true.

'It's good of you to agree to see us,' said Hunter.

Payne shook his head, his head waggling about on his thin neck.

'Always happy to help the law,' he said.

Nolan got out his notebook and pen.

'So,' said Hunter. 'About Bruno Dawkins?'

'Oh, the boy?' The Reverend Payne leaned in. 'I knew the woman who looked after him. Not his mother at all. She confessed that to me.'

'What was her name?'

'Nora Dawkins. Bad business really. She didn't even have the poor child baptised, you know.'

'You say Bruno wasn't her child? Then whose child was he?'

'This is where it gets interesting,' said the reverend with relish.

Nolan was busy taking notes.

'There were powerful criminal gangs in those days. Still are, I suppose, but there was a sort of swagger to them then. They were almost *acceptable*, do you know what I mean? Greeted housewives in the street, patted little children on the head. They were respected. Like the Kray twins. They were like film stars. Well they *mixed* with film stars. High-ranking politicians. Members of the high church. It was all rather scandalous.'

'And . . . ?'

'There were the Richardsons, and the Delaneys, and the Carters, and the Krays, yes, everyone remembers them, don't they. Others too. They dominated the city of London.'

This criminal list seemed to excite Payne. His thin hands twitched on the blanket; his eyes danced with glee.

'So who's child . . . ?' prompted Hunter.

'It was her sister's child. Who incidentally was also mother to one of these awful gangster types who ruled the East End. Poor Nora, she acted with the best of intentions you know, but I think she was completely out of her depth. She'd never had children, never had any interest in them, and here she was, taking on a child, thinking no doubt that it was the Christian thing to do.'

'But why didn't the child's mother raise him?' asked Nolan.

'Because he was *illegitimate*,' said Payne in a loud whisper. 'Wrong side of the blanket, you see? Queenie Carter's own children were adults when she had what I suppose you would call a "fling" with a travelling salesman. She had to keep the thing secret so she came down from London to Brighton and stayed with her sister until the baby was born. And then Nora was supposed to get rid of it, take it to the police, consign it to the care system.'

'But she didn't?' asked Hunter.

'No. Silly woman changed her mind at the last moment and kept it. Struggled to know what to do with it, really. Confided in me about it. I said to her that she had done a very bad thing, and she had to tell Bruno – when he was old enough to understand – about his real parentage. And of course I told her that she must discuss the matter with her sister, that it must all be resolved.'

'Right. Very good.' Nolan was scribbling busily. 'And did she?'

The Reverend Payne's face fell. His lips trembled.

'No,' he said. 'She never got the chance. Poor Nora must have been far more tormented by all this than I realised. I failed her. I felt terrible about it. I still do.'

'So what happened?' asked Hunter.

'It was in all the papers. A scandal. Afterwards, I did wonder what had happened to the boy but he was nowhere to be found – and until this day, I haven't discussed this with a soul. Not even with the police. Perhaps I was wrong. I don't know. I just hoped the boy was all right. I only met him a time or two. He was silent, watchful. Poor child. Nora had quite turned him against the Carter family and no doubt he did feel let down by them. Betrayed, even. I did wonder if he might have taken himself off to London. Got in with the wrong crowd. So many young people do, don't they.'

'Yes, but what happened to Nora?' asked Nolan.

'Nora?' The Reverend Payne's pale blue eyes opened very wide. 'That poor woman! She must have been so tormented by it all. With the best will in the world, I'm sure she could clearly see she'd made a terrible mistake.'

'And?' said Hunter.

'She threw herself off Margate cliffs.'

# 115

Max went out, telling Annie that he was taking Tone with him. He was going over to see Chris at the Shalimar, make sure everything was OK there now.

'Fine,' she said, seeing him off at the door.

Three-quarters of an hour after Max had departed, someone else was knocking at the door. Annie came downstairs and went and said cautiously: 'Who is it?'

'It's Bruno Dawkins,' said a voice on the other side of it.

Annie opened the door a crack. 'What do you want?'

'I need to talk to you. It's important.'

Layla was halfway down the stairs, her face anxious. 'Who is it?' she asked.

'Nobody,' said Annie. 'Go back upstairs.'

Layla didn't. She came and stood by Annie.

Annie turned back to Bruno. 'So talk.'

'Can I come in?'

Annie looked beyond Bruno to the gate. One of Max's boys was there, watching what was happening at the front door. The man followed Bruno inside the house and stood there in the hall.

Layla was eyeing up the blond man standing there.

'Hello,' she said.

'Hi.'

Annie ushered the pair of them into the kitchen and they all sat down at the table.

'What did you want to talk to me about?' she asked.

*Pick a side,* thought Bruno. It was time to do that, at last. He was looking around the kitchen, his eyes interested.

'I've been here before,' he said. 'To this house.'

'Oh?' said Annie, wondering what this was all about.

'It was a long time ago.' Bruno's eyes fastened on Annie's face and there was something in his expression that was almost pleading. 'What was she like, Queenie Carter? Really?'

Annie frowned at him. 'Personally, I don't know. She was dead before I arrived on the scene.'

'Right.' He looked crestfallen, almost childlike in his disappointment.

'What are you doing here, today?' asked Annie.

'Oh yes. Yes.' He gave a smile full of sweetness. 'There was a note posted through the letterbox of your Holland Park place a few days ago,' said Bruno.

'Yes,' said Annie. 'There was.'

'I did that.'

Annie's hand slipped into her pocket, fastened on the slim handle of the kiyoga. Was she going to have to shout for that handy-looking chap out in the hall? She hoped not.

'I know that,' she said.

Bruno smiled. 'The book of remembrance. I should have thought of it.'

'But you didn't.'

'No. The note wasn't intended as a threat,' said Bruno, holding up his hands in a 'peace' gesture. 'It was a warning. Not for you. For Max.'

'Right.' A warning for *Max*? 'And . . . ?'

'Why would you be warning Dad?' interjected Layla.

'Long story.' Bruno smiled faintly.

'We've got all bloody day. Spit it out,' said Annie, her grip on the kiyoga not loosening for an instant. 'No. Wait. First, answer me a question, will you?'

Bruno nodded, his eyes growing wary.

'Are you . . . are you Max's brother?' Annie asked him. 'Are you the one who paid Jaime to find him in nineteen-seventy in Majorca?'

Bruno was silent. Then he straightened in his chair and said: 'Why would you think that?'

Annie stared straight into Bruno's eyes.

'When Max was in his twenties, his mum Queenie had an affair with a company rep. Maybe that's even why his dad left, I don't know. Maybe she was *always* playing around. Anyway. Not long after the rep quit the scene, she went to stay with her sister Nora in Brighton. Max told me that she was gone for a good couple of months, maybe a bit more – time enough for her to have a mid-life baby and leave it there.'

Bruno's face flushed, but he said nothing.

'It was you, wasn't it?' Annie went on. 'You sent Jaime the goat boy down onto the cliffs to find Max. You told Jaime you were Max's brother and you paid him to look.'

'And?' said Bruno.

'Here's what I think. You work for the Delaney mob – or what's left of them, anyway. I don't know why. Maybe revenge for what Queenie Carter did, abandoning you. But, Bruno, they're bad, bad people. They've chased me. They've killed people. I think they probably killed Steve Taylor. Maybe you even helped them.'

Bruno swallowed hard. 'A long time ago, I had to pick a side. I was hurt and I was angry and I think . . . I think

I picked the wrong one,' he said finally. 'Look, the note? I warned Max because the truth is, he's family, all right? But I spent years hating him. You're right about that. The Carters dumped me. And he gave the order to kill Nora, the poor cow. She at least *tried* to look after me, which is more than *they* ever did.'

'Max wouldn't do that. She was family too.'

'Well, whatever – he did it. And I was bitter, you know? Life had been bad enough when I was with her, but after that I was completely alone. I had *no one* and that was Max's fault. And so I joined up with the Delaneys.' Bruno's skin flushed again, turning the birthmark on his cheek darker. 'I had an affair, I suppose you would call it. With Tory Delaney. I was almost happy with him, for the first time ever. And then Max killed him.'

'No. No! You've got that wrong,' said Annie. 'I know every-one thought that at the time, but it wasn't true.'

'Really?' Bruno looked sceptical.

'Yes. Really. Damn, I even thought it *myself* for a while, but eventually the real killer came to light.'

'Who the hell was it then?' asked Bruno.

'Kieron Delaney. Tory's brother.' She shuddered as she looked at him. 'Bruno, you fell in with a real nest of vipers there. None of the Delaneys are to be trusted.'

'I know that,' he said broodingly. 'But once you're in with them, it's like a trap. You can't get out.' His mouth twitched in a smile. 'Not *alive*, anyway.'

# 116

As Tone was driving, weaving through traffic, Max was thinking that something wasn't adding up. He thought of Annie in the pool, of making love to her. Thought of Steve, dead. His best mate. People like that, you only met them once in your life if you were lucky. You never expected to lose them. The pain of losing Steve ate at him.

And the photos! The red-haired man on the doorstep of Steve's house, Annie's reaction to that. That *face*. Hard. Predatory. Was he the one who poisoned Jaime? One twin in Majorca doing that, the other chasing Annie up the beach?

'Traffic's a fuckin' nightmare today,' said Tone. 'I'll cut through.'

Tone was steering the car down a side street, accelerating briskly, then out onto a main road – and then something hit them hard, from the side.

The impact of the collision was jarring, mind-numbing.

Instantly, the engine cut out.

Max's head struck the window, hard. Then he sat there, dazed, aware of the warm wetness of blood trickling down his face. Tone was slumped against the wheel, unmoving. The car's horn was blaring.

'Tone?' Max managed to get out.

No answer.

Max felt consciousness wavering, a low droning hum seeming to fill his head, blackness closing in.

Someone was opening the door beside him.

Someone . . .

A sharp sting in his neck.

Then he was gone.

## 117

Everything fell into place for Annie then. The mysterious 'brother' paying Jaime to find Max after the finca explosion back in the Seventies. The familiarity she felt whenever she looked at Bruno, the feeling that she knew him, saw Max in him.

She found herself staring at his face as she sat across the table from him. There was the birthmark on his left cheek, a slight imperfection but overall it did little to detract from his good looks. His nose – it was the same, that piratical Carter hook. Max's nose. Queenie's, too. Annie had seen that in the portrait hanging in the front room.

'You look like him. You *do*,' said Annie.

'What the hell is this?' demanded Layla. 'What's he saying? That he's Dad's brother? My *uncle*?'

'I thought Max had abandoned me,' said Bruno. 'But he didn't, did he? He didn't even know I existed. I've thought about all this, over and over. It's plagued me for years. So I had to come here today, I had to tell you. I had to let you know because it's getting too dangerous.'

'Well . . . why haven't you shown yourself to Max? Told him? And how could you be his brother and he be unaware of it. How is this *possible*?' demanded Annie.

'Queenie – Max's mother – had me when Max and his brothers were grown up. She had an affair with a travelling salesman. A shameful hole-in-the-corner thing, and I was the result.'

Annie was frowning. 'So she didn't bring you up?'

'No. She didn't. Apparently the plan was to give me up to the adoption people, but her sister Nora raised me instead. It wasn't exactly a barrel of laughs, but she tried I suppose.'

'And . . . ?' Annie prompted when he hesitated.

'For a long time I thought that Max was my enemy. I hated him. He had everything I wanted. A mother who adored him, not a stone-cold stand-in who could never really be bothered. And there were other things that turned me against him. Nora was supposed to have topped herself, thrown herself off a cliff, but I know she never did. I saw Jonjo and Steve Taylor in Nora's house in Brighton one night. I *know* they did her. And I was convinced Max ordered her death.'

'He wouldn't do that,' said Annie, appalled that he should think so.

'That was it, you see. It didn't fit with the man I'd been watching all this time, the man I *thought* he was. Strike out at a woman? And one he was related to? I thought it would be beneath him. I always sort of *admired* him, you see. He was so damned *cool*. I wanted to be like him and I hated him for being the loved son, the *wanted* one – unlike me.'

Annie was digesting all this. Her one real worry was the note. All along, they'd thought it was for her. But no – according to Bruno it was aimed at Max. *Max* was the one who could be in danger.

'Why were you warning Max?' she asked Bruno. 'What were you warning him *of?*'

Bruno shook his head. 'There are things you don't know about. Things you maybe thought were dead and buried, but I'm telling you, they're not.'

'What do you mean?'

'I mean Redmond Delaney.'

# 118

Annie stared at Bruno. '*What?*' she said faintly.

Bruno nodded. She watched his hands on the table, saw the nails chewed down to the quick. They were trembling, very slightly. What the hell . . . ?

'But Redmond's dead,' she said.

'No. He isn't. It's true you know. I swear it,' said Bruno. 'He's alive. And he has his twin Delaney cousins, Seamus and Cormac, with him.'

'But I saw it happen! I was in Scotland when he died and . . .'

Bruno shook his head. 'He survived. He ought to have died, he *should* have died. I wish he had. But he didn't.'

Annie took a breath. This was a nightmare. Then she thought of the man chasing her up the beach, the man standing on the doorstep of the Parliament Hill house the other day. 'These cousins. Big men, are they? Athletic types? Fortyish? Red hair fading to grey? Sharp faces. Hard bastards?'

Bruno was staring at her face. 'Yes! You've seen them?'

'Yes,' said Annie grimly. 'I have.'

'Then you know I'm telling the truth.'

Annie felt as if she was sinking into a spiralling pit of anguish. She looked across at Layla.

'Where did your dad say he was going?' Annie asked, feeling a gnawing worm of worry in her gut. Max had told her, but she hadn't been paying attention.

'Over to see Chris at the Shalimar.'

Annie glanced at her watch. 'He should be there by now. Shouldn't he?'

'I should think so.'

'Wait.' Annie went out into the hall and picked up the phone and dialled the Shalimar's number, all the while keeping her eye on the open door into the kitchen, on her daughter sitting there at the table with Bruno.

*Max's brother.*

Who might be their friend – or their enemy, in disguise.

Ellie answered after three rings. 'Ellie, is Max there?'

'No, he's not.'

*Redmond, alive? Alive and gunning for Max?*

Annie felt her mouth go dry. 'Is Chris expecting him? Had they arranged anything?'

She heard Ellie mumble something, a deep male bass voice answering. Ellie was talking to Chris. Presently, he came on the phone. 'Annie?'

'Chris? You expecting Max?'

'No. Why'd you say that?'

'Maybe he was just going to call in at the club after doing something else first,' she said. 'He said he was coming to see you.'

'Well, he hasn't shown up yet. You tried the Parrot? The Palermo?'

'No. I'll do that now.'

'I'll stay by the phone here. I'll let you know if he does come. Shout if you need me.'

'Will do.' Annie rang off and phoned through to Janice at the Blue Parrot. Max wasn't there, said Janice, and he wasn't expected. Annie gave her Queenie's number, told her to phone if Max did show. Then she tried the Palermo. He wasn't there either and they weren't expecting to see him there today, why was she asking?

'No reason. If he shows, call me.' She rattled off Queenie's number, then hung up.

'Problems?' asked Max's boy by the front door, who'd been listening in to all this.

'I don't know.' Annie was thinking fast. She went to the hat stand and rummaged in a coat pocket hanging there. Then she snatched her coat down off the hook and went back to the kitchen. She looked at Bruno. Did she dare trust him? 'Bruno, you got a car?'

'Yeah, sure.'

'Layla, you stay here in case the phone rings. Bruno – with me. We're going to trace his route over to the Shalimar, maybe they've had a breakdown, who knows.'

'Mum . . .' started Layla, worried, starting to get up.

'No. You *stay here*.' Annie indicated the man by the door. 'You stay too. Layla – keep him close, don't go out. Bruno – come on.'

# 119

Max came back to his senses by slow degrees. He was aware first of pain – his head was pounding and his cheek felt sticky with blood.

The crash came back to him.

*Tone?*

He blinked with sore eyes, looking around. He was in what looked like a cellar, white painted, glaringly lit by a single hundred-watt bulb. And he was tied up, tied to a chair. He strained against his bonds and felt rope cut into his wrists. Straining to look behind him, he could see a table. Instruments on there. Knives. *Scalpels.*

'I see you're back with us,' said a voice behind him.

There was the whir of a motor – and then a nightmare in a wheelchair came humming forward, into Max's line of vision.

The face was twisted, the left eye a black gaping hole. The left arm looked bent, wasted. And the legs were gone.

'Yes,' said Redmond. 'Me.'

Max shook his head, grimaced.

'Nothing to say?' asked Redmond in that soft Irish lilt.

'Yeah. Actually I have got something to say,' said Max.

'Go on.'

'Why don't you fuck off and die, like you were supposed to?'

Redmond gave a crooked smile. 'Yes, that was always the plan, wasn't it,' he said. 'I was supposed to die, but I seem to have a talent for staying alive, don't I. And so have you – up until now.'

'Yeah, yeah,' said Max. 'Get on with it then. Don't just sit there pecking my bloody head.'

'But why not? It's such fun.' Redmond frowned. 'What, do you think there's a way out of this for you? Not this time, I'm afraid.'

'People will be looking,' Max pointed out.

'*Will* they though?' Redmond considered that. 'What, you mean Annie? You think she'll search for you? But she never did, did she? Not even when you went missing for two years. She didn't search for you. Didn't much care, I suppose. Truth is, she left you to rot, and you know what? She'll do the same this time.'

There was a noise at the far end of the room. A lift? A motor started and Max heard the lift descending.

Redmond gave Max his death's-head smile.

'That will be Seamus and Cormac,' he said. 'Good. Now the fun can *really* begin.'

# 120

Annie and Bruno found the car down a side alley, halfway between Queenie's house and the Shalimar. Both the back passenger doors and the driver's door were flung wide open.

'Tone!' shouted Annie, seeing him slumped there, senseless, behind the wheel, his head covered in blood. She bolted out of the car before Bruno had even turned off the engine and ran to where Tone was. He looked awful, bleached of all colour. Desperately she felt for a pulse in his neck, expecting nothing. But it was there – faint but steady. Thank God.

'Phone an ambulance,' she said to Bruno. 'Hurry.'

While he did that, she looked in the back seat of the Jag; she opened the boot. Nothing. No Max. He was gone. But gone *where*?

'They're coming,' Bruno told her when he'd made the call. He was looking at Tone. 'Poor bastard. No sign of Max?'

'None.' Annie had to think straight. She had to focus, not panic. But God, it was hard. 'If somehow Redmond's managed to snatch Max . . .' She thought of the twins, the deadly twins . . . 'Where would he be taken?'

'That's easy I reckon. The Delaney place over in Battersea. The scrapyard.'

His words gave Annie a spasm of memory, acutely painful, terrifying. Long ago, she'd had a trip to that same yard. And nearly – so very nearly – she hadn't lived to tell the tale.

She felt fear grip her, nearly choking the breath out of her. A nightmare image of Steve, hanging dead off a canal bridge, shot into her brain. She thought of Max, who believed that once she had abandoned him, given up on him. This time, whatever the outcome, she wasn't going to let him think that. She *couldn't*.

'You're sure?'

'Yeah. Redmond's favourite playground.' Bruno's smile was a wince, a flinching-back from things he'd seen and heard. 'You reckon we should get the police?'

'Not if we can sort this out ourselves,' said Annie. She showed Bruno the gun she'd taken out of Max's raincoat pocket back in Queenie's hallway. She could hear an ambulance's siren, coming closer. Tone would be OK, she hoped. But could she trust Bruno, whose loyalties were so divided, or was he leading her straight into a trap? He could be. She didn't know. Everything he'd told her could be a pack of lies. But, right now, she didn't have much choice.

If Max was in trouble, she had to go on. Had to trust her instincts.

She handed Bruno the kiyoga.

'You take this. Come on. Let's get over there.'

# 121

Hunter's intention, after visiting Reverend Payne, had been to talk to Annie Carter about what he'd discovered – but he never got the chance. When Nolan pulled up outside the old Carter house in Bow they saw her and a blond man speeding away from it in a car.

'Follow it,' snapped Hunter.

Nolan did. He followed Bruno's progress, right up to the point where Bruno and Annie found Max Carter's crashed Jag down a side alley. But they didn't linger there. Minutes, then they were back in the car and Nolan was on their tail again in the thick of the traffic.

'Don't bloody lose them,' said Hunter, who was radioing through the details of the crashed Jag, ordering up an ambulance for its driver, only to find a call had already gone in.

'I won't,' said Nolan, but minutes later he did. '*Fuck*,' he said.

Hunter got on the radio again, put out an APB on Bruno's car.

'Pull in,' he said to Nolan grimly. 'Just park up.'

'Fuck it. Sorry, sir.'

Six minutes later, the radio crackled into life. Bruno's car was found parked outside a Battersea scrapyard. Control gave Hunter the address. Nolan started the engine and floored the accelerator.

## 122

Going into the Delaneys' scrapyard was revisiting a bad, bad dream. There were piles of rusted scrap metal – cars, fridges, old gates – everywhere. There were cranes, and there was the car crusher. God, she remembered that. There was a handy-looking guard on the big padlocked steel gate, a whip-thin Dobermann Pinscher, a killing machine on four legs, at his side.

Seeing Bruno, the guard let them in. And there, coming down the steps from the static office at the back of the yard, were the twins Cormac and Seamus – one marked by Annie's double strike with the kiyoga, the other not. They walked over and Bruno said: 'See? I said I'd bring her, and I did.'

Annie looked at Bruno. She had put her trust in him, but now she wondered with an icy thrill of fear – had she been mistaken?

The scarred twin grabbed her roughly by the arm and started leading her across the concreted yard, heading not for the office but down an alleyway beside it to the house. Inside a tiny room at the front of it there was a desk littered with piles of invoices. Last year's calendar still hung on the wall beside a stopped clock. There was dust everywhere.

The twins took her and Bruno straight through there and to a door at the back of the room, which led into a lift. One twin closed the metal cage at the door and the lift sank down, painfully slowly, juddering all the way, clanking, metal cogs squealing, just one floor. Then the lift door opened and they all stepped out into a big white-painted cellar, brightly and starkly lit by just one bare overhead bulb.

*It's like a dungeon,* thought Annie with a shudder. She could feel cold sweat trickling down her back. She looked around in desperation, caught Bruno's eye. Friend or foe? She just didn't know. And where the hell was Max?

Her heart seemed to stall in her chest.

Oh Christ. He was there, tied up to a chair. Facing them, as they emerged from the lift.

The lift was going back up, its metal parts screaming. Max's eyes were open but dazed. There was bruising on his cheek, blood trickling down from a cut on his brow. The unmarked twin walked over to where Max was tied, grabbed a handful of his hair and yanked his head back hard. The twin was grinning, like this was the best fun ever. Beyond Max, Annie could see a table, laid out with surgical instruments.

*Enough,* she thought.

She pulled Max's old .45 gun out of her coat pocket, released the safety catch and placed the muzzle up against the head of the marked twin who was standing right next to her. As he felt something very cold and hard pressing up against his already wounded temple, he froze.

'Hello again,' said Annie, and pulled the trigger.

# 123

Nothing happened.

Annie yanked the trigger again. A click – and nothing.

The twin turned, a snarl on his face. He grabbed the gun and swung it. It caught Annie on the cheek and she reeled back, stunned, falling to the floor. Pain erupted and she had the dizzying sensation that she was about to pass out. She gulped down air. The high metal whine of the lift gears had stopped; the lift was up on the ground floor again, just off that shabby little office. She could hear clanking, the metal cage doors being pulled back. Someone was up there. Someone was going to come down.

She came to her knees. Shakily, she got to her feet, her face throbbing hotly. Bruno caught her arm, supporting her. Then – unexpectedly – he sagged under her weight. He turned, swinging the kiyoga hard. It struck the twin who was now holding Max's gun straight between the eyes with a sharp *crack*, shattering his nose. He howled in pain as blood gushed down his nostrils. Cupping both hands to his face, he staggered back and Bruno came at him again, swinging the kiyoga in a wide arc, catching the top of his head.

The twin collapsed to the floor and lay still.

'That's a very handy thing to have about a person,' panted Bruno, looking admiringly at the kiyoga in his hand. 'But,

Mrs Carter, before you go to fire a gun you really should make sure it's loaded.'

'It should have been loaded. Max *keeps* that loaded, right by the door,' objected Annie. She felt like her cheekbone had swollen to twice its normal size. *Sometimes it misfires,* she remembered Max telling her. Of all the bloody times for it to do that!

Someone was coming down in the lift. Clanking and shuddering, it was descending again.

She picked up the gun, which had fallen from the hand of the man on the floor. She pointed it at the other twin who was standing beside Max's chair.

'Oi! Arsehole!' she shouted. It hurt but she didn't care. 'Step away from the chair.'

The twin grinned and shook his head. To her horror she saw that he now had a knife in his hand.

'That feckin' thing's not loaded,' he said, and, ignoring her, he turned toward Max.

Annie gave up a prayer and fired. The gun was an old Second World War item, a Smith and Wesson museum piece, but when it did work, by God it worked just fine.

The noise of the .45 bullet leaving the chamber was loud as a sonic boom in this confined space. The twin holding the knife to Max's throat shot backward as if hit by a truck, clutching at his shattered shoulder and screaming in agony.

'*Bruno* . . . ?' prompted Annie, and Bruno obligingly rushed forward and whacked him with the kiyoga while he was too injured to resist. He crumpled to the floor.

Annie dashed over to Max. 'You OK?' she asked him.

'Been better.' He winced. 'Cut the rope.'

Annie was looking for the knife. Where the hell was it?

The lift was wheezing and clanking; it was coming to a stop. Someone was pulling back the doors. She had to hurry.

*Where was the knife?*

'Bruno? Where's the knife?' she said urgently.

'I've got it,' said Bruno, snatching it up and lunging forward, slicing through the bonds that held Max.

Max staggered to his feet and then an ice-cold voice with a soft Irish lilt to it said: 'Oh look – a family reunion.'

The three of them turned and saw Redmond Delaney there. The wheelchair whirred out of the lift into the cellar and then stopped. There was a machine gun on Redmond's lap – and it was aimed at all of them.

## 124

'Well – this is nice,' said Redmond.

Annie was staring at him, shocked to the core.

'Bruno?' said Redmond. 'Come over here with me, where you belong. And well done, by the way. Getting her here. Good show.'

His eyes fell to the twin lying unconscious on the floor near him, then to the other one at the far end of the room, who was writhing and groaning in pain while clutching at his mangled shoulder.

'I do appreciate that you had to make it convincing,' Redmond said to Bruno.

Annie looked at Bruno. No, he was on *her* side. He'd proved it today. Hadn't he? But to her dismay, to her *horror*, Bruno left her and, tucking the knife into the waistband of his jeans, he walked over to stand beside Redmond.

'I can see that this surprises you, Mrs Carter,' said Redmond silkily. 'But this poor lost boy has been nurtured by my family for so long – and completely ignored by yours. I set a lot of store by family – I lost my own dear sister Orla in a plane crash in the Seventies, as you know.'

*No you didn't,* thought Annie. But that was something she would never speak about – not to anyone.

'So what did you expect, other than this poor boy turning on you?' Redmond went on.

'What the fuck?' asked Max.

Annie shook her head. 'Later,' she said.

'Yes but sadly there will *be* no "later", Mrs Carter. Not for either of you, anyway. I, of course, will go on. Some things have sustained me – most importantly, the notion of revenge. Revenge for the loss of my sister, for the ruin of my family. All those years of hatred, of loathing, and it's all boiled down to this final confrontation. It's incredibly pleasing, you know, the thought of taking everything away from you. You, Max Carter – I took your dearest friend and hanged him. The witnesses were a pity, but of course they had to be dealt with so that I could deliver the final *coup de grace* right here, today. I smashed up your clubs. Bruno helped. Dear Bruno. And here, today, this is where it ends at last. Because Max – may I call you Max? – I am going to kill your wife, Annie Carter. All you will be able to do is watch. And then, when you have suffered through *that* for what I consider long enough, then, Max Carter, I will kill *you*.'

Max was staring at the mangled remains of Redmond, his face impassive.

'You used Steve's death to lure me back to London,' he said.

'Correct,' said Redmond.

'But you've got one detail wrong,' said Max.

'Oh yes? And what is that?'

Max gave a dismissive nod in Annie's direction. 'She's not my wife. She's my *ex-wife*. And I don't give a flying fuck about her. So go ahead. See if I care. Shoot her.'

## 125

'You're bluffing,' said Redmond.

'Am I? I don't think so,' said Max.

'But look what a devoted wife she is,' said Redmond. 'Of course, last time, she abandoned you. I do understand how that must have rankled. Two years in the wilderness, weren't you, and then you get home and what do you find? She's bedded a new man. A Mafia don no less. Constantine Barolli. That must have been pretty hard to forgive, I suppose – wasn't it? Yes, surely it was. But this time, you have to admit it – she's come up trumps, hasn't she. Come dashing to your rescue. And made a fairly good job of it too, but so sad that she's walked right into a trap of my making and now – well – are you *sure* you want me to shoot her, Mr Carter?'

'I'm sure,' said Max.

'Max?' Annie was turning toward him. 'What . . . ?'

Redmond lifted the muzzle of the machine gun, taking aim at Annie.

'No second chances with this, Mr Carter. Say you're sure and I'll go ahead. Really, I don't care one way or another. The choice is yours.'

He was going to do it. And Max was going to let him!

'You bastard,' she said to Max.

'Yeah. That's me,' he said and then to Redmond: 'I'm sure. Go on. Do it.'

Redmond lifted the gun, aimed.

Annie shut her eyes. This was it.

She saw Bruno move, fast as lightning. Something *zipped* out of his hand and struck the light switch at the side of the room.

Instantly the light went out, plunging them all into darkness.

And the lift was going up again.

# 126

Annie was blinking, blind in the pitch blackness, when someone grabbed her and pushed her to the floor, sending her stumbling over the twin with the shoulder injury. She fell to her knees behind the man. Then she heard noises, clanking, squealing. She was going to hear them in her nightmares for months to come – she knew it. The lift was coming down again.

The lift stopped. The metal doors squealed open. Suddenly the light came back on. She stared around, squinting, trying to make sense of what had just happened – and there was Max, untied, over by Redmond, snatching the gun out of his hands while Bruno leaned in with a thin-bladed knife, pressing hard up against Redmond's throat.

Behind them, three men were stepping out of the lift. Three dark-coated, immaculate men, two of them standing back a little, and the third . . .

'*Alberto?*' said Annie.

'Hiya, Stepmom,' he said. 'Max,' he said cordially.

'About bloody time,' said Max.

'Oh I dunno. Looks like you have the situation under control.'

Annie struggled back to her feet. She clambered over the man she'd shot. He grabbed at her feebly but she eluded him and gave him a well-aimed kick in passing. *Bastard.*

And *what* had Max said just now?

'"I don't give a flying fuck about her"?' she said furiously, advancing on the little tableau near the lift. 'What the hell was *that*?'

'Just buying time,' said Max calmly. He looked at Redmond, then over at Alberto. 'Well, Golden Boy, what now?'

'We'll handle it,' said Alberto, and his two companions grabbed hold of Redmond and yanked his chair back, toward the lift.

'"Just shoot her, see if I care"?' Annie raged on.

'That gun was never going to fire,' said Bruno. 'I fixed it earlier. And – um – I told Max I'd done it. And obviously – he believed me.'

'You *what*?' Annie rounded on him.

'Redmond was showing the damned thing off to the twins. He said he had something special to do with it and I knew he was fixed on you Carters. I could see something bad coming – so I removed the firing pin.'

'I wish you all in hell!' shouted Redmond.

'See you there then,' said Max.

'And was that you who shoved me? Yes. It was. You *shoved* me,' said Annie to Max. 'And you didn't *know* the damned thing wouldn't fire, did you.'

'Yes I did. It's true, what Bruno said. He spoke to me yesterday and told me he'd been fixing Redmond's arsenal of guns. Took quite a risk to do it, too.'

'He *what*? Well why didn't you tell me?'

'I'm telling you now.'

'This isn't over!' yelled Redmond. 'You think you've seen the last of me? You haven't!'

'I think you'll find Max pushed you to get you behind matey over there, to give you whatever cover he could,' said

Bruno. Seeing both Annie and Max turn toward him with angry expressions, he shrugged. 'Just saying.'

'Should we do something about him?' wondered Annie aloud, her gaze wandering back to the twin at the far end of the room. 'And this one?' She nudged the nearer one with her toe.

The lift doors were being pulled shut. Through the cage, they could see the two big black-coated men, and Alberto, and Redmond's ruined face, twisted with impotent rage.

'Nah,' said Max. 'Fuck 'em.'

## 127

Hunter and Nolan arrived at the Delaney scrapyard just in time to see a black limousine pulling away from the front of it. The metal gates were standing open. No guards about. No dogs. No nothing.

'Shall we go in?' said Nolan, and then Hunter tapped his arm and nodded toward three people who were emerging from the house at the back of the yard.

It was a bloodied Max Carter. Annie Carter followed, and Bruno Dawkins. They came out through the gates, got in Bruno's car, and he drove away.

'Boss?' Nolan was champing at the bit, eager to follow.

'No,' said Hunter firmly. 'Leave it.'

'What now?' asked Nolan, disappointed.

'Back to the station.'

'But the limo . . . ?'

'Forget the bleeding limo, Nolan. That's above your pay grade.' Hunter heaved a sigh. 'And mine.'

★

Next morning, bright and early, DCI Hunter assembled his team in the station and addressed them over the cases of Steve Taylor, the hanging man on the canal bridge, and the book boat man tied to his own anchor chain, and Mr Halliday, drowned in his own boat.

'We've had confessions from Cormac and Seamus Delaney,' Hunter summed up. 'They're laid up in hospital at the moment, but I anticipate that they are going to be tucked away at Her Majesty's pleasure for a long, long time.'

'Did they act independently?' asked one of the team, who was now busy taking down the gruesome array of photos from the wall behind Hunter's desk.

'They didn't implicate Redmond Delaney in any way,' said Nolan.

'And where is he now?' asked another team member.

'We don't know the answer to that,' said Hunter, who was pretty convinced that the Mafia had snatched him, and good luck to them.

'So – case closed then, sir?' asked Nolan.

'Looks like it.'

# 128

Bruno dropped Annie and Max not at Queenie's old place but back, on Annie's say-so, at the Holland Park house. She phoned through to Layla straight away, let her know they were all OK.

'Home sweet home,' she said, looking around her with satisfaction.

Max was watching her face. 'You love this place,' he said.

'I do.' Annie turned to Bruno. 'Come along in, Bruno.'

But he just stood there on the doorstep.

'Nah,' he said at last. 'Think I'll pass.'

Annie glanced at Max, then at Bruno, thinking that Max ought to ask him to stay, but Max didn't say a word.

'So what are you going to do now?' she asked Bruno.

He shrugged. 'Dunno. Maybe make myself scarce for a while until everything cools down.'

'Where will you go?' she asked.

*Still* nothing from Max.

'Travel around for a bit,' said Bruno. He flicked a look at Max, then away. 'Few months. Egypt maybe. Always fancied that.'

Annie nodded. Silence descended.

'Well,' she said, 'you're always welcome here. *More* than welcome. Isn't he, Max?'

'It's your house,' said Max.

'I'll be off,' said Bruno, and left.

Annie closed the front door. 'What a graceless bastard you are,' she said to Max.

'What did I do?' asked Max.

'It's what you didn't do. That man saved your life. Twice.'

'You don't understand.'

'Damned right I don't.'

'It shook me, all right?' Max said suddenly. 'The thought of my old mum doing something like that, dropping a bastard sprog in middle age. Now what can I say? It's a fact. So yes, he's my brother. I admit to that. But don't expect me to feel easy about it. And don't expect me to be bloody pleased, because I'm not.'

Annie sighed. 'Come down to the kitchen. Let's get that cut cleaned up.'

## 129

The following afternoon, Annie and Max went to visit Tone in hospital. He was sitting up in bed, groggy but otherwise OK; his head was swathed in bandages and the table in front of him was piled high with car magazines and a basket full of fruit. Ellie and Chris were there, sitting one on either side of him like bookends, and when the Carters came in, they stood up and Ellie gave Annie a warm hug.

'You all right, both of you? Tone's been telling us about the car smash, what little he can remember of it, anyway.'

'I'll fill you in on the rest later,' said Annie, and Chris and Ellie took their leave.

'Doing OK are you?' Max asked Tone.

'Yeah. What about you?' Tone indicated Max's head, which was sporting a large plaster. 'Thought you'd be laid here in the next bed after that.'

Max told Tone that the Delaney mob had snatched him and taken him to the scrapyard, where Annie and Bruno had tracked him down.

'Who's this Bruno?' Tone asked.

Annie opened her mouth to speak.

'Friend of ours,' said Max. 'What do the docs say about your head then?'

'Concussion. Nothing bad. One more night in here, then I'm out.'

They stayed at the hospital with Tone for an hour, then left.

'A *friend* of ours?' Annie queried as they left the building.

'What the hell else was I supposed to say?'

'Maybe the truth.' But she understood. He thought that the truth would make his mum look bad.

'What now?' she asked. 'Home?'

'Nah, let's go somewhere and eat. Celebrate being alive?' He grinned.

Annie shuddered. 'He was going to do it. Wasn't he.'

Max took her arm. 'He was. But he didn't manage it. We're still here. And he . . .' Max shrugged. 'Well, who knows.'

'Alberto will see to it,' said Annie.

'Amen to that.'

# 130

That same evening, Layla was sitting alone in the Holland Park house watching TV. She nipped down to the kitchen to make herself a coffee and when she came back upstairs she felt a cool draught sweeping through the big marbled hallway. She heard a noise – faint, tinkling, a soft fairy noise. She froze at the side of the hall and looked up. The crystal droplets on the chandelier above her head were moving softly in the breeze – and the front door was standing wide open.

'Hello?' she said shakily. 'Somebody there?'

No answer. There was no one here with her tonight because her parents had told her about what had happened at the Delaney scrapyard, that all their current problems were resolved. But were they wrong?

She went over to the door, paused a moment looking out at the black night sky, listening to the noises of traffic, distant sirens. Then she closed the door, shivering, and hurried across the hall and into the drawing room, shutting the door behind her.

There was a man standing in front of the fireplace.

A shriek escaped her.

He was tall, and blond. As she came into the room he turned and stared at her with bright laser-blue eyes.

'Hi Layla,' said Alberto.

'Oh my God,' said Layla, shocked, spilling her coffee onto the rug.

Alberto came across the room and caught her hand. 'Steady. You'll scald yourself.' He took the coffee, put the mug down on an occasional table and straightened up. 'You OK?'

From fright Layla was catapulted into fury. He'd scared her half to death.

'OK?' she shot out. 'No I'm not bloody OK. What the hell d'you think you're doing, creeping about in here?'

Alberto half-smiled. 'This place always did feel like home,' he said. 'Sorry.'

It was such a shock, seeing him. Layla was groping for something to say, and what came out of her mouth was: 'You warned off DS Nolan.'

'Oh, that?'

'Yes that.'

'What, you want me to apologise?'

'That would be nice.'

'All right. Then I do.'

'Mum said you were at the Delaney scrapyard yesterday,' said Layla.

'I was. Just helping out.'

'So it's over then? Whatever blew up, whatever happened about Steve, it's over?'

'Done and dusted.'

'Good.' She let out a shaky sigh and sat down. Her legs felt unsteady. He had really, really scared her.

'But what about us?' asked Alberto. 'You didn't even say goodbye. You just left.'

'I thought it was the best thing to do.'

'You don't love me anymore then?'

Layla let out a hiss of pain. 'Don't be ridiculous,' she snapped out. 'Of course I do.'

'So the business with that cop? Nolan?'

'You've been spying on me.'

'Yeah. So what was that?'

'That was . . . he's very sweet, DS Nolan. He's not like you.'

'Oh, and that's good is it?'

'I thought . . . I was just trying it out, OK? *Could* I feel the way I feel about you, with someone else? I wanted to. I *needed* to.'

'And? Could you?'

'No. I bloody couldn't.'

'Well that's a relief.'

'Is it? Not to me.'

'Are you going to get your ass over here and kiss me?' Alberto asked.

'No! I couldn't go back to that again, you know. All that moving around. Being scared all the time. I'm a homebody. I like to stay in one place.'

'Noted.'

'Yes, that's all very well, but are you really hearing what I'm saying?'

'Yes. I am. I've missed you.' His face clouded and for the first time ever, she saw him look uncertain. 'Honey . . . I didn't know what to say to you, about the baby. I knew you were hurting. I was too. But I couldn't seem to say what I *wanted* to say about it, and you cut me dead. You know you did. I wanted to say that I was there for you, that I would do anything to protect you from pain like that again.'

Layla said nothing. She was afraid to speak, very close to tears.

'Kiss me.'

'Fuck's sake.'

'Come on, you know you want to,' said Alberto.

'No. I don't.'

Alberto started to smile. 'Puckering up here.'

'Bastard,' said Layla, but she was smiling too, as she went into his arms.

★

When Annie and Max got back from dinner later in the evening, Max sauntered through to the drawing room and poured a brandy.

'Layla upstairs?' he asked, as Annie followed him in.

She went upstairs to Layla's room, calling her name, expecting she'd turned in early. But the bed was empty and so was the en suite bathroom. She checked the wardrobe, but that was empty too. All Layla's stuff was gone. Annie came back downstairs and it was only then that she saw the note on the hall table. She picked it up and went into the drawing room, unfolding it.

'Isn't she up there?' asked Max. Then he saw the note. 'What's that?'

'No. She's not upstairs. And this,' Annie said, feeling anxious now, 'is a *pizzino*. Look. Just numbers. Let me see . . .'

They sat down and deciphered Caesar's code.

The message said:

*Gone with Alberto*

*L*

# SIX MONTHS LATER . . .

## 131

'You look,' said Ellie, kissing Annie's cheek, 'utterly fabulous.'

'You don't think the cream's too much? Too bridey?'

Annie and Ellie were standing outside in the foyer with a neatly suited and booted Tone in attendance, checking each other out – Ellie was in her favourite shade of cherry red, wearing a swishing chiffon dress that floated around her in a cloud; her hat was loaded with pink, white and scarlet cabbage roses. More of the same roses were in the small bouquet Annie was holding. She was wearing a beautifully cut cream silk suit, killer heels, no hat. A garland of roses pinned up her dark hair.

'Bridey? Well for God's sake, why would it? You are, after all, a bride.'

Annie held up two fingers. 'Second time,' she said. 'Same man. Am I completely mad?'

'Probably,' said Ellie.

'Not reassuring.' Annie thought of her daughter, how she would have loved this. 'I wish Layla could have been here.'

'She's back with him then? For keeps?'

'Yes,' said Annie, but in all honesty she couldn't say that she was entirely sure about that. Her daughter had the same taste as she did for hot, dodgy men. She just hoped that it would all somehow come good for Layla – and for Alberto, too.

The registrar, a tiny little bespectacled man in an immaculate brown suit, popped his head around the door and stared at the two women, Ellie in her elaborate red ensemble, Annie in her exquisitely cut cream suit.

'Don't you two look lovely! Is the groom here yet?'

'He's here,' said Chris, just coming into the foyer with Max.

Max came over to Annie and kissed her mouth.

*Can't live with him, can't live without him,* thought Annie.

'Hi,' she said, smiling into his eyes, thinking how handsome he was and how much she loved him.

'You look great,' he said.

'Shall we press on?' said the registrar.

# 132

After the wedding they honeymooned in 'their' place, the little family-run hotel in Illetas where they ate too many elaborate dinners and drank far too much wine.

'You're such a cheap date,' Max laughed at her, because she couldn't hold her drink at all and was woozy after a couple of glasses.

During the day they did nothing but laze naked on their sun-drenched balcony or lie in the shade of their suite to make love. Later on they went up to visit Benito at the monastery, to tell him the rest of the story, then to stand silent at Jaime's graveside, which had been dug out of a quiet cool corner, deep in the monastery catacombs.

'He saved my life,' said Max.

But Annie shook her head. 'He saved your life because Bruno paid him to.'

Max said nothing to that. Even now, he still refused to discuss Bruno.

But Benito had one last thing to tell them. After the tragedy of Jaime's death, he'd made inquiries around the area and a different story had emerged.

'What do you mean?' asked Max.

'That poor boy,' sighed Benito. 'Always so hungry for money – having had so little of it all his life.'

'What happened?' asked Annie.

'He'd been getting into bad company around Palma harbour. He'd been working for one of the Russian oligarchs who moored his floating gin palace there and . . .' Benito hesitated.

'Go on,' prompted Max.

'Jaime become entangled with the gangster's life. Such a glossy life, so far removed from everyday reality. The yachts, the five-star food, the hedonistic lifestyle. It was all so seductive to a poor boy like Jaime had been all his life. And then he started an affair with the man's very glamorous young wife. When he did that, he signed his death warrant,' Benito told them. 'This man was very proud, very possessive. Jaime trod on his toes and paid a high price.'

'And the woman? The wife?' asked Annie.

Benito shrugged. 'Who knows? I heard she disappeared. Maybe she survived. Maybe not.'

'So Jaime's death had nothing to do with me,' said Max, feeling the weight of the guilt lifting from his shoulders.

'Nothing at all, my friend,' Benito assured him.

'That Russian son of a bitch could have killed all three of us – not just Jaime,' said Max.

'I don't suppose he cared much about that,' said Benito. 'He wanted to get Jaime, who had cost him his marriage. That was all that concerned him.'

Max and Annie said their farewells to Benito later in the day, went back to the hotel, fell into bed with the song of the cicadas ringing in their sun-dazed ears, and slept in each other's arms.

# 133

After two lazy weeks in Majorca, they went home to Holland Park.

'Rosa not back yet then?' asked Max as they dropped their cases in the hall and gratefully closed the front door behind them.

'Not yet, no.' Annie turned to Max, thinking how much she loved him, admiring his dark mahogany suntan and the way the depth of it made his eyes glitter. He came over to her, kissed her.

'What?' he asked.

'I might sell it. This place.'

'Really?'

'Maybe. Providing you sell that old place in Bow too. Then we could get something else, something together.'

'We'll see.'

★

Days later, they took flowers to Queenie's grave – pink roses, her favourite. They also took some pink ones for Eddie, and red ones for Steve.

As they stood at Steve Taylor's graveside, Annie said: 'What about Kirsty?'

'Kirsty?' Max shrugged. 'It's not against the law, being a money-grubbing little tart.'

'I thought she must be involved.'

Max shook his head. 'She wasn't. And sometimes shit just happens. She's not the nicest woman in the world, she manipulated the situation to her advantage. So she should have scooped the jackpot.'

Annie was thoughtful, staring down at the bare earth on the grave, imagining Steve – their strong silent gladiator, who had stood beside them through so much – slumbering beneath. She shivered.

'Do you think Bruno's with her now? With Kirsty?' she asked Max.

'No.'

Annie looked at him, her attention sharpening. 'You say that as if you're certain. And what was that – what did you mean – *should* have scooped the jackpot? Kirsty has, surely.'

'That's because I am certain.' Max gave a thin smile. 'And I'm certain about Kirsty being left out of the will, too. I meant to tell you – Kirsty *didn't* inherit the farm.'

Annie frowned. 'But what about the new will?'

Max shook his head. 'They found another one, more recent.' He gave a low laugh. 'It seems Kirsty wasn't the only one spreading the love around. While she was cheating on Steve with Bruno, Steve had a little something of his own going on.'

'You're kidding me.'

'I'm not. Guess who?'

'How should I know?'

'She worked at Carter Security . . .'

'Latipa? The cleaner?'

'Nope. Remember little Julie in the office?'

Annie did. Pretty little blonde Julie, trusted with a key to the premises, in floods of tears over Steve's death.

'Julie! Good God.'

Max was nodding and grinning too. 'She gets everything. And Kirsty? Nothing at all.'

Annie was silent for a beat, taking it in. Then she said: 'About Bruno. I know it's a sore subject . . .'

Max's grin vanished. 'Then drop it,' he said.

'Whatever your mum did and however much it upsets you, none of that is Bruno's fault.'

'I know that.'

'He's in awe of you, Max. He's been following you around half his life, just hoping for a glimpse of you.'

'And working for the Delaneys.'

'Yes, well, that's true. And he may have thought of getting back at you in some way because of what happened with Nora – and Tory Delaney too.'

'You know I had no part in any of that.'

'Yes, but I think he wanted to approach you, to *know* you. He followed us out to the finca, didn't he, in nine-teen-seventy. Why? He didn't do us any harm. In fact, he did good. He sent Jaime to find you.'

'Just drop it,' said Max, so she did.

# 134

All sorts of things were happening. There was a For Sale board up at Queenie's old house, lots of viewings, and then an offer, which Max accepted. Some smaller items had been ferried out of the house and into Holland Park – things like Queenie's portrait, which Annie had shipped over and hung in Max's dressing room. Then the sale fell through and Max decided to take the house off the market, until things picked up.

'Nice?' said Annie, hustling Max into his dressing room one day and showing him Queenie's portrait, hanging in pride of place at the far end of the room under a picture light.

Max stood there and stared at the portrait of his mother.

'Yeah,' he said. 'Very nice.'

'If I can forgive you for pushing me away like you did, maybe you can forgive Queenie for falling in love?'

'Do you think that's what it was?'

'It must have been horrible for her. Because he abandoned her, didn't he? Left her to clean up the mess.'

Max said nothing. He stared at Queenie's image.

'I wonder where Bruno is now?' said Annie.

'Who knows?'

A week later, they heard that Cormac and Seamus Delaney had been nailed by the police for the murders of Steve Taylor, Stan Halliday and Cyrus Toynbee – and Bruno turned up at the front door.

# 135

'Hi,' he said, when Annie opened the door to him.

He looked the same as ever. Bad hair job, brassy blond with black roots. The strawberry birthmark bright on his cheek. His beautiful, beautiful face, so like Max's. He was wearing a tan leather jacket and faded jeans and – this broke her heart – his eyes were sad and hopeful, like a dog who's been kicked too many times but lies whimpering in a corner, longing to be shown some love.

'Bruno! Come in.'

'Is Max here?' he asked, and she could see that he was nervous of a positive answer but wanting it all the same.

She ushered him in the door, over to the drawing room and inside. Max was there, standing by the empty fireplace.

'Bruno's come to see us,' she said, her voice sounding falsely cheery, even to her own ears.

'So I see,' said Max.

*Be nice to him,* Annie's eyes pleaded.

'Why don't you give us a moment,' said Max to Annie.

She didn't want to, but she left the room. She didn't even listen at the door.

★

'So – how are you?' said Max to Bruno.

'Fine. Fine! You?'

'I'm OK.'

Silence.

Then Max said: 'This is hard to get my head around.'

'Yeah. Me too.'

'I thought all my brothers were dead.'

'And yet – here I am!' Bruno shrugged.

'We don't have the same father.'

'No. I guess we don't.'

'But the same mother.'

'That's right.'

Silence.

Then Bruno said: 'You're going to hate me.'

'Oh? Why's that?'

'Because I was *there*,' Bruno said. 'On the night the Delaney mob robbed your house in Surrey. I didn't know what they were planning or even who lived there but I was there, with them. It was my fault she died.'

Max shook his head slowly. 'No. That was *my* fault. I gave an order and it wasn't clear enough. Someone else died as a result and I don't think she ever got over the shock of that.'

'You mean Nora. You mean when Jonjo and Steve Taylor came and took her away.'

'I told Jonjo to talk to her. That's all. I swear it.'

'Maybe we should both stop blaming ourselves,' said Bruno. 'There's not a damned thing either one of us can do about any of it now.'

'You're right. In fact, I think what you should do right now . . .'

'Yes?' Bruno eyed Max anxiously. He was going to tell him to crawl off and die. He knew it.

'I think you should come over here and hug your brother. Since – against all the odds – it turns out you have one.'

Bruno started to smile. 'Really?'

'I won't offer a second time.'

Bruno went to Max, stood in front of him, unsure.

Max opened his arms.

Bruno went into them and felt, finally – at last – that he'd come home.

He laughed. And Max came as close as he ever would to crying. He hugged his brother hard.

When Annie came back into the room, she saw the two men embracing – and she smiled.

## END

# ACKNOWLEDGEMENTS

To all my friends and fans who have – in whatever small or large way – helped in the production of this book. Thank you, pals. All best wishes. Jx